HARRY POTTER AND RESISTANCE

Although rule breaking in *Harry Potter* is sometimes dismissed as a distraction from Harry's fight against Lord Voldemort, *Harry Potter and Resistance* makes the case that it is central to the battle against evil. Far beyond youthful hijinks or adolescent defiance, Harry's rebellion aims to overcome problems deeper and more widespread than a single malevolent wizard. Harry and his allies engage in a resistance movement against the corruption of the Ministry of Magic as well as against the racist social norms that gave rise to Voldemort in the first place. Dumbledore's Army and the Order of the Phoenix employ methods echoing those utilized by World War II resistance fighters and by the U.S. Civil Rights movement. The aim of this book is to explore issues that speak to our era of heightened political awareness and resistance to intolerance. Its interdisciplinary approach draws on political science, psychology, philosophy, history, race studies, and women's studies, as well as newer interdisciplinary fields such as resistance studies, disgust studies, and creativity studies.

Beth Sutton-Ramspeck, Associate Professor Emerita of English at the Ohio State University at Lima, received her doctorate in English, with a minor in Women's Studies, from Indiana University. The author of *Raising the Dust: Literary Housekeeping in the Writings of Charlotte Perkins Gilman, Sarah Grand, and Mary Ward* (2004), and the editor of three novels, she has published numerous articles and presented at conferences about Victorian literature and about *Harry Potter*.

HARRY POTTER AND RESISTANCE

Beth Sutton-Ramspeck

NEW YORK AND LONDON

Designed cover image: Getty

First published 2023
by Routledge
605 Third Avenue, New York, NY 10158

and by Routledge
4 Park Square, Milton Park, Abingdon, Oxon, OX14 4RN

Routledge is an imprint of the Taylor & Francis Group, an informa business

© 2023 Beth Sutton-Ramspeck

The right of Beth Sutton-Ramspeck to be identified as author of this work has been asserted in accordance with sections 77 and 78 of the Copyright, Designs and Patents Act 1988.

All rights reserved. No part of this book may be reprinted or reproduced or utilised in any form or by any electronic, mechanical, or other means, now known or hereafter invented, including photocopying and recording, or in any information storage or retrieval system, without permission in writing from the publishers.

Trademark notice: Product or corporate names may be trademarks or registered trademarks, and are used only for identification and explanation without intent to infringe.

ISBN: 978-1-032-31989-6 (hbk)
ISBN: 978-1-032-31987-2 (pbk)
ISBN: 978-1-003-31226-0 (ebk)

DOI: 10.4324/9781003312260

Typeset in Bembo
by Newgen Publishing UK

CONTENTS

Preface: *TERFs, Texts, and Thanks* — vii

Introduction: I Solemnly Swear I Am Up to No Good: Rule Breaking as Resistance — 1

1 "Made to Be Broken": The Laws, Rules, and Norms of the Magical World — 30

2 "Filth! Scum! By-products of Dirt and Vileness!": "Mudbloods," Dirt, Privilege, and Systemic Oppression in the *Harry Potter* Series — 55

3 "How Dare You Defy Your Masters?": Rules, Roles, and Resistance in the Potterverse's Domestic Realm — 85

4 "Creative Maladjustment": Creativity and Resistance in the *Harry Potter* Series — 119

5 "Do You Really Think This Is about Truth or Lies?": Honesty and Resistance in the *Harry Potter* Series — 145

Epilogue: "Mischief Managed"? — 166

Works Cited — *174*
Index — *189*

PREFACE
TERFs, Texts, and Thanks

I did not plan to write a book. Originally, seeking a topic for a 2011 conference focusing on creativity, I chose *Harry Potter* because I was teaching a class in the books at the Lima campus of the Ohio State University, so *Harry Potter* was on my mind. When I hunted for examples of creativity in the series, I discovered that its most creative characters are rule breakers. Later, on learning that Edinboro University's Ravenclaw Academic Conference, within driving distance of Lima, accepted student papers, I decided to attend with several of my stellar students and to reprise my own paper. The following year, when I wanted to take another group of students to Edinboro, I needed a second paper of my own. This one was about the Imperius Curse. Once you have two papers, you consider writing more, and then you wonder how you might bring them together. Rule breaking was the thread connecting my ideas.

The 2016 Presidential election upended everything. The kinds of corruption, racism, xenophobia, authoritarianism, lies, and cruelty that had been *Harry Potter*'s fictional nods to mid-twentieth-century fascism suddenly were echoed in every day's news. By early 2017, I had participated in the Women's March on Washington and joined a northwest Ohio political group, dedicated to peacefully resisting the Trump administration's worst policies. Alongside my critical and theoretical reading about *Harry Potter*, I was reading about tyranny, racial justice, and alternative facts; I saw more and more connections. One day it hit me that Dumbledore's Army and the Order of the Phoenix were doing what I was doing: they weren't just breaking rules; they were resisting unjust rules and systems; they were, in the late Congressman John Lewis's words, making "good trouble." And as I learned more for my book about resistance (and creativity, disgust theory, race theory, and care ethics), I was also learning to be a more effective member of the resistance. After years of being sorted into Ravenclaw or Hufflepuff—and occasionally Slytherin—suddenly, and to my great surprise, I started being sorted into Gryffindor. Apparently, I was developing more courage and chivalry than I had thought possible. So while this book was not originally intended as political, it has become that way. It is not written as a how-to book about resistance, but I hope aspiring advocates for a politics of tolerance and care will find inspiration in Dumbledore's Army and its methods.

The So-Called "TERF Wars"

Unfortunately, another current issue has also become relevant to *Harry Potter*. Any book about the series needs to confront the hippogriff in the room, and one must speak respectfully to the hippogriff—often called J. K. Rowling's TERF Wars—to avoid being attacked or, worse, expelled. *Harry Potter* fans and scholars are frequently asked our response to Rowling's comments about transgender people, so I need to address the question upfront. However, as it is not central to my book's arguments, I will be brief.

First, because it's important to listen to what people have to say for themselves, not just what people say about them (see *The Daily Prophet!*), I urge anyone who has not done so to read Rowling's own account, on her webpage. In the wake of these and other statements, many have called her a "TERF," which stands for "trans-exclusionary radical feminist." Some former fans have sworn off the series altogether, and a few even burned the books. For handy links to Rowling's tweets and other comments up to January 2022 and reactions to them, I recommend Abby Gardner's long article on Glamour.com. I also recommend Brie Hanrahan's point-by-point response to the arguments Rowling makes. At the end of this preface, you will find a selected bibliography of these and some other useful articles addressing issues raised by the controversy. Please judge for yourself.

As Gardner's summary shows, most public responses to Rowling's comments have been negative, with a few supportive exceptions. After having taught the series for more than fifteen years, I know many, many fans, and nearly all of them reject Rowling's views; those in the LGBTQ+ community feel particular pain and a sense of betrayal. The world of academic *Harry Potter* studies has been roiled nearly as much as the general fan community. Judging from my own observations of *Harry Potter* scholars, the vast majority disagree with Rowling's positions. A few scholars have stopped writing about the series altogether, but they seem to be the exception. To explain our continued work, scholars often cite literary theorist Roland Barthes's 1968 essay "The Death of the Author," which I rush to say is not about literal death but makes the argument that, metaphorically, the author dies when their writing begins. What matters is the reader's interaction with the text, which exists independently of its writer or the writer's supposed "intentions." That said, and although I was first trained to interpret texts without regard to the author, I had stopped observing that principle, and this book, most of which was drafted long before the "TERF" controversy arose, sometimes supports interpretations by citing Rowling's comments about the text and its backstories. I have not removed such material from this book.

The author of *Harry Potter* has contended that the books "are a prolonged argument for tolerance, a prolonged plea for an end to bigotry" ("J. K. Rowling at Carnegie Hall").[1] I could not agree more, which is why I do share with so many others the puzzled disappointment at her remarks about transgender women. As Cecilia Konchar Farr argues, that readers continue to use the series to promote acceptance and social justice represents "a pretty serious coup" (xxi)—or in my book's terms, resistance.

The series also vividly promotes the value of free speech, as did the author in a 2016 address to the writers' organization PEN America in which she commented on then-candidate Donald Trump: "His freedom to speak protects my freedom to call him a bigot. His freedom guarantees mine" (McCarthy). On that Rowling and I agree.

A Note on Texts

I could devote an entire chapter to the TERF controversy and the arguments on both sides, but, as I have emphasized, this book is not about Rowling. It also is not about the *Harry Potter* movies or the *Fantastic Beasts* movie franchise or *Harry Potter and the Cursed Child*, though each of these is mentioned in passing. This is a book about the *Harry Potter* books. I am a scholar of literature; I prefer the books to the movies, and I am far more qualified to analyze literature than film, so I am sticking with the books. As an American who taught the books for several years using the American (Scholastic Press) editions of the books, I have opted to use American editions. In my parenthetical citations, I use the following abbreviations:

SS	*Sorcerer's Stone*
CS	*Chamber of Secrets*
PA	*Prisoner of Azkaban*
GF	*Goblet of Fire*
OP	*Order of the Phoenix*
HBP	*Half-Blood Prince*
DH	*Deathly Hallows*
FB	*Fantastic Beast and Where to Find Them*

Some background information comes from the official *Harry Potter* site *Wizarding World*, which, when it appears in the text, is always italicized, to distinguish it from references to the wizarding world—lower case and no italics—which is a useful way to talk about the magical community—or for that matter to distinguish it from the theme park, though that is not mentioned in this book.

Thank You

One of the most profound lessons of *Harry Potter* is that few ventures succeed without help from friends and allies; this one is no exception, and I have many people and institutions to thank for their help along the way.

The project would never have begun if not for the Ohio State University's support, beginning with my program coordinator, John Hellmann, who suggested I teach a class about *Harry Potter*. The students in those classes and the insights they developed in their papers and in class discussions were a constant inspiration. A few of them are cited in the body of this book, but all of them were amazing and illustrate that a teacher learns from her students every day. As I began to write about the series, Ohio State paid my way to several conferences and awarded me a research leave. Ohio State librarians Tina Schneider and Zack Walton provided invaluable assistance at critical moments.

The warm and supportive world of *Harry Potter* scholarship has brought me many productive *Harry Potter* discussions at conferences and in private messages and social media exchanges. Some of these communications are directly cited in this book, but here I would like to extend my thanks to (alphabetically) Tracy Bealer, Laurie Beckhoff, Chris Bell, Lauren Camacci, Janet Brennan Croft, Louise Freeman Davis, Cecilia Konchar Farr, Corbin Fowler, John Granger, Tolonda Henderson, Janice Liedl, Patrick McCauley, Kathryn N. McDaniel, Katherine Sas, Emily Strand, Karen Wendling, and Lana Whited. Apologies if I overlooked anyone.

Earlier versions of my work on creativity and on the Imperius Curse appeared in the book *The Ravenclaw Chronicles: Reflections from Edinboro*, edited by Corbin Fowler, whose feedback was invaluable. Excerpts from those essays are published with the permission of Cambridge Scholars Publishing.

As many thanks as there are *Harry Potter* quotations in this book to Tia Ruark, who helped me acquire e-texts of the novels. Tia is also quite possibly the funniest reader of "hott" bad novels and helped make the first crazy road trip to Edinboro Potterfest even goofier than it already was.

Many thanks to Talia Schaffer, who steered me toward recent material about care ethics and whose brilliant application of that material inspired my own.

Thank you to Louise Freeman, who generously helped me research the scientific angles of the TERF debate and who generously shared a pre-publication copy of her essay about witches. Similar thanks to Tolonda Henderson and Mark-Anthony Lewis who also shared their essays before publication.

I am particularly indebted to Lana Whited, Maya Fischhoff, and especially Kathryn McDaniel, who kindly gave me invaluable feedback about the book manuscript. Their suggestions inspired new ideas and saved me from several embarrassing mistakes. Any remaining errors are, of course, my own.

I have been fortunate to work with Routledge Publishers and am grateful for the generous comments from anonymous readers who recommended the project for publication while also suggesting valuable additions and necessary deletions. Thank you to Senior Editor Michelle Salyaga, for her enthusiastic shepherding of my proposal; to Editorial Assistant Bryony Reese, for her prompt assistance about dull but important matters like contracts and fun stuff like the cover design; to Production Editor Louise Peterken, for her well-informed questions about my manuscript and well-informed answers about indexing; to copy editor Himalda Martin at Newgen Publishing, for her sharp eyes that saved me from multiple embarrassing errors; and to Newgen Project Manager M. Aishwariya, for her patience and kind answers to my many questions about the copy editing.

Since early 2017, my political friends have buoyed my spirits and kept up my hopes, starting with Wendy Chappell-Dick, rabble-rousing organizer extraordinaire, who booked buses to the 2017 Women's March on Washington and invited me along. Before we left, Wendy was literally the only person I knew among the 102 passengers; two days later, I had several new friends and, having seen dozens of *Harry Potter*–inspired protest signs, had the first glimmerings of my book's new focus. The following month I joined AHEAD (Allen & Hardin [Counties] for Election Action & Democracy) and became an organizer myself. I don't know how I would have made it through the years after the 2016 election without our version of Order of the Phoenix, whose members have included (alphabetically again) Jim Bode, Kerry Bush, Wendy Chappell-Dick, Sheila Coressel, Jenny Donnelly, Alice Donohue, Mary Drzycimski-Finn, Elizabeth Eley, Cris Elstro, Maya Fischhoff, Emily Fisher, Dylan Gross, Teresa Heath, Kim Lane, Sue Metheney, Holly Norton, Eugene Paik, Leslie Rigali, Jennifer Robertson, Lisa Robeson, Carla Thompson, and Rochelle Twining; many of them share enthusiasm for *Harry Potter*, and even those who don't have been among my most supportive cheerleaders. Thank you all.

As with every project I have completed, I am grateful to my family: my daughter Lee, without whom I might never have begun reading the series: she was eight when news of *Sorcerer's Stone* was still traveling by word of mouth; we read the first four volumes together. And my husband Doug, who, despite not being a *Harry Potter* fan, has provided the world's best sounding board for my ideas and only occasionally mocked me for using words like "Muggle" or "*Expelliarmus*." Thank you, Doug, for nearly fifty magical years, the best proof of everything Dumbledore ever said about the power of love. This book is for you. Always.

Note

1 But see Tolonda Henderson's brilliant analysis of deadnaming and other trans-exclusionary themes in the series.

Works Cited and Selected Annotated Bibliography of Materials about the Controversy Surrounding J. K. Rowling

Rowling's Positions

Rowling, J. K. "J. K. Rowling at Carnegie Hall Reveals Dumbledore Is Gay, Neville Marries Hannah Abbott, and Much More." Interview, 20 Oct. 2007. The Leaky Cauldron www.the-leaky-cauldron.org/2007/10/20/j-k-rowling-at-carnegie-hall-reveals-dumbledore-is-gay-neville-marries-hannah-abbott-and-scores-more/. Accessed 24 Jan. 2022.

———. "J. K. Rowling Writes about Her Reasons for Speaking Out on Sex and Gender Issues." www.jkrowling.com/opinions/j-k-rowling-writes-about-her-reasons-for-speaking-out-on-sex-and-gender-issues/. The author explains the five main reasons for her positions: impacts of trans activism on biomedical research; its effects on children's education; free speech concerns; the impacts of transitioning on young people; and, because Rowling herself is a survivor of sexual violence, concern for the safety of "natal girls and women."

Direct Responses to Rowling's Positions

De Hingh, Valentijn. "I'm Trans and I Understand JK Rowling's Concerns about the Position of Women. But Transphobia Is Not the Answer." Translated by Hannah Kousbroek. *The Correspondent* https://thecorrespondent.com/702/im-trans-and-i-understand-jk-rowlings-concerns-about-the-position-of-women-but-transphobia-is-not-the-answer/788222918340-a4270c13. Accessed 23 Feb. 2022. A trans-woman's complex autobiographical response to the controversy.

Ferber, Alona. "Judith Butler on the Culture Wars, J. K. Rowling and Living in 'Anti-Intellectual Times.'" Interview, *The New Statesman*, 23 Sep. 2020, www.newstatesman.com/uncategorized/2020/09/judith-butler-culture-wars-jk-rowling-and-living-anti-intellectual-times. Accessed 30 Sep. 2020. A foremost gender theorist weighs in on the relationship between feminism and trans rights.

Gardner, Abby. "A Complete Breakdown of the J. K. Rowling Transgender Comments Controversy." *Glamour* 3 Jan. 2022. www.glamour.com/story/a-complete-breakdown-of-the-jk-rowling-transgender-comments-controversy. Accessed 13 Feb. 2022. A summary, with links, of Rowling's statements and some of the responses.

Hanrahan, Brie. "A Reasonable Person's Guide to the J. K. Rowling Essay." *Medium*, 20 June 2020. https://medium.com/@briehanrahan/a-reasonable-persons-guide-to-the-j-k-rowling-essay-6bd9e2d638ad. Accessed 13 Feb. 2022. A thorough, point-by-point response to Rowling's long blogpost.

Henderson, Tolonda. "Chosen Names, Changed Appearances, and Unchallenged Binaries: Trans-Exclusionary Themes in *Harry Potter*." *Harry Potter and the Other: Race, Justice, and Difference in the Wizarding World*, edited by Sarah Park Dahlen and Ebony Elizabeth Thomas, UP of Mississippi, 2022, pp. 164–177. Interprets themes in the series itself as trans exclusionary, thus prefiguring the author's more recent comments.

McCarthy, A.J. "J. K. Rowling Defends Free Speech—and Donald Trump." Slate.com, 17 May 2016. https://slate.com/human-interest/2016/05/j-k-rowling-defends-donald-trumps-right-to-be-bigoted-and-free-speech-video.html. Accessed 28 Feb. 2022. A brief summary of Rowling's speech to PEN America, in defense of free speech, along with a video of the speech itself.

Steinberg, Neil. "Beating up J. K. Rowling won't help." *Chicago Sun Times*, 1 Jan. 2022. https://chicago.suntimes.com/columnists/2022/1/1/22857270/jk-rowling-transgender-comments-harry-potter-reunion-hbo-max-cross-dressing-steinberg. A plea for tolerance for all by a columnist and fan.

Research Concerning Issues Raised During the Debate

Ainsworth, Claire. "Sex Redefined." *Nature*, vol. 518, no. 7539, Feb. 2015, pp. 288–91. Explains that "Sex can be much more complicated than it at first seems" and lays out factors that contribute to a person's place in the spectrum from male through intersex to female.

Barthes, Roland. "The Death of the Author." *Image, Music, Text*. Translated by Stephen Heath, Hill, and Wang, 1977, pp. 142–48. Argues that interpretation of a text should proceed without concern for what the author may have said elsewhere.

Bauer, Greta R. et al. "Do Clinical Data from Transgender Adolescents Support the Phenomenon of 'Rapid Onset Gender Dysphoria'?" *Journal of Pediatrics*, vol. 243, Nov. 2021, pp. 224–27. This recent study, conducted to test findings Rowling describes in her post, looks at data from teens and finds no evidence for an epidemic of sudden transitions; nor did transitioning teens suffer from more depression, or other mental illness, or neurodevelopmental disorders (including autism) than did teens with "longstanding experiences of gender dysphoria" (Bauer et al. 3).

Bustos, Valeria P. et al. "Regret after Gender-affirmation Surgery: A Systematic Review and Meta-analysis of Prevalence." *Plastic and Reconstructive Surgery. Global Open.* vol. 9, no. 3 e3477, 19 Mar. 2021, doi:10.1097/GOX.0000000000003477. Finds that the rate of transgender people regretting medical interventions is approximately 1%.

Faulker, Doug. "Maya Forstater: Woman Wins Tribunal Appeal Over Transgender Tweets." *BBC News*, 10 June 2021. Explains the judgment by Britain's Employment Appeal Tribunal; Rowling's tweets had supported Forstater, who won her appeal.

Ghorayshi, Azeen. "Doctors Debate Whether Trans Teens Need Therapy before Hormones." *The New York Times*, 18 Jan. 2022. Lays out current arguments in this controversy.

Hasenbush, Amira, Andrew R. Flores, and Jody L. Herman. "Gender Identity Nondiscrimination Laws in Public Accommodations: A Review of Evidence Regarding Safety and Privacy in Public Restrooms, Locker Rooms, and Changing Rooms." *Sexuality Research & Social Policy: A Journal of the NSRC*, vol. 16, no. 1, 2019, pp. 70–83. A peer-reviewed UCLA study finds no evidence that attacks increased after the passage of laws that guaranteed bathroom access to transgender people.

Montañez, Amanda. "Beyond XX and XY." *Scientific American*, vol. 317, no. 3, Sept. 2017, pp. 50–51. A chart that illustrates how "A host of factors figure into whether someone is female, male, or somewhere in between."

Murchison, Gabriel R., M. Agénor, S. L. Reisner, et al. "School Restroom and Locker Room Restrictions and Sexual Assault Risk among Transgender Youth." *Pediatrics*, vol. 143, no. 6, June 2019. Finds that transgender youth who were prevented from using restrooms and locker rooms corresponding to their gender identity reported being sexually assaulted at substantially higher rates than transgender youth generally.

Olson, Kristina R. "When Sex and Gender Collide." *Scientific American*, vol. 317, no. 3, Sept. 2017, pp. 44–49. A Princeton developmental psychologist explains studies of children whose biological sex and gender identity don't align.

Serano, Julia. "Origins of 'Social Contagion' and 'Rapid Onset Gender Dysphoria.'" *Whipping Girl*, 29 Nov. 2021, http://juliaserano.blogspot.com/2019/02/origins-of-social-contagion-and-rapid.html Accessed 7 Mar. 2022. A timeline tracking the history of the idea Rowling discusses that gender dysphoria is a "social contagion"; the ideas were developed on four websites hostile to gender-affirming practices rather than in science.

INTRODUCTION

I Solemnly Swear I Am Up to No Good: Rule Breaking as Resistance

One Saturday morning in Harry Potter's third year at Hogwarts School of Witchcraft and Wizardry, Fred and George Weasley pull him aside and, with a "mysterious wink" from Fred and a "beaming" look from George, they present Harry with what they call "the secret of our success" (PA 190, 191). The gift appears to be no more than an old piece of blank parchment—until the user pronounces the words, "I solemnly swear I am up to no good" (192). This "bit of old parchment" (191) is, of course, the Marauder's Map, which allows a user to view (nearly[1]) every room and corridor of Hogwarts Castle, including several secret passages, and to see the whereabouts of everyone inside the Castle. As Fred and George explain, when Harry finishes using the map, he should "Just tap it again and say, 'Mischief managed!' And it goes blank" (194).

The oxymoronic phrase "Mischief managed" epitomizes rule breaking in the series. On the one hand, we think of mischief as playful misbehavior, ranging from harmless pranks to destructive criminality. Mischief is chaotic, even anarchic, but to "manage" something is not just to accomplish it, or, as the spell suggests, to complete it. It also means to regulate or even organize it. At first, Harry uses the map, as the twins expect, for innocuous juvenile mischief: to sneak without permission into Hogsmeade village, where he visits Honeydukes sweet shop and tries butterbeer. But then, concealed beneath his invisibility cloak, he overhears a conversation not intended for his ears, about Sirius Black's supposed betrayal of Harry's parents; thereupon, Harry's "mischief" and rule breaking take on a more serious cast. By the end of the school year, the map has revealed the presence in the castle of Peter Pettigrew, the actual betrayer of James and Lily Potter; and Harry has learned the truth about the treachery that led to their murder. By breaking numerous school rules, Ministry regulations, and social norms, Harry saves two

DOI: 10.4324/9781003312260-1

lives and advances the process of resisting and ultimately defeating Voldemort. He has taken important early steps in a career of resistance. The map and, to an even greater degree, the cloak begin as aids to juvenile rule breaking but ultimately serve as crucial nonviolent means of resisting and overcoming Voldemort and the wider corruption he embodies.

This book argues that the *Harry Potter* series celebrates rule breaking as a manifestation of resistance to corrupt rules, social norms, and institutions. Indeed, the series illustrates the ways that both recorded statutes and the unwritten rules that are social norms can become corrupt and thus invite being broken. A problem with rules and norms is that they tend to over-simplify. For this reason, the health of any system requires questioning the status quo and challenging the injustices implicit in outworn ideologies and corrupt systems. The book also argues that at the core of the series is an emphasis on the complexity of motives and behaviors and of our understanding of good and evil. Sometimes even members of the resistance employ questionable methods. And while the wizarding world is obviously fictional, the series, like most good fantasies, comments on complex real-world issues, real-world ethical and political dilemmas.

"Not a good kid"? The Controversies about Harry's Rule Breaking

In 2002, the Cedarville, Arkansas, school board voted 3–2 to remove *Harry Potter* books from the school library, allowing access only to students who had their parents' permission. Board members' justification: the books promote witchcraft and could encourage "juvenile delinquency." "[B]ooks teaching that sometimes rules need to be disobeyed," they contended, "should not be allowed in the school" (DeMitchell and Carney 163). The school district was subsequently sued, losing the suit on First Amendment grounds, but some parents and critics continue to say that frequent rule breaking makes the series "inappropriate" for children. In his book *Harry Potter and the Bible*, for example, Richard Abanes points out that by the end of Chapter 12 of *Harry Potter and the Sorcerer's Stone*, "Harry has disobeyed Hogwarts' codes at least seven times without suffering any consequences" (35).[2] Likewise, in an online review of the *Prisoner of Azkaban* movie, Peter T. Chattaway worries about the series' "questionable, and highly subjective, morality," especially that Harry "exhibits a flagrant disregard for the rules, even when they have been put there for his own safety, and nearly always seems to get away with it." And Christian fantasy author Bryan Davis complains that Harry "is not a good kid. He lies, he cheats, he steals, and he's never punished for it. In fact he gets worse as the series goes on." Moreover, in the series, Davis observes, it's "cool to break the rules"; by contrast, "every rule-keeper is portrayed in a bad light. Every authority figure is portrayed as a buffoon" (quoted in LeBlanc). Although the furor has died down since the final books and movies were released, to this day the series is condemned for encouraging rule breaking and glorifying the occult—for of course sympathetic depiction of witchcraft itself violates fundamental rules of certain segments of Muggle culture.

Before we dismiss such criticism as missing the point, we should acknowledge that not all rule breaking in the series is virtuous. Of course, most of the ways Voldemort and his followers defy wizarding norms are morally indefensible—and unequivocally depicted that way. But consider the Weasley twins' pranks: though entertaining and generally harmless, they are rarely, at least early in the series, examples of principled civil disobedience. Fred and George's juvenile mischief includes nicking food from the kitchens, skipping class, or tormenting someone—like Dudley Dursley—who gets on their bad side. Indeed, viewed from ten thousand feet, the episode of Dudley and the Ton-Tongue Toffee is little more than bullying the fat kid. To be sure, as the series progresses, the twins' anarchic mischief challenges Dolores Umbridge's authoritarian rule at Hogwarts, and some merchandise they originally intended as joke items is later repurposed to fight Death Eaters—for example, shield cloaks and decoy detonators. Later, we will need to consider Dumbledore's youthful advocacy of "wizard dominance" over Muggles and Harry's own use of Unforgivable Curses. For now, it's important to grant that not all rule breaking is okay—nor always overtly questioned in the series.

Still, most critics are sympathetic to literary rule breaking. Alison Lurie, in her classic study *Don't Tell the Grown-Ups: Subversive Children's Literature*, argues that "Most of the great works of juvenile literature are subversive in one way or another: they express ideas and emotions not generally approved of or even recognized at the time; they make fun of honored figures and piously held beliefs; and they view social pretenses with clear-eyed directness" (4). The protagonists of the best children's books, from *Tom Sawyer* to *Mary Poppins*, from *Peter Rabbit* to *Peter Pan*, Lurie asserts, are defined by disobedience and bad behavior. If nothing else, "subversive" children's books have a long history of popularity. Ron W. Cooley points out that much of classic adult literature, from *Antigone* to *Huckleberry Finn*, is premised on rebellion against unjust authorities and that Northrop Frye observed "how often the action of a Shakespearean comedy begins with some absurd, cruel, or irrational law ... which the action of the comedy then evades or breaks" (qtd. in Cooley 29).

Addressing *Harry Potter* more directly, other critics celebrate its depiction of rule breaking. Vandana Saxena, for example, approaches the "subversive" in *Harry Potter* from a different angle than mine, addressing the ways that both fantasy and adolescence are "queer," in that they "denaturalize" cultural categories (29–33) and contest "norms that constitute identity" (179). Tenille Nowak, recognizing that "The rule-breaking by Harry and his friends and the inconsistency of the consequences for doing so present[s] a serious problem for parents trying to teach their children that they must conform to the rules," argues, as do several other critics,[3] that parents and educators can use the books to explore decision making about rules in complex situations (21). Edmund Kern, for example, argues that often in *Harry Potter*, the "rules don't always serve larger moral principles" (96), which the series, in turn, elucidates. Several critics use Lawrence Kohlberg's model of stages of moral development to explore characters' rule breaking.[4] Another perspective that comes close to my own approach is that of Noel Chevalier, who analyzes "Rowling's critique of the institutions of power in the wizarding world, and Harry's place as a heroic resistance figure, on the side of moral right, but not necessarily on the side of order and conformity" (398). Chevalier describes the series as a "critique of systems of authority that define the wizarding world" (400).

A few critics contend the series is not subversive enough. Jack Zipes, writing before the series was completed, saw in it "the same sexist and white patriarchal biases of classical fairy tales" (186). Nicholas Tucker, another early naysayer, saw a "distinctly backward looking quality" in that "contemporary social issues [meaning 'drugs, alcohol, divorce, or sexual activity of any kind'] do not exist in [the first three] Potter books" (221). Rebecca Skulnick and Jesse Goodman, among others, note that "For all of his compassion and identification with those characters from the lower rungs, [Harry] never questions the gender, class, or European hegemony of his world" (263). Critics like Zipes, Tammy Turner-Vorbeck, and Andrew Blake are troubled, with some justification, by manufactured hype surrounding sales of the books, as well as the movies and consumer products marketed to fans which promote the "commodification of childhood," and, Turner-Vorbeck argues reinforce "hegemonic, hierarchical middle-class social and cultural values" (20).[5] A number of critics question the gender politics of the books. Many of these, as well as other critics, are troubled by the racial politics of the series and remain concerned that the series never resolves the problem of house-elf slavery.[6]

While I concede that there is plenty to criticize in the *Harry Potter* series and will address several of these objections in later chapters, I contend that, for the most part, Harry and his allies' rule breaking is neither antisocial nor reactionary. Moreover, to portray a flawed world—and magical culture is severely flawed, marred by racism, sexism, class bias, and other injustices—is not to endorse those shortcomings. The early critics, more astute observers than preteen Harry, recognized those flaws before Harry, but as the series progresses, Harry and the reader learn to look critically at wizarding culture and recognize the need to resist its injustices.[7]

Why Not Just Obey?

Setting aside the literary advantages of conflict, one might reasonably ask why Harry *can't* be a "good kid" who follows the rules. What's wrong with obedience? To be sure, one should obey rules that contribute to safety or the public good. As it happens, Harry never cheats at Quidditch and manages, even in battle, never to cast the worst of the Unforgivable Curses, *Avada Kedavra*.[8] When Harry does something genuinely bad—slashing Draco Malfoy with the *Sectumsempra* spell—a furious Snape orders, "You wait here for me," and "It did not occur to Harry for a second to disobey" (HBP 523); granted, when Snape returns and orders Harry to bring his textbook, Harry hides the potions book and borrows Ron's, but he does accept punishment for the more serious wrong-doing of using a dark curse. He says, "I wish I hadn't done it, and not just because I've got about a dozen detentions" (HBP 530). In *Chamber of Secrets*, when he and Ron fly the Weasleys' Ford Anglia to Hogwarts, they are punished in multiple ways—and both recognize that this rule breaking was unnecessary and had serious consequences. Even Dumbledore, himself rather lax about rules, threatens to expel them if they do anything similar—and Harry is too ashamed to look him in the eye. Harry certainly respects Dumbledore's authority—most of the time, including when he reluctantly plies Dumbledore with the lethal potion in the Horcrux cave in *Half-Blood Prince*. Significantly, in the final volume, he openly grapples with whether to accept Dumbledore's mission, ultimately actively choosing to trust his mentor. Harry's obedience is not unquestioning.

For obedience is not always or necessarily a good thing, as we have learned from incidents like the 1968 My Lai massacre and most notoriously, Adolf Eichmann's Nuremberg defense that he was just "following orders." Sadly, Eichmann may have been on to something; and principled disobedience may be the exception. In Stanley Milgram's famous obedience experiments at Yale University, devised in the wake of the Nuremberg Trials, test subjects were instructed to administer increasingly powerful electric shocks to an unseen "student" (an actor) they were supposedly teaching, each time the student answered questions incorrectly. In the original experiment, 65% of subjects continued administering shocks up to the highest level, marked "Danger," where the student appeared to have passed out or possibly died. Milgram and others repeated the experiment with numerous variations, concluding that most people will follow orders, even orders they feel uncomfortable with or that have destructive consequences, when they consider the source of the orders is a legitimate authority, when they can deflect responsibility onto that authority, and when the victim is distanced from the teacher. Where does "legitimacy" derive from? In Milgram's experiments, authority was signaled by the experimenter's lab coat. In real-world military and political situations, people look to the chain of command. Theoretically, for children, adults are legitimate authorities; but are they always? Psychologist Herbert C. Kelman and sociologist V. Lee Hamilton found that crimes of obedience occur, consistent with Milgram's findings, in three circumstances: when people feel they have no choice other than to obey orders from an authority they consider legitimate; when the order is perceived as part of a routine operation in which the person feels they have some formal role; and when the victim is dehumanized or not perceived as having an individual identity. In Harry Potter's fictional world, both Muggles and literally non-human magical beings like giants, goblins, and house-elves are routinely dehumanized and treated accordingly.

In the wizarding world, obedience at its most extreme is a curse—the Imperius Curse—one of only three Unforgivable Curses, along with *Avada Kedavra* and Cruciatus, the killing curse and torture curse. The spell's name derives from the

Latin *impero* (to order or command) or *imperium* (absolute power, dominion) and is related to English words like *imperative* (demanding obedience). When Mad-Eye Moody demonstrates the Imperius Curse in Defense Against the Dark Arts class, he describes it as "Total control," adding, "'Years back, there were a lot of witches and wizards being controlled by the Imperius Curse' ... and Harry knew he was talking about the days in which Voldemort had been all-powerful. 'Some job for the Ministry, trying to sort out who was being forced to act, and who was acting of their own free will' (GF 213). *Imperio*'s "total control" distinguishes it from other control curses and potions, which affect only parts—albeit important parts—of the target's will: memory (*Obliviate*), ability to keep secrets (*Veritaserum*), erotic desire (*Amortentia*), and so on. Those under the Imperius Curse *must* obey—are "forced to act" according to another's will, including engaging in behaviors that would otherwise be completely unnatural for them, ranging from the trivial—like Moody's tap-dancing spider—to the fundamental. In *Harry Potter and the Deathly Hallows*, for example, the Imperiused Minister of Magic Pius Thicknesse "leads" a puppet government that Voldemort controls.

Further, Moody makes a crucial distinction between being "forced to act" and "acting under their own free will." We later find out that Moody—actually Barty Crouch, Junior, in disguise—learned this distinction first-hand by enduring the Imperius Curse for many years. He describes himself as "enslaved," and even Winky the house-elf considered it a "life of imprisonment" (GF 686). Once Barty is freed from the curse and Voldemort Imperiuses his father, the elder Crouch is, in his son's words, "imprisoned, controlled," while the son describes himself as "released. I awoke. I was myself again, alive as I hadn't been in years" (GF 688). The Imperius Curse is such an extreme form of obedience that it denies the victim his very identity. Moral responsibility, moreover, depends on free will.

At a pivotal moment for the resistance, Dumbledore anticipates a time when students will "have to make a choice between what is right and what is easy" (GF 724). Choosing to obey can be easier than disobeying, as symbolized when "Moody" demonstrates the Imperius Curse on Harry in class: "It was the most wonderful feeling. Harry felt a floating sensation as every thought and worry in his head was wiped gently away, leaving nothing but a vague, untraceable happiness. He stood there feeling immensely relaxed" (231). To passively obey requires no consideration. When Moody tells him to jump on a desk, Harry's first impulse is to "ben[d] his knees *obediently*, preparing to spring" (231; emphasis added), but his second is to consider the order's merits:

> Why, though? Another voice had awoken in the back of his brain.
> Stupid thing to do, really, said the voice.
> *Jump onto the desk....*
> No, I don't think I will, thanks, said the other voice, a little more firmly ... no, I don't really want to....
>
> (231–2)

To "fight" the Imperius Curse is overtly to question the wisdom of the orders and then to disobey them. It can be difficult, symbolized by the pain in Harry's knees when he resists jumping. Moody/Crouch explains that "The Imperius Curse can be fought ... but it takes real strength of character, and not everyone's got it" (GF 213). In the cemetery scene in *Goblet of Fire*, Voldemort hits Harry first with the Cruciatus Curse and then with the Imperius Curse and with Cruciatus again, but Harry vows, "he wasn't going to obey Voldemort" (GF 661). Harry's capacity to resist the Imperius Curse shows the "strength of character" that makes him heroic. The flip side is whimpering that one was "forced" to obey, like Wormtail (PA 374), or has "no choice," like Draco Malfoy (HBP 591)—the Eichmann defense—though at least Draco, unlike Wormtail, is protecting those he loves.

Understanding Milgram's and subsequent studies' findings that people will choose to obey "legitimate" authority is assisted by sociologist Max Weber's distinction among three kinds of authority people consider legitimate: traditional authority, such as monarchies; legal-rational authority, based on laws; and charismatic authority. Although the Ministry of Magic promulgates plenty of rules, regulations, and laws, its authority seems based primarily on traditions, for when Dumbledore uses legal reasoning during Harry's expulsion hearing in *Order of the Phoenix*, Cornelius Fudge is thoroughly nonplussed. Charismatic authority derives from the outsized personality of a leader, who, at the most extreme, is perceived as having superhuman or, appropriately, "magical" powers. The series features two charismatic leaders who challenge traditional authority: Voldemort and Dumbledore. Voldemort better fits Weber's ideas, however, as he engineers a complete though covert overthrow of the Ministry, largely through sheer power of personality. Significantly, Voldemort also has a trait that more recent analysis has linked to charismatic leaders: narcissism.[9] Dumbledore, too, inspires tremendous personal loyalty, but though graced with charisma, Dumbledore has refused the position of Minister, precisely because, he says, "I had learned that I was not to be trusted with power" (DH 717).

In Weber's view, a charismatic leader's followers resemble devoted disciples who obey accordingly. The Death Eaters are Voldemort's "followers." As Dumbledore recalls, adolescent Tom Riddle "[r]igidly controlled" his Hogwarts companions (HBP 362), whom Dumbledore hesitates to call "friends"; later he describes Death Eaters as "servants" or "henchmen" under Voldemort's "command" (HBP 444–45). The cult-like Death Eaters' preferred sobriquets for their leader, "the Dark Lord" and "Lord Voldemort," evoke not only (Muggle) aristocracy but also divinity. Snape describes Voldemort to Bellatrix in quasi-religious terms: "If he had not forgiven we who lost faith at that time, he would have very few followers left" (HBP 26–27), and "The Dark Lord's word is law" (HBP 32).

If there were any doubt of the horrors of unquestioning obedience to a charismatic leader, one need only read that moment in Voldemort's perverse incarnation ceremony when Wormtail cuts off his own hand at Voldemort's behest. Professor Quirrell, controlled to the point that Voldemort is literally inside his head, is left to die after he fails to kill Harry. The snake Nagini benefits no more than Quirrell or Wormtail from her obedience. Christopher E. Bell says of Nagini, "Because she is an animal and cannot dissent, she is a direct metonym for blind allegiance; she is the only servant Voldemort has that he completely trusts, and she defends Voldemort up to the very moment she gets her head cut off, without questioning" ("Heroes" 84). It is the rare and influential character—Narcissa Malfoy, Regulus Black, and of course Severus Snape—who disobeys Voldemort's wishes. In short, disobeying is often quite difficult, even when no Imperius Curse is involved, but unquestioning obedience is shown to be dangerous in every way. Harry's disobedience is one of his strengths.

What Is "Resistance," and How Does it Apply to Harry Potter?

My book is not just about rule breaking but about rule breaking as "resistance," a term some might question. Thus Lori Campbell, who acknowledges that Harry "personifies the larger resistance of the Order of the Phoenix against Voldemort" (303), sees his behavior as neither principled nor political but as mere adolescent rebellion. Similarly, Lakshmi Chaudhry contends that Harry has "no interest in the larger issues at stake in the resistance against Voldemort" (6). Skulnick and Goodman hold that the novels send the message that "one can become a civic leader without having to reconstruct the institution's hegemonic structure" (272). Granted, Skulnick and Goodman advanced their interpretation before the publication of the final three volumes, but they overlooked some already-obvious flaws in Hogwarts, the wizarding world, and its underlying cultural norms—which I will shortly be discussing in more detail—as well as how Harry and his friends challenge those flaws. From a different perspective, Richard Garfinkle contends that although Voldemort is a "petty tyrant," opposing him is not a political act because Voldemort is not a political actor. He is merely "interested in flashy exercise and the showing off of power, not in the systematic repression of a truly dangerous dictator" (183). Garfinkle, too, wrote before the release of the final volume, in which Voldemort takes over all of Britain's magical power structures: the Ministry of Magic, Gringott's Bank, the *Daily Prophet*, and Hogwarts. Moreover, Garfinkle wrote before the presidency of Donald Trump demonstrated the ways personal narcissism can shade into systemic oppression and inspire a cult-like following that can nearly topple a democracy. Furthermore, many of these critics overlook Sirius Black's crucial observation: "the world isn't split into good people and Death Eaters" (OP 302); Voldemort and his followers are hardly the only characters who embody repressive politics. Political corruption and social injustice appear early in the series in institutions that, superficially, oppose Voldemort. Harry both observes and resists that corruption. The critic whose approach most nearly resembles my own is Tracy L. Bealer, who in her brilliant analysis of *Order of the Phoenix* identifies Harry's work as political "resistance" and argues that "the abilities both to love and to resist evil require individuals to negotiate a balance between order and disorder, structure and chaos" ("(Dis)Order" 176–77). As Bealer observes, success against Voldemort depends, practically and philosophically, on collaboration and emotional connections. Bealer does not, however, address rule breaking.

What, then, do I mean when I say that Harry not only breaks rules but "resists"? Historically, *resistance* calls to mind movements against the Nazis during World War II. It is practically a truism of *Harry Potter* studies that the series is replete with references to Hitler's Germany. Everyone from scholars to creators of internet memes has noted Grindelwald's and Voldemort's Hitler-like attitudes and Voldemort's secret "half-blood" background, Grindelwald's defeat in 1945, the registration and removal of "mudbloods," the murders of Muggles and "race traitors," and even Draco Malfoy's Aryan appearance.[10] Rowling herself has said she modeled Voldemort on Hitler and Stalin ("New Interview"; "Harry Potter: The Final Chapter"). If Voldemort echoes Hitler, it stands to reason that Voldemort's opponents resemble Hitler's—the resistance.[11] Subsequent to World War II, "resistance" has been applied to movements ranging from campaigns for social justice within existing systems to those promoting regime change or attempting to expel a colonial occupier: from movements for democratic rights in India, China, eastern Europe, and Latin America, to the anti-apartheid movement in South Africa, to the Arab Spring uprisings, to the civilian mobilization against the Russian invasion of Ukraine; and, in the US, from the mid-twentieth-century civil rights and antiwar movements to opposition to the Trump administration.[12]

Nevertheless, "resistance" is a term people routinely use for social or political action, though one that hardly anyone stops to define. Sometimes it merely means "protest"; other times, it stands for a full range of activities that *push back* against repressive/oppressive power. A few definitions have been advanced. According to the US Defense Department, "Resistance is an organized effort by some portion of the civil population of a country to resist the legally established government or an occupying power and to disrupt civil order and stability" (qtd. in Biggers, 4). Despite being rather circular ("Resistance is an organized effort … to resist"), this definition covers many possibilities. It includes responses to both a "legally established" government and an illegitimately "occupying" one, but in either case, those resisting are civilians; it also conveys anxiety about resistance as something intended to "disrupt order and stability." Sociologist Kurt Schock, more sympathetically, defines civil resistance as "the sustained use of methods of nonviolent action by civilians engaged in asymmetric conflicts," specifically "groups resisting various forms of oppression and injustice" (277). Crucial to Schock's concept of resistance is that power is "asymmetric": the authorities are disproportionately powerful and "not averse to using violence to defend their interests"—an apt description of Voldemort and the Death Eaters, but also of the Ministry of Magic under Cornelius Fudge and Rufus Scrimgeour. A definition that applies nicely to the Order of the Phoenix and its junior branch, Dumbledore's Army, comes from political scientists Erica Chenoweth and Maria J. Stephan: "The term *resistance* implies that the campaigns of interest are noninstitutional and generally confrontational in nature. In other words, these groups are using tactics that are outside the conventional political process (voting, interest-group organizing, or lobbying)" (12). British magical culture seems to lack most conventional political channels, so it stands to reason that magical resistance is outside them.

Political scientists who study "resistance movements" most often, like Schock, mean nonviolent actions and, with few exceptions, are different from those studying revolutions, though some explore conditions under which nonviolent protest becomes violent insurrection.[13] The *Harry Potter* series, of course, culminates in violence—the Battle of Hogwarts—and features other violent clashes, such as that in the Department of Mysteries or the pursuit of the seven Potters that begins *Deathly Hallows*. Significantly, in all these episodes, the other side instigates violence. Notably, Voldemort's death is brought about when his spell rebounds against himself, deflected by Harry's defensive spell, vividly realizing the assertion by Gene Sharp, political scientist and advocate of nonviolent resistance to tyranny, that nonviolent action is a kind of political jiu-jitsu. Indeed, for the most part, the magical resistance remains nonviolent except in self-defense. On the other hand, to call the Battle of Hogwarts revolutionary is not inaccurate; after all, it overthrows the puppet government controlled by Voldemort. It fits Peter Calvert's definition of a revolution as "A process in which the political direction of a state becomes increasingly discredited in the eyes of either the population as a whole or certain key sections of it" and is followed by "A change of government .. by the use of armed force" (4). Many political theorists distinguish resistance and revolution from a third phenomenon, the coup, which, says Charles Tilly, involves little "significant structural change" (220). Voldemort's takeover is a coup: after all, aside from Scrimgeour's replacement by Pius Thicknesse as Minister of Magic, the changes at the Ministry are at first so subtle that few people realize Voldemort has taken charge. To be sure, the long-term outcomes of the Battle of Hogwarts are not revealed within the pages of the series, but we have Rowling's extracanonical remarks: "The Ministry of Magic was de-corrupted, and ... the discrimination that was always latent there was eradicated." Moreover, the dementors are removed from Azkaban, Harry is appointed to run the Auror Department, and Hermione works for social justice at the Ministry of Magic ("J.K Rowling Web Chat"). In short, the Battle of Hogwarts is a revolution that instigates both structural and ideological change.

The Value of Crime

While obedience can in some cases be socially harmful, sociologist Émile Durkheim contended that actual crime is an inevitable, even beneficial part of healthy societies, as conflict between what a culture considers acceptable or criminal helps define and strengthen social norms. However, says Durkheim, crime is also essential for progress, creating new norms. He offers Socrates as an example: "According to Athenian law, Socrates was a criminal, and his condemnation was no more than just. However, his crime, namely, the independence of his thought, rendered a service not only to humanity but to his country. It served to prepare a new morality and faith which the Athenians needed" (71). Innovative thinkers or revolutionaries may be perceived by their contemporaries as criminals, and punished accordingly, as were American Revolutionaries, World War II resistance fighters, or Martin Luther King, Jr, but their challenges to the status quo render a valuable service to their communities. To be sure, "the boy who lived" is no Socrates; but nor is he, as Vernon Dursley believes, a candidate for St. Brutus's Secure Center for Incurably Criminal Boys. As I will discuss more fully in Chapter Four, Harry's violation of wizarding norms, which makes him Undesirable Number 1, is consistent with the kind of "societal creativity" that reimagines society. In the language of creativity studies, Harry and the Order of the Phoenix defy the Zeitgeist. That includes both discriminatory wizarding social structures and patriarchy.

Care Ethics, Carol Gilligan, and Resistance to Patriarchy

For my study of resistance in *Harry Potter*, I have been inspired, in part, by care ethics, a multidisciplinary scholarly approach that, as Daniel Engster and Maurice Hamington explain, "challenges us to rethink the nature and purpose of politics … in terms of what is necessary for promoting and sustaining good personal care"(1). Theories of care ethics start with the assumption that people are relational and interdependent. Thus, as Fiona Robinson explains, "care must be recognized as a social responsibility, an attribute of citizenship" (308); care is not, that is, a purely private feel-good emotion but something that politics and policy must address. Moreover, as Engster and Hamington note, care ethics "eschews simplistic judgments about right or wrong"—or, I would add, rules or rule breaking—"isolated from all context" (1).

Foundational ideas of care ethics were conceived separately in the 1980s by Carol Gilligan, Nel Noddings, and Sara Ruddick, and subsequently developed by philosophers, political scientists, sociologists, and others. In Gilligan's groundbreaking 1982 work, *In a Different Voice*, she takes issue with theories of moral development, such as those by Jean Piaget and Lawrence Kohlberg, that studied boys and overlooked girls and which argued that an "ethic of rights" is more mature than an "ethic of care." In this early work, the ethic of care is implicitly feminine. Gilligan identifies it as a "moral imperative that emerges repeatedly in interviews with women": "an injunction to care, a responsibility to discern and alleviate the 'real and recognizable trouble' of this world." This contrasts with men's moral imperative, which "appears rather as an injunction to respect the rights of others and thus to protect from interference the rights to life and self-fulfillment" (100). As Amanda Cawston and Alfred Archer observe, in care ethics, the "moral outlook places caring for others at the heart of morality. According to Gilligan, this moral outlook is just as legitimate a form of moral reasoning as one that prioritizes rules and principles" (457).

In subsequent writings, Gilligan—like other care ethicists—argues that an ethic of care is not solely feminine but is "quintessentially human" (*Birth* 61), a position consistent with Dumbledore's insistence on the power of love to overcome hate. Gilligan's recent books, including, most obviously, *Joining the Resistance*, address resistance directly, showing how psychological "resistance" to silencing relates to mounting a political challenge to patriarchy, which she identifies as a force antithetical to democracy: *patriarchy*, as Gilligan uses the term, is "those attitudes and values, moral codes and institutions, that separate men from men as well as from women and divide women into the good and the bad" (*Joining* 177). Patriarchy pressures both boys and girls to suppress their desire for genuine relationships with one another; patriarchy reinforces the erroneous idea that autonomy and distance are masculine, while caring is feminine (or "sissy") and less than, a form of weakness. By categorizing some qualities as masculine and others as feminine, then privileging the masculine ones, patriarchy creates hierarchies, identifying men as superior to women and finding some men superior to others—and in the magical world, humans superior to other magical beings. Gilligan's writings celebrate resistance to patriarchy, "resistance in the sense of resistance to disease; resistance as political resistance—speaking truth to power" (*Joining* 105–6). "Love," writes Gilligan, practically channeling Dumbledore, "is the enemy of patriarchy, crossing its boundaries, dissolving its hierarchies, and thus challenging its most fundamental assumptions about how things are and how things have to be" (*Joining* 42). That is, an ethic of care is inherently a form of resistance to patriarchy, both patriarchy's psychological manifestations and its socio-political manifestations. Indeed, argues Gilligan, "Within a *patriarchal* framework, care is a feminine ethic. Within a *democratic* framework, care is a human ethic" (*Joining* 22; emphasis Gilligan's).

How does all this apply to *Harry Potter*? Most simply, one might identify Percy Weasley's fondness for rules, delight at being a prefect and then Head Boy, and willingness to place ambition before family as perfectly illustrating a statement Gilligan makes in *In a Different Voice*: "While women ... try to change the rules in order to preserve relationships, men, in abiding by these rules, depict relationships as easily replaced" (44). Gilligan's more recent work identifies such extreme respect for authority and hierarchy with patriarchy, which damages both sexes equally though in different ways: patriarchal systems tend to silence girls, who conceal their identities in the quest for relationships; for boys, patriarchy impairs relationships. Where Percy's rigidly following rules alienates his family, Hermione's rule breaking forges and strengthens friendship. In Book One, Hermione lies about the troll to protect Ron and Harry, and thereafter the trio are friends. When, in the later pages of *Deathly Hallows*, Percy chooses his family over the Ministry, his choice represents both joining the political resistance and resisting the pressures of patriarchy. The epilogue and some of Rowling's interviews indicate that Percy never abandons his fondness for rules, but at least he is no longer rejecting his family. Just as an ethic of care can be embraced by men, patriarchal attitudes are not exclusive to them: an authoritarian fondness for hierarchies, oppressing those considered "inferior," and suppression of caring are traits shared by Dolores Umbridge, Bellatrix Lestrange, and other female members of the Black family—all of whom Harry and his allies resist in various ways. Although Dumbledore, in his commentary on "The Tale of the Three Brothers," observes that "No witch has ever claimed to own the Elder Wand" (*Tales* 106), Umbridge and Bellatrix would no doubt relish wielding that phallic symbol of superiority and domination.[14]

Voldemort, the wizard who went, in Hagrid's words, "As bad as you could go" (SS 54), is in many obvious senses the ultimate rule breaker in the series. And yet, considering the iron control he maintains over his followers, he is also the quintessential ruler. With his contempt for love, authoritarianism, devotion to hierarchy, and oppression of those he considers inferiors, he also perfectly exemplifies the worst aspects of patriarchy, which he is incapable of resisting. Gilligan's arguments about adolescent development offer insights into how Tom Riddle became Voldemort. Granted, there are also important socio-political explanations. Susan Hall argues, for example, that "The weakness of the rule of law within the wizard world creates a vacuum, which Voldemort—who offers a perverted, dictatorial version of order—exploits" ("Harry" 148). Bell makes a strong case that Voldemort breaks the rules because, on the one hand, he has been "Othered his entire life," which has fostered a sense that the system is rigged, and on the other hand, as Slytherin's descendant, he finds the limits he has experienced "not only unjust but unrighteous based on suppositions about the social order" that someone of his birth is superior ("Riddle" 46). Thus, Bell observes, "the ease with which Voldemort is able to dehumanize is entirely the constructed fault of the Wizarding world itself"—its inequality, racism, and exploitation of "lesser" beings (61). Rowling has told audiences that a major foundation of Voldemort's evil is that he was conceived without consent when his father was controlled by a love potion.[15] One could also speculate that Tom has several genetic strikes against him: the heritage of Slytherin, the Gaunts' inbreeding, and Tom Riddle, Sr.'s character.

These explanations have merit, but care-based theories offer additional perspectives on Voldemort's multifaceted situation. *Harry Potter and the Half-Blood Prince* invites readers to speculate about how Tom Riddle's early childhood might have contributed to the making of Lord Voldemort. Rowling has commented, "of course, everything would have changed if Merope had survived and raised him herself and loved him" ("J.K. Rowling Web Chat"), and she has decried

> how much measurable brain damage is done when a child is taken from its mother and placed in an institution. And when I say measurable, you can scan the brain and you will see that pathways haven't been made, and you can never get that back.
>
> (*Women*)[16]

Thus, it is legitimate to examine Tom's childhood at Wool's Orphanage, whose conditions, observed by Harry in the Pensieve, are superficially satisfactory: it is "shabby but spotlessly clean," and Mrs. Cole, its director since before Tom's arrival, seems "harassed" but "more anxious than unkind" (HBP 264). Nevertheless, it is a "rather grim, square building surrounded by high railings" and has a "bare courtyard"—hardly a warm, nurturing environment (HBP 263). The bareness and shabbiness suggest a lack of funding, the operation seems understaffed, and Mrs. Cole has a drinking problem. Although we can only infer the kind of babyhood Tom experienced, a good guess, given insufficient staff, is that he was held considerably less than most babies, and on top of that, "He was a funny baby too. He hardly ever cried" (HBP 267). In a family situation, a "good baby" who rarely cries will be cuddled, talked to, and played with, but in an understaffed institution, a child who doesn't compete for attention may get none. Moreover, this little boy was certainly "odd," so not surprisingly he "scared the other children" (HBP 267) and possibly some staff. Whether his lack of friends came before or after he scared people is not revealed, but by the time Dumbledore meets him he is hostile, isolated, secretive, and unusually self-sufficient.

In his work studying pathological responses to loss, psychologist John Bowlby has observed that children placed in situations of extreme detachment from others, who are discouraged from expressing their distress, will resist initially, but if their protests fail, will "shut away all the feeling they have about their loss" (406). A stoicism some might interpret as evidence of recovery is actually a sign of trauma (Gilligan and Snider 51). Such traumatized children disconnect themselves from others both emotionally and physically (Gilligan and Snider 55). As Gilligan and coauthor Naomi Snider observe, the result is children who focus on accumulating power and material things, which in a boy may easily be mistaken for the kind of independence and autonomy—even success—which "mirrors the pseudo-independence of manhood, which in patriarchy is synonymous with being fully human" (55–6). These children's angry despair is rarely expressed toward those responsible for their loss of connection but instead is repressed, often "projected onto others—typically someone weaker" (51). That is, such children may, like young Tom, bully other children. Moreover, "To avoid the pain of further loss, children raised in environments of emotional scarcity or adversity may sacrifice the hope or deny the very possibility of love" (Gilligan and Snider 59). Gilligan and Snider note that the more damaged children will "disconnect from their emotional desires and capacities" (63). In the most extreme cases, emotional detachment leads to criminality. How like the experience of the orphaned Tom Riddle! His rejection of love, his domination of others, his collecting of material trophies, and even the division of his soul (similar to what classical psychoanalysts call dissociation) are all forms of psychological resistance to his human need for connection, or "resistance in the sense of ... a reluctance to bring into consciousness things kept out of awareness" (*Joining* 105–6). Ironically, the types of rule breaking Voldemort embraces follow the script—the "rules"—of the most toxic forms of masculinity.

Harry, by contrast, resists the "rules" of masculinity. Why Harry emerged surprisingly unscathed from the trauma of losing his parents is not explained in the text, though Rowling has said, "what I wrote about Harry having been incredibly loved in his earliest days is measurably true: that literally will have given him protection that no one can undo. His brain will have developed in a way that Voldemort's brain didn't because Voldemort was from the moment of his birth institutionalized" (*Women*). Perhaps, too, Petunia was more attentive to her daughter's orphaned baby than she is when we meet Harry at eleven. Mrs. Figg, who babysits Harry frequently, treats him kindly. As Talia Schaffer points out in her discussion of caregivers in Victorian fiction, care is not just an emotion but an action, and in many instances, what matters is that a caregiver, whether they are emotionally engaged or not, fulfills the needs of the person cared for; ironically, as Dumbledore observes in *Half-Blood Prince*, the Dursleys, with their dearth of emotional "care" for Harry, may have better fulfilled his needs than they did the over-indulged Dudley's (55). Whatever the explanation, from the first times we see Harry, he is responding compassionately to a boa constrictor's imprisonment and unconsciously using his magic not to bully others but to resist bullying—regrowing his hair after a bad haircut and escaping to the roof of the school kitchen. Patrick McCauley theorizes that such events suggest that "rebellion against injustice can begin even before we are conscious of it" (46). Harry's response to privation is to be drawn immediately to motherly Molly Weasley at King's Cross Station and to empathize with Ron's poverty, delighting in sharing treats. Harry's responses are less like those typical of adolescent boys in patriarchy—withdrawing from relationships—and more like adolescent girls—an inclination toward self-sacrifice. Indeed, a small but important body of scholarship addresses the ways that the series interrogates the entire definition of masculine and feminine.[17] Strict gender binaries are challenged through Hagrid's mothering of Norbert the dragon, his pink umbrella, and fondness for knitting and cooking; and Dumbledore's partiality for knitting patterns; not to mention the many male characters who embrace an ethic of care.

Harry, Resistance, and the Ethic of Care

Harry's first forays into rule breaking seem unconnected to "resistance." He and Ron arouse Argus Filch's ire on their first morning, by attempting to force the door to the forbidden third-floor corridor, but only because they are lost. Harry's second infraction occurs during his first flying lesson when he violates Madam Hooch's injunction not to move, retrieving Neville's Remembrall from Draco Malfoy. He is standing up to a bully, but to call that "resistance" seems like a stretch—until we recall that a crucial element of the ethic of care is responding to others' needs and feelings. Nevertheless, in the early books, even when Harry breaks rules that interfere with his quests to protect others and, directly or indirectly, to fight Voldemort, any "resistance" is far from obvious. The word "resist," when it appears, is used only in a sense like "resist temptation"—for example, "Resisting the urge to take a look, Harry walked on by" (*CS* 198). Yet even in the first book, Harry breaks some rules on principle. When Hermione warns that he could be expelled for pursuing the Sorcerer's Stone, Harry's response shows that he's thinking well beyond house points or his own personal loss:

> "SO WHAT?" Harry shouted. "Don't you understand? If Snape gets hold of the Stone, Voldemort's coming back! Haven't you heard what it was like when he was trying to take over? There won't be any Hogwarts to get expelled from! He'll flatten it, or turn it into a school for the Dark Arts! Losing points doesn't matter anymore, can't you see? D'you think he'll leave you and your families alone if Gryffindor wins the House Cup? If I get caught before I can get to the Stone, well, I'll have to go back to the Dursleys and wait for Voldemort to find me there, it's only dying a bit later than I would have."
>
> (270)

Aside from his misunderstanding of Snape's role, Harry shows a surprisingly well-developed grasp of the stakes involved: Although he has been working all year to win house points, he is willing to lose them and even to sacrifice enrollment at Hogwarts, the first place in his memory that he considers home—in Schaffer's terms, a care community. Recognizing, moreover, that his life is in danger from Voldemort no matter what, he employs an ethic of care in thinking of "you and your families" and Hogwarts's very existence—and predicting with uncanny accuracy the Hogwarts of Book Seven. Protecting the stone is more to Harry than an "adventure" that happens to break a few school rules. Harry is already part of a resistance.

The concept of "resistance" becomes psychologically more complex as Harry learns to "resist" dementors (PA 188). The form his Patronus takes embodies care—Harry's longing for his father—and while the thoughts and memories Harry conjures to create the Patronus vary through the series, many concern his friendship with Ron and Hermione: emotional caring beats back isolation and depression. Resistance takes yet another psychological aspect in *Goblet of Fire*, when Mad-Eye Moody puts the Imperius Curse on students in Defense Against the Dark Arts class, "to see whether they could *resist* its effects" (GF 230; emphasis added). Not jumping onto a desk is hardly a matter of ideological principle, but since the curse can force people to do far more serious things than jump on desks or imitate a squirrel, this form of resistance has significance beyond the personal and psychological.

The word "resist" is also used to describe Occlumency in *Order of the Phoenix*: Snape tells Harry, "I am about to attempt to break into your mind [...] We are going to see how well you resist. I have been told that you have already shown aptitude at resisting the Imperius Curse. ... You will find that similar powers are needed for this" (534). Ironically, Harry does *not* succeed as well at Occlumency, though probably not due to lack of "aptitude," since he does, during his very first lesson, keep Snape from entering his thoughts about Cho; and, a couple of weeks later, Harry manages to enter Snape's childhood memories. Harry fails at Occlumency, partly, of course, because the piece of Voldemort's soul within him creates no ordinary connection, a fact that is not yet revealed in this volume. Also, Harry doesn't practice because he is curious about the closed door he sees in his/Voldemort's visions—a bad reason. Mostly, he is reluctant to perfect Occlumency because the foray into Voldemort's consciousness saved Arthur Weasley's life. Ironically, Voldemort exploits Harry's failure to close his mind, his "saving-people-thing" (OP 733), and his love for Sirius—all closely related—when he manipulates Harry into believing that Sirius is captive at the Ministry and lures Harry to the Hall of Prophecy, ultimately causing Sirius's death. While disobeying Dumbledore's directive to practice Occlumency has terrible consequences in *Order of the Phoenix*, in *Deathly Hallows* the open channel allows Harry to track Voldemort's actions and attitudes. Connection proves a weapon of espionage and resistance. Moreover, when it does become necessary to close his mind to Voldemort so that Harry can plan how to get the remaining Horcruxes, he "clutched his head, trying to help it *resist*" (500; emphasis added)—and succeeds.

That is, Harry's resistance to Occlumency reveals a paradoxical strength. Occlumency requires one to "let go of all emotion" (OP 535). Snape sneers that those, like Harry, who cannot resist Legilimency are "Fools who wear their hearts proudly on their sleeves, who cannot control their emotions, who wallow in sad memories and allow themselves to be provoked this easily—weak people, in other words" (OP 536). In Snape's view, emotion is weak, a classic patriarchal perspective. Harry denies that he is weak, but it takes Dumbledore to explain that when Voldemort enters Harry's consciousness at the climax of the battle in the Ministry, it is Harry's emotion, his grief at Sirius's death, that repels Voldemort's attack: "'There is no shame in what you are feeling, Harry,' said Dumbledore's voice. 'On the contrary ... the fact that you can feel pain like this is your greatest strength'" (OP 823). Later, Dumbledore adds, "That power also saved you from possession by Voldemort, because he could not bear to reside in a body so full of the force he detests. In the end, it mattered not that you could not close your mind. It was your heart that saved you" (OP 844). Dumbledore understands that Voldemort's and Snape's "control" over emotion, though empowering in classic patriarchal terms, is only superficially so.[18] Likewise, Gilligan has noted the "ability to read other minds"—speaking metaphorically of course—is another way of describing empathy (*Joining* 64). As Bealer has observed, love is the one form of magic available to Muggles (186).

During the scene in which Dumbledore makes these statements, following Sirius's death, Harry repeatedly shouts a statement psychologist Niobe Way often observes in adolescent boys: "I don't care." Way comments that boys who say this certainly do care—as does Harry—but are protecting themselves from feeling betrayal and loss. Not wishing to be vulnerable, because they associate vulnerability with being feminine or gay, the more these boys care, the more they insist they do not. Like Gilligan, Way links this response to patriarchy: "when experiences of betrayal are mixed with the dictates of masculinity and maturity (i.e., emotional stoicism and autonomy), boys often end up alone" (Way 198). Of course, when Harry insists, "I don't care," Dumbledore replies, accurately, "Oh yes, you do.... You have now lost your mother, your father, and the closest thing to a parent you have ever known. Of course you care" (OP 824). By listening to Harry, even allowing him to angrily smash Dumbledore's belongings, and by (finally) providing Harry with information that he should have known years before, Dumbledore helps Harry come to terms with his emotions, so that Harry handles losing Sirius far more effectively than he had handled Cedric's death, a trauma he had faced with no one to talk to. Way's and Gilligan's analyses of adolescent boys' struggles with caring not only support the idea that Harry's ability to care represents resistance to patriarchal pressures but also that Snape's and Voldemort's capacity to suppress feelings of betrayal and grief embodies the fundamental weakness of traditional masculine autonomy.

We know, of course, that Harry survives his final encounter with Voldemort in the Forbidden Forest because, as he says, "I was ready to die to stop you from hurting these people"—because of care (DH 738). But perhaps less noticed is that Harry's final advice to Voldemort expresses care: "before you try to kill me, I'd advise you to think about what you've done.... Think, and try for some remorse, Riddle. [...] It's your one last chance [...] it's all you've got left.... I've seen what you'll be otherwise.... Be a man ... try ... Try for some remorse" (741). Remorse, as Hermione had explained, is the sole "way of putting yourself back together" after splitting your soul to create a Horcrux by committing murder (DH 103). Harry has seen Voldemort's maimed soul during his King's Cross Station near-death experience, where the fragment of Voldemort's soul seemed both "indecent" and "shameful" (706), but also, significantly, "small and fragile and wounded" (707) and "pitiful" (706)—inspiring pity—that is, care. Dumbledore, of course, famously advises, "Do not pity the dead, Harry. Pity the living, and, above all, those who live without love. By returning, you may ensure that fewer souls are maimed, fewer families are torn apart" (DH 722). Dumbledore also repeatedly assures Harry that Voldemort's soul fragment is "beyond either of our help" (706–8). Perhaps what we are to understand is that while the soul fragment is beyond *Harry's* help or pity, the living Tom Riddle is another matter. He can himself "Try for some remorse," as Harry reminds him. Nearly certain that the phallic Elder Wand will not function for Voldemort, who "won't be killing anyone else" (38), Harry compassionately offers Voldemort a way to avoid his own destruction. Instead of taking the advice,

Voldemort is, as we know, "killed by his own rebounding curse" (744). Notably, Harry advises Voldemort that to "try for some remorse" would be to "Be a man." No doubt the distinction is partly between being human and being reptilian, and perhaps the language is taunting Voldemort regarding his manhood, but another interpretation is possible, that this remark mirrors the resistance to gender norms throughout the series. However much Voldemort might imagine that to "Be a man" means isolation and domination, Harry has learned that manhood entails caring for and protecting others, even self-sacrifice.

As Gilligan points out, patriarchy is all about hierarchy, while democracy is premised on equality. When Harry defeats Voldemort, patriarchy is obviously not destroyed along with him, but some of the separations and hierarchies he symbolizes are temporarily undermined in the Great Hall, as "nobody was sitting according to House anymore: All were jumbled together, teachers and pupils, ghosts and parents, centaurs and house-elves, and Firenze lay recovering in a corner, and Grawp peered in through a smashed window, and people were throwing food into his laughing mouth" (DH 745). In resisting Voldemort, Harry and his allies have also resisted patriarchy, and, for a time at least, have triumphed.

Traditional Political Resistance in *Harry Potter*

In and after *Order of the Phoenix*, "resistance" gets political, in the traditional sense, and the term is applied in familiar ways. There are striking parallels between anti-Hitler resistance movements and the Order of the Phoenix—including the small resistance cell comprised of Harry, Ron, and Hermione. Mid-twentieth-century resistance fighters engaged in espionage, not unlike Arthur Weasley's, Kingsley Shacklebolt's, and Tonks's work within the Ministry or Lupin's infiltrating the werewolves allied with Fenrir Greyback. Small groups of World War II resistance fighters engaged in sabotage and organized protests—like the Weasley twins disrupting Umbridge's control over Hogwarts in *Order of the Phoenix*, or Luna, Neville, and Ginny writing graffiti and standing up to the Carrows in *Deathly Hallows*. Resistance cells created underground publications and radio broadcasts, not unlike the *Quibbler* and *Potterwatch*. Just as members of the World War II resistance hid Jews and other endangered individuals, so Harry, Ron, and Hermione extricate Mary Cattermole and other Muggle-borns from the Muggle-born Registration hearings and encourage them and their families to leave the country. They also release POWs (Luna, Griphook, Dean, and Mr. Ollivander), and of course they break into the Ministry and Gringotts to retrieve the weapons that are Horcruxes.

The Order of the Phoenix resists not only Voldemort but also those who impede opposition to Voldemort, specifically Fudge, Umbridge, and their supporters. By the end of *Goblet of Fire*, the Ministry's corruption is unmistakable, as, for the second year in a row, Fudge authorizes inflicting the Dementor's Kiss without a trial or public testimony, this time on young Barty Crouch, who might otherwise have provided crucial information about Voldemort's return and the plot against Harry. *Order of the Phoenix* begins with more evidence of corruption: an orchestrated dementor attack; the subsequent expulsion threat and Wizengamot tribunal that nearly rejects Harry's self-defense case; a Ministry-orchestrated smear campaign against Harry and Dumbledore; and Umbridge's arrival at Hogwarts, ostensibly to teach Defense Against the Dark Arts, but actually, as Undersecretary to Fudge, to interfere with students' learning. Fudge had asserted that to admit that Voldemort is back would "start a panic that will destabilize everything we have worked for these last thirteen years" (GF 707). His (misplaced) distrust of Dumbledore's motives is fully consistent with the US Defense Department's interpretation of resistance as an effort to "disrupt civil order and stability" of an established government. Even more to the point, from Fudge's perspective, Voldemort's return could mean the "end of my career" (GF 708). When Umbridge denies that students need to learn to fight Voldemort, she is propping up Fudge's power.

Harry's initial rebellion against Umbridge, talking back in class and insisting that Voldemort has indeed returned, might be considered an individual act of conscience, not a collective one, for, at this point, few students share his knowledge about Voldemort. Punished cruelly and unjustly, Harry stubbornly endures and opts not to report the abuse, even to his friends, much less to the school administration, considering it a "private battle of wills" (269). But as social justice researcher Leroy H. Pelton observes, the Milgram experiments demonstrate the power of example: participants in the presence of dissenters who refused to administer shocks were less likely to administer shocks themselves, and in similar experiments, having *previously* observed someone who disobeyed increased the likelihood of disobedience (153). Thus, the very act of standing up to Umbridge in class begins the collective resistance—bookended, two years later, by Neville's explanation for talking back to Alecto Carrow: "The thing is, it helps when people stand up to them, it gives everyone hope. I used to notice that when you did it, Harry" (DH 574).

Many who study resistance describe some tactics as *performances* in their means of getting the attention of authorities and inspiring people to join the resistance; Martin Luther King, Jr., carefully orchestrated protests with media coverage in mind. Sociologist Hank Johnston identifies the "full cast of players in protest performances, the onlookers, the counter-protesters, the police, the military, and other agencies of social control" ("Analyzing" 5–6). Each of these "players" can be matched with characters in the series. Performance items include everything from street speakers to sit-ins, occupations, mass marches, protest signs, and badges—like those Hermione creates for S.P.E.W. (the Society to Promote Elvish Welfare). Hermione's early methods, learned presumably from Muggle protests, translate poorly to the magical world, but the Weasley twins are masters of splashy protests, such as their creation of—appropriately—a swamp in the Hogwarts entrance hall. Then, when Umbridge authorizes Filch (an "agent of social control" in Johnston's terms) to whip them, they stage a dramatic exit from Hogwarts, cheered by "tumultuous applause," to open their shop (OP 675). Watching one of the twins' rockets fly by, Hermione remarks, "happily, 'd'you know . . . I think I'm feeling a bit . . . *rebellious*" (OP 634). Harry, too, performs, though less theatrically, when he argues in class about Voldemort's return, when he tells prospective D.A. members about his run-ins with Voldemort, and even when he is interviewed in the *Quibbler*. Later, *Potterwatch* is a performance, and even though the intentions are to be secretive, the incursions into the Ministry and Gringotts, climaxed by the dramatic escape on the dragon, end up having large audiences, effectively inspiring wider resistance.

Ironically, Umbridge's methods of suppressing resistance motivate the very rebellion she seeks to prevent. She refuses to teach practical defensive spells, both to conceal Voldemort's renewed threats and out of fear that Dumbledore will form "his own private army, with which he will be able to take on the Ministry of Magic" (OP 303). While the young people rightly consider Fudge's fear of Dumbledore, in Ron's words, "the stupidest thing I've ever heard" (OP 303), when they organize to learn forbidden skills, they select their group's name, the D.A., to "stand for Dumbledore's Army because that's the Ministry's worst fear, isn't it?" (OP 392). Dumbledore's comment to Harry the following year applies as well to the backlash against Umbridge and Fudge as it does to Voldemort: "Voldemort himself created his worst enemy, just as tyrants everywhere do! Have you any idea how much tyrants fear the people they oppress? All of them realize that, one day, amongst their many victims, there is sure to be one who rises against them and strikes back!" (HBP 510). In agreeing to lead the D.A., Harry's thoughts are about fighting Voldemort but also about resisting Ministry tyranny—not just about adolescent rule breaking. This is principled resistance. To be sure, it starts as a sort of study group, but the young people practice forbidden skills, so by definition the group is *rebellious*—the word in Harry's mind as he speculates that Professor McGonagall would not allow them to use her classroom for meetings. Once the group is formed, "The knowledge that they were doing something to *resist* Umbridge and the Ministry, and that he was a key part of *the rebellion*, gave Harry a feeling of immense satisfaction" (OP 350; emphasis added). Notably, too, Dumbledore's Army, unlike the Ministry, has an elected leader—Harry—and a name its members vote to adopt. It welcomes students from any of the Hogwarts Houses. Its democratic structure implicitly rejects Ministry authoritarianism and exclusivity, as is often the case in resistance movements against oppression.

In *Deathly Hallows*, after Voldemort overthrows the Ministry, Lupin uses the language of "resistance" to describe the situation. By Imperiusing the new Minister, Pius Thicknesse, Voldemort has created a puppet state with classic totalitarian features but a veneer of lawfulness. No one is sure exactly whether Voldemort is in charge, making people afraid to speak up. As Lupin explains, "Voldemort is playing a very clever game. Declaring himself might have provoked open rebellion: Remaining masked has created confusion, uncertainty, and fear." Under these circumstances, to discourage "open rebellion," the Ministry demonizes

Harry to undermine his influence: "Now that Dumbledore is dead, you—the Boy Who Lived—were sure to be the symbol and rallying point for any *resistance* to Voldemort. But by suggesting that you had a hand in the old hero's death, Voldemort has not only set a price upon your head, but sown doubt and fear amongst many who would have defended you" (DH 208; emphasis added). To sow division, the occupied Ministry employs propaganda about Harry because he is a particularly unifying symbol of "resistance" or even "open rebellion."

Later in *Deathly Hallows*, Lupin publicly identifies Harry with a "resistance" struggle, in an interview on *Potterwatch*—whose name shows Harry's power as a symbol. Asked by Lee Jordan if he believes that Harry is still alive, Lupin replies emphatically:

> There is no doubt at all in my mind that his death would be proclaimed as widely as possible by the Death Eaters if it had happened, because it would strike a deadly blow at the morale of those resisting the new regime. "The Boy Who Lived" remains a symbol of everything for which we are fighting: the triumph of good, the power of innocence, the need to keep resisting.
>
> (DH 441)

Lupin twice uses the word *resist* to convey Harry's significance and to rally the resistance by naming it and by strengthening the morale he understands the Death Eaters wish to suppress.

Hermione as a Resistance Leader

Although Dumbledore organizes and leads the Order of the Phoenix and Harry leads Dumbledore's Army, Hermione is the primary instigator of student resistance, beginning with her efforts advocating for house-elves and accelerating when she encourages Harry to form the D.A. Hermione provides the moral conscience and has a gift of expanding a situation's moral context from the immediate to the systemic. Arguably, this begins in *Chamber of Secrets*, when she suggests brewing Polyjuice Potion to find out who opened the chamber. She concedes, "We'd be breaking about fifty school rules" (159) but insists, "*I* don't want to break rules, you know. *I* think threatening Muggle-borns is far worse than brewing up a difficult potion" (165). As when in Book One Harry asserts that preserving Hogwarts is more important than following Hogwarts rules, here Hermione weighs two ethical principles: stealing is bad, but killing people is much worse. She chooses to break one ethical code to preserve the more important one.

Hermione obviously takes the lead in promoting elf rights. To be sure, many arguments have been made about the insufficiencies of S.P.E.W.,[19] one of the most pointed being Farah Mendlesohn's. Writing prior to the publication of *Order of the Phoenix*, Mendlesohn grumbles, "Radicalism, as embodied in Hermione, is irrational, ignorant, and essentially transient. ... [P]ositive action to change matters is always ascribed at best to foolishness and at worst to evil intent" (306). As it happens, Rowling shares some of Mendelsohn's skepticism about Hermione, describing her early efforts as "quite self-righteous" and noting her "blunders towards the very people she's trying to help"; however, Rowling's "heart is entirely with her" as she goes through "a growing-up thing, … realizing you don't have quite as much power as you think you might have and having to accept that" (Interview with Evan Solomon). Nevertheless, it is Hermione who consistently raises the level of discussion from a particular grievance to a political issue. While Harry sympathizes with Dobby and frees him from the Malfoys and then, in *Goblet of Fire*, pities Winky, only Hermione speaks up in Winky's defense—confronting a group of powerful Ministry wizards. Afterward, she protests to Mr. Weasley with such passion that he replies, catching her drift, "Hermione, I agree with you, … but now is not the time to discuss elf rights" (GF 139). When she learns about the Hogwarts house-elves, Hermione's thoughts turn practical and political: working hours, wages, sick leaves, and pensions. She determines methods for "making a stand about elf rights" (GF 194), and within the first week of classes attempts to organize her classmates to change the situation. S.P.E.W. has both political and economic goals: "changing the law about non-wand use, and trying to get an elf into the Department for the Regulation and Control of Magical Creatures, because they're shockingly underrepresented" (225).

Hermione's plans and methods, workable though they might be in a functioning Muggle democracy, fall flat in magical Britain and even inspire ridicule, though as Bharati Kasibhatla points out, Hermione is mocked because she "challenges the very structure that the others are trying to protect" (123). In Chapter Three, I have more to say about house-elves themselves, but for now the important point is that Hermione recognizes that their enslavement transcends the individual situations of Dobby, Winky, or even the Hogwarts house-elves but represents a systemic problem: "'It's people like *you*, Ron,' Hermione began hotly, 'who prop up rotten and unjust *systems*, just because they're too lazy to—'" (GF 125; emphasis added). Jackie C. Horne has observed, "[Hermione's] campaign on behalf of elf-rights starts not when she witnesses an individual elf suffering or mistreated, as did Harry, but rather when she recognizes how her own privileges as a student at Hogwarts are supported by the labor of others" (84-5). That Hermione is ridiculed illustrates, as Katrin Berndt points out, that "rebels are often perceived as obnoxious trouble-makers before they succeed in introducing a new order" (165). And that she continues despite the ridicule proves that the Sorting Hat was right: she has the courage and chivalry of a true Gryffindor. Bryccham Carey rightly notes that S.P.E.W.'s methods become untenable as the wizarding world increasingly abandons the rule of law itself. To be sure, no "new order" arrives for house-elves as the series ends, but Hermione does successfully raise her friends' consciousness. Harry, hearing how Hokey the house-elf was falsely blamed for Hepzibah Smith's death, exclaims indignantly, "because she was a house-elf." The narrator adds, "He had rarely felt more in sympathy with the society Hermione had set up, S.P.E.W." (HBP 439). Hermione has enabled Harry to recognize both systemic discrimination and the wisdom of organized political action to counter it. What is ineffective for a fourteen year-old whose only social justice knowledge comes from the Muggle world nevertheless suggests an activist career path for an adult witch. As Rowling revealed in her July 2007 web chat, "Hermione began her post-Hogwarts career at the Department for the Regulation and Control of Magical Creatures where she was instrumental in greatly improving life for house-elves and their ilk. She then moved (despite her jibe to Scrimgeour) to the Dept. of Magical Law Enforcement where she was a progressive voice who ensured the eradication of oppressive, pro-pureblood laws."

In *Order of the Phoenix*, Hermione is the first student to infer that Umbridge's speech at the start-of-term feast "means the Ministry's interfering at Hogwarts" (214) and the first to challenge her teaching methods. And although she is, typically, concerned about her O.W.L. exams, when she proposes that Harry teach defense lessons, one of her first comments is "this is much more important than homework!" (OP 325); as she speaks, "her face was suddenly alight with the kind of fervor that S.P.E.W. usually inspired in her" (325)—that is, like she's focusing on principle. As she explains her idea and suggests including fellow students, she once again addresses principles: "I really think you ought to teach anyone who wants to learn. I mean, we're talking about defending ourselves against V-Voldemort ... it doesn't seem fair if we don't offer the chance to other people" (OP 332). By including others, Hermione transforms personal rule breaking into organized shared resistance whose efficacy only grows.

Subtler Resistance in *Harry Potter*

Nor does the only resistance in the series occur among insurgents in the Order of the Phoenix and Dumbledore's Army. Sharp, the political scientist, contends that non-cooperation is one of a resistance movement's most powerful tools. In the magical world, some who publicly comply with the Ministry engage in non-cooperation. These include whoever causes rainfall in the Ministry offices of important Death Eaters and even the workers compiling pamphlets about the dangers of "Mudbloods," who covertly call Umbridge "the old hag" (DH 249) and cheerfully interrupt work to examine the Decoy Detonator Harry deploys as a distraction. Moreover, as sociologist Johnston points out, one subtle form of resistance is "refusal decisions" among those enforcing social control in an authoritarian state ("Analyzing" 13). In China, for example, Communist Party members whose families attend underground Christian churches often look the other way (9). Refusal decisions and other types of "porous" social control appear here and there in the series. For example, Kingsley Shacklebolt, nominally heading the search for Sirius, is instead quietly "feeding the Ministry information that Sirius is in Tibet" (OP 95). When the Weasley twins detonate fireworks at Hogwarts (a classic resistance tactic in its own right), "Professor Umbridge spent her first afternoon as headmistress running all over the school answering the summonses of the other teachers, none of whom seemed able to rid their rooms of the fireworks without her." A "beaming" Professor Flitwick explains, "I could have got rid of the sparklers myself, of course, but I wasn't sure whether I had the *authority*" (OP 633–4). Outwardly supporting the acting headmistress' authority, the professors nevertheless undermine her control. Similarly, two years later, the professors avoid referring students to the Carrows for punishment (DH 573). Among them, only Hagrid and McGonagall are Order of the Phoenix members.

Some refusal decisions reflect political scientist Karen Stenner's finding that when people with "authoritarian dispositions" are coping with personal trauma, like financial distress, family illness, crime victimization, or loss of a loved one, that reduces their authoritarianism (32). Thus Mr. Crouch, out of love for his dying wife and possibly even a bit for his son, helps break young Barty out of Azkaban, dramatically undermining Ministry authority despite his assiduous efforts to present himself as inflexible against Voldemort's followers. Narcissa Malfoy, too, is not technically a Death Eater but is so closely allied that her attempts to protect Draco could be seen as "refusal decisions." Though not aiming to forestall Voldemort's goal of killing Dumbledore, Narcissa works to undermine his means: having Draco perform the murder. Evidence that her small act of rebellion is "great treachery to the Dark Lord" is her admission to Snape, when she seeks his help, that "the Dark Lord has forbidden" her to speak of the plan (HBP 32). Yet speak she does, and even binds herself and Snape in an "unbreakable vow" that he will undertake the murder if Draco cannot, to save Draco's life. For Narcissa, Draco's safety outweighs all else. In the final Forbidden Forest scene, in the wake of numerous family setbacks under Voldemort's rule, she makes the refusal decision to lie that Harry is dead. She makes that act of resistance because she cares more about her son than any ideology or leader. To be sure, Narcissa's family loyalty is at times difficult to distinguish from pride in pureblood lineage, but genuine love seems to outweigh all else. Snape, of course, engages in the most extreme non-cooperation with Voldemort. Care considerations outweigh patriarchal rules considerations.

To complicate matters, some might argue that there are two resistance movements, one led by Dumbledore—and later, Harry—and the other led by Voldemort, who, along with his Death Eaters, successfully resists and overthrows the Ministry of Magic. From a Death Eater perspective, blood purity is a just cause, and a government that tolerates "mudbloods" (who in their view do not count as true wizards or witches) and "race traitors" is, accordingly, illegitimate. Given that the Minister of Magic is not, in many instances, an elected position, installing Thicknesse is perfectly consistent with Ministry practice. Hence, from this perspective, overthrowing Scrimgeour's Ministry is a just insurrection and the Order of the Phoenix are seditious terrorists. Rooting out such dissident radicals, who want to assassinate Voldemort, the government's leader, is fully justified. Harry, that is, deserves his label of "Undesirable No. 1," and characters like Narcissa Malfoy are, likewise, traitors. Of course, Thicknesse is literally a puppet leader, under an Imperius Curse, not really the Minister of Magic; Voldemort's puppet government is most accurately described as an "occupying" force. But it's also true that when the Ministry under Thicknesse's supposed leadership systematically imprisons its enemies, it merely perpetuates injustices begun under previous Ministries. The difference lies only in whom the Ministry imprisons and what laws it accuses them of breaking. Harry resists both.

A Marauder's Map of the Book's Geography

Resistance, then, involves breaking rules, but obviously not all rule breaking is beneficial—nor is all rebellion. Not all trouble is what Congressman John Lewis would consider "good trouble," nor is all mischief bad. The rest of this book explores some of the ways *Harry Potter* confronts these ambiguities and invites its readers to distinguish juvenile mischief from principled resistance.

Chapter One, "Made to Be Broken," charts out rules, regulations, laws, and norms that Harry and his allies resist. These include the laws of magic, which, like Muggles' scientific laws, are essentially unbreakable—or broken only at great peril. The crucial difference between Voldemort and Dumbledore, the two most powerful wizards of their era, is that Dumbledore, who himself treats most rules cavalierly, respects a magical law that Voldemort cannot even perceive, that love is "a force that is at once more wonderful and more terrible than death, than human intelligence, than forces of nature" (OP 843). The rules of Quidditch, which Harry respects, represent regulations at their most arbitrary and static, reflecting problems with more important rules of the magical world. Hogwarts's school rules seem to function primarily as testing grounds for Harry's ethical choices; moreover, enforcement of school rules is arbitrary and inconsistent. That inconsistency pales by comparison, however, with the inconsistency with which the Ministry of Magic administers laws and decrees. The Ministry is undemocratic; many of the laws are trivial or unjust; and it applies laws unevenly, giving preferential treatment to some and discriminating against others. In short, the rules structuring British wizarding culture represent a level of systemic injustice that practically demands resistance.

The second chapter, "'Filth! Scum! By-products of Dirt and Vileness': 'Mudbloods,' Dirt, Privilege, and Systemic Oppression in the *Harry Potter* Series," focuses primarily on unwritten rules—social norms—that shape wizarding culture. The magical world is marred by wizard privilege, analogous to real-world white privilege. Wizards dominate other beings, from house-elves to Muggles; and "purebloods" have more privilege than "mudbloods." This language reflects a pattern in the series, of imagery and language about dirt and cleanliness. Anthropologist Mary Douglas, in her 1966 study *Purity and Danger*, argues that "dirt" is culturally defined. Recent research on disgust has found correlations between xenophobia and disgust sensitivity—repulsion by things considered dirty and contaminating. Privileged social in-groups label members of out-groups as "dirty," to justify class divisions, authoritarianism, and genocide. In the wizarding world, those who are most offended by impurity and dirt—such as so-called "mudbloods"—are, of course, Voldemort and his sympathizers. What characters assess as dirty and disgusting ultimately says more about the characters' value systems and the prevailing social system than about the person or object being assessed. By the same token, cleaning may be obsessive like Petunia Dursley's or shade into Voldemort's ethnic cleansing; yet it may also express love, as when houses are cleaned for special occasions. In a culture premised on hate, oppressing others for being "dirty" is the "norm," but cleaning in the service of love represents resistance. Likewise resisting oppressive unspoken norms requires recognizing privilege. The chapter concludes with an analysis of Ron Weasley's gradual recognition of his privilege and his progress, however halting and incomplete, toward anti-racism.

Chapter Three, "'How Dare You Defy Your Masters?' Rules, Roles, and Resistance in the Potterverse's Domestic Realm," explores resistance among two analogous groups that seem least likely to rebel: house-elves and housewives. Although enslaved and ostensibly submissive, house-elves "have a powerful magic of their own." The exceptions to the norm of the "happy house-elf," like Dobby and Kreacher, illustrate that far from being "natural," house-elf enslavement is a matter of ancient enchantments. The issue of "natural" capacities of elves is explored by analogy with John Stuart Mill's classic discussion in *The Subjection of Women* of similarities between slavery and women's subordination. Some elves do manage to rebel. That they generally comply can be attributed to another aspect of their power: their love of their families. House-elves' protective love is one of several analogies to domestic women in the series. A "relational feminist" approach illuminates the "power the Dark Lord knows not": sacrificial love can resist and ultimately overcome the patriarchal oppression embodied in Lord Voldemort.

In the fourth chapter, "'Creative Maladjustment': Creativity and Resistance in the *Harry Potter* Series," I explore the ways the magical resistance movement illustrates what Martin Luther King, Jr., called "creative maladjustment" in the face of "things in our society to which we should never be adjusted." The chapter explores creative ways Harry and his allies refuse to adjust to systemic problems in magical culture. The "maladjustment" of rule breakers in the magical resistance movement exemplifies core traits of creativity: it is both "novel" and "useful." Their approaches illustrate a crucial trait of creativity, "divergent thinking," in that they break the "rules" of wizarding culture. Ironically, some of the most creative characters in the series include malevolent rule breakers—Dolores Umbridge, Rita Skeeter, and Lord Voldemort himself, "creator" of Horcruxes. But the magical resistance is ultimately more creative, for they defy the wizarding status quo.

Some forms of creative invention may raise questions about lying and truth, the topic of Chapter Five, "'Do You Really Think This Is about Truth or Lies?' Honesty and Resistance in the *Harry Potter* Series." One might imagine that a rule breaker like Harry would use lying as a major resistance tool. Indeed, he and his allies do lie. But official lies and censorship are the modus operandi in the wizarding world's corrupt autocracy. Thus, to assert the truth, as Harry does, for example by insisting that Voldemort has returned, represents a radical rebellion—for which Dolores Umbridge sadistically punishes him. Umbridge and the Ministry of Magic subscribe to a relativistic, constructivist approach to truth: the truth is what those in power say is true. Harry, by contrast, insists on facts that correspond to actually observed realities. Meanwhile, as the *Daily Prophet* becomes little more than state-run media, alternative outlets like the *Quibbler* and *Potterwatch* gain importance as alternative voices that foster resistance.

The book's brief epilogue "Mischief Managed?" notes that however satisfying we may find the defeat of one charismatic leader, it does not end the underlying social problems that brought him to power in the first place. The systemic oppression of house-elves cannot be conquered in a single generation and requires a revolution in wizard ideology. Moreover, even good wizards do bad things: Dumbledore dabbles in authoritarianism and attempts to justify it with "empty words" about the Greater Good; for a time, Harry, too, flirts with Unforgivable Curses "for the Greater Good." The wizarding world, like our own, is full of ambiguities, but that makes considered resistance all the more important.

Notes

1 The important exceptions are, of course, the Room of Requirement and Chamber of Secrets.
2 While, technically, this statement is accurate, it distorts the truth, since two chapters later, Harry, Hermione, Neville, and Draco are all caught violating curfew, receive detentions, and lose fifty house points each, finding themselves ostracized as a result. Here and elsewhere, rule breaking certainly has consequences.
3 These include Glanzer, Griesinger, Kern, Neal, and Moshe Rosenberg.
4 See the work of Edmund N. Kern and two pairs of researchers: Lana A. Whited and M. Katherine Grimes, and Wendy N. Law and Anna K. Teller.
5 Other critics who point out flaws in the Potterverse include many of the authors of articles in the important early essay collections, especially Elizabeth E. Heilman's *Harry Potter's World* (2003), in which Turner-Vorbeck's essay appears; and Giselle Liza Anatol's *Reading Harry Potter* (2003).
6 I discuss critiques of the series' racial politics in Chapter Two and the unresolved house-elf problem in the Epilogue.
7 See Karin E. Westman on the ways the series' third person limited point of view depicts Harry's moral growth.
8 See the epilogue on Harry's decision to use the Cruciatus and Imperius Curses in *Deathly Hallows*.
9 On Voldemort as a malignant narcissist, see Prinzi, pp. 154–57. On charismatic leaders and narcissism, see, for example, the work of Jerrold M. Post.
10 See, for example, Castro, Prinzi, Reagin, and Wente.
11 See McDaniel, "Dumbledore's," on parallels between Dumbledore's Army and a nonviolent World War II student resistance group, The White Rose Society. This essay, which I discovered after my book was drafted, discusses many of the same correspondences I identify between the wizard resistance and historical resistance.

12 Among the thousands of signs at the Women's March on 21 January 2017, and at the young people's March for our Lives' gun control marches on 24 March 2018, among others, a remarkable number have featured *Harry Potter*-related slogans, as do numerous t-shirts and protest buttons.

13 Further complicating matters, scholars such as Erica Chenoweth and Orion A. Lewis distinguish the resistance from revolution by whether the civilian resistance is armed; but of course in the Potterverse, all magical humans are "armed" with wands, weakening that distinction for our purposes.

14 Although I have since seen the idea elsewhere, I remain grateful to my student Victoria Gonzalez for first calling my attention to the phallic implications of wands.

15 In a web chat, Rowling explains that Riddle's conception under the influence of Amortentia is "a symbolic way of showing that he came from a loveless union" and that "it shows coercion, and there can't be many more prejudicial ways to enter the world than as the result of such a union" ("J. K. Rowling Web Chat").

16 Many care theorists would disagree with Rowling here, arguing that paid care—as opposed to family-based care—is not necessarily inferior if it is not relegated to under-funded institutions with overworked and underpaid staff. Rather, "Our moral obligations to care for others ... generate collective responsibilities to organize our political, economic, international, and cultural institutions at least in part to support caring practices and care for individuals in need" (Engster 2).

17 See, for example, Camacci, "Multi-Gaze" and "Prisoner"; Gallardo-C and Smith; Groves, ch. 7; Anne Collins Smith; and Wolosky, "Gendered."

18 Rowling has said that Draco Malfoy "would be very gifted in Occlumency," because he "is very capable of compartmentalizing his life and his emotions, and always has done. So he's shut down his pity, enabling him to bully effectively. He's shut down compassion[;] how else would you become a Death Eater?" ("Leaky," Part Two).

19 Meredith Cherland, Rachel McCarthy James, Bharati Kasibhatla, Jeanne Hoeker LaHaie, and Christine Schott, among others, fault Hermione's activism or the depiction of it, or both. I agree with Kathryn N. McDaniel ("Real") that its greatest impact, at least within canon, is on Ron and Harry's attitudes—and the readers'. One might argue that despite her good intentions, Hermione only makes a difference for the house-elves themselves when she interacts personally with an individual, Kreacher. In that regard, her weaknesses and strengths in working for house-elves illustrates Nel Noddings's observation that "Those who care about others in the justice sense must keep in mind that the objective is to ensure that caring actually occurs. Caring-about is empty if it does not culminate in caring relations" (*Starting* 24).

1
"MADE TO BE BROKEN"
The Laws, Rules, and Norms of the Magical World

The word *resist* is a transitive verb: a person resists *something*: temptation, an opponent, or political oppression. Frequently, resistance entails breaking unjust laws or rules. To analyze issues surrounding rule breaking and resistance in *Harry Potter*, we need to consider what rules and laws exist in the Potterverse and some of their implications. To a great degree, magical rules resemble Muggle rules, ranging from the scientific to the political, from school- to home-based, from sports rules to unwritten social norms. The legitimacy of magical rules ranges from the (generally) unquestionable—the scientific (laws of magic)—to the arbitrary but acknowledged—athletics—to the arbitrary and ill-conceived—many school and Ministry regulations and wizarding social norms. The depiction of these rules and norms invites readers to evaluate them and by implication to assess which should be observed and which resisted.

Laws of Magic and "what's at stake"

Let's start with laws of magic, which are both the most immutable and most mysterious of wizard laws, comparable to Muggle scientific laws. Granted, when Muggles use the term "laws" for scientific principles, it means something very different than legislative statutes that require human enforcement. It is also true that no one in the Potterverse directly refers to "scientific" laws, because principles of magic draw on a Medieval world view antedating the scientific revolution. Just to add to the fun, magical phenomena shatter some Muggle scientific laws: consider apparition, *Wingardium Leviosa*, or the permeable wall at Platform 9 ¾. Nevertheless, as the characters gain magical knowledge, we hear about principles resembling science—and sometimes called "laws." These include Golpalott's Third Law, in potion-making, which, as Hermione recites,

DOI: 10.4324/9781003312260-2

"states-that-the-antidote-for-a-blended-poison-will-be-equal-to-more-than-the-sum-of-the-antidotes-for-each-of-the-separate-components" (HBP 374). During the trio's final adventures, they contend with the fact that "food's one of the five exceptions to Gamp's Law of Elemental Transfiguration": it cannot be created from nothing but must be retrieved from known sources (DH 578). We can deduce that other laws of magic include that people cannot be brought back from death and that some spell damage cannot be healed—such as George's lost ear or Dumbledore's cursed hand. Something akin to a law of magic apparently compels Peter Pettigrew's demise, anticipated four years earlier when Dumbledore had explained, "When one wizard saves another wizard's life, it creates a certain bond between them. [...] This is magic at its deepest, its most impenetrable, Harry. But trust me . . . the time may come when you will be very glad you saved Pettigrew's life" (PA 427). More overtly, Mr. Ollivander explains that "Subtle laws govern wand ownership" (DH 494).

These principles of magical reality resemble the law of gravity or Newton's laws of motion, statements that describe how things behave in (magical) nature, phenomena that, presumably, witches and wizards have repeatedly observed. We can assume a magical law, like a scientific law, always applies if the circumstances are consistent; one cannot "break" such a law, unlike a human-written statute. Although laws of magic cannot be broken, effective wizardry depends on critical thinking about them. That the name "Unspeakables" is given to wizards who work in the Department of Mysteries, the closest thing in the wizarding world to a scientific research institute, suggests an unhealthy suppression of information about underlying magical principles. Thus, it is fitting that the closest people to experimental scientists in the series are the rule-breaking Weasley twins.[1]

A magical law that shades into an official Ministry regulation concerns time travel. In *Prisoner of Azkaban*, Professor McGonagall allows Hermione to use a Time-Turner so she can take more than one class at the same hour. She warns Hermione, however, not to be seen and not to change the past in any other way, because "awful things have happened when wizards have meddled with time" (PA 399). Thus, when Dumbledore encourages Harry and Hermione to rescue Sirius Black and Buckbeak the hippogriff by going back in time, he warns, "Miss Granger, you know the law—you know what is at stake. . . . *You—must—not—be—seen*" (393). Accordingly, Hermione insists to Harry, "We're breaking one of the most important wizarding laws! Nobody's supposed to change time, nobody!" (PA 398). And yet, at Dumbledore's instigation, they do just that. While magical laws surrounding time can be broken, unlike, say, Gamp's Law of Elemental Transfiguration, doing so is so risky that statutes governing it are scarcely necessary; nevertheless, the Ministry tightly controls access to Time-Turners.

Noel Chevalier sees the study of magic as comparable to the study of science and argues that readers gradually realize that magic—like science—cannot itself solve ethical and social problems; this is Rufus Scrimgeour's point when, in response to the Muggle Prime Minister's asking why the Ministry of Magic can't use magic to fight Voldemort, Scrimgeour replies, "The trouble is, the other side can do magic too" (HBP 18). But while magic alone can't solve ethical problems, understanding the laws of what Dumbledore calls "magic at its deepest" seems crucial for avoiding magic's most severe ethical pitfalls. This is illustrated in Dumbledore's commentary on the story of "The Warlock's Hairy Heart" in *The Tales of Beedle the Bard*, in which he seems to identify another law of magic only indirectly described in the seven novels of the *Harry Potter* canon. In the story, a warlock, to avoid feeling love or grief, magically locks his heart in a box in a dungeon. Dumbledore compares the warlock's locking his heart away to creating a Horcrux:

> Although Beedle's hero is not seeking to avoid death, he is dividing what was clearly not meant to be divided—body and heart, rather than soul—and in doing so, he is falling foul of the first of Adalbert Waffling's Fundamental Laws of Magic:
> Tamper with the deepest mysteries—the source of life, the essence of self—only if prepared for consequences of the most extreme and dangerous kind.
> And sure enough, in seeking to become superhuman this foolhardy young man renders himself inhuman.
>
> (58–9)

As the commentary suggests, Voldemort's creation of Horcruxes, like the warlock's hairy heart, violates this "fundamental" law, in that Voldemort "tamper[s] with the deepest mysteries—the source of life" when he splits his soul by committing murder. As Horace Slughorn warns, splitting the soul is "against nature" (HBP 498).

Dumbledore's interpretation also explains that the warlock's story illustrates "one of the greatest, and least acknowledged, temptations of magic: the quest for invulnerability. Of course, such a quest is nothing more or less than a foolish fantasy. No man or woman alive, magical or not, has ever escaped some form of injury, whether physical, mental or emotional. To hurt is as human as to breathe" (*Tales* 55–6). These insights, surely meant to apply to Voldemort, are consistent with Carol Gilligan's observation that under patriarchy, men are encouraged to cut themselves off from their capacity to care, from their vulnerability, greatly to their detriment, for "Vulnerability, once associated with women, is a characteristic of humans" (*Joining* 43). With the attempt to become invulnerable, with an incomplete soul, Voldemort does become less human—and ultimately not invulnerable at all, a fact he cannot grasp. In this case, breaking the law does not pay. These laws are neither made nor enforced by humans, and as such seem to require more respect.

This discussion of magical laws points to a crucial difference between the two most powerful wizards of Harry's time: Dumbledore and Voldemort, both rule breakers. Voldemort attempts to break such fundamental laws as the "source of life" and completely fails to understand that love is "a force that is at once more wonderful and more terrible than death, than human intelligence, than forces of nature" (OP 843). For all his skills, he lacks understanding of magical laws or the costs of breaking them. Dumbledore learned from the consequences of his youthful desire to become the invulnerable master of Death—though he briefly forgets the lesson in his attempts to access the Resurrection Stone. Generally, though, Dumbledore applies fundamental laws of magic as means to defeat evil. Respecting magic's "deepest mysteries," he readily overlooks minor human rules about curfews and even important ones about time travel, but in the interest of larger ethical principles such as saving innocent lives. Voldemort, by contrast, has no qualms about killing or torturing, no respect for magical laws that don't enhance his own power, and a surprising fondness for creating new rules like forbidding people from saying his name.

Quidditch Rules and Rule Breaking and the Wizarding World's "Particular Character"

Early in *Harry Potter and the Half-Blood Prince*, Hermione jinxes Cormac McLaggen with a Confundus charm during Quidditch tryouts. McLaggen "sh[oots] off in completely the wrong direction," missing a save, and as a result, Ron lands the position of Keeper on Gryffindor's team (225). When I have asked students about this incident, the consensus is that Hermione has cheated but that the narrative makes light of the incident, which mostly shows Hermione's growing affection for Ron. Moreover, they say, McLaggen doesn't deserve the Keeper position, for he is arrogant and a poor sport; when he finally does play Keeper, McLaggen almost single-handedly loses the match for Gryffindor by knocking out Harry with a Bludger. Students argue that Hermione jinxes McLaggen not to create an unfair advantage; she only wants to make Ron happy. So while underhanded, it is not, strictly speaking, cheating.

As cheating incidents go, Hermione's Confundus charm is relatively trivial, especially in a world threatened by Voldemort's overwhelming evil. And yet cheating in sports may tell us more than may at first seem apparent. As Rick Reilly observes in his 2019 book *Commander in Cheat*, "the way Trump does golf is sort of the way he does a presidency, which is to operate as though the rules are for other people." Observes Reilly, "Golf is like bicycle shorts. ... It reveals a lot about a man" (12). Unlike laws of magic, the rules of games have neither natural origin, mysterious significance, nor strictly speaking, practical purpose. And yet, of course, rules make any sport what it is, which is why people treat them so seriously. Furthermore, Rowling has suggested that studying Quidditch teaches a great deal about magical culture: "I had been pondering the things that hold a society together, cause it to congregate and signify its particular character and knew I needed a sport" (Furness).

Judging from *Quidditch through the Ages* and the rampant cheating during the Triwizard Tournament, wizards have a cavalier attitude toward sports rules—a sardonic commentary both about the "particular character" of the wizarding world and about Muggle sports. Kenilworthy Whisp, putative author of *Quidditch through the Ages*, asserts that "Rules are of course 'made to be broken'" (28), hardly surprising when we consider that Quidditch has only one referee to the fourteen players who compete in a large horizontal space (a 500×180 ft oval) with no vertical limit (*Quidditch* 17, 27). By contrast, an NBA basketball game has three officials for the ten players on the 50×94 ft court. Notably, while there are seven hundred possible Quidditch fouls, the full list of fouls is kept secret, lest players "get ideas" (*Quidditch* 28). Perhaps that could happen, but a rule book no one can see invites arbitrary officiating, a weakness not unrelated to wider problems with magical enforcement of rules and laws.

Nevertheless, Harry never commits any of the possible fouls.[2] That is partly because fewer Quidditch fouls can be committed by a Seeker, and indeed Seekers are more likely to be targets of fouls than are players in other positions. Further, Harry is more skilled than most players he competes against and can win by playing fair; moreover, his attitude toward Quidditch approaches reverence, and judging from his indignation at other players' fouls, he considers fair play a point of honor. Indeed, for Ulrike Kristina Köhler, Harry's affinity for Quidditch is part and parcel of his role as "the embodiment of the idea of the English gentleman" (16), and "Harry's aptitude for sports is bound up with fair play" (17). Nevertheless, Harry is not above "psyching out" his teammates and opponents. For example, knowing that the luck potion Felix Felicis is banned in sports, Harry does not, in fact, spike Ron's pumpkin juice before a big match, but by allowing him to think so, he boosts Ron's confidence and thus his performance. (Much of Felix's effect seems to be psychological in any case.) Harry will also distract an opposing Seeker by pretending to see the Snitch—a completely acceptable strategy.

That is not to say Quidditch never involves ethical lapses. Far from it. Harry's presence on Gryffindor's Quidditch team in his first year directly violates Hogwarts rules, and McGonagall witnesses Harry's flying skills after he flouts Madam Hooch's warning that anyone who mounts a broom in her absence will be expelled. In Rebecca Skulnick and Jesse Goodman's view, "Harry's choice to fly underscores a major trait of civic heroism: rules may be broken when their rupture serves to uphold rather than subvert the cultural values embedded in the institution. The need for a talented Seeker was more important to the maintenance of Hogwarts's society than to the upholding of the broom-flying rule." Hence, McGonagall's motives "may be interpreted as immoral. ... Potter characters frequently act out of selfish intentions but they always remain 'good' so long as their acts do not threaten the demise of Hogwarts" (268). McGonagall, like many at Hogwarts and elsewhere, allows sports fandom to overrule more important considerations, but, in Skulnick and Goodman's view, her choice helps establish for readers the importance of Hogwarts as a nexus of ethical standards. That is, the series supports an old-fashioned boarding school value system that esteems athletic competition above all else.

There are, however, other ways to interpret this incident. For one thing, Harry's reason for flying, to protect Neville's Remembrall against Malfoy's bullying theft, is well-intended disobedience. Furthermore, Malfoy has a point that the rule against first years having brooms is arbitrary. Thus, this early incident invites readers to weigh a rule's value—in this case, not very high—against another ethical principle: bullying is wrong, and defending others against it is important: Harry's virtue is rewarded. From yet another perspective, Christopher E. Bell has noted that Harry's making the team is one of many occasions when he gets away with things other students would not, because he has a "patently ridiculous amount of privilege" ("Does Harry"), and Harry's participation in Quidditch, as Bell and others have argued, reflects wizard social stratification. When Harry lands the Seeker position, he not only violates the rule about first years having brooms but is presented with a Nimbus Two Thousand that arouses the envy of every other student. There is no indication of who pays for it. Farah Mendlesohn describes Quidditch as "a rich man's sport: like Polo, in which the expense of horses limits participation to those with money or those sponsored by money, Quidditch players with old brooms can never compete with those in possession of the latest technological marvels" (297). This analysis overlooks the fact that every member of the financially strapped Weasley family excels at Quidditch, but access to good equipment is crucial. Harry may not exactly "cheat," but he benefits from fame, his professors' rule-bending, inherited wealth, and a wealthy godfather. Ironically, when Draco's wealthy father supplies the Slytherin team with Nimbus Two Thousand and Ones, apparently in exchange for Draco's becoming Seeker, he is repeatedly mocked for "buy[ing] his way' on the team" (CS 167). Although these inconsistencies are not always called out, it's worth remembering that to depict hypocritical or ethically questionable behavior is not necessarily to endorse it.

Corruption in sports is an important theme in *Goblet of Fire*. Ludo Bagman, head of the Department of Magical Games and Sports, openly solicits bets on the World Cup Finals, including from minors, then cheats the Weasley twins by paying them in Leprechaun gold—equivalent to knowingly passing counterfeit money. Later, although Bagman is a Triwizard Tournament judge, he bets on Harry and keeps trying to feed him clues about the tasks. As William P. MacNeil observes, Bagman is "a compulsive punter, who plays fast and loose with any and all rules when money is involved" (548)—evidence that rule breaking is not uniformly depicted as admirable in the series. Mad-Eye Moody—who also offers Harry advice while claiming he won't "show favoritism"—assures him that "Cheating's a traditional part of the Triwizard Tournament and always has been" (344, 343). Of course, Moody is actually Barty Crouch, Jr., who, in the ultimate breaking of rules and with the intention of delivering Harry to Voldemort, puts Harry's name in the Goblet, makes sure Dobby overhears him talking about Gillyweed, and turns the Triwizard Cup into a Portkey. Still, "Moody's" observation about the "tradition" of cheating seems reliable, given that Hagrid shows the dragons to both Harry and Madame Maxime and that Igor Karkaroff's scoring is clearly biased. This rampant cheating provides a critique both of wizard culture and of corruption in Muggle sport, notorious for biased scoring, gambling by participants, and violent riots. To be sure, Harry does not seek help except when Hermione helps him master the *Accio* command. Moreover Harry only "cheats" to assist others: communicating his knowledge about the dragons to Cedric, attempting to rescue Hermione and Gabrielle during the second task, and insisting on sharing the "win" with Cedric—however badly that ultimately works out for Cedric. Still, Harry does benefit from others' cheating. Overall, wizard athletics are corrupt, and Harry remains mostly oblivious to the corruption. Rather, his skill as a Quidditch Seeker is depicted as contributing practically and symbolically to his quest to defeat Voldemort.

Finally, Quidditch, like much of magical culture, suffers from stagnation. According to *Quidditch through the Ages*, Quidditch rules were set down in 1750 and have hardly changed since (27). Muggle sports constantly evolve: two recent examples are changing rules for tiebreakers in tennis and for penalty kicks in soccer (football). We change rules to increase safety, encourage sportsmanship, and make games more watchable—all issues with Quidditch. Rules also change when technology changes, and indeed one of the few ways Quidditch has changed is the rapid improvement of broomsticks, yet the rules remain the same. Quidditch's inertia reflects the "particular character" of a culture stuck somewhere between the seventeenth and nineteenth centuries in everything from its technology to its education to its legal system.

Points, Punishments, and Power: The Problems with Hogwarts's School Rules

Most of the rules Harry breaks early in the series are Hogwarts's school rules, and thus it is primarily through these that readers are introduced to questions of ethical choice. Christian author Richard Abanes finds Harry's choices problematic, contending that when Harry sneaks into the library's Restricted Section to learn about Nicolas Flamel, "rather than following any objective standard of right and wrong (i.e., Hogwarts' rules), Harry lets his own self-interests and subjective rationalizations determine his actions" (34–5). I think it is fair to counter that if Harry only cared about "self-interests," he would focus on Quidditch and treacle tarts, while avoiding three-headed dogs. Yes, Harry breaks school rules constantly but if school rules reflected an "objective standard of right and wrong," as Abanes says, then every school would have the same dress code and the same hall pass and restroom rules. True, an objective standard of right and wrong is identified in *Half-Blood Prince*, as Dumbledore informs young Tom Riddle, "Thieving is not tolerated at Hogwarts" (273), but that's hardly a rule exclusive to Hogwarts or any other school. (It is also true that Hermione steals ingredients to make Polyjuice potion.) In other cases, Hogwarts's rules are among the series' most arbitrary: why, for example, are cats, owls, and toads allowed but not other animals traditionally identified as "familiars," such as ferrets or dogs? How do Ron and

Percy get away with Scabbers the rat? Why are first years prevented from having brooms and both first and second years forbidden from going to Hogsmeade, and everyone forbidden from having screaming yo-yos—especially in light of the many dangerous creatures, plants, potion ingredients, and spells the students routinely encounter? Such examples encourage readers to question which rules are legitimate and which are arbitrary or even counterproductive. In nearly every case, the school rules Harry breaks seem trivial in comparison to larger principles at stake.

Every time Headmaster Dumbledore gives his start-of-term notices, he subtly indicates that he doesn't take the rules very seriously. In *Sorcerer's Stone*, he begins:

> "First years should note that the forest on the grounds is forbidden to all pupils. And a few of our older students would do well to remember that as well."
> Dumbledore's twinkling eyes flashed in the direction of the Weasley twins.
> "I have also been asked by Mr. Filch, the caretaker, to remind you all that no magic should be used between classes in the corridors."
>
> (SS 127)

Granted, Dumbledore then warns students not to enter the third-floor corridor where, we later learn, a vicious three-headed dog guards Nicolas Flamel's Sorcerer's Stone, but the first announcement is undercut by Dumbledore's good-humored acknowledgment that the twins sneak into the "forbidden" forest unscathed and by attributing to Filch, rather than claiming for himself, the rule forbidding magic in the hallways. By Harry's fourth year, Filch's list of prohibited objects numbers 437 items, and "The corners of Dumbledore's mouth twitched" as he announces the list (GF 183). Yet Dumbledore is sometimes firm about rules, as when he sternly warns Tom Riddle,

> At Hogwarts … we teach you not only to use magic, but to control it. You have—inadvertently, I am sure—been using your powers in a way that is neither taught nor tolerated at our school. You are not the first, nor will you be the last, to allow your magic to run away with you. But you should know that Hogwarts can expel students, and the Ministry of Magic—yes, there is a Ministry—will punish lawbreakers still more severely. All new wizards must accept that, in entering our world, they abide by our laws."
>
> (HBP 273)

Young Tom has already used magic to torture children and kill small animals, so this warning is appropriate, yet Dumbledore describes Hogwarts rules as a subset of broader magical codes; he mentions nothing about curfew or the library's Restricted Section. Concerning those rules, Dumbledore is notoriously lax. On more than one occasion, Dumbledore realizes that the trio are at Hagrid's under the invisibility cloak (which Dumbledore has made sure Harry possesses)—thus violating the rule against leaving the castle—but instead of subtracting House points, he offers indirect advice. Hogwarts's Headmaster is, ironically, its biggest rule breaker.

Early on, Hogwarts's discipline seems straightforward and mostly fair. House points are awarded for "triumphs," primarily exemplary classroom behavior, and lost for violating rules. Wanting to win the House Cup, students work hard in class and avoid breaking rules—or at least being caught breaking rules—to avoid losing both points and the approval of fellow House members. But early on, the point system is shown to be flawed, when Snape arbitrarily takes points from Harry for "breaking" a nonexistent rule against taking a library book outside; in *Prisoner of Azkaban*, Snape actually deducts points when Hermione knows an answer, for being "an insufferable know-it-all" (172). Moreover, exactly why one transgression costs five points and another fifty is never specified, nor why some offenses are overlooked and others cost points and lead to detentions. Why does repeatedly violating curfew in Chapter Twelve of *Sorcerer's Stone* culminate in a mild conversation about the nature of the Mirror of Erised, while in Chapter Fifteen curfew violation results in a potentially life-threatening nighttime encounter with Voldemort in the Forbidden Forest? Dumbledore's awarding Gryffindor precisely enough points to defeat Slytherin at the end of Harry's first year is only the most frequently cited example of how random the system can be in practice.

However arbitrary the punishments, most are no harsher than Harry's having to go through old files containing his dead father's name or Ron's having to polish trophies without magic. Until Harry's fifth year. That is when Dolores Umbridge takes charge, in the name of the Ministry, and she brings Ministry authoritarianism with her, driven by "her furious desire to bring every aspect of life at Hogwarts under her personal control" (OP 551). In class, Umbridge discourages questions or independent thought. Her "Educational Decrees" limit freedom of association by banning clubs and freedom of information by banning the *Quibbler* and forbidding faculty "from giving any information that is not strictly related to the subjects they are paid to teach" (551). She corrupts the prefect system into an "Inquisitorial Squad" overtly aimed at punishing her and her student allies' opponents. She sadistically perverts the mundane school punishment of writing "lines," with her magical quill that carves the students' script into their skin so that they write in their own blood. She grants Filch approval to horsewhip student rule breakers, and she almost uses the forbidden Cruciatus Curse on Harry, wearing a "nasty, eager, excited look on her face that Harry had never seen before" (OP 746). In the name of enforcing her decrees, she authorizes harsh physical treatment even of faculty—Hagrid and McGonagall. Information that Umbridge had authorized the dementor attack on Harry and Dudley earlier in the year confirms that her ostensible devotion to rules is a complete fraud, poorly concealing her thirst for power, not to mention her pleasure in others' pain. A similar regime arises in the seventh year, with Death Eaters Alecto and Amycus Carrow chaining and beating students and routinely inflicting the "Unforgivable" Cruciatus Curse and even making students "practice" it on fellow students who have earned detentions (DH 573). The similarities underscore Sirius's point that "the world isn't split into good people and Death Eaters" (OP 302). One might easily conclude that the characters who most enthusiastically support school rules—Umbridge and Filch, Percy Weasley, and the Carrows—are among the series' least likable.

Not coincidentally, the only years when students actively resist the Hogwarts administration are the years when Umbridge and the Carrows control discipline. It is of course under Umbridge's watch that Dumbledore's Army is formed and that the Weasley twins set off fireworks and create a swamp in the entrance hall. In *Deathly Hallows*, members of the D.A. write graffiti like "*Dumbledore's Army, Still Recruiting*" and speak forbidden truths, such as Terry Boot's shouting news of the Gringotts break-in or Neville's asking Amycus Carrow how much Muggle blood she has. By the time Harry, Ron, and Hermione return to the castle, more than twenty student resistance fighters are bivouacked in the Room of Requirement. The transition to a battle against Voldemort occurs smoothly because the movement against repressive school rules and against repressive Ministry policies has become the same.

Wizard Government and Law: Inconsistency, Incompetence, and Injustice

Skulnick and Goodman contend that "like much of children's literature, Harry's world is devoid of much ambiguity. Dumbledore's Hogwarts is good whereas Voldemort and his followers are evil" (262). Though written before all the books had been published, the observation represents a common view that the series concerns a simple battle between forces of metaphysical good (Harry and Hogwarts) and forces of metaphysical evil (Voldemort), a battle focused on Hogwarts. However, Skulnick and Goodman's interpretation overlooks the considerable ethical ambiguity of wizard culture. Sirius' observation that "the world isn't split into good people and Death Eaters" (OP 302) applies particularly well to the Ministry of Magic. While I would not go as far as Bell, who describes the wizarding world as a dystopia ("Riddle" 51), it is certainly deeply flawed. Many of its shortcomings derive directly from its legal and political structures, which create, as Chevalier says, "a world so highly regulated and defined by the strictness of its laws that it always seems in danger of collapsing under the weight of its own rules" (399). Paradoxically, one could also argue, like Susan Hall, that, in fact, "The wizard world is not governed by the rule of law" ("Justice" 72). The flaws of wizard government also powerfully reinforce Maurice Hamington's argument that governments should focus more on caring for their people than on getting and maintaining power, that caring for individuals' needs should transcend "unyielding external moral rules" resembling those in a game (272).

An observant reader notices cracks in the magical world's facade early in Book Two, when Harry realizes that house-elves are enslaved and the Ministry could expel him without investigating who performed the hover charm at the Dursleys' residence. We also learn early in *Chamber of Secrets* that Arthur Weasley wrote the law against bewitching Muggle artifacts, building in a loophole allowing him to tinker with them himself. This seems a benign quirk, but it prefigures deeper problems with regulating justice. Later in *Chamber*, Hagrid is sent to Azkaban without trial, and we learn he was expelled in his third year because Tom Riddle framed him for murdering Myrtle Warren (Moaning Myrtle). Four years later we learn that this was only the first time Riddle successfully implicated the innocent—especially those he considered inferior, like Hagrid and Hokey. But as early as Book Two, we get hints that the Ministry tolerates corruption, oppression, injustice, and arbitrary punishment.

Many critics[3] have examined the numerous flaws in the wizard legal system, but here is a quick summary: First, although the process of writing laws is unclear, it seems to be the task of bureaucrats and the Minister of Magic rather than of any elected body. We gather this from Arthur Weasley's responsibility for the law on enchanting magical objects, from Umbridge's having written anti-werewolf legislation that prevents Remus Lupin from getting a job, and from Mr. Crouch's actions during and after Voldemort's first rise to power. Nowhere do the novels refer to a wizard legislative body, though *Wizarding World* identifies the Wizengamot as "an organisation that predates the Ministry of Magic and nowadays functions as a combination of court and parliament" ("Order"). While a limited set of "beings" are deemed of "sufficient intelligence to understand the laws of the magical community and to bear part of the responsibility of shaping those laws" (FB xxii), in practice the "part of the responsibility" allowed them seems severely limited. Furthermore, in describing the Minister of Magic, on *Wizarding World*, Rowling writes, "All matters relating to the magical community in Britain are managed solely by the Minister for Magic, and he has sole jurisdiction over his Ministry." This comment on relations between the Minister and the Muggle Prime Minister confirms the impression conveyed elsewhere of a figure with considerable power. Moreover, he is not always elected:

> The Minister for Magic is democratically elected, although there have been times of crisis in which the post has simply been offered to an individual without a public vote (Albus Dumbledore was made such an offer, and turned it down repeatedly). There is no fixed limit to a Minister's term of office, but he or she is obliged to hold regular elections at a maximum interval of seven years. Ministers for Magic tend to last much longer than Muggle ministers. Generally speaking, and despite many a moan and grumble, their community is behind them in a way that is rarely seen in the Muggle world. This is perhaps due to a feeling, on the part of wizards, that

unless they are seen to manage themselves competently, the Muggles might try to interfere.

("Ministers")

No doubt the magical community has undergone many periods of "crisis" that could be used to justify granting the Minister autocratic powers, but abandoning democracy any time a crisis occurs seems a precarious way to maintain a stable and fair government. Concern for Muggle interference seems specious, since few Muggles know wizards exist, much less how they govern themselves. Timothy Snyder, in *On Tyranny*, quotes the Federalist Papers: "where annual elections end, tyranny begins" (30). The warning is apt.

The danger of a government whose laws are not made by a representative legislature is illustrated by an exchange during Harry's Wizengamot hearing for performing magic in the presence of a Muggle, for which he has been threatened with expulsion from Hogwarts. Dumbledore tells Fudge:

> "In your admirable haste to ensure that the law is upheld, you appear, inadvertently I am sure, to have overlooked a few laws yourself."
> "Laws can be changed," said Fudge savagely.
> "Of course they can," said Dumbledore, inclining his head. "And you certainly seem to be making many changes, Cornelius."
>
> (OP 149)

This exchange reveals that when a Minister of Magic—in this case, Fudge—finds a law inconvenient to his own interests, he can simply change the law, and not necessarily in the interest of greater justice. Because readers identify with Harry in this scene, it effectively shows that the Ministry is not necessarily on his side—or on that of other wizards under its control.

As for wizard laws themselves, aside from laws resembling Muggle laws—such as those establishing as Unforgivable the curses causing torture and murder—magical laws seem to come in two forms that frequently overlap: those regulating the use of magic and those regulating interactions with Muggles. The law whose administration we see most closely is the Decree for the Reasonable Restriction of Underage Sorcery, which Harry learns about soon after finding out he is a wizard[4] and encounters again shortly before his second year:

> As you know, underage wizards are not permitted to perform spells outside school, and further spellwork on your part may lead to expulsion from said school (Decree for the Reasonable Restriction of Underage Sorcery, 1875, Paragraph C).
>
> We would also ask you to remember that any magical activity that risks notice by members of the non-magical community (Muggles) is a serious

offense under section 13 of the International Confederation of Warlocks' Statute of Secrecy.

(CS 21)

This message indicates that the Decree's main purpose is to maintain secrecy, though, according to *Wizarding World*, another is "to keep potentially dangerous or hazardous magic out of inexperienced hands prior to their proper education" ("What are the differences"). While the reasons for the law are arguably legitimate, its application is imprecise. After all, Harry is threatened with expulsion without an investigation to determine whether he performed the magic. Presumably, Dobby knows this, as his presence on Privet Drive is against his masters' interest, and he would fear severe punishment. Ministry enforcement of the Decree is also inconsistent, as Harry learns the next year when he loses control and angrily inflates his aggravating Aunt Marge like a balloon. Although this is a worse offense than levitating and dropping a pudding, it is brushed aside by Fudge himself:

> "Oh, my dear boy, we're not going to punish you for a little thing like that!" cried Fudge, waving his crumpet impatiently. "It was an accident! We don't send people to Azkaban just for blowing up their aunts!"
> But this didn't tally at all with Harry's past dealings with the Ministry of Magic.
> "Last year, I got an official warning just because a house-elf smashed a pudding in my uncle's house!" he told Fudge, frowning. "The Ministry of Magic said I'd be expelled from Hogwarts if there was any more magic there!"
> Unless Harry's eyes were deceiving him, Fudge was suddenly looking awkward.
> "Circumstances change, Harry.... We have to take into account ... in the present climate ..."

(PA 45)

Although Aunt Marge is a vile bigot who had been spewing cruel things about Harry and his parents, Harry recognizes that his violation was egregious, deserving punishment. Fudge's awkward inconsistency would be suspicious enough if it weren't further contradicted twice, the first time minutes later, when Harry asks Fudge for permission to visit Hogsmeade. Fudge flatly replies, "rules are rules," and refuses to sign. Later we learn that both decisions are based on fears that Harry will be attacked by Sirius Black, but their inconsistency is no less blatant.

Following Harry's fourth year, Fudge contradicts himself yet again, when Harry saves himself and Dudley from dementors—a clearly justifiable use of magic for self-defense—and immediately receives notification that "The severity of this breach of the Decree for the Reasonable Restriction of Underage Sorcery has resulted in your expulsion from Hogwarts School of Witchcraft and Wizardry.

Ministry representatives will be calling at your place of residence shortly to destroy your wand" (OP 26–7). Harry is summoned to a hearing—to take place *after* the sentence of expulsion and destruction of his wand is carried out. Such capriciousness casts doubt on the entire magical legal system.

The Ministry of Magic is depicted in ways largely designed to score satiric points. The source of most of its problems is that nearly every Ministry department somehow enforces the International Statute of Wizarding Secrecy, which was signed in 1689 and fully instituted in 1692 (DH 318; Rowling, *Quidditch*, 16), a product of the witch burnings of the fifteenth through seventeenth centuries. Arguably, complete segregation between the magical and non-magical worlds only exacerbates distrust and prejudice on both sides; and Hall argues that separation from Muggle culture before the Enlightenment explains the magical world's lack of basic political principles like individual liberty, equality before the law, separation of powers, or checks and balances ("Justice" 65). The Statute requires considerable regulation and increases the responsibilities of departments dealing with transportation, control of magical creatures, misuse of Muggle artifacts, and magical catastrophes, many of which involve Muggle witnesses. Muggles who inadvertently witness magic must be dealt with by the Muggle-Worthy Excuse Committee, the Office of Misinformation, and the Accidental Magic Reversal Squad, one of whose main tools is the Obliviate charm, which erases memories; that is, many of these departments are dedicated to legally sanctioned abuse of Muggles. The Department of International Magical Cooperation, akin to the British Foreign Office or the American State Department, seems focused on trivia like cauldron thickness and flying carpets. The Department of Magical Games and Sports is run by Bagman, who has the job primarily because he was a popular professional athlete. Bagman is incompetent, loses track of employees, and openly bets on the sports he should, theoretically, be supervising even-handedly.[5]

Perhaps the most troubling Ministry department is Magical Law Enforcement. It includes Arthur Weasley's Misuse of Muggle Artifacts Office and, later, the Office for the Detection and Confiscation of Counterfeit Defensive Spells and Protective Objects, which Arthur heads. Magical Law Enforcement includes the Improper Use of Magic Office, responsible for registering Animagi and sending letters of warning regarding underage magic. Presumably, it eventually includes Umbridge's Muggle-born Registration Commission, which, in addition to its fundamental evils, also fosters self-serving corruption, as Runcorn's ousting of Dirk Cresswell for being Muggle-born opens his position in the Goblin-Liaison Office for another corrupt bureaucrat (DH 245). The Department of Magical Law Enforcement certainly includes the Magical Law Enforcement Squad—analogous to Muggle police—which keeps order at the Quidditch World Cup. Magical Law Enforcement, more alarmingly, employs "Hit Wizards" to deal with dangerous criminals like Sirius (PA 208). "Hit Wizards" strongly suggests a force that shoots first and asks questions later—if at all—and echoes the worst Muggle police misconduct. This squad is distinct from the Aurors, who specialize in capturing dark wizards.

Generally speaking, Aurors are depicted positively. Some of our favorite characters are Aurors: Alastor Moody, Nymphadora Tonks, and Kingsley Shacklebolt; both of Neville Longbottom's parents were Aurors. The Aurors' mission, to catch Death Eaters and other dark wizards, makes them Harry's allies. And of course, Harry's own ambition is to become an Auror. But there is ethical ambiguity to the Aurors as well. Sirius reports that when Mr. Crouch headed the Department of Magical Law Enforcement during the First Wizarding War against Voldemort and his supporters, "The Aurors were given new powers—powers to kill rather than capture, for instance.... Crouch fought violence with violence, and authorized the use of the Unforgivable Curses against suspects. I would say he became as ruthless and cruel as many on the Dark Side" (GF 527). In other words, the Aurors engaged in extra-judicial killings and torture. There could be no clearer illustration of the principle that "the world isn't split into good people and Death Eaters."

In addition, under Crouch's leadership, Aurors apparently engaged in genocide against the giants, if we read between the lines of Rita Skeeter's reporting: "many of the giants who served He-Who-Must-Not-Be-Named were killed by Aurors working against the Dark Side" (GF 439). This looks suspicious, considering wizards' anti-giant bias and the fact that Aurors were not bothering to capture enemies but killed them. By contrast, Dumbledore had, in Hagrid's words, "argued against the killin' of the last giants in Britain" (OP 429), and after Voldemort's return sends Hagrid and Madame Maxime as "envoys," as he explains to Fudge, less "Voldemort will persuade them, as he did before, that he alone among wizards will give them their rights and their freedom!" (GF 708). During the First Wizarding War, the Aurors helped enforce policies that denied giants not just rights but their very existence. The Aurors allied with Dumbledore during the second wizarding war show no anti-Giant bias, but a corrupt Ministry readily encouraged Aurors to exert unfettered, dangerous (not to mention counterproductive) power.

Aurors and Magical Law Enforcement seem to have more license to search and surveil without a warrant than does Muggle law enforcement in democratic countries. While it is true that "Moody" in Book Four is an imposter, Snape doesn't question his claim of "Auror's privilege" to search Snape's office or "keep an eye" on him—only protesting that Dumbledore trusts him (GF 471). When Hagrid and Maxime travel to recruit the giants, they are "tailed" (426). Moreover, Hagrid—still forbidden to use magic because the Ministry won't accept evidence that Riddle, not he, caused Myrtle's death—knows he can't be seen using magic because "the Ministry'd be lookin' fer a reason ter run us in" (OP 425–6). The "Trace" on underage wizards supposedly ensures they don't reveal their abilities to Muggles, but it is highly intrusive. Later, the "taboo" placed on the name "Voldemort" allows his followers to locate the person who said the name and to neutralize protective spells. And although the Ministry seems only tangentially interested in evidence, when they do pursue it, they use questionable methods like Veritaserum—presumably a potion resembling Sodium Pentothal—to coerce confessions. Once Voldemort takes control, the Cruciatus Curse also becomes a common interrogation technique.

If there are problems with wizard policing, there are even more problems with what should be the next stage: legal trials. The case of Buckbeak the Hippogriff in *Prisoner of Azkaban* prepares readers to question wizard justice. Hoping to get Hagrid fired, Malfoy trumps up the accusation that Buckbeak attacked him during Hagrid's class. After Draco brings the injury on himself by ignoring instructions about how to interact with a hippogriff, he lies about the injury's severity and complains to his father, who uses his influence at the Ministry—influence in itself corrupt since it is based on large monetary gifts—to make a formal complaint to the Committee for the Disposal of Dangerous Creatures. The very name, featuring "Disposal" and "Dangerous," indicates pre-judgment. Hagrid's only assistance defending Buckbeak is from an underage witch (albeit the brilliant Hermione), who can only help prepare but not assist at the hearing itself. And when the Committee rules against Hagrid and orders Buckbeak's execution, the "appeal" is a fiction, as "From sneering comments Harry overheard, Malfoy was certain Buckbeak was going to be killed" (PA 316). The executioner—one of Lucius's fellow Death Eaters—is brought to the "appeal," and Fudge comes along because "The Committee for the Disposal of Dangerous Creatures required a witness to the execution of a mad hippogriff" (PA 319–20)—hardly signs of an unbiased appeals process.

In the wizarding world, punishment is typically rendered without an adequate hearing. In *Chamber of Secrets*, Hagrid is sent to Azkaban merely because Fudge, though acknowledging lack of evidence, had been "under a lot of pressure. Got to be seen to be doing something" (CS 261) about attacks on Muggle-borns. This and Buckbeak's story prepare readers to believe that Sirius's imprisonment in Azkaban may not necessarily indicate his guilt. Moreover, the witnesses who might have cleared Sirius at the time were Muggles whose memories were modified before they could testify and who, because of prejudice against Muggles, would not have been considered adequate witnesses in any case. This is not an isolated example, as Sirius attests: "I wasn't the only one who was handed straight to the dementors without trial" (GF 527). When Sirius is captured at the end of Book Three, Fudge, the sole decision-maker about the irrevocable verdict of having the dementors suck out Sirius's soul, refuses to hear testimony that would clear him. Furthermore, as Dumbledore observes, the current potential witnesses in Sirius's defense are underage wizards and a werewolf, whose testimony would not be considered reliable. Sirius only escapes because Harry and Hermione break Time-Turner rules to save him and Buckbeak. The following year, Fudge does succeed in summary justice against young Barty Crouch, ordering a Dementor's Kiss without consulting anyone, without a hearing, and without appeal. Each of these injustices and potential injustices increasingly justifies Harry's resisting the authorities responsible.

46 "Made to Be Broken"

Even after Fudge is replaced by Scrimgeour, the Ministry continues to punish people without sufficient evidence, including feckless Knight Bus conductor, Stan Shunpike. As Arthur Weasley remarks,

> of the three arrests we've made in the last couple of months, I doubt that one of them is a genuine Death Eater [. . .] I mean, anybody who has actually interviewed [Stan] agrees that he's about as much a Death Eater as this satsuma . . . but the top levels want to look as though they're making some progress, and "three arrests" sounds better than "three mistaken arrests and releases."
>
> (HBP 331)

Unfortunately, it is not just authoritarian states that habitually jail someone, anyone, to create the impression of progress against a notorious crime. The situation here, though, is exacerbated by the fact that the Ministry sends Stan and the other, unnamed accused, to Azkaban without a trial.

We do see some trials, but not fair ones. Harry is tried for an offense he certainly committed: performing underage magic in front of a Muggle—the same offense Fudge had previously waved aside. The second offense is surely justified as defending himself and his cousin, but, as Fudge said two years before, "circumstances change" (PA 45). The changed "circumstances" are that Fudge feels threatened by Harry's information about Voldemort, so the hearing before the entire Wizengamot is in an intimidating dungeon used to try criminals bound for Azkaban. Fudge reschedules the hearing—obviously intentionally—so Harry will be late. No defense counsel is provided, and, though a minor, Harry enters the courtroom alone. Fortunately, Dumbledore shows up—even though he, too, was intentionally not informed of the earlier time or changed location. He provides witnesses that Harry would not otherwise have had and argues Harry's case brilliantly, and enough members of the Wizengamot are fair-minded that Dumbledore's arguments prevail. Sadly, though, the fact that Harry benefits from effective representation is atypical—another example of his privilege.

When, via the Pensieve, we see trials for more serious offenses, not one defendant has counsel or can call witnesses. Moreover, Mr. Crouch acts as both prosecutor and judge. There is a jury of sorts, the "Council of Magical Law," but the verdict is based primarily on emotion, not on testimony. Igor Karkaroff's and Ludo Bagman's hearings differ in the mood of the onlookers, hostile to Karkaroff and friendly to Bagman. Neither trial features evidence, but despite serious accusations, Bagman's jury, composed of Quidditch fans, refuses to convict and cheers his acquittal. Afterward, a juror speaks up: "'We'd just like to congratulate Mr. Bagman on his splendid performance for England in the Quidditch match against Turkey last Saturday,' the witch said breathlessly" (GF 593). This is far from equal treatment under the law.

One need not be a lawyer to recognize the problems with the mass sentencing hearing for Bellatrix, Rodolphus, and Rabastan Lestrange, and young Barty Crouch, for torturing the Longbottoms. It is presided over by Barty's own father, an obvious conflict of interest. As Sirius says, the "trial" "wasn't much more than an excuse for Crouch to show how much he hated the boy" because "Anything that threatened to tarnish his reputation had to go; he had dedicated his whole life to becoming Minister of Magic" (GF 528). The sentence to life in Azkaban is driven by emotion: Mr. Crouch's face expresses "pure hatred" toward his son; there is "spit flying from his mouth" (GF 594, 596), while the jury's "faces [are] full of savage triumph," and "The crowd was jeering, some of them on their feet" (GF 595, 596), no doubt because "The Longbottoms were very popular." Dumbledore explains: "Those attacks caused a wave of fury such as I have never known. The Ministry was under great pressure to catch those who had done it. Unfortunately, the Longbottoms' evidence was—given their condition—none too reliable" (GF 603). The Ministry is once again finding someone, anyone, to prosecute because it is "under pressure." Everyone sitting in judgment has strong emotional connections with the victims or the accused. None would be allowed to participate in an ordinary Muggle trial; their vindictive behavior illustrates why. The evidence is so shaky that Dumbledore admits he has "no idea" whether any of the accused is guilty (GF 603). MacNeil describes the trial as one of those "curial performances beloved of totalitarian regimes, the show trial, where legality is staged as a show of governmental force" (550). MacNeil also notes that these scenes provide no new *information* about Bagman, Karkaroff, or Crouch; thus, their function is not expository but thematic (548). That theme is the cruel unfairness of wizard "justice."

Wizard justice is even more perverted after Voldemort takes over the Ministry, when Umbridge controls the Muggle-Born Registration Commission. She likely wrote the laws; she presides over the hearing, where she presumes the guilt of everyone in front of her, asks all the questions, passes judgment on each case, and assigns punishment—imprisonment in Azkaban. All this even though the charge of "stealing magic" is nonsensical; for, as Ron says, "if you could steal magic there wouldn't be any Squibs" (DH 209). Yet while the laws themselves are more overtly discriminatory after Voldemort's ascension, the legal process remains consistent with his predecessors' approach—which speaks volumes about wizard law.

Finally, the routine punishment, imprisonment at Azkaban, the prison presided over by dementors, is cruel and unusual by any standard. Because dementors, described as "sightless, soul-sucking fiends" (GF 23), drain people's happiness, imprisonment in Azkaban is effectively psychological torture: most prisoners go insane and, eventually, die of despair. According to Sirius, most people imprisoned in Azkaban "go mad in there, and plenty stop eating in the end. They lose the will to live. You could always tell when a death was coming, because the dementors could sense it, they got excited" (GF 529). After eleven years at Azkaban, Sirius's eyes have a "deadened, haunted look" (GF 331), even though he could counter the dementors' power somewhat by transforming into a dog. That Muggle-borns are sentenced to Azkaban—where some die—simply on account of blood status represents yet another parallel to Hitler's regime.[6] Rowling has observed, "The use of Dementors was always a mark of the underlying corruption of the Ministry, as Dumbledore constantly maintained" ("J.K Rowling Web Chat"). The analysis echoes Amnesty International's assessment: "Torture does not occur simply because individual torturers are sadistic, even if testimonies verify that they are. Torture is usually part of the state-controlled machinery to suppress dissent" (4). It is dementors' nature to suck people's souls; the state's crime is to use them. In a provocative essay, Tracy Bealer invites readers to consider that the Ministry has "cultivated and weaponized the dementors' natural predilections to create fearsome and debilitating prison guards," even intentionally keeping them hungry to make them more effective, exploiting them to support a surveillance state that "nurtures an ever-present threat of emotional and physical punishment for non-compliance" ("Consider" 40, 42).

What wonder that Harry and his friends resist the Ministry at every turn? In the face of the Ministry's railroading of Stan Shunpike, Harry refuses to cooperate with the Ministry's public relations efforts (HBP 346). When Hermione and Harry rescue Buckbeak and Sirius, they not only break the rule about time travel but actively undermine Ministry "justice," as does releasing Muggle-borns awaiting "justice" in *Deathly Hallows*. Hermione defiantly responds to Scrimgeour's question, "Are you planning to follow a career in Magical Law, Miss Granger?" with the retort, "No, I'm not ... I'm hoping to do some good in the world!" (DH 123–4). That Hermione pursues a career in Magical Law in the post-Wizarding-War Ministry ("J.K Rowling Web Chat") confirms her sincerity, as this profession only meets her standards of "do[ing] some good" after the Ministry is thoroughly reformed.

Compounding the problems with wizarding political and legal structures is the absence of any check by a free press. As I will discuss more fully in Chapter Five, the *Daily Prophet*, though occasionally critical of the Ministry, more frequently serves as its propaganda arm, and in all cases is more focused on selling copies than on uncovering the truth about public affairs. Because of its focus on pleasing readers, it is less an influence on public opinion than subject to popular whim. Indeed, a notable feature of the magical world is the power of public opinion and the social norms that shape it.

Unwritten Rules: What Is "Perfectly Normal"?

As every *Harry Potter* fan knows, the books begin, "Mr. and Mrs. Dursley, of number four, Privet Drive, were proud to say that they were perfectly normal, thank you very much. They were the last people you'd expect to be involved in anything strange or mysterious, because they just didn't hold with such nonsense" (SS 1). Immediately thereafter, "strange" and "mysterious" things happen all around the

Dursleys, mostly related to their nephew Harry, who is anything but "normal"—from a Muggle perspective. By his magical nature, Harry, like the magical world generally, breaks unwritten rules of Muggle culture. Thus the series' first page establishes a central theme: the question of what is "normal" or "abnormal"—or, for that matter, "strange." Who decides, and what are the implications of the social norms that define any culture? What Vernon Dursley considers "normal" has little in common with "normal" in the magical realm, and the juxtaposition invites readers to question both sets of norms. As John S. Nelson observes, the series' early emphasis on conforming to what is "normal" effectively introduces an "everyday politics" familiar to young readers, long before we encounter issues we ordinarily identify as "political" (91).

Political scientist Karen Stenner argues that the authoritarian dynamic is fundamentally a concern for maintaining social norms—variously defined. Authoritarians of all times, places, or political stances share a "familiar triad of racial, political, and moral intolerance: the tendency to glorify some 'in-group' and to denigrate 'out-groups,' ... to venerate and privilege a set of ideas and practices, and to reward or punish others according to their conformity to this 'normative order'" (1). Authoritarians rush to stamp out "misbehavior," that is, violations of these norms: "minimizing difference requires *others'* obedience and conformity, which necessitates someone to obey, something to conform to, and ... some system of collective authority and constraint, and some conception of who 'we' are to which the system applies" (18). However different they may otherwise be, the Dursleys and Malfoys share this authoritarian inclination to discriminate against anyone who violates their in-group's norms. Even in the absence of authoritarianism, social norms act as powerful controls: consider the ostracism Luna Lovegood faces, simply for being unconventional. Indeed, while rule breaking often comes naturally to teenagers, most shy away from violating peer norms; doing so requires tremendous courage, Dumbledore's message when he awards Neville the crucial House Cup winning ten points at the end of *Sorcerer's Stone*.

Harry, who by his very existence violates Muggle norms, spends his early years in magical culture trying to master the unwritten norms of the wizard in-group—and also violating them, first unwittingly, and then, increasingly, intentionally. Harry's first response to magical culture—like that of readers—is wonderment. It seems a refreshing change from the Dursleys. Sure, there is evil, personified by Voldemort, but the magical world seems fundamentally aligned with goodness. Wanting to fit in, Harry spends the early books feeling insecure about his grasp of wizard norms and eagerly learning the ropes. But gradually we and Harry realize that the magical world is as judgmental as the Muggle world and equally inclined to treat cruelly those considered "other," which, readers soon realize, start with Muggles like ourselves. Unlike Voldemort, whose propensity to cruelty is reinforced by the worst magical customs and who aspires to take over the system and amplify it, Harry, as he comes to understand dominant wizarding cultural attitudes, increasingly resists them. Guided partly by his own instincts and partly by Hermione, he rejects not only the corruption of the magical world's official rules but also many unwritten norms, with their prejudices and discrimination. Researchers of social movements observe that one way movement activists motivate new supporters is by establishing new interpretive "frames" that help "people come to see old injustices in new ways" (Johnston, *What*, 65). As outsiders, Harry and Hermione bring fresh perspectives that help their friends question taken-for-granted frames of reference about matters like elf rights. In the terms of the creativity research examined in Chapter Four, they "defy the Zeitgeist." Analysis of this defiance will be at the core of subsequent chapters, but I want to look quickly at one of the first wizard customs Harry encounters—one of the first unwritten rules he breaks, at first inadvertently but soon intentionally: the taboo against saying "Voldemort."

Unwillingness to say Voldemort's name is nearly universal in wizard culture. Even Minerva McGonagall, as she and Dumbledore await Hagrid's arrival with baby Harry, twice mentions "You-Know-Who," prompting this response from Dumbledore, the first of several similar conversations, and also the first time "Voldemort" is used:

> "My dear Professor, surely a sensible person like yourself can call him by his name? All this 'You-Know-Who' nonsense—for eleven years I have been trying to persuade people to call him by his proper name: *Voldemort*." Professor McGonagall flinched, but Dumbledore, who was unsticking two lemon drops, seemed not to notice. "It all gets so confusing if we keep saying 'You-Know-Who.' I have never seen any reason to be frightened of saying Voldemort's name."
>
> "I know you haven't," said Professor McGonagall, sounding half exasperated, half admiring. "But you're different. Everyone knows you're the only one You-Know- oh, all right, *Voldemort*, was frightened of."
>
> (SS 11)

Once Voldemort consolidates power, in *Deathly Hallows*, the name becomes jinxed, as Ron explains: "Now they've put a Taboo on it, anyone who says it is trackable—quick-and-easy way to find Order members!" (390). Traditionally, "taboo," which has its origins in Tongan customs observed during Captain James Cook's eighteenth-century travels, has referred to something forbidden because it is too sacred for ordinary people. Before the jinx, attitudes toward "Voldemort" resemble most taboos, a cultural norm or an indication of a personality cult.[7] Rowling has compared the taboo's power both to fears raised by gangsters and to folklore taboos in which "your name is something that can be used magically against you if it's known. It's like a part of your soul" ("Leaky," Part Two). After Voldemort's ascendancy, saying the name summons a brutal mercenary force called "Snatchers." The logic is that it is "only people who were serious about standing up to him, like Dumbledore, who ever dared use it" (DH 390). That is, the jinx uncovers resistance fighters. It also breaks defensive spells. Thus, once the name becomes magically "Taboo," there are practical reasons not to use it, but had that been true before Voldemort's disappearance, Dumbledore would surely have acknowledged it. The barrier to using the name, as McGonagall concedes, is simply fear.

Of course, "You-Know-Who" only works as an identifier if the person addressed does know, which is why Hagrid reluctantly shares the name with Harry, but only following a long wind-up, after which he returns to "You-Know-Who":

> "It begins, I suppose, with—with a person called—but it's incredible yeh don't know his name, everyone in our world knows—"
> "Who?"
> "Well—I don' like sayin' the name if I can help it. No one does."
> "Why not?"
> "Gulpin' gargoyles, Harry, people are still scared. Blimey, this is difficult. See, there was this wizard who went . . . bad. As bad as you could go. Worse. Worse than worse. His name was . . ."
> Hagrid gulped, but no words came out.
> "Could you write it down?" Harry suggested.
> "Nah—can't spell it. All right—*Voldemort*." Hagrid shuddered. "Don' make me say it again."
>
> (SS 54)

Large and intimidating as Hagrid appears, his obvious difficulty telling the story reinforces that Voldemort and his name inspire terror.

Coming from outside wizard culture, Harry struggles to remember to avoid the name; as a result, he violates the prohibition and must correct himself repeatedly: "Vol-, I mean, You-Know-Who." As he explains to Ron on the Hogwarts Express, "I'm not trying to be *brave* or anything, saying the name … I just never knew you shouldn't. See what I mean? I've got loads to learn" (SS 100). What he is learning is neither an official rule nor established knowledge but a social convention, for using the name need not require courage, as there is no danger. Ironically, as Harry adjusts to the norm, "He was starting to get a prickle of fear every time You-Know-Who was mentioned. He supposed this was all part of entering the magical world, but it had been a lot more comfortable saying 'Voldemort' without worrying" (SS 107). Dumbledore confirms Harry's perception at the end of Book One, advising, "Call him Voldemort, Harry. Always use the proper name for things. Fear of a name increases fear of the thing itself" (SS 298). Thereafter, Harry follows his original instincts and says, "Voldemort." Harry learns both to say "Voldemort" and a larger principle: to question social norms. Dumbledore not only leads the active resistance later in the series but models resistance to irrational norms throughout the series.

Voldemort, as we know, has several sobriquets, the most proscriptive being "He-Who-Must-Not-Be-Named," which Harry first hears from Mr. Ollivander as he learns about the matching wand cores: "The wand chooses the wizard, remember. . . . I think we must expect great things from you, Mr. Potter. . . . After all, He-Who-Must-Not-Be-Named did great things—terrible, yes, but great" (85). In response, Harry "shivers," whether at the comparison, at Ollivander's description of Voldemort's power, or at the way he identifies Voldemort is unclear. This is the only time in *Sorcerer's Stone* that suggests that the name is actually forbidden, but the idea appears frequently in *Chamber of Secrets*, which is also, of course, the book in which we learn that "I am Lord Voldemort" is an anagram of "Tom Marvolo Riddle," and that "I fashioned myself a new name, a name I knew wizards everywhere would one day fear to speak, when I had become the greatest sorcerer in the world!" (CS 314). Voldemort suppressed his birth name and spread fear of his chosen name. As Dobby explains, "The Dark Lord, before he changed his name, could be freely named, you see?" (CS 339). It is from Dobby that we first hear the phrase "The Dark Lord" (CS 15), which he presumably learned from the Malfoys. It is the Death Eaters' preferred euphemism, reflecting their elitism and near worship of their charismatic leader. Ordinarily, Dobby's preferred term is "He-Who-Must-Not-Be-Named"—highly appropriate for a creature who spends his life being forbidden from doing things.

In other words, the characters' ways of referring to Voldemort say a great deal not only about magical culture but about them as individuals.[8] Notably, Hermione says the name the first time when she is trying to talk Harry into teaching defensive spells:

> "Harry," she said timidly, "don't you see? This . . . this is exactly why we need you. . . . We need to know what it's r-really like . . . facing him . . . facing V-Voldemort."
>
> It was the first time she had ever said Voldemort's name, and it was this, more than anything else, that calmed Harry.
>
> (OP 328)

Knowing that Harry says the taboo name to express defiance, Hermione musters the courage to show similar rebelliousness, which helps persuade Harry to endorse her plans. Hermione once again voices the name at the organizing meeting for the D.A., with powerful results:

> "I want to be properly trained in Defense because . . . because . . ." She took a great breath and finished, "Because Lord Voldemort's back."
>
> The reaction was immediate and predictable. Cho's friend shrieked and slopped butterbeer down herself, Terry Boot gave a kind of involuntary twitch, Padma Patil shuddered, and Neville gave an odd yelp that he managed to turn into a cough. All of them, however, looked fixedly, even eagerly, at Harry.
>
> (OP 340)

The students' reaction is partly to news of Voldemort's return, but the effort it takes for Hermione to say "Voldemort," for the second time and publicly, suggests that the name itself causes shrieks, twitches, shudders, and yelps. It also helps cement the students' interest. Thus, Harry's and Hermione's publicly flouting an important social convention has a major impact on organizing the student resistance movement, reflecting findings of obedience studies that those who observe others defying questionable expectations are more willing to do the same.

Significantly, in the final showdown of *Deathly Hallows*, Harry repeatedly uses "Riddle," not "Voldemort." Perhaps, having just cast the *Protego* charm across the Great Hall, Harry is avoiding the jinx that breaks protective enchantments, but he seems confident that, as he tells Voldemort, "You won't be able to kill any of them ever again. Don't you get it? I was ready to die to stop you from hurting these people ... I've done what my mother did. They're protected from you. Haven't you noticed how none of the spells you put on them are binding?" (738). So Harry uses the name with the same defiant confidence he previously had saying, "Voldemort." Tom Riddle had changed his name to erase connection with his "filthy Muggle father's name" (CS 314), but Harry will have none of that, taunting Voldemort with his own racism, spitting out the paternal surname in overtly challenging tones:

> "You don't learn from your mistakes, Riddle, do you?"
> "*You dare—*"
> "Yes, I dare," said Harry. "I know things you don't know, Tom Riddle. I know lots of important things that you don't. Want to hear some, before you make another big mistake?"
>
> (DH 738)

In this climactic scene, Harry schools Voldemort about wand lore, the need for remorse, and especially the power of love, saying the hated father's name, "Riddle," six times while giving Voldemort a chance to learn, to repent, before his curse rebounds against him and Harry triumphs. Challenging the magical world's taboo against saying Riddle/Voldemort's name represents a core piece of Harry's ultimate victory.[9]

Social norms and unwritten rules are powerful, sometimes more powerful than formal laws. That one of Voldemort's earliest acts when he seizes power is to codify an unwritten rule against speaking his name into a statute enforced by mercenaries illustrates both the authoritarian nature of his governance and the significance of the social pressure surrounding his name. He and his minions do much the same thing when they create laws and commissions to validate the most elitist and discriminatory of social attitudes in the wizarding world. Because of the power of these norms and attitudes in magical culture, much of the next few chapters will be devoted to them and to the ways they are resisted.

Notes

1 It is also disturbing that the Department of Mysteries is so readily corrupted after Voldemort's takeover that it quickly issues "research" indicating that magical ability only occurs among those with magical parents (DH 209)—though, to be sure, this may be *Daily Prophet* propaganda; either way, with essentially no scientific training, credulous *Prophet* readers may well believe this obviously false statement. Contemporary Muggles can be forgiven for noting parallels to false "science" about vaccines and masks—and the disinformation machines that promote it. Moreover, as Susan Hall observes, the isolation of wizards from Muggles and goblins creates "artificial barriers to technical advance" among wizards ("Marx" 282–3).

2 We are told explicitly that Harry's catching the Snitch in his mouth in his first match "hadn't broken any rules" (SS 191), but it is a fine example of Harry, as usual, getting away with something that is at least aberrant.

3 See, for example, Hall, "Harry Potter" and "Justice"; MacNeil, "Kidlit." Many legal issues in the Harry Potter series are explored in the excellent collection, *The Law and Harry Potter*, edited by Thomas and Snyder.

4 In response to Harry's interest, during his first visit to Flourish and Blotts, in a spell book that would teach him how to curse Dudley, Hagrid comments, "I'm not sayin' that's not a good idea, but yer not ter use magic in the Muggle world except in very special circumstances" (SS 80).

5 One final Ministry department is less about policy or law and more about research: The Department of Mysteries. Perhaps it would be accurate to say that this department explores how the "laws of magic" work.

6 The deaths of Muggle-borns at Azkaban could be predicted even without confirmation in the "Dolores Umbridge" entry in *Wizarding World*.

7 Not all taboos relate to things considered sacred; other taboos forbid behaviors that arouse cultural disgust. Very few Muggle taboos are legally enforced. The exceptions are behaviors like pedophilia. One might argue that in some cultures behaviors like abortion, drug use, and drinking face legally enforced taboos. See Chapter Two on the role of disgust in wizarding culture.

8 For example, the fact that Ginny's singing valentine addressed to Harry in *Chamber of Secrets* describes him as "*The hero who conquered the Dark Lord*" (238) is a clue that she is possessed by Voldemort, as the Weasley family habitually uses the euphemism "You-Know-Who."

9 See, however, Tolonda Henderson's "Chosen Names" on the parallels with deadnaming trans people and the author's own inability to challenge norms of traditional gender binaries.

2

"FILTH! SCUM! BY-PRODUCTS OF DIRT AND VILENESS!"

"Mudbloods," Dirt, Privilege, and Systemic Oppression in the *Harry Potter* Series

The most difficult rules to resist may be the "rules" people rarely think about because they are so widely understood: a culture's unwritten norms. Harry Potter has been in the wizarding world for a year before he encounters the word "mudblood," though, to be sure, on his first day in wizard culture he hears Draco Malfoy remark, "I really don't think they should let the other sort in, do you? They're just not the same, they've never been brought up to know our ways. Some of them have never even heard of Hogwarts until they get the letter, imagine. I think they should keep it in the old wizarding families" (SS 78). As an outsider who had also "never even heard of Hogwarts" and has no clue about "our ways," Harry recoils from this opinion, but only gradually does Harry—and the Muggle reader—learn that Draco's personal bigotry reflects what we might call "pure-blood privilege" and systemic oppression of Muggle-borns and non-wizards. Fighting Voldemort then becomes, implicitly and eventually explicitly, resistance to structural injustices. In this chapter, I will explore how metaphors of dirt and cleanliness permeate the series' depictions of systemic racism and wizard privilege. Through its identification with "Mudbloods" and other out-groups, the series challenges and complicates the "normal" binary of "filth" vs. "purity," in which dirt is bad and cleanliness is good. Resistance to this unwritten "rule" is central to the series.

In the Potterverse, magical blood status operates as a metaphor for race, with the notion of "pure-blood" superiority standing in for white racism. To be sure, there are many troubling aspects to the series' handling of literal race dynamics, most notably that the default race, that of the main characters, is white, while only the racial and ethnic background of secondary characters is noted.[1] This is only one concern raised as part of much broader critiques of the racial politics of the series by such critics as Raymond I. Schuck, who argues that the series'

DOI: 10.4324/9781003312260-3

ostensible antiracism is belied by its "white hero premise," where the unprivileged groups can only be saved by a protagonist from the privileged group; Soma Das, who argues that the depiction of the Patil twins supports "maintaining status quo, reinforcing gender and racial stereotypes, and tokenism" (45); Kristen Cole, who argues that Hogwarts's practices reify Eurocentrism and androcentrism; and Giselle Liza Anatol, who argues that the books "wobble between seeking a way out of the imperialist agenda and experiencing a certain nostalgia for the safety and security attributed to the empire" ("Fallen" 174) and that Rowling's "inconsistent rendering of what it means to be an Other to society's hegemonic forces weakens the explicit antiracism theme of the books" ("Replication" 109).[2] These are legitimate and important arguments; my primary concern here, however, is with the metaphor of dirt in the series' depiction of blood status, privilege, and discrimination, and the ways the metaphor contributes to its depiction of resistance.

Wizard privilege is the magical world's version of "white privilege," a term Peggy McIntosh popularized. McIntosh's 1988 article, "White Privilege and Male Privilege: A Personal Account of Coming to See Correspondences through Work in Women's Studies," describes "an invisible package of unearned assets" enjoyed by white people and not shared by people of color who are otherwise similar economically, socially, or politically (17). Crucially, these "unearned assets" are "invisible"—invisible, that is, to those who benefit from them. Thus, "whites are taught to think of their lives as morally neutral, normative, and average, and also ideal, so that when we work to benefit others, this is seen as work that will allow 'them' to be more like 'us'" (19). To be sure, many poor white people bristle at being called "privileged," which is where the concept of intersectionality helps. No one has a single identity, so a white person may be disadvantaged by gender, sexuality, economic status, religion, age, size, physical ability, education, immigration status, or other factors, singly or intertwined. In the wizarding world, magical ability is a primary source of privilege, with hierarchies from pure-blood, half-blood, Muggle-born, and Squib, to Muggle; magical humans have more privilege than goblins, centaurs, and house-elves. Race, class, and gender have less potency in wizard culture than in Muggle culture but are far from irrelevant. As a wealthy, straight white pure-blood male, Draco Malfoy's privileges multiply.

The existence of "wizard privilege" is confirmed with just a few examples analogous to McIntosh's. McIntosh observes, "I can easily find academic courses and institutions which give attention only to people of my race" (21). All Hogwarts students take History of Magic, in which, by definition, Muggles and nonhuman magical beings figure only as "Others," usually adversaries. Wizard culture, after all, enforces a form of Apartheid, a radical separation between those born with magical ability and those who are not. The Ministry of Magic's primary function is to enforce the separation. Squibs, non-magical folk born into magical families, are hidden away as shameful (as Ariana Dumbledore was rumored to have been), excluded from magical culture (like Arabella Figg), or mocked (like Argus Filch). Muggle-born witches and wizards endure suspicion or condescension.

And the Muggle majority are routinely manipulated and ridiculed, even by those who don't engage in Muggle-baiting or murder.[3] Nonhuman magical beings are second-class citizens, considered adversaries—like goblins—or overlooked entirely. Magical education acknowledges none of this. Only Hermione notices that "Not once, in over a thousand pages, does *Hogwarts, A History* mention that we are all colluding in the oppression of a hundred slaves!" (GF 238); indeed, "Wizarding history often skates over what the wizards have done to other magical races" (DH 506). Ironically, the permanent residents of Hogwarts, who are there not to be educated but to be exploited, go virtually unnoticed.[4] Prior to their second year at Hogwarts, neither Harry nor Hermione knows about "the existence of their race," in McIntosh's words (19).

Another advantage white people experience, without thinking about it, is "I can do well in a challenging situation without being called a credit to my race" (McIntosh 31). Of course, wizards define "race" less by appearance than by magical ability—wizard vs. Muggle or Squib. Thus Muggle-born Hermione inspires statements like Slughorn's: "Oho! '*One of my best friends is Muggle-born, and she's the best in our year!*' I'm assuming this is the very friend of whom you spoke, Harry?" (HBP 186). Slughorn has insisted, "You mustn't think I'm prejudiced!" (HBP 71), but his surprise reveals an implicit bias familiar in Muggles who know that bigotry is unacceptable but haven't examined their unconscious preconceptions as closely as they might. For explicit bias, Malfoy provides the series' first case. From him, we first hear the term "mudblood," an epithet reflecting a long tradition of expressing fear of the Other through the language of dirt and disgust.

In her seminal 1966 study *Purity and Danger*, anthropologist Mary Douglas defines dirt as "matter out of place." "Dirt," she writes, "is never a unique, isolated event. Where there is dirt there is a system. Dirt is the by-product of a systematic ordering and classification of matter, in so far as ordering involves rejecting inappropriate elements" (35). That is, each culture defines what is "out of place" and inappropriate, tries to control it, based on its own systems, then calls that matter "dirt" or "dirty." Wizard culture is no different. Thus, what characters in *Harry Potter* consider dirty and disgusting ultimately says more about the characters, their value systems, and wizarding cultural systems than about the person or object being assessed.

Dirt—or what characters identify as dirt or filth—takes many forms. A word search in digital copies of the books reveals hundreds of references to dirt and related concepts like mud, dust, clutter, untidiness, debris, mess, rubbish, grime, slime, squalidness, impurity, filth, scum, pollution, stench, decay, taint, dung, and puke. Dirt in the series includes, of course, literal earth in gardens or on Quidditch pitches, which sometimes gets on people's clothes or faces or gets tracked into the castle, where, out of place, it incenses Argus Filch. References to human waste or decay sometimes appear for comic effect and sometimes to inspire fear. But most interesting, in my view, is "dirt" reflecting moral and social value systems, in terms like "impure," "scum," and "mudbloods."

In this chapter, I will discuss, first, the ways the books reverse expectations by associating dirt with positive things (and cleanliness with negatives), as well as the use of dirt as misdirection, to challenge readers' expectations. Then I will offer an overview of the growing field of disgust studies and explain what responses to "moral dirt" and "mudbloods" suggest about Voldemort and the Death Eaters. As it does in many other areas, the series challenges preconceptions about dirt—but not always. Dirt, like so many other issues in *Harry Potter* and like life itself, is a messy issue. Next, I will look at the series' multifaceted depiction of cleaning, which is both a reaction to dirt (however that is defined) and an expression of love—and thus a form of resistance. Finally, I will look at the evolution of Ron Weasley, from a boy with no concept of his wizard privilege to a budding antiracist.

The Dirt on Dirt in *Harry Potter*

We generally assume that dirt is bad. Historian William A. Cohen points out that "In a general sense, [the word] *filth* is a term of condemnation, which instantly repudiates a threatening thing, person, or idea by ascribing alterity [otherness] to it. Ordinarily, that which is filthy is so fundamentally alien that it must be rejected; labeling something filthy is a viscerally powerful means of excluding it" (Cohen ix). In Harry Potter's world, things are not that simple. Indeed, dirt often carries positive connotations. From the beginning, readers identify with Harry, with his "untidy" hair, by contrast with the "tidy," bourgeois, "perfectly normal" neighborhood of Number 4 Privet Drive, which is typified by Aunt Petunia's obsessive cleaning. Hagrid, also lovable—if intimidating—from the first, endears himself the more when, in telling Harry how his parents died, he "suddenly pulled out a very dirty, spotted handkerchief and blew his nose with a sound like a foghorn" (SS 55). The Leaky Cauldron is "grubby looking" (68). Hedwig is unquestionably "matter out of place" at the Dursleys', where she brings back dead mice that would have horrified Petunia had she entered Harry's room to vacuum (SS 88); but Hedwig is his first birthday present since his parents' death, arguably, his first friend. As Keri Stevenson observes, Hedwig's presence represents "a rebellion against the rigidity of order and normality that the Dursleys try to enforce" (121). Among the first things Harry notices about Ron is a black smudge on his nose (SS 98). Later, Harry is charmed by the homey Burrow (a name suggesting a home in the earth/dirt), with its cluttered kitchen and "litter of old Wellington boots and rusty cauldrons" around its back door (HBP 81). The Sorting Hat is so "extremely dirty" that "Aunt Petunia wouldn't have let it in the house" (SS 117). In one of the series' most moving moments, Harry digs Dobby's grave by hand, without magic, sweating, his muscles aching, his hands "covered in mud and Dobby's blood" (DH 482).

In some cases, dirt shares the very essence of magic. Polyjuice Potion in a cauldron is a "slow-bubbling, mudlike substance" (HBP 185), echoing the Biblical tradition that humans were created from dust or clay (Genesis 2:7; Isaiah 64:8). It is the appropriate raw material from which to generate any individual's bodily form. In a spell evoking postmortem return to dust, the corpse-like "horror figure" representing Dumbledore (171), that emerges when one enters number twelve Grimmauld Place in *Deathly Hallows*, "explode[s] in a great cloud of dust" (171). At Ollivanders, "The very dust and silence ... seemed to tingle with some secret magic" (SS 82). Thus, the books break the usual rules by associating dirt not with the unappealing but with love and magic.

That is not to say that dirt is always unambiguously positive or cleanliness always bad. Indeed, the books frequently exploit readers' preconceptions that dirt indicates evil—and sometimes those preconceptions prove correct: Knockturn Alley and the Gaunts' house are as evil as their shadows and grime imply. And in the final book, Harry's near-death experience is in King's Cross Station, only, he observes, it is "a lot cleaner and empty," and Harry's hands are "clean" and "unblemished" (712). More on this later.

Other times, descriptions exploit readers' preconceptions about dirt to remind us that things are not always what they seem. The potions textbook Slughorn lends Harry appears "old and dirty and dog-eared" (HBP 193), and Harry is initially annoyed that the "Half-blood Prince" has "scribbled all over the pages, so that the margins were as black as the printed portions" (189). When Madam Pince the librarian sees the book, she is appalled that it is "Despoiled! ... Desecrated! Befouled!" (308). Of course, this "graffitied" (220) book proves not worthless but extremely "illuminating" (376). Likewise, the Hogshead Pub seems "dodgy," with its "very dirty room that smelled strongly of something that might have been goats," its floor covered with "what seemed to be the accumulated filth of centuries" (OP 335), and its barman "wiping out a glass with a rag so filthy it looked as though it had never been washed" (OP 338). This is a classic misdirection, of course, for the barkeep is Aberforth Dumbledore. Another misdirection is Snape's greasy hair and, in the memory Harry glimpses in the Pensieve, gray underpants.

Crucially, many things designed to be overlooked by Muggles are shabby, dirty, or disused. Portkeys are "Unobtrusive things, [...] so Muggles don't go picking them up and playing with them ... stuff they'll just think is litter" (GF 70), like the "moldy-looking old boot" that transports Harry's group to the World Cup (GF 71). St. Mungo's Hospital for Magical Maladies and Injuries is concealed by the storefront for a closed department store, Purge and Dowse Ltd., which has a dusty door and a "shabby, miserable air" (OP 483). This method of hiding magic in plain sight is a subtle dig at Muggles' Dursleyish fixation on the latest shiny new thing and a reminder not to judge superficially. Muggles' refusal to see magic in plain sight is among their least admirable qualities.

And then there is Professor Lupin, mocked by Draco because "He dresses like our old house-elf" (PA 141). Dobby, we recall, wore an old, "filthy" pillowcase when he was enslaved by the Malfoys. Lupin's robes are not dirty, but they resemble items linked to dirt and rubbish: they are "extremely shabby," "patched and frayed" (PA 74, 141). In short, he is poor; Draco habitually conflates poverty and dirt, as when he insults the "smell" of the Weasley's supposed "bin" or "hovel" (OP 412)—classist remarks disproved by Molly's domesticity. When Lupin is first seen, sleeping on the Hogwarts Express, he appears insignificant, belying the fact that, at the full moon, he becomes a fearsome predator and at other times is a dynamic teacher and powerful wizard.

Disgust Sensitivity and the Wizarding World

Once Lupin is revealed to be a werewolf, he becomes a social outcast, an object of fear and disgust. The relatively new and growing field of disgust studies sheds light on this and other aspects of *Harry Potter*. Theorists about dirt and disgust fall into two basic camps: scholars who identify dirt with permanent, biological or psychological realities; and scholars who agree with Douglas that human attitudes toward "filth" are primarily learned and vary with cultural and historical circumstances. They point out that small children put almost anything in their mouths; they don't learn disgust until three or four years old.[5] Dietary and sexual taboos vary among cultures. Biologists and many psychologists argue that disgust provides evolutionary advantages, protecting us from disease. While the biological approach offers useful information, the cultural approach is more relevant to *Harry Potter*.

Recently, psychologists have observed that politically conservative people have greater "disgust sensitivity" than others, specifically, three kinds of disgust: "interpersonal disgust (i.e., the feeling produced by drinking from the same cup as someone else); core disgust (the response to maggots, vomit, dirty toilets, etc.); and animal-reminder disgust (reactions to corpses, blood, anything that evokes our animal nature)" (Hurst). People with greater disgust sensitivity are "more tolerant of social inequality and score higher on measures of authoritarianism, have more conservative attitudes toward sex," including homosexuality, are more likely to have anti-immigrant attitudes, and are "more likely to identify as politically conservative" (Inbar et al. 537). They are frequently disgusted by actions that break rules or norms that matter to them.

People who are obsessively clean and respectful of authority, classically described as having "anal retentive" personalities, are described by Ernest Becker, in his book *The Denial of Death*, as troubled by their animal nature: "Excreting is the curse that threatens madness because it shows man his abject finitude, his physicalness, the likely unreality of his hopes and dreams" (Becker 33). According to Becker, "anal" people resist contradictions and ambiguities and prefer "their symbols pure, their Truth with a capital 'T'" (32). Although the terms have changed since Becker wrote in the 1970s, his theories are confirmed by recent, controlled studies that find connections between obsessive-compulsive disorder and disgust sensitivity (feces are a universal disgust stimulus).[6] Narcissa Malfoy provides an interesting case in point. In the earlier books, Narcissa seems in a state of perpetual disgust. Observing her at the World Cup, Harry thinks, "she would have been nice-looking if she hadn't been wearing a look that suggested there was a nasty smell under her nose" (GF 101). That expression—presumably a wrinkled nose, retracted lips, and lowered eyebrows—is universal, one reason theorists, beginning with Darwin, have associated disgust with unwholesome smells and tastes.

By contrast, Fred and George Weasley, probably the series' most anti-authoritarian characters (Freud might call them "anal expulsive personalities"), appeal to customers—mostly kids and Order of the Phoenix sympathizers—with products that run heavily toward the disgusting. These include dungbombs, Nosebleed Nougats, Puking Pastilles, trick wands that turn into pairs of briefs, and "edible dark marks—they'll make anyone sick!" (HBP 117–18). Weasleys' Wildfire Whiz-Bangs write "swearwords in midair of their own accord" (OP 632). When the twins release fireworks in rebellion against Dolores Umbridge, "a sparkler floated past the tower, still resolutely spelling out the word POO" (OP 634). To these products, the movie version of *Half-Blood Prince* adds "Nautious [sic] Jumping Snakes" and "Demon Dung Crackers." In a direct parody of Voldemort and an overt suggestion of anal retentiveness, the twins' store window displays "a gigantic poster, purple like those of the Ministry, but emblazoned with flashing yellow letters":

> WHY ARE YOU WORRYING ABOUT
> YOU-KNOW-WHO?
> YOU SHOULD BE WORRYING ABOUT
> U-NO-POO —
> THE CONSTIPATION SENSATION
> THAT'S GRIPPING THE NATION!
>
> (HBP 116)

Of course, this appeals to young readers' distinctly scatological sense of humor. Such humor challenges social taboos surrounding elimination; it subverts convention and deflates the powerful and the pompous. In general, laughter eases stress that arises when people are afraid; moreover, associating a frightening person or event with something considered ridiculous or disgusting strips the frightening thing of its power; for this reason, such humor empowers those who deploy it.[7] Even more relevant, in this instance, is how pointedly the "U-No-Poo" joke hits Voldemort at his most sensitive point, conflating anal retentiveness/constipation/disgust sensitivity/authoritarianism with Voldemort's discomfort with his own physicality.

When Fred and George occasionally feel disgusted, it is with the conventional, the hierarchical—or rules themselves. They are "revolted at the very idea" of being a prefect, George explains, because "It'd take all the fun out of life" (PA 62). When Ron is named prefect, they reiterate their abhorrence: "'Oh, Mum's going to be revolting,' groaned George, thrusting the prefect badge back at Ron as though it might contaminate him" (OP 162).

The characters we like express "Moral disgust"—but their disgust reflects social value systems we can endorse: Arthur Weasley remarks "disgustedly" that torturing and killing Muggles is "fun" for Death Eaters (GF 143). On a more mundane level, Lee Jordan complains about a "revolting foul," a "disgusting bit of cheating," by the Slytherin Quidditch team (SS 188); the Hogwarts house-elves are disgusted by Winky's drunkenness (GF 538). Professor McGonagall refuses to be intimidated by Amycus Carrow, instead looking down at him "as if he were something disgusting she had found stuck to a lavatory seat" (DH 593). We delight in McGonagall's disgusted response to Umbridge's evaluation of Harry's course work: "'What, this thing?' said Professor McGonagall in a tone of revulsion, as she pulled a sheet of pink parchment from between the leaves of Harry's folder" (OP 664). Indeed, Umbridge inspires a great deal of disgust: "Harry was revolted to see the enjoyment stretching her toadlike face as she watched Professor Trelawney sink, sobbing uncontrollably" (OP 595). Ron is revolted to learn of Umbridge's version of "lines" (OP 272). These disgusting situations range from relatively petty misbehaviors to betrayal to outright cruelty.

"Muggles are like animals, stupid and dirty"

By contrast, Voldemort's allies and sympathizers justify cruelty by expressing "moral disgust" consistent with a very different socially defined value system. David Livingstone Smith, in his study *Less than Human: Why We Demean, Enslave, and Exterminate Others*, notes that during World War II, propaganda on *all* sides portrayed the enemy as subhuman, with analogies to dogs, pigs, apes, vermin, rats, bats, viruses, and cockroaches. Disgust is often about "policing the boundary between ourselves and nonhuman animals, or our own animality" (Nussbaum 89). Accordingly, people consider animal secretions like feces, mucus, semen, or menstrual blood to be contaminating. Psychologists Paul Rozin, Jonathan Haidt, and Clark McCauley observe that "humans display in most cultures a strong desire to be seen as qualitatively distinct from other animals, that is, to be 'more than animals'" (13). Of course, as philosopher Martha Nussbaum notes, not all animals repulse us. No one, she observes, is disgusted by dolphins, and we admire animal traits like strength and agility. Rather, negative analogies between humans and animals emphasize traits considered subhuman, and, in turn, people compare members of out-groups to nonhumans to justify ill-treatment. Thus Voldemort brags to Harry that Lily's love "did not prevent me stamping out your Mudblood mother like a cockroach" (DH 739). The analogy identifies her as disgusting and vulnerable.

Under Voldemort's influence, dehumanizing the Other becomes official Ministry policy.[8] Umbridge's xenophobic pamphlet on "MUDBLOODS and the Dangers They Pose to a Peaceful Pure-Blood Society" depicts a rose—a purity symbol—"strangled by a green weed with fangs and a scowl" (DH 249), an image suggesting a snake—a frequent stimulus of disgust and fear responses—to convey the supposedly contaminating "half-breed" traits. At Hogwarts, under Voldemort, Muggle Studies becomes compulsory, and its teacher, Alecto Carrow, preaches that "Muggles are like animals, stupid and dirty." In the spirit of war propaganda, Muggles are blamed for "dr[iving] wizards into hiding by being vicious toward them." Thus, Ministry policies oppressing Muggles and mudbloods are "how the natural order is being reestablished" (DH 574).

Alecto replaces the murdered Muggle Studies professor, aptly named Charity Burbage, whose supplanted curriculum Voldemort describes with the language of filth, contamination—and Nazi propaganda: Voldemort says, "Not content with corrupting and polluting the minds of Wizarding children, last week Professor Burbage wrote an impassioned defense of Mudbloods in the *Daily Prophet*. Wizards, she says, must accept these thieves of their knowledge and magic. The dwindling of the purebloods is, says Professor Burbage, a most desirable circumstance.... She would have us all mate with Muggles ... or, no doubt, werewolves" (DH 12). The word "mate," of course, conflates Muggles with animals and adds sexual disgust to words like "corrupting" and "polluting."

The term "mudblood" is the series' strongest allusion to traditional associations of out-groups with filth. When Malfoy first calls Hermione a "filthy little mudblood" (CS 112), Ron explains, "mudblood" is a "really foul name for someone who is Muggle-born" (CS 115). Ron's word "foul" is, ironically, a synonym for "filthy," and, to add to the paradox, Ron calls it "a disgusting thing to call someone" (CS 116): what one considers filthy and disgusting depends on one's own value system. Ron's explanation that the term denotes "Dirty blood, see. Common blood" (CS 116) adds an elitist element. Instead of being "pure," the blood of Muggle-born wizards is polluted with dirt, filth, and commonness.

The converse of "mudblood" is, of course, "pure-blood." Ironically, blood purity's loudest advocate (literally) is the portrait of Walburga Black, whose denunciations of *"MUDBLOODS! SCUM! CREATURES OF DIRT!"* echo through the filthiest house imaginable. Similarly, the Horcrux from Tom Riddle's diary emerges, ironically, in what amounts to a chamber pot of secrets (accessed through a bathroom's drains) to explain why he rejected his given name: "You think I was going to use my filthy Muggle father's name forever? I, in whose veins runs the blood of Salazar Slytherin himself? I, keep the name of a foul, common Muggle ... ?" (CS 314). Here, Riddle uses the language of "pure" blood and emphasizes both dirt and disgust in describing miscegenation between a witch and a Muggle. As Smith explains it, Nazis deployed the idea of "blood purity" because, of course, Jews look like Aryans—just as Muggles and Muggle-borns look like wizards—so the "taint" must be both fundamental and invisible. Smith observes, "Of course, Jews did not wear their subhumanity on their sleeves. They were regarded as insidiously subhuman. Their ostensible humanity was, at best, only skin deep" (4–5). In Nazi Germany, "The mystical notion of blood-borne subhumanity was the basis for laws against miscegenation (Hitler compared ethnically mixed marriages to 'unions between ape and human'). The Nazi publication

The Subhuman states that Aryan nations that are 'tainted by the mixing of blood' are thereby destroyed" (Smith 160).

Language linking dirt and racial Others persists. During 2018's hysteria about a "caravan" of Central American asylum seekers, the internet site Puppet String News posted, "2,267 Caravan Invaders Have Tuberculosis, HIV, Chickenpox and Other Health Issues."[9] Fox News commentator Tucker Carlson claimed in 2019 that the Potomac River "has gotten dirtier and dirtier and dirtier and dirtier. I go down there, and that litter is left almost exclusively by immigrants" (Plott). COVID-19 inspired anti-Asian rhetoric that focused on dirt, disorder, and infection. CNN reporter Jeff Yang quoted social media posts that claimed that the Chinese "eat anything and everything and infect the world with viruses" and called the Chinese "dirty people who can't keep order." All of this was complicated by findings that hand hygiene was one of the few methods of curbing spread of the coronavirus. Sadly, the disproportionate impact of COVID-19 on U.S. communities of color was too often blamed not on their over-representation among "essential workers" with high exposure to the disease nor on a history of inadequate access to health care—but on poor hygiene. A state Senator from Ohio, Stephen Huffman, speculated, "Could it just be that African Americans, or the colored population, do not wash their hands as well as other groups?" (Gabriel). Dehumanization of supposedly "dirty" out-groups is illustrated by Donald Trump's July 27, 1919, tweet that Baltimore, Maryland, is "a disgusting, rat and rodent infested mess" and "no human being would want to live there." The implication was that Baltimore residents, 66% of whom are people of color, are not human. Finally, the Black Lives Matter demonstrations of summer 2020 inspired Eric Trump to describe protesters as not Americans, but "animals": "when you see these animals literally taking over our cities, burning down churches, this isn't America. That's not what Americans do" (Brennan).

In *Harry Potter*, treating the Other as a disgusting animal is not just for Death Eaters. Aunt Marge Dursley, who once gave Harry dog biscuits as a Christmas present, shows her character by insulting both Harry and his dead parents: "'You mustn't blame yourself for the way the boy's turned out, Vernon … If there's something rotten on the *inside,* there's nothing anyone can do about it. … It's one of the basic rules of breeding,' she said. 'You see it all the time with dogs. If there's something wrong with the bitch, there'll be something wrong with the pup—'" (CS 25). Marge can't resist rendering Harry and his parents as subhuman, using classic racist tropes: "'It all comes down to blood, as I was saying the other day. Bad blood will out. Now, I'm saying nothing against your family, Petunia'—she patted Aunt Petunia's bony hand with her shovel-like one—'but your sister was a bad egg. They turn up in the best families. Then she ran off with a wastrel and here's the result right in front of us'" (PA 28). Aunt Marge is reputedly named after Margaret Thatcher—who notoriously voiced "people's" fear of "being swamped by people with a different culture." If, as Christopher C. Bell theorizes in his conference presentation "You Have Your Mother's Eyes," James Potter was Black,

Marge's insult about Harry's "bad blood" and describing James as a "good-for-nothing, lazy scrounger" (PA 28) could be interpreted as a slur conflating his race and his (supposed) socioeconomic status.

Marge's insults anticipate Voldemort's language regarding Tonks and Lupin's marriage. After he mockingly congratulates Bellatrix and Narcissa, Bellatrix replies, "She is no niece of ours, my Lord ... We—Narcissa and I—have never set eyes on our sister since she married the Mudblood. This brat has nothing to do with either of us, nor any *beast* she marries" (DH 10; emphasis added). Voldemort happily adopts the "beast" metaphor, asking Draco, "Will you babysit the cubs?" (DH 10). Then, he rapidly moves from derision to didacticism: "Many of our oldest family trees become a little diseased over time," he counsels, advising Bellatrix, "You must prune yours, must you not, to keep it healthy? Cut away those parts that threaten the health of the rest. [...] And in your family, so in the world ... we shall cut away the canker that infects us until only those of the true blood remain" (DH 10–11). Not to put too fine a point on it, Voldemort advocates genocide (or at least *ethnic cleansing*[10]), starting with his followers' family members, and he justifies it using the language of disgust, disease, infection, and identifying non-pure-bloods as lower life forms—beasts and diseased plants.

Systemic Racism in the Magical World

The phrase "systemic racism" adapts the word *systemic* from medical terminology, to describe a disorder affecting not just a localized area but the entire "social body." That is, racism is not merely a personal flaw but is built into social institutions. Systemic racism infects policies in government and law enforcement and in institutions like banking, education, and healthcare. Thus, Draco's personal bigotry reflects a broader social reality. Wizard privilege and pure-blood privilege are not merely personal but systemic, and indeed magical folk like the Weasley family who reject personal bigotry against Muggles and Muggle-borns still benefit from the wizarding world's systemic racism. Wizard privilege is codified in wizard law, in clause three of the Code of Wand Use: "*No non-human creature is permitted to carry or use a wand*" (GF 132). There is an entire Department for the Regulation and Control of Magical Creatures to enforce this rule and others that subordinate magical nonhumans. Clause three denies powerful magical beings like centaurs, goblins, and house-elves "the possibility of extending [their] powers" with a wand (DH 488). Once Voldemort controls the Ministry, the rule is extended to Muggle-born witches and wizards, on the false pretext that "magic can only be passed from person to person when Wizards reproduce. Where no proven Wizarding ancestry exists, therefore, the so-called Muggle-born is likely to have obtained magical power by theft or force" (DH 209). That is, a Muggle-born witch or wizard—a "mudblood"—is automatically guilty of a crime. The penalty is to be stripped of one's wand—reduced to the status of a "non-human creature"—and sent to Azkaban. Naturally, Muggle-born children are barred from

Hogwarts. Once Voldemort seizes power, Muggle killings increase as he carries out an idea advanced by a cousin of Sirius's mother, who had advocated legalizing "Muggle-hunting" (OP 113). And why not? In the introduction to *Fantastic Beasts and Where to Find Them*, "Newt Scamander" comments, "We are all familiar with the extremists who campaign for the classification of Muggles as 'beasts'" (xiii). As Scamander explains, "beast" is distinguished from the official legal term "being," defined in 1811 as "any creature that has sufficient intelligence to understand the laws of the magical community and to bear part of the responsibility of shaping those laws" (xii). Indeed, as Juliana Valdes Lopes observes, the distinctions between "beings" and "beasts" are politically rather than biologically based (180). This is systemic racism at its most virulent.

Even before Voldemort's takeover, wizard law-enforcement discriminated against nonhuman or half-human magical individuals. For example, part-giant Hagrid is hustled away to Azkaban without a hearing, purely on suspicion of opening the Chamber of Secrets. Hokey the house-elf is convicted of poisoning her mistress, Hepzipah Smith—who was in fact killed by Tom Riddle—because, as Dumbledore explains,

> "the Ministry was predisposed to suspect Hokey —"
> "— because she was a house-elf," said Harry.
> (DH 439)

There is also workplace discrimination. When Dumbledore hires Lupin, his lycanthropy is kept secret, for good reason: once it is revealed, parents demand his termination. The problem is not just parents; we learn in *Order of the Phoenix* that Umbridge "drafted a bit of anti-werewolf legislation two years ago that makes it almost impossible for him to get a job" (302); the timing suggests she made official—systemic—the parents' unofficial bigotry. In Harry's fifth year, Dumbledore hires Firenze the centaur over Umbridge's objections—later she calls centaurs "Filthy half-breeds! ... Beasts! Uncontrolled animals!" (755) and asserts that they have "near-human intelligence" (754). Fellow Divination professor Trelawney scornfully calls Firenze "the horse" and "the nag"—to students. Talk about a toxic work environment! As Mark-Anthony Lewis observes, nonhuman and part-human Hogwarts employees suffer all the disadvantages of being tokens: not fully belonging to the wizard community and outcast from their community of origin.

Systemic racism at Hogwarts follows a typical Muggle pattern. Although Muggle-borns and the occasional part-human attend the school, no nonhumans attend, further limiting their ability to develop their powers, as Lopes has pointed out (182). As McIntosh notes, one marker of white privilege is "I can remain oblivious of the language and customs of persons of color who constitute the world's majority" (20). Hogwarts graduates are similarly oblivious. The curriculum completely overlooks the servant class (house-elves); merpeople are virtually unknown; and goblins appear in Magical History only as enemies and Others. Students never learn, for example, how goblins understand ownership of goblin-made valuables, which might clarify the Goblin Wars Professor Binns lectures about. Students' tactless comments when Firenze joins the faculty show how little they have learned about centaurs, despite centaurs' obvious gifts and despite many living close by: Lavender Brown says, "There are *more of you*?" and Dean Thomas asks, "Did Hagrid breed you, like the thestrals?" (OP 601). To be sure, older Hogwarts students may take Muggle Studies, but even before Alecto Carrow takes over, the course is problematic. As Joanna Lipińska observes, Muggle Studies resembles cultural anthropology, with Muggles treated as

> a kind of primitive culture, a curiosity that can be studied and whose technical solutions surprise with the level of advancement for such a simple civilization that has no real professional tools (magic).
>
> It is not that all wizards intentionally treat Muggles as something inferior, but the way they look upon them resembles the nineteenth-century Eurocentric way of treating other cultures.
>
> (119)

In other words, the course, like History of Magic, reinforces a privileged ethnocentric view that magical culture is "normal," despite encompassing a small minority of humans—never mind the cultures of other magical beings. Since wizards and Muggles interact constantly and much of the magical legal code is premised on (hostile) relations with Muggles, Muggle Studies is an inadequate elective. Even supposed specialists in Muggles, like Arthur Weasley, know surprisingly little about Muggle culture and technology, and Arthur's fond comment, "Bless them" (GF 96), is kind but condescending. Magical culture seems indifferent to knowledge gaps, however, because "wand carriers" have more power than other "beings."

Similarly, at Hogwarts, werewolves are studied as a threat. When Snape substitutes in Lupin's Defense Against the Dark Arts class, he assigns students to write an essay on "the ways you recognize and kill werewolves" (PA 173). A lesson based on the premise that one kills a werewolf immediately upon recognizing one promotes neither tolerance, equality, nor justice. Snape's intention is to "out" Lupin—and cost him his job.

It's Complicated

Werewolves represent a particularly interesting case study in dirt, disgust, and interrelationships between the human and the animal. Fenrir Greyback, the werewolf who "infected" Lupin, has dirty, disgusting traits: in the *Deathly Hallows* capture scene, his face is "covered in matted gray hair and whiskers," indicating poor grooming; "his breath [was] foul in Harry's nostrils as he pressed a filthy finger to the taut scar" (DH 452). In addition, "Harry could smell a powerful mixture of dirt, sweat, and, unmistakably, blood coming from him. His filthy hands had long yellowish nails" (HBP 593). He also has "pointed brown teeth"—animalistic and discolored—and "sores at the corners of his mouth"—indicating disease, possibly an STD (DH 450). Infection is not merely suggested; for Greyback, Lupin tells Harry, "regards it as his mission in life to bite and to *contaminate* as many people as possible; he wants to create enough werewolves to overcome the wizards" (HBP 334; emphasis added). No one is imagining or inventing Greyback's evil. Greyback's behavior helps explain, though not excuse, why parents fear a werewolf teacher. Before Lupin is revealed to be a werewolf, of course, he is popular with nearly all students except Malfoy. Revelation of his lycanthropy changes only one piece of knowledge, yet he is immediately unemployable. That one werewolf is malevolently aggressive and dangerous does not necessarily mean another has the same traits, as Lupin, unlike Greyback, has spent a lifetime attempting to control his condition. As Travis Prinzi has observed, werewolves, like other characters in the series, are defined by their choices (57).

The *Harry Potter* books fundamentally challenge disgust at animal-human connections in many ways, from the respectful portrayal of centaurs and merpeople to our sympathy for Lupin and our admiration for Animagi. Nevertheless, Rowling deploys disgust—partly for humorous effect—in describing creatures like trolls and ghouls. The troll in Book One has "a foul stench" like "a mixture of old socks and the kind of public toilet no one seems to clean" (SS 174). The Weasley family ghoul, who makes "[a] horrible, half-sucking, half-moaning sound," has "an unpleasant smell like open drains" (DH 97). Harry is "revolted" at the sight—albeit because of the deforming spell that makes it appear to have Spattergroit, which is, literally, contagious (DH 98). Even Grawp, Hagrid's half-brother, has "filthy, bare feet," and a horrified Harry takes him at first for a boulder (OP 693); this proves to be more a case of misdirection, as Grawp eventually proves to be another gentle giant.

Surely Rowling made Peter Pettigrew/Scabbers/Wormtail a rat rather than a cat, bunny, or another small animal, to leverage the associations of rats with treachery and betrayal—and with dirt, disease, and infection. The Marauder nickname Wormtail, not something like Whiskers or Squeaker, emphasizes one of a rat's least appealing traits—worms disgust many people. The name Scabbers, too, has negative connotations suggesting disease. Descriptions reinforce Peter's ratlike—and dirty—qualities: "His skin looked grubby, almost like Scabbers's fur, and something of the rat lingered around his pointed nose and his very small, watery eyes" (PA 366). Assigned to work as Snape's servant, he is described as "scurrying" from a room (HBP 24). Not surprisingly, Voldemort, though willing to exploit Wormtail, derides his animal traits, his "filthy little friends," and "curious affinity with rats" (GF 655). Moreover, the narrative hints at homosexuality, first when Ron "with the utmost revulsion," exclaims, "I let you sleep in my *bed*!" (PA 373). Later, in Snape's memory, Peter's fascination with James seems excessive:

> James was still playing with the Snitch, letting it zoom farther and farther away, almost escaping but always grabbed at the last second. Wormtail was

> watching him with his mouth open. Every time James made a particularly difficult catch, Wormtail gasped and applauded. After five minutes of this, Harry wondered why James didn't tell Wormtail to get a grip on himself, but James seemed to be enjoying the attention.
> …
>
> "Put that away, will you?" said Sirius finally, as James made a fine catch and Wormtail let out a cheer. "Before Wormtail wets himself from excitement."
> Wormtail turned slightly pink but James grinned.
>
> OP 644–5

While James watches girls, Peter watches James, and can't "get a grip on himself." Peter's reactions are implicitly sexual: his open mouth, gasp, blush, and the possibility of "wet[ting] himself from excitement." Even "Wormtail" sounds like sexual slang. A reader could wonder whether a jealous, rejected Peter was willing to sacrifice Lily and Harry much as Snape was willing to sacrifice James and Harry. These hints associating Peter with homosexuality contrast with Rowling's extracanonical comments that Lupin's lycanthropy represents AIDS and that Dumbledore is gay,[11] for the dominant attitude of the series is rejection of filth-based disgust and the intolerant attitudes that accompany it.

"My mother can't have been magic, or she wouldn't have died": Animal-Reminder Disgust, Race, and Fear of Death

Perhaps what disgust-sensitive humans most wish to ignore about our similarities with animals is that animals die and decay. As Nussbaum theorizes, disgust reflects "a wish to be a type of being that one is not, namely nonanimal and immortal. [Disgust's] thoughts about contamination serve the ambition of making ourselves nonhuman, and this ambition, however ubiquitous, is problematic and irrational, involving self-deception and vain aspiration" (102). This irrational ambition for immortality, this disgust by intimations of mortality, which are, in turn, associated with "contamination and filth," is precisely what we see in Voldemort and what he encourages in his followers. Voldemort's denial of death is a lifelong issue. As a child, he assumes, "My mother can't have been magic, or she wouldn't have died" (HBP 275). Moreover, he has a vexed relationship not only with his "half-blood" heritage but with his own corporeal form. While he goes to considerable trouble to rebuild a body, the spell he designs to get it requires "impure" materials he disdains—dust from his Muggle father's corpse, (half)-blood from Harry, and flesh from the rat-like "servant" Wormtail. And though Voldemort revels in having a body—an intensely white body—after the perverse incarnation scene that is his "rebirthing ceremony," he expresses ambivalence: "I was willing to embrace mortal life again, before chasing immortality. I set my sights lower . . . I would settle for my old body back again, and my old strength" (GF 656). For Voldemort—

who, ironically becomes more snakelike, less human as he divides his soul—to have a physical human body is to "settle." Voldemort's attitude echoes racist concepts of Aryan mental and spiritual superiority, reinforcing "the inescapable corporeality of non-white peoples, while leaving the corporeality of whites less certain" (Dyer 24). In this conception, white people are closer to "the pure spirit that was made flesh in Jesus, their spirit of mastery over their and other bodies, in short their potential to transcend their raced bodies" (Dyer 24–25).

Voldemort's desire for immortality—and eagerness to kill others to achieve it—complements his simultaneous revulsion and fascination for dead bodies, from his father's corpse to Inferi, to Bathilda Bagshot's corpse inhabited by Nagini—not by Voldemort himself. Voldemort's intense disgust reactions to death and what he considers filth are illuminated by Richard Dyer's description of white people's "special relation with death" (208). Dyer theorizes that traditional veneration of the dead white body comes from "a deep conviction of the reality of transcendence" (209). For Dumbledore, the soul transcends the body by going "On" (DH 722). For Voldemort, however, separating the (white) body and the soul reflects his "superiority" to the Muggle body. And Rowling complicates the duality by describing Voldemort's mangled soul, in the King's Cross scene, as taking "the form of a small, naked child, ... its skin raw and rough, flayed looking" (DH 706); in contrast, Harry, with his "clean, unblemished hands," wears robes that are "soft, clean, and warm" (712, 706). Rowling is deploying traditional Christian symbolism of the purity of souls—in contradistinction to bodies. Dumbledore says Voldemort would not have understood the Resurrection Stone because "whom would he want to bring back from the dead? He fears the dead. He does not love" (DH 721). Harry can defeat Voldemort, Dumbledore explains, because Harry "had accepted, even embraced, the possibility of death, something Lord Voldemort has never been able to do" (DH 711). Harry is "the true master of death, because the true master does not seek to run away from Death. He accepts that he must die, and understands that there are far, far worse things in the living world than dying" (DH 720–21). Love, that is, transcends fixations on dualisms of dirt and cleanliness.

Cleaning: Sometimes Repression, Sometimes Resistance

Where you have fear of dirt, you inevitably have cleaning. Like the books' depiction of dirt, their portrayal of cleaning away "filth" is multifaceted, complex, and frequently paradoxical. Cleaning is depicted as sometimes trivial, too often fraught with racism and "ethnic cleansing." As with dirt, a character's attitude toward cleaning indicates the "system" that defines what they consider "out of place," in Douglas' terms, and how they imagine dealing with it. Thus, some characters clean to control a threatening "impurity," while others clean as gestures of care for family and friends.

"Filth! Scum! By-products of Dirt and Vileness!" **71**

In the magical world, as in the real world, cleaning protects from literal contamination and disease and removes literal messes. Hence the PSA at St. Mungo's: "A CLEAN CAULDRON KEEPS POTIONS FROM BECOMING POISONS" (OP 484). Although Filch is personally unlikeable, maintaining Hogwarts's basic cleanliness is necessary and no doubt frustrating. When Harry tracks mud from the Quidditch pitch, Filch complains Harry's "crime" has created "an extra hour of scrubbing" (CS 126), and he stocks Mrs. Skower's All-Purpose Magical Mess Remover by the crate (GF 304), though the product may not be that magical: Filch cannot scrub away the foot-high message "Enemies of the Heir, beware." As a Squib, Filch cannot use spells like Scourgify and Tergeo, so house-elves probably perform most of Hogwarts's domestic labor. The bitter Filch does excel at maintaining a "highly polished collection of chains and manacles" (CS 125).

As we have seen, extreme disgust sensitivity and fear of dirt are linked to obsessive-compulsive disorder. Petunia, with her panicky fear of contamination by Harry's "abnormality," exemplifies cleaning at its worst, and her obsessive fixation on cleanliness only increases. In the early books, she cleans to prepare for guests like Aunt Marge and Vernon's prospective client Mr. Mason, but by Book Four she is "compulsively straightening cushions" (GF 41). By *Order of the Phoenix*, her "surgically clean kitchen" has "an oddly unreal glitter" (37, 25). Seeing it, Tonks observes, "Very *clean,* aren't they, these Muggles?" (OP50). A bit later, she remarks, "Funny place, ... it's a bit *too* clean, d'you know what I mean? Bit unnatural." Significantly, when Tonks (whose resistance to wizarding disgust norms culminates in marriage to a werewolf) sees Harry's messy room, she remarks, "Oh, this is better" (OP 51). A year later, we find "Harry's aunt, wearing rubber gloves and a housecoat over her nightdress, clearly halfway through her usual pre-bedtime wipe-down of all the kitchen surfaces" (HBP 46). Someone who can't sleep without cleaning surfaces that are already "surgically clean" has a problem. Even when the Dursleys are removed from the home in the final volume, Petunia's concern for her family's safety doesn't distract her from leaving behind a "pristine kitchen" (DH 47). Tonks's observation that Petunia's kitchen is a "[b]it unnatural" reflects Petunia's disgust sensitivity and her reluctance to admit her connection to "weirdos" and "freaks" (DH 669).

Compulsive cleanliness is not exclusive to Muggles, though the impeccably neat Mr. Crouch is said to "pass" as a Muggle particularly effectively. Crouch is

> a stiff, upright, elderly man, dressed in an impeccably crisp suit and tie. The parting in his short gray hair was almost unnaturally straight, and his narrow toothbrush mustache looked as though he trimmed it using a slide rule. His shoes were very highly polished. Harry could see at once why Percy idolized him. Percy was a great believer in rigidly following rules, and Mr. Crouch had complied with the rule about Muggle dressing so thoroughly

that he could have passed for a bank manager; Harry doubted even Uncle Vernon would have spotted him for what he really was.

(GF 90)

Crouch's straight part reflects the unbending and "unnatural" way he treats his son and his house-elf. As we have seen, Crouch, a staunch defender of the status quo, when he headed the Department of Magical Law Enforcement, encouraged systemic police misconduct. This is reminiscent of a certain germophobic American President, who described cities as "rat-infested" and who advised police, "Please don't be too nice" to suspects. Defense of "law and *order*" can lead to systemic disregard for the rule of law.

Similarly, Cornelius Fudge indirectly aids Voldemort to avoid "the prospect of disruption in his comfortable and ordered world" (GF 707). Dolores Umbridge's neatness correlates with authoritarianism and xenophobia. Umbridge has "neat mousy hair"; her Educational Decrees feature "a neat and curly signature" (OP 351). Umbridge's "neatness" and excessive femininity seem at first to contradict her fierce treatment of her supposed inferiors, but they reflect her repressive personality and, of course, her distaste for "part-humans" and "mudbloods."

Cleaning itself is frequently depicted negatively. Early in the series, Harry's domestic labor—frying bacon and cleaning windows—symbolizes his downtrodden Cinderella-like status (SS 19, CS 10). Later, as punishment, Ron must do "Muggle cleaning" to polish trophies (CS 119). Snape particularly enjoys denigrating cleaning as a form of humiliation, mocking Sirius for remaining at number twelve Grimmauld Place where only cleaning takes place, punishing Harry by making him scrape tubeworms off desks (CS 146), and forcing Wormtail to clean and serve drinks (HBP 23–24). To be sure, Snape himself suffered from a particularly unpleasant episode of humiliation-through-cleaning, when James Potter literally washed Snape's mouth out with soap, as retribution for Snape's calling Lily a "mudblood."

But there is more to cleaning in *Harry Potter* than obsessiveness, drudgery, and humiliation. Like much else in the series, cleaning can be connected to love—and love with resistance. An instructive example is Sirius's evolving attitude toward cleaning. When Harry first arrives at Grimmauld Place, Sirius complains about "all [Snape's] snide hints that he's out there risking his life while I'm sat on my backside here having a nice comfortable time . . . asking me how the cleaning's going—" (OP 83). Snape's comments reflect a traditionally masculine scorn of "women's work," and Sirius readily accepts that value system. In fact, not Sirius but Molly and the young people do most of the cleaning. At Christmas time, by contrast, Sirius, "no longer their sullen host of the summer," instead "worked tirelessly in the run-up to Christmas Day, cleaning and decorating with their help, so that by the time they all went to bed on Christmas Eve the house was barely recognizable"; significantly, "a great Christmas tree … blocked Sirius's family tree from view" (OP 501). Now, cleaning is not a humiliating obligation but communicates hospitality and love.

Number twelve Grimmauld Place is a site of contention between competing ideas about filth and cleanliness, as the portrait of Walburga Black shrieks like a deranged housewife about "filth"—meaning, however, anyone lacking "pure" wizard blood—while remaining oblivious to the house's literal decay and dirt (partly punning on "grime" and "mold," among other possibilities). When Harry first arrives just pages after Tonks's comment about the Dursleys' "unnatural" cleanliness, he is struck by the "damp, dust, and a sweetish, rotting smell" (60). When Molly, Sirius, and the children set out to "decontaminate" the place (117), the challenge seems ordinary enough: the drawing room's walls are "covered in dirty tapestries" and "The carpet exhaled little clouds of dust every time someone put their foot on it" (101). But being a wizarding home, that carpet is infested with buzzing doxies (tiny, hairy, four-handed, venomous fairies); and the house has a "murderous old ghoul lurking in an upstairs toilet" (118).

Various physically dangerous artifacts are objective correlatives for the philosophically dangerous concept of blood purity: Lupin helps "repair a grandfather clock that had developed the unpleasant habit of shooting heavy bolts at passersby" (OP 118)—suggesting that the house, though stuck in the past, can be returned to a less intolerant present. Order members are attacked by an "unpleasant-looking silver instrument, something like a many-legged pair of tweezers, which scuttled up Harry's arm like a spider when he picked it up, and attempted to puncture his skin." Ironically, "Sirius seized it and smashed it with a heavy book entitled *Nature's Nobility: A Wizarding Genealogy*" (OP 116), a book tracking "pure" bloodlines that is subsequently discarded but retrieved by Kreacher and, appropriately, later joins the books Hermione "borrows," finding information there about the Peverell family. Battles are not won by destroying, discarding, or hiding books. Also discarded but retrieved by Kreacher: the Horcrux locket. Cleaning is a mixed bag.

While the Burrow's clutter is endearing, Molly Weasley devotes considerable time to cleaning up after her enormous family. One of the first things we see upon meeting the Weasleys is Molly cleaning a smudge off Ron's nose, rubbing until it turns pink; Ron tries to wriggle free, the twins tease, and the smudge remains through the Sorting Ceremony. We immediately recognize a close family with a loving mother, and the gesture is no less appealing for being futile—in contrast to Petunia's cleaning, so successful but so sterile, or Wool's Orphanage, where Tom Riddle grew up, "spotlessly clean," but loveless (HBP 264). As Molly welcomes Harry to her family, she starts doing his laundry, with "freshly laundered robes" (OP 163) mentioned at the beginning of every book beginning with *Goblet of Fire*. These many instances all characterize Molly as expressing love not only with delicious cooking but with washing.

Cleaning to express love is not just for moms. When a grief-stricken Hagrid drops a milk jug, Hermione steps in immediately, "hurrying over and starting to

74   "Filth! Scum! By-products of Dirt and Vileness!"

clean up the mess" (PA 327–28). Hagrid simultaneously scolds and grooms Harry when Harry misses his fireplace the first time he uses the Floo network: "'Yer a mess!' said Hagrid gruffly, brushing soot off Harry so forcefully he nearly knocked him into a barrel of dragon dung outside an apothecary" (CS 54). When Hermione bursts into tears about Mad-Eye's death, Ron rushes to comfort her through a small act of cleaning:

> One arm around Hermione, he fished in his jeans pocket and withdrew a revolting-looking handkerchief that he had used to clean out the oven earlier. Hastily pulling out his wand, he pointed it at the rag and said, "*Tergeo.*"
> The wand siphoned off most of the grease. Looking rather pleased with himself, Ron handed the slightly smoking handkerchief to Hermione.
> (DH 94–5)

Hermione, in turn, washes as she packs for the Horcrux quest: "I'm nearly done, I'm just waiting for the rest of your underpants to come out of the wash, Ron" (DH 115).

Some cleaning to express love marks a special occasion, notably when the topsy-turvy Weasley household gets put in order for Bill and Fleur's wedding:

> Harry had never seen the place looking so tidy. The rusty cauldrons and old Wellington boots that usually littered the steps by the back door were gone, replaced by two new Flutterby bushes standing either side of the door in large pots ... The chickens had been shut away, the yard had been swept, and the nearby garden had been pruned, plucked, and generally spruced up, although Harry, who liked it in its overgrown state, thought that it looked rather forlorn without its usual contingent of capering gnomes.
> (DH 106–7)

Gnomes, though theoretically pests, add to the Burrow's lived-in, homey quality; fortunately, we know from previous books that they will return. Later wedding scenes show the beautiful results of these preparations. One reason for the cleaning had been misplaced anxiety about Fleur's family, who turn out to have exactly the right attitude toward housework and visiting: "The Delacours, it soon transpired, were helpful, pleasant guests. They were pleased with everything and keen to assist with the preparations for the wedding. ... Madame Delacour was most accomplished at household spells and had the oven properly cleaned in a trice" (DH 108). Being half veela doesn't prevent Madame Delacour from cleaning the oven.

Being well groomed conveys love and being loved; conversely, poor grooming may reveal neglect or depression. In a photograph of Luna and her late mother, "Luna looked rather better-groomed in this picture than Harry had ever seen her in life" (DH 417). Young Snape is already "dirty-haired" (DH 665) and wears mismatched, ill-fitting clothes and gray underpants. By contrast, young James Potter is "slight, black-haired like Snape, but with that indefinable air of having been well-cared-for, even adored, that Snape so conspicuously lacked" (671). Grooming also reveals one's state of mind. When Sirius is at Azkaban and in hiding, his face "had been gaunt and sunken, surrounded by a quantity of long, black, matted hair—but the hair was short and clean now, Sirius's face was fuller, and he looked younger, much more like the only photograph Harry had of him, which had been taken at the Potters' wedding" (GF 331). Later, feeling stuck in Grimmauld Place, Sirius is "unshaven," with "a slightly Mundungus-like whiff of stale drink about him" (OP 475). His poor grooming reflects his depression.

One can deduce house-elves' state of mind from their apparel's design, condition, and cleanliness. Enslaved by the Malfoys, Dobby wears a "grubby," "filthy old pillowcase" (CS 15; GF 375). Freed, he wears garments that are "clean and well cared for" (GF 377). Similarly, Kreacher's appearance expresses his distaste for serving Sirius and later Harry: a "filthy rag tied like a loincloth" (OP 107). But when treated kindly, "Nothing in the room … was more dramatically different than the house-elf who now came hurrying toward Harry, dressed in a snowy-white towel, his ear hair as clean and fluffy as cotton wool" (DH 225). Winky, while working for Mr. Crouch, wears a neat "tea towel draped like a toga" (GF 97). Freed (against her will), she becomes depressed, abuses butterbeer, and "had allowed herself to become so filthy that she was not immediately distinguishable from the smoke-blackened brick behind her. Her clothes were ragged and unwashed" (GF 536). For house-elves, whose identity is defined by housework, including cleaning, cleanliness and good grooming convey caring and being cared for.

One expression for cleaning—to "wipe"—describes both cleaning and concealment, sometimes both. When Snape detains Harry after Harry throws mud on Draco from beneath his invisibility cloak, "Harry followed him downstairs, trying to wipe his hands clean on the inside of his robes without Snape noticing" (PA 282). Magical wiping occurs when the trio prepare to cross snow-covered grounds from a secret visit to Hagrid, and he reminds them, "don' forget ter wipe yer footprints out behind yeh!" (OP 439). Each is wiping away evidence of rule breaking. This is true of the Marauder's Map, as George cautions,

> "Don't forget to wipe it after you've used it—"
> "—or anyone can read it," Fred said warningly.
> (PA 193)

Hogwarts students use similar magic to deceive Umbridge: "Harry's interview had been bewitched to resemble extracts from textbooks if anyone but themselves read it, or else wiped magically blank until they wanted to peruse it again" (OP 582). Once again, "wiping" the document hides rule breaking—so the wiping becomes part of the resistance.

In short, sometimes cleaning amounts to resisting rules; other times, breaking rules and violating accepted norms inspire disgust. The real and apparent contradictions do not render irrelevant the series' depiction of dirt and cleanliness. Rather, they challenge reductive binaries. In a culture premised on hate, cleaning as care (not rejection or exclusion) represents resistance. Simultaneously, oppressing others for being "dirty" is all too "normal." And part of resisting the unspoken rules of "normality" is learning to recognize and resist privilege.

Resisting Privilege—Defending and Redeeming Ron Weasley

Why would Ron Weasley need defending? Everyone loves Harry's funny best friend, don't they? Actually, no. Ron has inspired harsh criticism because he repeatedly abandons Harry just when Harry needs his loyalty most and because he habitually defends some of the wizarding world's least savory characteristics: exploiting magical creatures, treating goblins as second-class citizens, and enslaving house-elves. Ron is a virtual poster boy for wizard privilege and racism. As Jennifer Cross remarked during a conference session on "The Banality of Evil: Collaborators and Appeasement," "Don't even get me started about Ron Weasley." When I told a student the topic of this section, she instantly responded, "Good luck with that!"[12]

To be sure, Ron deserves criticism. He can be thin skinned and easily provoked, insecure, jealous of his siblings and his best friend, insensitive toward Hermione, and sexist in general; even when he tries to understand women, his guide book seems focused on manipulation. These flaws are exacerbated in the movies, which frequently reduce his character to the funny bits and give Hermione some of his most sympathetic lines—such as her explanation of the term "mudblood." While much of Ron's behavior is indefensible, he is a dynamic character who grows and develops, arguably, more than Harry himself. Ron's changing attitudes are central to the series' depiction of the need to question and resist accepted social norms. By the end of the series, while by no means perfectly antiracist, Ron is at least trying.

Ron is an ordinary kid and a product of his family, which, despite its "blood traitor" status, is also a product of wizard culture. Even good-hearted Molly wants a house-elf to ease her domestic load, is slow to warm to Fleur, and distrusts a patient suffering a werewolf bite, in her husband's ward. Ron begins the series oblivious to wizard culture's systemic problems. The key word here is "oblivious." Sensitive to his family's poverty, he resembles poor white Muggles who are incredulous at being called privileged because their very real disadvantages hamper their awareness of their "unearned assets." Ron is poor, but also both pure-blood and male. Thus, though well-meaning and troubled by overt discrimination, Ron is the epitome of "wizard privilege"; questioning hegemonic wizard ideology simply doesn't occur to him.

At first, Ron seems like a fount of inside information: from Ron Harry learns about collecting Chocolate Frog cards, the joys of Quidditch, the merits of the Hogwarts Houses, and a bit about the Malfoys. Ron's perspectives seem nicer than Draco's, so it's easy for a first-time reader to overlook Ron's first unconscious statement of wizard prejudice:

> "Are all your family wizards?" asked Harry, who found Ron just as interesting as Ron found him.
> "Er–yes, I think so," said Ron. "I think Mum's got a second cousin who's an accountant, but we never talk about him."
>
> (SS 99)

Ron at this stage is an "interesting" new friend who knows the world Harry is entering. Learning at this stage that wizards feel about Muggles much the way the Dursleys feel about wizards seems an amusing illustration of the relativity of "normal." But more alert readers must notice that Dursleyish refusal to talk about relatives who are "different" is hardly admirable.[13] While Ron remains a source of information, ironic distance from his authority increases as his information becomes less about candy and Quidditch and more about cultural values. Ron's first big cultural blind spot appears in Book Two, when the Weasleys' perspective on house-elves is undercut by Harry's experience with Dobby. Later, the young men's bumbling interactions with girls and Ron's mental blocks about Quidditch make us increasingly distrust his instincts. Ron is no longer a reliable authority.

Although Hermione is mocked as a "know it all," Ron has a habit of making authoritative pronouncements that he claims "everyone knows"—"everyone" meaning people raised in wizarding families. "Everyone knows" is Ron's version of Vernon Dursley's "Perfectly normal, thank you very much." "Everyone knows," Ron says, that "Dragon breeding was outlawed by the Warlocks' Convention of 1709," though when Harry, who is obviously not "everyone," asks, "But there aren't wild dragons in *Britain*?" Ron replies matter-of-factly, "Of course there are" (SS 230–31). As late as the final book, Ron assumes everyone knows Elder Wands' reputation:

> "One of those superstitions, isn't it? ... You must've heard them. My mum's full of them."
> "Harry and I were raised by Muggles," Hermione reminded him.
>
> (DH 414)

Moreover, Ron has so internalized wizard prejudices that despite his fondness for Lupin and Hagrid, he instinctively recoils on learning of their werewolf and giant identities. To Lupin, Ron gasps, "*Get away from me, werewolf!*" (PA 345). Similarly, when Harry asks Ron to explain his response to Hagrid's overheard confession,

> [Harry] knew immediately, from the look Ron was giving him, that he was once again revealing his ignorance of the wizarding world. Brought up by the Dursleys, there were many things that wizards took for granted that were revelations to Harry, but these surprises had become fewer with each successive year. Now, however, he could tell that most wizards would not have said "So what?" upon finding out that one of their friends had a giantess for a mother.
>
> (GF 429)

The key phrase is "took for granted." Ron explains to Harry, "they're just vicious, giants. It's [...] in their natures, they're like trolls ... they just like killing, everyone knows that" (GF 430). That description would be more persuasive if we didn't in fact know Hagrid! Ron's nonsensical, racist generalization derives from his wizard privilege: witches and wizards are "normal"; and giants, like all other magical beings, are "less than." Forgetting he knows one half-giant, Ron falls back on what he "knows" of giants—second-hand stereotypes.

Another fact Ron takes for granted becomes crucial when the trio infiltrate the Ministry—that "everyone from Magical Maintenance wears navy blue robes" (DH 229). Lacking that information, because Ron had taken for granted that "everyone knows," they fail to prepare for the attendant responsibilities of Ron's planned impersonation of Reg Cattermole. Reg's appearance and job, significantly, a job all about cleaning, invite readers to underestimate him—as Ron certainly does. But Ron's experience literally walking in Reg's body provides an important stage in his growth. Reg, introduced as "Mr. Magical Maintenance," is a "small, ferrety-looking wizard," who looks "thoroughly downcast" (DH 238) and is easily intimidated by the ostensibly unintimidating Mafalda Hopkirk (actually Hermione). Reg, it seems, is both timid and easily tricked. First, he compliantly eats one of the Weasley Twins' Puking Pastilles; then he lets "Malfalda" persuade him to seek help at St. Mungo's. After impersonating Reg, Ron speculates, "I didn't get the feeling Reg Cattermole was all that quick-witted, though, the way everyone was talking to me when I was him" (274).

However, consider counterevidence, beginning with Reg's timidity toward "Mafalda." Alert readers recognize her name from the letters Harry receives from the Improper Use of Magic Office, responding to Dobby's mischief at the Dursleys' and again to Harry's producing a Patronus to protect Dudley. Thus, Mafalda is a relatively powerful Ministry bureaucrat, responsible for enforcing Ministry rules, and therefore someone Reg would naturally fear on the day of his wife's hearing for a supposed rules violation. Indeed, "Mafalda" (Hermione) is later enlisted to take notes at Reg's wife's trial. No wonder he looks "rather alarmed" and reluctantly takes the "sweet" that "Mafalda" "aggressively" proffers (DH 238). He complies in what he imagines is his wife's best interest.

To be sure, others at the Ministry treat Reg disrespectfully. When Yaxley spots "Reg" (Ron) on the elevator, he orders Reg to stop the rain in his office despite knowing perfectly well—unlike Ron—that Reg's wife is currently being questioned; indeed, Yaxley uses that knowledge as a cudgel to ensure Reg's compliance:

> "if *my* wife were accused of being a Mudblood," said Yaxley, "—not that any woman I married would ever be mistaken for such filth—and the Head of the Department of Magical Law Enforcement needed a job doing, I would make it my priority to do that job, Cattermole. Do you understand me?"
>
> "Yes," whispered Ron.
>
> "Then attend to it, Cattermole, and if my office is not completely dry within an hour, your wife's Blood Status will be in even graver doubt than it is now."
>
> (DH 244)

As a department head, Yaxley considers Reg beneath him, but as Sirius once advised, "If you want to know what a man's like, take a good look at how he treats his inferiors, not his equals" (GF 525). His treatment of Reg reveals Yaxley to be bigoted, cruel, and autocratic. And the more Yaxley deploys the language of "filth" to deride Mary Cattermole and, by extension, her husband, the more we should look for Reg's strengths.

Reg is treated as inferior, not because he is but because of elitist beliefs in blood purity and other illegitimate sources of status—including class-based contempt for maintenance workers. Ron's confusion, rather than indicating Reg's own incompetence, explains how he is treated while impersonating Reg. When ordered to "sort out" Yaxley's office, Ron's response is "Raining . . . in your office? That's—that's not good, is it?" and a "nervous laugh" (DH 243). Ron has no idea how to solve the problem, though Hermione suggests several solutions—that Ron needs to have explained more than once. Once the friends separate at the Ministry, Harry worries that "Ron was struggling to do magic that Harry was sure was beyond him" (DH 248); indeed, when Harry next sees him, "a soaking-wet and wild-eyed Ron got in" the elevator. A conversation between the disguised Ron and his father ensues:

> "I couldn't stop it, so they've sent me to get Bernie—Pillsworth, I think they said—"

"Yes, a lot of offices have been raining lately," said Mr. Weasley. "Did you try Meteolojinx Recanto? It worked for Bletchley."

"Meteolojinx Recanto?" whispered Ron. "No, I didn't. Thanks, D—I mean, thanks, Arthur."

(254–5)

This exchange shows that although Ron has no idea how to remove the jinx, other Magical Maintenance workers do, so probably the real Reg Cattermole does too. The magic required for the task, though "beyond" Ron, is in Reg's skill set. As too frequently happens, Ron assumes others feel as he does, in this case, not terribly "quick-witted." As it turns out, those who do the care work of cleaning up messes and repairing malfunctioning systems have powers others may not imagine or appreciate. Reg looks "ferrety," but domestic ferrets—a species closely related to weasels—are intelligent, affectionate animals. Typically, Arthur Weasley is the exception who treats Reg respectfully. While Ron worries whether the Cattermoles escaped, the evidence seems reassuring. Using apparition, Reg gets to St. Mungo's and back surprisingly quickly, considering that he had been so ill he collapsed. When we next see him, as Harry and company are helping Mary Cattermole and the other Muggle-borns to escape, "The real Reg Cattermole, no longer vomiting but pale and wan, had just come running out of a lift" (266).

This brings us to the core of Reg's story. Reg is introduced as "downcast"; and even after eating a Puking Pastille, he is determined to enter the Ministry: "'No—no!' He choked and retched, trying to continue on his way despite being unable to walk straight. 'I must—today—must go—'." Ron, who infers that Reg is "Keen on his job" (DH 239), does at least wonder why Reg is carrying his robes in a bag: "Weird he wasn't wearing them today, wasn't it, seeing how much he wanted to go?" (DH 240). But, of course, Reg is dressed formally, looks "downcast," and acts "keen" to get inside the Ministry to support his wife, the mother of his three children. Had he not encountered "Mafalda" and her spiked sweets, he would have been there, and he joins Mary as quickly as possible. Understandably confused as they both are by Ron's impersonation, their devotion to each other and their children is unmistakable. Mary has learned what to do from Harry, masquerading as Runcorn: "he's told all of us to leave the country, I think we'd better do it, Reg, I really do, let's hurry home and fetch the children and—" (264); and Reg has demonstrated his ability to apparate. Thus although Reg is identified initially—and dismissively—as "Mr. Magical Maintenance," associated "merely" with cleaning and repair, in the end Reg Cattermole is another representative of the motivating power of love.

While Reg's story is far from essential to the novel's core plot, it receives a surprising amount of emphasis, perhaps because it shows Ron's developing empathy. After they escape the Ministry, Ron is suffering from a painful splinching, but the Cattermoles are his first concern:

"What d'you reckon happened to the Cattermoles? [...] Blimey, I hope they escaped," said Ron [...] "God, I hope they made it.... If they both end up in Azkaban because of us ..."

Harry looked over at Hermione and the question he had been about to ask—about whether Mrs. Cattermole's lack of a wand would prevent her Apparating alongside her husband—died in his throat. Hermione was watching Ron fret over the fate of the Cattermoles, and there was such tenderness in her expression that Harry felt almost as if he had surprised her in the act of kissing him.

(DH 274–5)

Hermione's intensely tender response signals this moment's importance in Ron's development. Instead of focusing on the Horcrux whose retrieval was the excursion's main goal (the next question *Harry* asks), Ron worries about people he had never met before that morning. To be sure, Ron's concern may be enhanced because he, like Reg, loves a Muggle-born witch. But we might speculate that Polyjuiced walking in Reg's shoes has helped Ron glimpse his own privilege.

Pure-blood privilege and wizard privilege, like white privilege, need not entail active discrimination; Ron can deplore Muggle-baiting and yet unconsciously benefit from privilege. Privilege, as McIntosh explains, and as we see in the wizarding world, is *systemic*, not merely personal. And it can be difficult for the privileged to perceive. McIntosh writes,

> One factor seems clear about all of the interlocking oppressions. They take both active forms that we can see and embedded forms that members of the dominant group are taught not to see. In my class and place, I did not see myself as a racist because I was taught to recognize racism only in individual acts of meanness by members of my group, never in invisible systems conferring racial dominance on my group from birth.
>
> (26)

From early on, when Ron becomes livid at Draco's calling Hermione "mudblood," we see Ron rejecting overt bigotry. Where he falls short is in recognizing the "invisible systems," too readily accepting what "everyone knows." As Ibram X. Kendi explains,

> What's the problem with being "not racist"? It is a claim that signifies neutrality: "I am not a racist, but neither am I aggressively against racism." But there is no neutrality in the racism struggle. The opposite of "racist" isn't "not racist." It is "anti racist." ... One either believes problems are rooted in groups of people, as a racist, or locates the roots of problems in power and

policies, as an antiracist. One either allows racial inequities to persevere, as a racist, or confronts racial inequities as an antiracist.

(9)

Looked at this way, Ron, for all his rejection of mistreating non-pure-bloods, remains a racist.

When, in their fourth year at Hogwarts, Hermione had taken an antiracist stance supporting house-elves, Ron mocked her efforts. Hermione's retort shows that she understands precisely what's at stake: "It's people like *you,* Ron," Hermione began hotly, "who prop up rotten and unjust *systems*, just because they're too lazy to—" (GF 125; emphasis added). By the end of *Deathly Hallows*, Ron remains imperfectly aware of his privilege and the systems operating in wizarding culture, but he has conquered many of his worst impulses. He is sufficiently "troubled" by Kreacher's story to change his view of him (DH 198). Later, Hermione says to Griphook, "'Did you know that we've wanted elves to be freed for years?' (Ron fidgeted uncomfortably on the arm of Hermione's chair)" (DH 489). Why does that matter? While I'm not a basketball fan, I like a statement by San Antonio Spurs coach Gregg Popovich: "there has to be an uncomfortable element in the discourse for anything to change. Whether it is LGBT, women's suffrage, race, [it] doesn't matter. People have to be made to feel uncomfortable; especially white people. We still have no clue what being born white means" (Gaines). So while Ron's uncomfortable fidgeting is parenthetical, it's a clue to his development. The best-known change, of course, is his concern for the house-elves during the Battle of Hogwarts. He, not Hermione, suddenly stops and says, "we should tell them to get out. We don't want any more Dobbies, do we? We can't order them to die for us—" (DH 625). Hermione's passionate kiss, after years of ambivalent reciprocation of Ron's romantic advances, testifies that she considers this genuine and radical progress. To be truly "antiracist," someone needs to take action, and Ron does that.

That is not to say that Ron becomes flawless. For example, he is tempted by the Elder Wand—an unseemly attraction to the crudest kind of phallocentric power. For Harry and Hermione, who grew up outside wizard culture, recognizing its problems is comparatively easy. For Ron, Harry's welcomed guide to what "everyone knows" about wizard ways, questioning wizarding norms is a gradual, lurching process the attentive reader can follow through seven volumes. Institutions (and people) must evolve, not just stick with old rules. Ron, therefore, as a member of an old wizard family who evolves, is not a "bad guy." His slow and uneven evolution exemplifies the promise of renewal for wizard culture. Ironically, it is Harry who fails to question the system. Recovering from the Battle of Hogwarts, Harry is "wondering whether Kreacher might bring him sandwich" (DH 749).

The *Harry Potter* books do not embody a simple duality in which all privileged wizards are evil and all the oppressed are good, or where all dirt is good and all cleanliness is bad. Though generally sympathetic to the dirty, the series also depicts situations in which dirt is disgusting and good things are pure. But the characters whom we admire grapple with privilege and avoid oversimplifications about dirt that deny life's or humanity's complexities. Indeed, one important aspect of the magical resistance movement is its implicit rejection of simple binaries of dirt and cleanliness. Thus, it is notable that Dumbledore's signature advice to Harry, not to fear death, is also, implicitly, not to fear things associated with death, including the fragile, mortal body and all the traits that make it, by some lights, "filthy." Those who insist on purity of body or ideology deny the messiness of the human condition: love, by contrast, embraces multiplicity and flaws. The series itself is messy, sometimes inconsistent, and certainly breaks a lot of rules. That is part of what makes it lovable.

Notes

1 The casting of Noma Dumezweni as Hermione in *Harry Potter and the Cursed Child* has inspired a rethinking of *Potter* characters' race; fan art and fan fiction had anticipated these changes.
2 Other important discussions of race in the series include those by Karen A. Brown, Elaine Ostry, Laurie Barth Walczak, and several authors of essays in the 2022 collection *Harry Potter and the Other: Race Justice, and Difference in the Wizarding World*, edited by Sarah Park Dahlen and Ebony Elizabeth Thomas; unfortunately this book became available too late for me to incorporate its findings into my own work.
3 A case in point is the routine use of the Obliviate spell on Muggles exposed to magic, even though memory modification is shown to cause brain damage, exemplified by its impact on Mr. Roberts at the World Cup, and on Bertha Jorkins and Gilderoy Lockhart. Karin L. Westman describes the Ministry "public policy" of treating wizards' "integrity of self [as] more valuable than a Muggle's" as "an exercise of privilege" (157).
4 See also Peter Dendle on the other magical creatures, from trolls to dragons, that the magical community exploits.
5 A *Wizarding World* essay mocks the idea that anti-Muggle disgust is inherent. One supposed indicator of pure-blood status is "an aversion to Muggles observable even in the pure-blood baby, which supposedly shows signs of fear and disgust in their presence"; the essay then says this and the other indicators (including dislike of pigs) "have no basis in fact" ("Pure Bloods"). These comments match those of Muggle researchers, who have observed that infants react with facial expressions of disgust only to tastes and smells (bitterness and, less intensely, sourness). Disgust responses even to feces and vomit rarely emerge until children are three or four; and social disgust not until seven or eight (Sawchuk 79–82).
6 On these connections, see, for example, Curtis; Olatunji et al.; Whitton et al.
7 I am grateful to Andrea Morales for calling this aspect of humor to my attention.
8 Complicating matters, Lauren Camacci, in "The Face of Evil," argues that the series employs tropes of physiognomy and phrenology to depict evil characters as ugly, frequently dehumanizing them with animal metaphors.

9. PolitiFact described the claim as "Mostly False," noting that in Tijuana there were "three confirmed cases of tuberculosis, four cases of HIV/AIDS and four separate cases of chickenpox" (Valverde).
10. The United Nations defines ethnic cleansing as "planned deliberate removal from a specific territory, persons of a particular ethnic group, by force or intimidation, in order to render that area ethnically homogenous" (quoted in Walling, pp. 48–49). Voldemort's and the Death Eaters' goal of homogeneity fits this definition, but since wizards, Muggles, and Muggle-borns all inhabit the United Kingdom, the only possible ways to physically remove Muggle-borns are murder and imprisonment; the expulsion of giants from Britain better fits the UN's definition. That said, terror, including murdering individuals, is one method of encouraging people to leave an area. As Carrie Booth Walling explains, "All genocide involves ethnic cleansing, because the physical elimination of a people by definition means physical displacement. However, the reverse is not true: ethnic cleansing does not equate with genocide, although it may be its precursor, and it may involve 'genocidal acts'" (50).
11. On Lupin's lycanthropy as a metaphor for HIV, see "Remus Lupin" on *Wizarding World*. On Dumbledore as gay, see "J. K. Rowling at Carnegie Hall." Jonathan A. Rose takes this concept further, exploring what the figure of "the werewolf can tell us about nonnormativity or queerness in more general terms" (155).
12. I am grateful to Ashley Meihls for this conversation.
13. It is also, as we later learn, inconsistent with Arthur Weasley's fondness for Muggles. Rowling has explained that the family rift occurred not because the accountant (or stockbroker) was a Squib but because he and his wife "had been very rude to Mr. and Mrs. Weasley in the past" (Rowling, "Mafalda").

3
"HOW DARE YOU DEFY YOUR MASTERS?"

Rules, Roles, and Resistance in the Potterverse's Domestic Realm

No rules are more rigidly enforced in the wizarding world than those imposed on house-elves—and no rules are less frequently questioned or broken. And yet Dobby, the first elf we encounter, appears in Harry's bedroom precisely because he is violating a central rule for house-elves by revealing his master's secrets. Thus, from the very beginning, the depiction of house-elves represents a meditation on rules, why they are followed, and what it means to resist them.

Despite its overt focus on challenging intolerance, the *Harry Potter* series has been accused both of accepting or even justifying house-elf slavery and of depicting women characters in stereotypical ways—and some critics conflate the two issues. In this chapter, I will argue that the seemingly powerless and submissive behaviors of house-elves and women characters are, upon closer examination, both powerful and rebellious. Moreover, in analogous ways, house-elves and witches have powers that wizards in authority ignore, often at their peril. In many cases, their power is a kind that patriarchy typically overlooks. Not necessarily as contented with subordinate positions as might seem, house-elves and domestic witches successfully resist patriarchal power by leveraging the "power the Dark Lord knows not" (OP 841).

Just by looking at titles, one can infer how critics assess the series' female characters: frequently viewing Hermione as representing feminist consciousness but generally characterizing depictions of adult women as antifeminist and even misogynist. Thus, an entire essay collection, edited by Christopher E. Bell, is called *Hermione Granger Saves the World: Essays on the Feminist Heroine of Hogwarts.*[1] On the other hand, in "From Sexist to (Sort-Of) Feminist: Representations of Gender in the Harry Potter Series," Elizabeth E. Heilman and Trevor Donaldson argue, as the title indicates, that the "the Harry Potter books, like many popular books for children, mostly reinforce gender stereotypes" (139). Heilman and Donaldson acknowledge that "the last three books showcase richer roles and more powerful

DOI: 10.4324/9781003312260-4

females" but contend that "women are still marginalized, stereotyped, and even mocked" in the series (140). Similarly, Jeanne Hoeker LaHaie, in "Mums are Good: Harry Potter and Traditional Womanhood," says the series suggests that to nurture is "the only appropriate role for an adult female" (143).

At a further extreme, in *Females and Harry Potter: Not All that Empowering*, Ruthann Mayes-Elma contends that Rowling's female characters remain unempowered because they comply with socially constructed gender rules that limit women: "what they are resisting is not the construction of gender that society has 'handed' them but instead the evil forces in the book" (103). This statement is, of course, patently contradictory since female characters who actively fight evil undermine the stereotype of the passive female victim. Mayes-Elma focuses on *Harry Potter and the Sorcerer's Stone* but states that in the first six books, Molly Weasley and Petunia Dursley are "very ineffective" mothers, whose sons don't appreciate them and take advantage of them (98). Mayes-Elma says nothing about Lily Potter. Similarly, John Kornfeld and Laurie Prothro argue that "by relying on stereotypical family roles and relationships to give us a few laughs, Rowling risks reifying family roles and relationships in the minds of her young readers." Among the stereotypes that inspire mockery, they contend, is the stay-at-home mother ("Comedy, Conflict" 189). In fairness, Kornfeld and Prothro wrote this in 2003, and their revised 2009 article addresses the value of home and acknowledges that Molly "emerges as a fierce protector (in addition to loving caretaker), rather than the stereotypical bemused (albeit magical) housewife of the first four books" ("Comedy, Quest," 133).[2]

The depiction of house-elf slavery has inspired even more negative commentary. Julia Park, for example, argues that, like Hagrid, house-elves function merely as comic relief, conveying a "middle-class patronizing attitude toward all types of laborers" (185). Closely related are accusations that the depiction of house-elves is racist.[3] William P. MacNeil argues that in depicting Hogwarts as supposedly post-racial, Rowling "more *dis*places than replaces racism, projecting its worst caricatures of racial 'Otherness' onto the house elves. Described as 'beaming, bowing and curtseying' [GF 329]—terms reminiscent of either wide eyed 'Uncle Toms' or giggling 'Oriental' houseboys—the house elves parallel, in their subservient status, the treatment meted out to, and behaviour expected of all 'subaltern subjects,' be they black, yellow or brown, by 'white mythology's' race power" (553). Jackie C. Horne describes the house-elves' speech patterns as "a patois closer to 1930s and 40s Hollywood misconceptions of 'darky' dialect than to any actual African-American speech pattern." Moreover, says Horne, "Even the house-elf Dobby, who desires and gains freedom, proves more an object of humor (as were many black characters in twentieth-century popular culture) than a model of what a free elf can accomplish" (81). Similarly, Farah Mendlesohn describes house-elves as "infantilised and the image is reinforced by the characterisation of Dobby as the 'happy darky,' making jokes, causing mischief, and of Winky, miserable when freed" (304); and Park complains, "There is nothing funny about slavery, and the author's depiction of an enslaved class as something to entertain her readers is reprehensible" (185). I confess that this angle puzzles me, as I see little humor, intentional or otherwise, in the depiction of house-elves' enslavement.

Finally, several critics address gender issues and house-elf issues together. Megan Farnel, who wisely finds the house-elves' plight exemplifies intersectionality among race, class, and gender, faults Rowling for not identifying the "broader causes" of their oppression (39). Vandana Saxena, identifying house-elves with a feminine domestic sphere, argues that the Dursleys treat Harry like a house-elf, and "to don the role of a masculine hero" he must "leave behind this sphere of lower order, the feminine realm of domesticity and enter the school, a space of intellectual pursuits—the elite and closed 'masculine' world. This elite order rests on the indispensable labor of the lower order that is embraced and shunned at the same time" (155, 156). Rivka Temina Kellner argues that house-elves represent "unemancipated and unempowered women of the past, and those in oppressive societies today." Moreover, she contends that, although the Potterverse contains many strong women, overall, "in the world [Rowling] creates the nuclear family structure is intensely traditional and patriarchal" (367).

These critics assume that women's domestic role is necessarily a locus of stereotypes, powerlessness, and marginalization. No doubt that is often true in portrayals of domestic women; moreover, for much of human history, what Adrienne Rich has called "the patriarchal institution of motherhood" has "ghettoized and degraded female potentialities" (13). Nevertheless, as Rich shows, "outlaws from the institution of motherhood" can reimagine mothering as empowering.[4] I contend that *Harry Potter* redefines the domestic by depicting domestic characters who break or transcend the rules/roles associated with their sphere. Both the feminized house-elves and the human characters linked to the domestic sphere—especially Molly Weasley and Lily Potter—embody a hidden power that reflects a revisionary feminist take on domestic power and resistance.

"Fair wages and working conditions": Liberal Feminism, House-Elves, and Traditional Domestic Womanhood

Kellner raises another objection: that by portraying house-elves as "stereotypical oppressed women," Rowling "projects an ambivalent attitude towards feminism" (367). While I will argue that the series' depiction of house-elves is feminist in ways Kellner overlooks, I also believe she is correct—up to a point. House-elves—a near rhyme with "housewives"—do resemble women in domestic roles. In *Harry Potter* we encounter four named house-elves—Dobby, Kreacher, Winky, and Hokey—two male, two female; nevertheless, house-elves, including the unnamed Hogwarts staff, are feminized: all except Kreacher have high, squeaky voices; and they wear domestic items, usually tea-towels, or, in Dobby's case, a pillowcase. As Kellner points out, house-elves have no surname, just as, traditionally, a married woman takes her husband's name. Kathryn N. McDaniel suggests that Winky's devotion to Mr. Crouch resembles that of a wife to an abusive husband ("Real" 74).[5] Most centrally, house-elves' primary job, indeed their very identity, is housework. As Hermione summarizes it, "You do realize that your sheets are changed, your fires lit, your classrooms cleaned, and your food cooked by a group of magical creatures who are unpaid and enslaved?" (GF 239). Aside from "classrooms," Hermione might be describing a traditional housewife's tasks. Winky's advice to Dobby resembles old-style advice to young unmarried women: "I says to Dobby, I says, go find yourself a nice family and settle down, Dobby" (GF 98).

Another similarity between house-elves and stereotypical housewives is seen in Kreacher's obsession with the Black family's possessions. I am reminded of Mrs. Tulliver's obsession with her china, monogrammed linens, and other "laid up treasures"—her "Teraphim, or Household Gods" as Eliot calls them in a chapter title of *The Mill on the Floss*. Sirius complains to Kreacher that "every time you show up pretending to be cleaning, you sneak something off to your room so we can't throw it out" (OP 109–10), and Kreacher's muttered explanation weirdly parodies Bessy Tulliver: "oh my poor Mistress, what would she say if she saw the house now, scum living in it, her treasures thrown out" (OP 110). Ironically, of course, Kreacher's obsessive hoarding ensures that Regulus's locket is not discarded and the Horcrux can be destroyed. Nevertheless, his behavior seems almost pathological, an obsession by someone with a limited perspective.

In her important essays, McDaniel argues persuasively that Rowling's house-elves resemble the 1950s housewives Betty Friedan describes in *The Feminine Mystique*: they have internalized the belief that their identity is completely tied up in their domestic lives, which, as Friedan showed, women clung to because the domestic role provides a sense of purpose. House-elves, like 1950s housewives, are constrained by a myriad of cultural messages. McDaniel argues that the depiction of an "elfin mystique" reflects the series' complexity, for to create a fictional world with flaws is not necessarily to endorse the flaws; rather, Rowling creates a wizarding world as imperfect as the Muggle world—"to highlight those aspects of the 'real world' that need to be attended to and changed" ("Real" 64).

An even stronger analogy than McDaniel's comparison between house-elves and Friedan's "Happy Housewife" is in philosopher John Stuart Mill's foundational text, *The Subjection of Women* (1869), which challenged his time's prevailing attitudes, advocating complete equality between the sexes and comparing Victorian women's condition to slavery.[6] Mill's explanations for women's subjection are particularly useful to explain the subjection of domestic house-elves, who are quite literally enslaved. Mill's analysis challenges core elements of women's traditional subjection—and of house-elf enslavement: the view that subjection is "natural" and that the subjected parties are content in their oppression.

Many readers are puzzled and disturbed by the attitude of Hagrid, who passionately champions the least lovable magical creatures, from dragons to Blast-Ended Skrewts; yet when Hermione invites him to join S.P.E.W.—the Society for the Promotion of Elvish Welfare—he refuses, explaining, "It's in their nature ter look after humans" (GF 265). This is not so far from the antebellum South's Doctor Samuel Cartwright's "medical" contention that American slaves, "[l]ike children," are "constrained by unalterable physiological laws, to love those in authority over them"; this love, he claims, is a "law of nature" (696). Mill describes a similar argument: "it will be said, the rule of men over women differs from all these others in not being a rule of force: it is accepted voluntarily; women make no complaint, and are consenting parties to it" (317). Mill answers this assertion, first, by noting that not all women did accept it: a few Victorian women sought better education, admission into "professions and occupations hitherto closed against them" (in elf terms, to be paid), and even the right to vote (317). In fact, one organization founded in 1859 and dedicated to finding women jobs in traditionally male professions like industry or office work was the Society for Promoting the Employment of Women—S.P.E.W.![7] These exceptions—mirrored, in the wizarding world, by Dobby—undermine arguments from "nature." A typical response to Mill's argument in his time would have resembled Hagrid's: "Yeah, well, yeh get weirdos in every breed. I'm not sayin' there isn't the odd elf [woman] who'd take freedom, but yeh'll never persuade most of 'em ter do it" (GF 265). Indeed, even educated Victorian women joined organizations like the Women's National Anti-Suffrage League; and women who sought education, economic freedom, and suffrage were called "unwomanly" and "unnatural." Even today, many women strenuously reject the label "feminist." Nevertheless, the existence of exceptions demonstrates that willing subjection, because not universal, is not, in fact, "natural."

In *The Subjection of Women*, Mill addresses precisely this question of "natural" subordination when he writes, "Some will object that a comparison cannot fairly be made between the government of the male sex and the forms of unjust power [absolute monarchy and slavery] which I have adduced in illustration of it, since these are arbitrary, and the effect of mere usurpation, while it on the contrary is natural. But was there ever any domination which did not appear natural to those who possessed it?" (315). In other words, those who benefit from slavery, male privilege—or white privilege or wizard privilege—neither notice it nor find it abnormal. Those in power generally perceive their power as "natural" and may not notice others' powerlessness—or consider it "natural."

Mill observes that entrenched systems of power—which would include the subjection of women and house-elves—are also considered "natural" because they have existed for so long: "So true is it that unnatural generally means only uncustomary, and that everything which is usual appears natural. The subjection of women to men being a universal custom, any departure from it quite naturally appears unnatural" (316). That is, we confuse custom—a purely social matter involving behavior—with "nature," because we assume that widespread behaviors are the only way. The same applies to wizard culture. Whether house-elf enslavement is "universal" is unknown, as we only see British house-elves in the novels; a few American house-elves appear in the first *Fantastic Beasts* movies. As to duration,

Hermione says that her library research reveals that "Elf enslavement goes back centuries" (GF 224), and Rowling said in an interview that their enslavement antedates Hogwarts's tenth-century founding: Helga Hufflepuff brought house-elves to the castle "to give them good conditions of work" (PotterCast). To be sure, longevity does not preclude a "natural" basis for house-elf slavery, but long custom is insufficient evidence, and anyway, as Christine Schott observes, a culture would hope to have advanced since the tenth century (268). Furthermore, what other job could a house-elf find? Dobby struggles for nearly two years to land paid employment of the kind he has done all his life; what chance would he have of being hired to do anything else? Dobby's dilemma resembles that of African American women, for nearly a century after emancipation: even those with advanced education found landing work other than domestic service nearly impossible (Harris 6–7). What a culture considers natural turns out to be systemic oppression.

"House-elves have got powerful magic of their own"

What, in fact, is house-elves' nature? Shortly after we meet Dobby, Fred Weasley explains, "house-elves have got powerful magic of their own, but they can't usually use it without their master's permission" (CS 28). Why, then, do so many astute readers assume house-elves are inferior? Shama Rangwala, for example, says house-elves are depicted as "inferior creatures, dirty and naked" (137). Estiningsyas Retno Windarti, in a post-colonial reading, argues they are a lesser species, "inferior to humans," and "dehumanized by having no power against the unjust wizarding society." But are house-elves indeed inferior? Slaves throughout history have been considered less-than human, and house-elves are literally a separate, smaller species, in a culture that treats all other magical species as less-than. Nevertheless, a case can be made that they have more magical power than humans—and occasionally even resist wizard oppression.

Consistent with the pattern that things in the Potterverse are not always as they appear, readers are encouraged to overlook house-elves' powers—as do most members of the magical community. After all, house-elves are very small, and their powerlessness so overt.[8] When we meet Winky, for example, she is hiding her eyes in terror of heights but remaining in place because, she avers, she has been ordered to save a spot for her master. She does *not* reveal that her presence had been her own idea, as she is accompanying the invisible Barty Crouch, Jr., who is attending the World Cup because Winky has persuaded Mr. Crouch to let him. The second time we see Winky, after the match, she is "fighting her way out of a clump of bushes," but "moving in a most peculiar fashion, apparently with great difficulty; … as though someone invisible were trying to hold her back … panting and squeaking as she fought the force that was restraining her." Harry condescendingly assumes she can't "run properly" because "she didn't ask permission to hide" (GF 124), and Hermione agrees that Mr. Crouch must have Winky "bewitched so she can't even run when they start trampling tents!" (GF 125). Only much later, during Barty's confession, do we learn that in the woods Winky really had been dragging an invisible wizard—Barty—who was resisting her, and that she was winning the struggle. But between our preconceptions about elves and our attention to Barty's treachery, readers overlook the evidence of Winky's control: when Barty produces the Dark Mark, he is in the woods because Winky "used her own brand of magic to bind me to her. She pulled me from the tent, pulled me into the forest, away from the Death Eaters" (687). Although Barty, an adult wizard at least twice Winky's size, has, unbeknownst to her, obtained a wand and regained magical strength, Winky's wandless but binding magic nearly overpowers him until she is stunned by the wands of several wizards simultaneously. This is extraordinary power, and since Barty describes being "enslaved" by her (686), it demonstrates that house-elves can turn the tables on wizards. Even more remarkably, it implies Winky could see beneath the invisibility cloak Barty had been "forced to wear ... day and night" for the dozen or so years she supervises him (GF 685); he only manages to steal Harry's wand because Winky is hiding her eyes. When all this is revealed, however, readers are so focused on Barty's other revelations and distracted by Winky's distress that we overlook the evidence of her strength, even though it explains so much.

Similarly, when we first meet Dobby, we're more struck by his mischief than by the fact that he achieves it without a wand. Wandless Dobby levitates a pudding, keeps Harry and Ron from entering Platform 9 ¾, and enchants a Bludger to attack Harry. Unlike wizards, house-elves can apparate within Hogwarts's grounds. It would be convenient to theorize that servants are exempted from the standard Hogwarts enchantments so they can do their jobs, but their inherently greater capability is confirmed when we learn that Kreacher apparated out of the Horcrux cave, a feat beyond both Dumbledore and Voldemort.

A sufficiently motivated house-elf can even harm a wizard: after Harry frees Dobby, Lucius Malfoy "lunge[s]" at Harry, and Dobby, merely raising "a long, threatening finger," "throw[s]" Lucius, a very powerful wizard with a wand, backward down a flight of stairs; then, Dobby intimidates him into leaving, with the words, "You shall not touch Harry Potter. You shall go now." Perhaps Dumbledore's presence constrains Lucius, but the passage suggests "Lucius Malfoy had no choice" because of Dobby, at whom he stares as he departs (CS 338). Less directly, of course, Kreacher's betrayal leads to Sirius's death.

Elves, after all, have not always been viewed as subservient or benevolent. Medieval medicine blamed elves for nightmares, madness, and "elf-sickness" (fever); elves supposedly exchanged healthy babies in their cradles for sickly or half-witted "changelings" (Simpson 79–80). The *Beowulf* poet observes that Cain's cursed descendants included "ogres and elves and evil phantoms / and the giants too who strove with God" (lines 111–12). These malevolent elves date from just before Hogwarts's founding, suggesting that the enchantments wizards laid on house-elves date from the same period and control an inherently rebellious spirit.[9]

House-elves' power and, possibly, former malevolence may explain why wizards instituted clause three of the Code of Wand Use: "*No non-human creature is permitted to carry or use a wand*" (GF 132), or as Griphook the goblin puts it, "Wizards refuse to share the secrets of wandlore with other magical beings, they deny us the possibility of extending our powers!" (DH 488). Even so, elves can disarm wizards, without a wand or a spoken spell: in one of his final acts, Dobby sends Narcissa Malfoy's wand flying, implicitly raising the question whether, having disarmed her, Dobby might have become master of her wand. We will never know. But if house-elves have this much power without wands, imagine how easily wand-wielding house-elves could control humans. Indeed, the fact that wizards forbid wand use suggests they fear elves' and goblins' power, considering it a challenge to their own. Hokey, Hepzibah Smith's house-elf, is readily framed for her mistress's death because, as Dumbledore tells Harry, "the Ministry was predisposed to suspect Hokey—," an observation Harry completes with "—because she was a house-elf" (HBP 439). Hokey's easy conviction indicates both bias and hidden fear of what motivated house-elves might do. Indeed in African American slave narratives, the mammy is sometimes "cunning, prone to poisoning her master, and not at all content with her lot" (Christian 5). As Mill observed, "What women by nature cannot do, it is quite superfluous to forbid them from doing" (329); and the same holds true of any creature—including house-elves. Though Hokey was innocent, when Kreacher betrays Sirius, he is, in part, resisting wizard injustice.

"But why don't you leave? Escape?" The Problem of the Contented Slaves

If, in a fair fight, wizards could lose to house-elves, what empowers wizards to grant or deny "permission"? And why don't house-elves rebel?[10] In *The Subjection of Women*, Mill notes that "the rule of men over women differs from [slavery and monarchy] in not being a rule of force" (317). Are house-elves enslaved by force? To Simone Weil, "force" is whatever "turned a person into a thing" (qtd. in Ruddick 164), an inclusive definition that applies nicely. Where wizards are concerned, "a rule of force" must include magical enchantments, but Rowling keeps this vague. When Dumbledore explains that "Kreacher is what he has been made by wizards," the immediate context is primarily Kreacher's treachery to Sirius: "Yes, he is to be pitied. His existence has been as miserable as your friend Dobby's. He was forced to do Sirius's bidding, because Sirius was the last of the family to which he was enslaved, but he felt no true loyalty to him. And whatever Kreacher's faults, it must be admitted that Sirius did nothing to make Kreacher's lot easier—" (OP 832). Dumbledore's explanation for Kreacher's disobedience is fourfold: first, Sirius's unkindness, but, second, Kreacher's "lot," which suggests an uncontrollable fate—something the series generally treats with skepticism. Third, the plural in "what he has been made by *wizards*" could mean attitudes instilled by the Black family but could also mean "wizardkind." Fourth, Kreacher is "bound by the enchantments of his kind" (OP 831), ambiguous words that suggest house-elf enslavement is not "natural" at all; rather, Kreacher's "lot" is some type of hereditary curse. However ancient those "enchantments" and whatever challenges might be associated with lifting them, the term suggests they are not inherent but imposed on "his kind," and hence reversible.

Clearly, house-elves are held in servitude by the degrading rule that they can only be freed if given clothing. Presumably, regular garb would reinforce house-elves' humanity. The fact that "The family is careful not to pass Dobby even a sock, sir, for then he would be free to leave their house forever" (CS 177) suggests the enchantment controls wizards as much as elves, since humans must be "careful" not to present clothing accidentally—as Lucius, inadvertently, does. This subtly reminds us that systemic oppression degrades not only the oppressed but the oppressors, but it still does not reveal how house-elf slavery is maintained.

Superficially, house-elves resemble the eponymous characters in the fairy tale "The Elves and the Shoemaker," who are similarly unseen, benevolent, fundamentally domestic—and naked. In the Grimm brothers' telling, the elves, who secretly sew shoes for a poor cobbler every night, are completely naked, until the shoemaker's wife sews them garments as a gesture of thanks. Upon receiving the gift, they are delighted and grateful; unlike Rowling's house-elves, once clothed, they disappear forever. As Jacqueline Simpson points out, the trope that an elf leaves once given clothes is consistent with traditional European "house spirits," but the depiction of an elf as "a downtrodden serf" is not (77). In the traditional tale, elfin nakedness is an incidental fact the shoemaker's wife kindly rectifies; in Dobby's case, it is an intentional form of control.

Moreover, house-elves' near nakedness seems a more salient trait than the complete nakedness of the traditional house spirit, reflecting Kenneth Clarke's classic distinction between the naked and the nude: "To be naked is to be deprived of our clothes, and the word implies some of the embarrassment most of us feel in that condition. The word 'nude', on the other hand, carries, in educated usage, no uncomfortable overtone. The vague image it projects into the mind is not of a huddled and defenseless body, but of a balanced, prosperous, and confident body" (3). Traditional house spirits, it could be argued, are nude; house-elves, however they may perceive themselves, are naked: "huddled and defenseless," and readers experience the attendant embarrassment. It must especially trouble adolescent readers insecure about their bodies. Nakedness—revisited in the Voldemort-controlled Ministry sculpture "Magic is Might" that features naked Muggles (DH 242)—contributes to the critique of the culture that enslaves house-elves—and prepares readers to see them, from the beginning, as powerless victims. House-elves are depicted in other ways that inspire sympathy. Their large eyes and heads and diminutive stature are childlike, traits researchers have argued create a "fundamental mechanism that helps to elicit caregiving" (Kringelbach, et al. 547). That almost instinctive response is only enhanced as Dobby reciprocates concern for Harry and his safety. Thus, while one can certainly criticize many aspects of house-elves' depiction, it's difficult to argue persuasively that the text condones their enslavement.

Nevertheless, few elves seem dissatisfied with their lot, and indeed when Mr. Crouch angrily frees Winky, she is devastated, pining for her master and crying into the butterbeer she drinks to the point of unconsciousness. And when Dobby says, "Dobby likes being free!" the hundred house-elves who cheerfully work at Hogwarts start "edging away from Dobby, as though he were carrying something contagious" (GF 378). Observing such behavior, nearly everyone who has grown up in wizard culture shares Ron's view that "They *like* being enslaved!" (GF 224; emphasis in original)—though the term "contagious" does suggest fear that desire for freedom may spread. Only Dumbledore and Arthur Weasley acknowledge that Hermione's indignation is correct, but each in his own way defers the issue.[11] House-elf slavery is thoroughly entrenched in wizard culture and ideology.

Mill indirectly explains how slavery is enforced when he acknowledges that women differ from slaves in that "The masters of all other slaves rely, for maintaining obedience, on fear; either fear of themselves, or religious fears" (318).[12] Yet few house-elves seem frightened: the Hogwarts house-elves need not fear Dumbledore; Hokey has no reason to fear Hepzibah Smith; Kreacher is brazenly rebellious; and Winky only becomes frightened when Crouch threatens her with freedom. Dobby, alone, fears the Malfoys, who fit Mill's label of the "brutish" master. The Malfoys encourage Dobby to punish himself for less-than-perfect service: "Sometimes they reminds me to do extra punishments" (CS 14). That is, they give orders, which a house-elf must obey. Although Dobby's punishments are harsh physical abuse, consistent with traditional slavery, it is significant that Dobby inflicts them on himself.

For in Orwellian fashion, house-elves self-punish merely for *thinking* of disobeying, such as when Dobby bangs his head on the window, shouting, "Bad Dobby! Bad Dobby!" apparently in response to Harry's remarking, "You can't have met many decent wizards." Dobby explains: "Dobby had to punish himself, sir ... Dobby *almost* spoke ill of his family, sir" (CS 14; emphasis added). That is, Dobby *thinks* ill of his family, whether he says so or not. Dobby's obviously horrifying self-abuse—banging his head and beating himself with a desk lamp for speaking ill of his family, shutting his ears in the oven door for warning Harry of danger—represent another reason to doubt that Rowling approves of house-elf enslavement. To be sure, Book Four complicates matters by introducing Winky and the happy Hogwarts house-elves.

What makes house-elf slavery unique is that the "enchantments of [their] kind" often render disobedience physically impossible: when, to establish that he is Kreacher's new master, Harry says, "Kreacher, shut up," it "looked for a moment as though Kreacher was going to choke. He grabbed his throat, his mouth still working furiously, his eyes bulging. After a few seconds of frantic gulping, he threw himself face forward onto the carpet ... and beat the floor with his hands and feet, giving himself over to a violent, but entirely silent, tantrum" (HBP 52–3).

The order silences Kreacher—but does not create fear. If anything, it intensifies Kreacher's rebelliousness. Unlike the Imperius Curse, an order to a house-elf constrains not the will but the physical capacity to carry out the will. Absent a direct order, house-elves can rebel, though the enchantment that forces them to punish themselves brutally disincentivizes disobedience.

Thus, Mendlesohn is incorrect that "elves do not resent their slavery: while Dobby may be happy, Winky hates freedom" (305). In fairness, Mendlesohn wrote this in 2001, before Kreacher's introduction, but Dobby's attitudes already suggest possibilities that Kreacher later confirms: dissatisfaction with enslavement is not confined to "weirdos." While Kreacher does not resent slavery *per se* (and happily contemplates his head being mounted on the Black family's stairway), both he and Dobby resent their masters. As Mill observed in 1860, "no enslaved class ever asked for complete liberty at once. ... It is a political law of nature that those who are under any power of ancient origin, never begin by complaining of the power itself, but only of its oppressive exercise" (317, 318). At first, Dobby seems untroubled by enslavement. Although when Harry meets him, Dobby clearly does not wish to stay with his as-yet-unidentified masters; he doesn't expect his servitude to end: when Harry asks, "why don't you leave? Escape?" Dobby responds, "A house-elf must be set free, sir. And the family will never set Dobby free . . . Dobby will serve the family until he dies, sir" (14). Once freed, however, Dobby is "over the moon about it" (GF 265). No doubt Kreacher would have been delighted if Sirius freed him, but only to serve Bellatrix Lestrange. When Harry inherits him, Kreacher insists, not on freedom, but that "Kreacher belongs to Miss Bellatrix, oh yes, Kreacher belongs to the Blacks, Kreacher wants his new mistress" (HBP 52). Kreacher's and Dobby's capacity to mentally reject their masters and their devious methods of rebelling show that elves have free will and their own opinions. Moreover, they can, with effort, rebel against specific abuses. Even Winky's drunkenness, McDaniel suggests, represents an unconscious (literally!) "state of protest of her condition," which, because she does not work, seems "transgressive" to other Hogwarts elves ("Real" 75). These are the first steps to rebelling against their "lot" more generally.

Evidence of house-elves' independent thinking emerges when Dobby and Kreacher disagree with their masters and act against them. Even Winky disagrees with Mr. Crouch's treatment of young Barty and persuades Crouch to grant his son privileges. Dobby's very presence in Harry's bedroom shows his discontent, as does his response to Harry's comment, "You can't have met many decent wizards." Kreacher is an overtly unwilling slave. In the first interaction we see between Kreacher and Sirius, Kreacher says the obligatory, "Whatever Master says," but mutters audibly, "Master is not fit to wipe slime from his mother's boots" (OP 109). Harry perceives, "It seemed that Kreacher did not dare disobey a direct order; nevertheless, the look he gave Sirius as he shuffled out past him was redolent of deepest loathing and he muttered all the way out of the room" (OP 110).

Kreacher is no more conciliatory when Harry inherits him, giving Harry his own "look of deepest loathing" (HBP 53) and giving him a package of maggots at Christmas (HBP 339). He insists that while Harry commands his actions, his will is his own, and does so in language reminiscent of Dobby's sentiments about "no decent wizard": "'Kreacher will do whatever Master wants,' said Kreacher, sinking so low that his lips almost touched his gnarled toes, 'because Kreacher has no choice, but Kreacher is ashamed to have such a master, yes—'" (HBP 421). Because Kreacher serves Harry unwillingly—as he served Sirius—Harry realizes that Kreacher will take advantage of any ambiguity in orders. When instructing Kreacher to follow Draco, Harry adds a detailed list of proscribed actions: "He thought he could see Kreacher struggling to see a loophole in the instructions he had just been given and waited. After a moment or two, and to Harry's great satisfaction, Kreacher bowed deeply again and said, with bitter resentment, 'Master thinks of everything, and Kreacher must obey him even though Kreacher would much rather be the servant of the Malfoy boy, oh yes'" (HBP 422). Apparently, he could betray Sirius, as Dobby could betray the Malfoys, because their masters neglected to order them directly not to.

We see, then, that house-elves think for themselves—and indeed Dobby, Kreacher, and even Winky have deeply-held—though opposing—belief systems. They possess more than "sufficient intelligence to understand the laws of the magical community and to bear part of the responsibility of shaping those laws"— legal "beings," by wizard definitions.[13] As Steven Patterson observes, their capacity for reason qualifies them to be treated as ends rather than means, in Immanuel Kant's ethics: deserving "every moral protection that we would owe to other human beings"—including freedom (109). But unlike goblins—or, for that matter, unlike women of Mill's time who petitioned Parliament for the franchise—elves seem to accept systemic subordination. Or do they? To be sure, Dobby's mission to save Harry from the basilisk in the Chamber of Secrets seems unrelated to house-elf enslavement, but one reason he wants to protect Harry is that Harry represents better conditions for house-elves:

> "Ah, if Harry Potter only knew!" Dobby groaned, more tears dripping onto his ragged pillowcase. "If he knew what he means to us, to the lowly, the enslaved, we dregs of the magical world! Dobby remembers how it was when He-Who-Must-Not-Be-Named was at the height of his powers, sir! We house-elves were treated like vermin, sir! Of course, Dobby is still treated like that, sir," he admitted, drying his face on the pillowcase. "But mostly, sir, life has improved for my kind since you triumphed over He-Who-Must-Not-Be-Named. Harry Potter survived, and the Dark Lord's power was broken, and it was a new dawn, sir, and Harry Potter shone like a beacon of hope for those of us who thought the Dark days would never end, sir."
>
> (CS 177–8)

This passage shows that Dobby has a sense of history and views himself as part of an oppressed class—"the lowly, the enslaved, we dregs of the magical world"—historicizing and generalizing in a way necessary if someone is to envision change. Dobby is taking what Mill described as the first step to challenging power: questioning conditions enabling its "oppressive exercise" and attempting, however inefficiently, to ensure those conditions aren't restored.

Dobby doesn't question that house-elves are "dregs," but he does question the Othering implicit in being treated like vermin.[14] Seeing Harry as a "beacon of hope" suggests possible changes for Dobby's "kind." Because Harry's defeating Voldemort promised a "new dawn" for his compatriots, Dobby willingly risks his own comfort and safety. That Dobby generalizes this way even though his own situation has not improved with Voldemort's disappearance indicates he understands social justice apart from his individual self-interest. Finally, referring to what Harry "means to *us*" implies Dobby believes he speaks for others; if true, Dobby may represent a forerunner of elfin resistance. By acting for the principle of maintaining the improved conditions enjoyed by his "kind," he shows an incipient revolutionary spirit.

Yet how do we explain nearly all house-elves'—and mid-Victorian women's—acceptance of subordination? In both cases, an explanation is less "nature" than nurture. Dumbledore insists, "it matters not what someone is born, but what they grow to be!" (GF 708). Similarly, regarding women, Mill explains,

> All causes, social and natural, combine to make it unlikely that women should be collectively rebellious to the power of men. They are so far in a position different from all other subject classes, that their masters require something more from them than actual service. Men do not want solely the obedience of women, they want their sentiments. All men, except the most brutish, desire to have, in the woman most nearly connected with them, not a forced slave but a willing one, not a slave merely, but a favorite. They have therefore put everything in practice to enslave their minds. ... The masters of women wanted more than simple obedience, and they turned the whole force of education to effect their purpose. All women are brought up from the very earliest years in the belief that their ideal of character is the very opposite to that of men; not self will, and government by self-control, but submission, and yielding to the control of others. All the moralities tell them that it is the duty of women, and all the current sentimentalities that it is their nature, to live for others; to make complete abnegation of themselves, and to have no life but in their affections.
>
> (318)

There are several applicable points here. Mill's term, "willing slaves," does describe nearly all house-elves. Ron, echoing Hagrid, Fred, and George, says, "Hermione—open your ears. ... They. Like. It. They *like* being enslaved!" (GF 224). House-elves know no other way: Winky says, "I is looking after the Crouches all my life, and my mother is doing it before me, and my grandmother is doing it before her" (GF 381). People—and presumably elves—generally fear the unknown and prefer the familiar. Service is all Winky has known "from the very earliest years," and service is all house-elves have known for centuries. We have no direct information about house-elf upbringing and training, but Hermione's explanation seems plausible: that house-elves like their lives because "they're uneducated and brainwashed" (GF 239). Mill argues that it is impossible to know women's actual nature—their true capabilities and interests—because they have lacked opportunities to discover and develop their talents. Few received training in subjects and skills other than those considered natural to them, while receiving intensive instruction in the domestic or ladylike. What the nineteenth century considered innate to women was a product of social conditioning: "What is now called the nature of women is an eminently artificial thing—the result of forced repression in some directions, unnatural stimulation in others. It may be asserted without scruple, that no other class of dependents have had their character so entirely distorted from its natural proportions by their relation with their masters" (324). One wonders what Mill would think of Winky.

Freedom makes Winky miserable. Hermione doesn't understand that Winky, "freed" against her will as "punishment" for supposed bad behavior, is not truly free, because she has neither chosen nor is prepared to choose freedom. Similarly, Hermione's ham-handed attempts to trick the Hogwarts elves into freedom, by leaving knitted caps in the Gryffindor common room, offends them, so they refuse to clean the area, increasing Dobby's workload. Thus Hagrid is correct that most house-elves are content and would, like Winky, be miserable if freed. This is not endorsing slavery. Rather, house-elves' terror of freedom demonstrates how thoroughly more than a millennium of enslavement can foster internalized racism that Brycchan Carey describes as "mind-forged manacles," William Blake's term for psychological or intellectual barriers to independent thought and action, including self-imposed barriers (Carey [2003] 104). House-elves' resistance to freedom shows how insidious slavery is. Thus, while it is true, as several critics note with disappointment, that the problem of house-elf slavery remains unresolved at the end of the series, we should hardly be surprised that the situation is so intractable.[15]

House-elves' devotion and self-sacrifice resemble how Victorian women, as Mill observed, were taught "to live for others; to make complete abnegation of themselves." As Virginia Woolf said of the Victorian "Angel in the House," "She sacrificed herself daily. If there was chicken, she took the leg; if there was a draught she sat in it—in short she was so constituted that she never had a mind or a wish of her own, but preferred to sympathize always with the minds and wishes of others" (237). Similarly, Winky insists, "House-elves is not supposed to have fun, Harry Potter" (GF 98). Woolf further notes of the Angel in the House, "Above all—I need not say it—she was pure" (237); Woolf of course refers not to the race purity that concerns wizards but to sexual purity. We hardly associate house-elves with sexuality,[16] yet Winky's "shame" at the idea of being paid for wife-like duties echoes the contrast between the assumed sexual purity of the Victorian wife—Mill's (unpaid) "willing slave"—and a prostitute: "'Winky is a disgraced elf, but Winky is not yet getting paid!' she squeaked. 'Winky is not sunk so low as that! Winky is properly ashamed of being freed!'" (GF 379). Winky, thinking of her mother and grandmother, mourns, "oh what is they saying if they knew Winky was freed? Oh the shame, the shame!" (GF 381). To Winky, freedom is the ultimate dishonor.

A Power of Their Own: House-Elf Love and Relational Feminism

As liberal feminists who saw male values as the norm, Mill and Woolf decried barriers to women's entering men's spheres of knowledge and power; hence, they overlooked strengths deriving from women's traditional spheres of power. Kellner makes a similar mistake when she argues that Rowling is ambivalent about feminism though she does widen the lens to three feminist approaches: Marxist feminism (house-elves as the proletariat), multicultural feminism (house-elves as "doubly oppressed" by the predominantly white, middle-class, patriarchal magical community [373]), and liberal feminism, epitomized by Hermione, whose unsuccessful efforts focus on education, public awareness, and legislative action to obtain economic and political "elf rights" equal to humans'. Kellner critiques liberal feminism's overlooking of physiological differences between the sexes and, by extension, between humans and house-elves, but she fails to consider another type of feminism, variously called difference feminism, cultural feminism, radical feminism, social feminism, domestic feminism, or—the term I find most useful for this context—relational feminism.[17] I have adopted "relational feminism" from Karen Offen's historical and (somewhat) cross-cultural attempt to define feminism.

Offen sorts historical feminisms into two basic "frameworks": individualist feminism and relational feminism. Individualist feminism—more often called "liberal feminism"—is the tradition of the best-known Anglo-American feminists, including Friedan, Mill, and Woolf. It seeks for women equal access to educational, economic, and political privileges enjoyed by men. It sees the individual as society's fundamental unit and advocates equal rights for all individuals, both male and female. Hermione's plans for S.P.E.W.—and its Victorian namesake—fit neatly into the liberal tradition: "to secure house-elves fair wages and working conditions" as well as "changing the law about non-wand use, and trying to get an elf into the Department for the Regulation and Control of Magical Creatures, because they're shockingly underrepresented" (GF 225). As liberal feminists want women to have the same rights as men, Hermione wants elves to have the same rights as witches and wizards.[18] After all, assuming that house-elves want to aspire to what humans consider "normal" perfectly exemplifies wizard privilege.

Relational feminism, which Offen also calls "familial feminism," sees not the individual but the family as society's fundamental unit. Relational feminists—who historically have outnumbered liberal feminists, despite being less well-known—assume there are fundamental differences between the sexes, and they seek "women's rights *as women*—(defined principally by their childbearing and/or nurturing capacities) in relation to men" (Offen 136). Relational feminists want women to have access to political and social power, to make distinctive contributions; relational feminists speak less of equal "rights" than of complementary "responsibilities." Valuing women's different interests and contributions, relational feminists, like individualist feminists, oppose subordination of women—or of women's values—to men. In fact, many relational feminists argue for the superiority of feminine values like nurturance and "maternal thinking." Thus, relational feminists dispute that domestic activities are, if freely chosen, inferior to activities that take place exclusively in the public sphere. They contend that business and government would benefit if women played greater roles, because women can contribute different types of expertise and because women are more ethical, less hierarchical, more collaborative, better listeners, and better at developing others' talents. In fact, research confirms the benefits of women's different contributions.[19] Another example of relational feminism—which may also apply to men—is care ethics. This includes Fiona Robinson's emphasis on a feminism that "emphasizes human interdependence and vulnerability" rather than focusing on individual economic empowerment (295) and Carol Gilligan's critique of individualistic, rights-based, hierarchical patriarchal values.[20]

Relational feminism offers insight into the women of *Harry Potter*, whom we will turn to shortly, but it also reveals another side of the meekest house-elf, Winky. Even after Mr. Crouch cruelly dismisses her, all Winky wants is to go "home" to take care of him. Readers know from the time that Crouch publicly berates and punishes Winky that the treatment is unfair, since she obviously did not create the Dark Mark. Only later do we learn that he blames Winky to conceal that his son cast the spell and to hide his culpability in Barty's escape. We also learn later of Crouch's pattern of betraying others to preserve his reputation and position. Winky tolerates this unfairness and blames herself rather than recognizing Crouch's hypocrisy and deflection of blame; indeed, she seems to crave more of the same. Winky's abject longing to return to slavery is the most disturbing depiction of house-elves, but it is a mistake to oversimplify it. The loyalty of elves like Winky to their masters can be explained by more than enchantments or centuries of socialization. Those explanations, though helpful, are too easy. As Ron observes of Winky, "She seems to love [Mr. Crouch]" (GF 383). One should never underestimate the influence of love in the Potterverse. Dumbledore describes love as "a force that is at once more wonderful and more terrible than death, than human intelligence, than the forces of nature" (OP 843). Love, of course, comes in many forms, from Lily Potter's selflessness to the love potion Amortentia, which, Horace Slughorn calls "probably the most dangerous and powerful potion in this room" (DH 186). It also includes house-elves' love of their masters. It is not at all unreasonable to treat house-elves' loves as like humans', following Dumbledore's explanation that Sirius's crucial error was that he never "saw Kreacher as a being with feelings as acute as a human's" (OP 832). It might even be said that like Victorian wives, Winky and Kreacher have, in Mill's words, "no life but in their affections." Love shapes house-elves' obedience to their masters, and unfortunately, as Farnel notes, facilitates their exploitation. Yet love—or its absence—also underlies house-elves' rare disobedience. Love, from a relational feminist perspective, is empowering, even, in some ways, for elves, though house-elf love is multifaceted.

Winky's loyalty is certainly the most disturbing. Her nearly doglike devotion to her abusive master almost justifies Peter Dendle's choice to include house-elves in his study of "Animal Stewardship" in the series. Practically as troubling, because the elf-animal parallel is so overt, is Kreacher's "life's ambition": to have his head mounted on the Black family staircase (OP 76). Ron's response, to call Kreacher a "nutter" and question whether he is "normal," is understandable—though it is more legitimate to question Sirius's aunt Elladora, who conceived "the family tradition of beheading house-elves when they got too old to carry tea trays" (OP 113)—treating house-elves as a combination of disposable tool, trophy, and family pet preserved through magical taxidermy.

While Winky remains loyal no matter how unkindly she is treated, Kreacher's loyalty and obedience are more transactional, illustrating that house-elves—like most of us—are fond of those who treat them nicely. Hermione argues that he is "loyal to people who are kind to him, and Mrs. Black must have been, and Regulus certainly was, so he served them willingly and parroted their beliefs" (DH 198). Kreacher's appreciation of kindness is hardly subtle: after Harry begins asking considerately for his aid, saying "Please" and "Thank you"—and especially giving Kreacher Regulus's locket—Kreacher's attitude and behavior completely reverse: he is friendly and the house is clean—as is Kreacher himself—and he makes Harry's favorite foods. As we have seen, cleaning can be an expression of love. Once well-treated, Kreacher becomes a "happy slave," loving both his master and his role. His ready compliance is almost as disturbing as Winky's abjection. Even when Kreacher leads the Hogwarts house-elves into battle, he invokes the masters he loves, not political principle, crying, "Fight! Fight! Fight for my Master, defender of house-elves! Fight the Dark Lord, in the name of brave Regulus! Fight!" (DH 734).

Although Kreacher's taking up arms (or kitchen utensils) to fight Voldemort is a political act of sorts, it suspiciously resembles his parroting of Mrs. Black's bigoted comments about Mudbloods. Still, he does generalize about Harry as "defender of house-elves." Kreacher's evolution from rebelling against Sirius, who treated him unkindly, to taking arms for a "defender of house-elves" is subtle, reminiscent of Mill's observation that "no enslaved class ever asked for complete liberty at once." But Kreacher takes the initiative, possibly even disobeying an order to leave

Hogwarts, for when Ron decides to warn the house-elves, to protect them from the battle, he uses the language of giving orders: "we should tell them to get out. We don't want any more Dobbies, do we? We can't order them to die for us—" (DH 625). Equivocal though Kreacher's actions may be, they, like Dobby's, suggest house-elves are capable of challenging oppression, to support their "family." Indeed, it's also possible that if the Hogwarts house-elves did get the order to get out, they may have disobeyed, for reasons resembling Dobby's. Griphook had commented to the trio, "As the Dark Lord becomes ever more powerful, your race is set still more firmly above mine! Gringotts falls under Wizarding rule, house-elves are slaughtered, and who amongst the wand-carriers protests?" (DH 489). As Dobby had acted to prevent the return of the time when house-elves were "treated like vermin" (CS 178)—presumably exterminated—so, too, do the Hogwarts' house-elves follow Kreacher's exhortation to "Fight the Dark Lord" by "hacking and stabbing at the ankles and shins of Death Eaters, their tiny faces alive with malice" (DH 735). After all, as Bethany Barratt observes, house-elves have previously shown "signs of being able to act in a coordinated and forcible fashion against the wishes of wizards when they so choose. In reaction to Hermione's suggestion they demand better working conditions, they quickly remove Harry, Hermione, and Ron from the Hogwarts kitchens" (51). Even Winky participates in the Battle of Hogwarts ("J. K. Rowling and the Live Chat").

As Carey (2009) points out, house-elves' behavior resembles the "grateful slave figure." The grateful slave is traditionally figured as over-emotional and irrational—certainly house-elf traits. According to George Boulukos, before the nineteenth century, gratitude was considered appropriate for "inferiors" within a hierarchical system, but as western cultures increasingly valued independence and embraced the idea of human equality, gratitude became less acceptable. As ideologies began to assume that poor white people should strive for independence, the belief that gratitude was appropriate for slaves was premised on an assumption that Black slaves were too irrational for independence. A slave's gratitude thus presumably expressed acceptance of inferiority. So to the extent that house-elves are over-emotional and their compliance with slavery is shaped by gratitude, their depiction seems to reinforce essentialist, hierarchical differences and thus justify slavery. But while Kreacher is motivated by gratitude for his master or mistress's kindness *as* masters, Dobby, by contrast, is grateful to be treated as an equal: upon being invited to sit, he bursts into tears, and when Harry apologizes for offending him, Dobby responds vehemently: "Offend Dobby!" choked the elf. "Dobby has *never* been asked to sit down by a wizard—like an *equal*—" (CS 13). Once again, Dobby's responses undermine interpretations that the series endorses slavery.

Yes, Kreacher obeys those to whom he is grateful for kind treatment and rebels against Sirius because of his *un*kindness. But Kreacher's behavior is more complex than that. Much of his rebelliousness derives from enduring loyalty to and sympathy for the person he considers his real mistress, who after all remains a voluble presence in the house. No doubt Walburga Black was despicable, but we can give

Kreacher credit for sympathizing, both that "Mistress was mad with grief, because Master Regulus had disappeared" (DH 197), and also that "Master [Sirius] was a nasty ungrateful swine who broke his mother's heart—" (OP 109). Kreacher complains that Sirius "comes back from Azkaban ordering Kreacher around, oh my poor Mistress, what would she say if she saw the house now, scum living in it, her treasures thrown out, she swore he was no son of hers and he's back, they say he's a murderer too—" (OP 110). While readers know Sirius is not a murderer and reject Walburga's politics, things, as usual, are complicated: naturally a mother would be disappointed that her son has rejected her and horror-stricken that he has been imprisoned for murder. Kreacher sympathizes with Walburga's unhappiness and shares her grief about Regulus.

Kreacher uses a version of "oh my poor Mistress" under two circumstances, both expressing family loyalty. And it is "family loyalty." When Dobby says, "Dobby almost spoke ill of his family" (CS 14), the phrase is ironically true: Dobby's ancestors, presumably for centuries, have served the Malfoys' ancestors. Winky, too, says, "I is looking after the Crouches all my life, and my mother is doing it before me, and my grandmother is doing it before her" (GF 381). We know the same is true of Kreacher's ancestors, through the macabre evidence of elf heads, all with Kreacher's snoutlike nose, mounted along the stairway. Kreacher invokes his "poor mistress," first, because "her" house contains "scum," "mudbloods," and "blood traitors," terms he learned from "his family" and Mrs. Black's portrait, which speaks of little else. He also invokes "my poor mistress" in response to the disposal of family heirlooms, notably the tapestry of the family tree. Kreacher says, "Mistress would never forgive Kreacher if the tapestry was thrown out, seven centuries it's been in the family, Kreacher must save it" (OP 110). No doubt keeping the tapestry is following orders ("Mistress would never forgive Kreacher"), but he also seems personally to treasure it. Not only did the Blacks value the tapestry, like other heirlooms Kreacher hoards, but also, it has links to Kreacher's own ancestors—perhaps for seven centuries or more—who have been inherited by and have cared for each generation of Blacks commemorated on the tapestry and have identified themselves with the family and the house itself; for house-elves "come with big old manors and castles and places like that" (CS 29). When Harry inherits number twelve, he inherits Kreacher. Kreacher is, in a sense, part of the house and may perceive himself that way.

House-elves in many cases see themselves as not just serving but also protecting their families. Winky has been "looking after" the Crouches, and when she hears that Crouch has been reported ill, she wails, drunkenly: "Master is needing his—*hic*—Winky!" (GF 537). Like Kreacher mourning his "poor mistress," Winky worries about her "Poor master, poor master, no Winky to help him no more!" (GF 382). Feeling needed can be part of feeling loved and valuable. It can be intrinsically rewarding. For this reason, Hagrid is correct that "Yeh'd be makin' 'em unhappy ter take away their work" (GF 265). As is sometimes true with humans, losing meaningful work can lead to depression and alcoholism; Winky, though not technically unemployed, considers herself to have lost her real work.[21] On the flip side, Kreacher, who initially seems averse to work, embraces work once he feels personally attached to Harry and his friends.

Winky's and other elves' love for their "families" is manifested in many ways that reflect the housewife/house-elf analogy. Kreacher, once he warms to Harry, treats him much as does Molly Weasley, whom we almost always see cooking, cleaning, and gently chiding her children: "'Shoes off, if you please, Master Harry, and hands washed before dinner,' croaked Kreacher, seizing the Invisibility Cloak and slouching off to hang it on a hook on the wall, beside a number of old-fashioned robes that had been freshly laundered" (DH 225). Similarly, when Dobby destroys Petunia's pudding, he explains with a "tragic look" and language resembling an affectionate parent explaining "consequences" to a wayward child: "Dobby must do it, sir, for Harry Potter's own good" (CS 19). For years, Winky acts almost like young Barty Crouch's surrogate mother. Her reaction to seeing Barty lying stunned on the floor of "Moody's" office at the end of *Goblet of Fire* resembles a bereaved mother's: "Her mouth opened wide and she let out a piercing shriek." Then "She flung herself forward onto the young man's chest. 'You is killed him! You is killed him! You is killed Master's son!'" (GF 683). As Barty recounts how he took advantage of Winky's unawareness that he was learning to resist the Imperius Curse and of her fear of heights, to grab Harry's wand, she chastises him like a mother or nanny might: "Master Barty, you bad boy!" (GF 686). Although Barty is over thirty, for Winky he remains a "boy" to protect or scold.

In supervising Barty, Winky was no mere passive servant. After his mother selflessly traded places with him in prison, Winky first nursed him back to health (GF 684) and then became his "keeper and caretaker." Not simply obeying orders, Winky advocated for Barty, implicitly allying herself with Barty's late mother. Indeed, it could be argued that in adopting this role, Winky deploys the kind of womanly "influence" that Victorian women embraced as their unique authority, the influence that Victorian relational feminists deployed as they moved domestic power into the public sphere. Winky "spent months persuading" Mr. Crouch to allow Barty to attend the World Cup (GF 685), arguing, Barty explains, that "my mother would have wanted it. She told my father that my mother had died to give me freedom. She had not saved me for a life of imprisonment" (686). So when Winky perches high in the stands, she is not, as Harry assumes, involuntarily suffering under orders: her presence with the invisible Barty is her idea, rather like a mother who takes her child on a carnival ride despite suffering from motion sickness. Later, during the Death Eaters' riot, Winky pulls Barty into the forest, like a mother pulling her child to safety.

Aurélie Lacassagne and Tanya Cook apply the concept of "othermother" to several characters—Petunia Dursley, Minerva MacGonnagall, Molly Weasley, and even Hagrid—who serve as Harry's surrogate mothers, creating a vision of mothering as powerful and empowering. Ironically, given that each borrows the term "othermother" from studies of African American women's culture, both critics overlook another significant othermother: Winky. Winky is not, of course, a fully independent actor but a slave and thus more closely resembles the othermothers discussed by Patricia Hill Collins, Stanlie M. James, and Rosalie Riegle Troester, who coined the term to describe African American women who step in when the biological mother is unavailable. Winky is almost literally a faithful, loving "mammy" figure. Lacking the stoic "endurance" of Dilsey from Faulkner's *The Sound and the Fury*, Winky's hidden strength, although real, is simply trampled on. That said, Winky acts willingly, out of love for both Mr. Crouch and "Master Barty"—a name a slave might use for a younger male in the master's family. Even her grief at being freed echoes nostalgic Daughters of the Confederacy propaganda described by Micki McElya, in which a newly emancipated woman exclaims that "Mammy loved her 'white baby' too dearly to accept her freedom" (57).

On balance, the depiction of Winky's love for her family and grief at Mr. Crouch's rejection is not, however, acceptance of that propaganda but contributes to a critique of house-elf enslavement. It justifies Dumbledore's description of love as "terrible" and Slughorn's as "dangerous," for it fosters oppression. Winky's years' long mammy-like role reinforces the cruelty of Crouch's casually disposing of her to protect his reputation and gives the lie to the myth of the mammy as a beloved family member. That perspective on the mammy, as Barbara Omolade observes, derived from sentimental Neo-Confederate myth-making, which depicted the mammy as a beloved figure with "great status and recognition in the personal memories of white families" (153). Neo-Confederates trotted out this myth of "the contented and well-cared-for slave as proof of benevolent paternalism" (McElya 11), but although Eugene D. Genovese has shown that a few individual mammies had great influence in their households, mammies generally "had no power in the society. They ruled and worked by whim. They were easily fired, demeaned, and demoted" (Omolade 153). Winky's dismissal is a wizarding world parallel.[22] Thus, the story of Winky's supervision of Barty does little to reframe slavery as nurturance and influence; rather, the family's betrayal of a devoted mother figure reinforces its general bad faith.

Dobby is the most important example of a house-elf motivated by love—motivated to resist. At the beginning of *Chamber of Secrets*, Dobby "sat with his great eyes fixed on Harry in an expression of watery adoration" (CS 13). After Harry frees him, Dobby hugs Harry, arguably at this point expressing more gratitude than love. Two years later, Harry gets an even more intense hug: "Next second all the wind had been knocked out of him as the squealing elf hit him hard in the midriff, hugging him so tightly he thought his ribs would break" (GF 375). Dobby's intense regard for Harry begins as gratitude but evolves beyond that. While not as passionate, Dobby's fondness for Dumbledore—partly occasioned by Dumbledore's willingness to pay him, give him days off, and permit him to call Dumbledore a "barmy old codger"—creates in Dobby a willingness to serve, directly contrasting his attitude toward the Malfoys: "Dobby likes Professor Dumbledore very much, sir, and is proud to keep his secrets and our silence for him" (GF380). So far, Dobby's responses, though affectionate, primarily reflect an appreciation for the kindness, which leads to gratitude, which leads to reciprocation.

As with Kreacher and unlike with Winky, unkind masters inspire Dobby's rebellion, but unlike either Winky or Kreacher, Dobby has not unquestioningly adopted "his family's" opinions, despite a long line of ancestors serving a family whose pureblood pride has endured for centuries. Dobby seems less troubled by cruel treatment—which he takes for granted—than he is by believing that Lucius Malfoy behaves like "no decent wizard" (CS 17). Even before meeting Harry, Dobby had determined that Harry must be safeguarded. Early on, of course, Dobby directly defies his masters, and his concern for Harry must be a matter of principles, not affection. To do the right thing, Dobby is already resisting unjust orders.

Dobby's motives for protecting Harry—and breaking rules—become increasingly personal. For example, during the Triwizard Tournament, Dobby brings Harry Gilly-weed even though he is breaking two rules—helping a champion and leaving his post in the kitchen—to protect Harry from losing his "Wheezy." Dobby again expresses concern for Harry's well-being in *Order of the Phoenix*: "'Harry Potter does not seem happy,' Dobby went on, straightening up again and looking timidly at Harry. 'Dobby heard him muttering in his sleep. Was Harry Potter having bad dreams?'" (OP 385). Although Dobby cannot directly aid Harry, he offers what he can: sympathy and concern. Free, eager to work for pay, Dobby nevertheless helps Harry without coercion or direct recompense. He had only reluctantly obeyed the Malfoys and had punished himself every time he mutinously protected Harry, but once Harry has freed him, he tearfully asserts, "Dobby is a free house-elf and he can obey anyone he likes and Dobby will do whatever Harry Potter wants him to do!" (HBP 421). In the end, Dobby freely gives his life for Harry: his last words, looking into Harry's eyes, are "Harry ... Potter" (DH 476). When Bellatrix chastises him for defying his masters, he declares, "Dobby has no master! ... Dobby is a free elf, and Dobby has come to save Harry Potter and his friends!" (DH 474). Dobby's death at Bellatrix's hands might be interpreted as a type of lynching, punishment for being uppity—and indeed, as Susan Howard observes, Dobby's disarming Bellatrix "signals a reversal in roles of the oppressor and oppressed" (46), one a slave owner cannot tolerate. And Dobby's rescuing Harry and his allies cleverly reverses the "white savior" trope.

Carey, who considers Dobby "unnecessarily obsequious," believes that "Rowling intends us to understand that servitude is the natural and inescapable condition of house-elves."[23] Dobby, Carey contends, has "only the freedom 'to obey who he likes' rather than the freedom to take direct control of his own actions" ([2009] 165). But when Dobby attempts to protect Harry from the basilisk, he defies not only the Malfoys but Harry's express wishes. If Dobby can resist enslavement and can, albeit with great effort, act independently of any wizard's demands, then servitude is not, after all, inescapable and "natural" for house-elves, any more than subordination is "natural" for women. Dobby's loyalty to Harry is freely chosen and based on love, as is his courageous mission to save Harry and his friends by returning to Malfoy Manor—surely the one place he would least like to be. Indeed, as Leroy Pelton points out in his study of resistance, "the greater the coercion [individuals] face, the greater will their courage have to be to overcome it" (156). Dobby is not only a free house-elf but a true Gryffindor.

Sacrifice and the "power the Dark Lord knows not"

Emily Griesinger has stated, "One of the lessons Harry learns throughout the series is that in the struggle between good and evil, sacrifice is necessary. The most difficult and costly sacrifices are motivated by goodness and unconditional love" (326). Griesinger applies this observation to Lily Potter and to the climaxes of *Sorcerer's Stone* and *Deathly Hallows*, but it also applies to house-elves. Other critics have, rightly, seen Dobby's death as a supreme act of self-sacrifice, but opinions differ about its implications. Howard argues that Dobby's death is "proof that he is a slave no more because he gains authority over his own life" (46), but Carey (2009) suggests that Dobby is an expendable "commodity" who merely sacrifices himself for a "new master" (Harry) rather than "living as a fully realized individual." Carey concedes that Rowling probably intended to portray Dobby as "a heroic free agent, a martyr for the cause, who willingly lays his life down in the service of a larger goal." But Carey places Dobby's death in the tradition of depicting slaves and former slaves whose violent deaths show that "freedom, or the attempt to seize freedom, leads violently to the grave" (167). Thus, Dobby's death is either retribution or an Uncle Tom-like martyrdom that functions primarily to facilitate the Ron-Hermione romance.

What Carey apparently overlooks is Jane Tompkins's powerful argument that *Uncle Tom's Cabin*, like other nineteenth-century sentimental novels, depicts self-sacrifice by women and slaves as emulating Christ's sacrifice. As such, the death of characters like Tom and little Eva is not passive victimhood but paradoxically conveys

> a philosophy, as much political as religious, in which the pure and powerless die to save the powerful and corrupt, and thereby show themselves more powerful than those they save. They enact, in short, a *theory* of power in which the ordinary or "common sense" view of what is efficacious and what is not ... is simply reversed, as the very possibility of social action is made dependent on the action taking place in individual hearts.
>
> (127–8)

This revisionist interpretation of "power" prefigures the "power the Dark Lord knows not," which Dumbledore repeatedly asserts is love. In *Harry Potter*, as in *Uncle Tom's Cabin*, "dying is the supreme form of heroism. ... [D]eath is the equivalent not of defeat but of victory; it brings an access of power, not a loss of it; it is not only the crowning achievement of life, it *is* life" (Tompkins 127). The freely embraced deaths of Dobby and Lily and Harry Potter convey "the idea, central to Christian soteriology, that the highest human calling is to give one's life for another" (Tompkins 128).

In Stowe's novel, the center of power is the domestic scene, exemplifying relational feminism, empowering women through rather than despite their relationships. Stowe's approach is overtly didactic. She states that her novel is designed to change America by appealing to readers' emotions:

> There is one thing that every individual can do,—they can see to it that *they feel right*. An atmosphere of sympathetic influence encircles every human being; and the man or woman who *feels* strongly, healthily and justly, on the great interests of humanity, is a constant benefactor to the human race. See, then, to your sympathies in this matter!
> (ch. 45; p. 624)

In this sense, it is true that the effect of Dobby's death on Ron's view of elf servitude resembles the intended impact of Uncle Tom's death. Travis Prinzi has argued persuasively that witnessing Dobby's sacrifice even more powerfully affects Harry, persuading him that if he too must die, good will come from it. Prinzi calls it "the most transformative moment in the entire series" (96).

Stowe's views on sentimental fiction's didactic power are not far from Rowling's idea about imagination's power, conveyed in her Harvard Commencement address:

> If you choose to use your status and influence to raise your voice on behalf of those who have no voice; if you choose to identify not only with the powerful, but with the powerless; if you retain the ability to imagine yourself into the lives of those who do not have your advantages, then it will not only be your proud families who celebrate your existence, but thousands and millions of people whose reality you have helped change. We do not need magic to change the world, we carry all the power we need inside ourselves already: we have the power to imagine better.
> ("Fringe")

Both authors contend that a compassionate understanding of powerless people's suffering has a real "influence" on the world—a term they share. Both authors deploy what Tompkins describes as the "pervasive cultural myth which invests the suffering and death of an innocent victim with ... the power to work in, and change, the world" (130). It is in this context that we should approach Lily Potter, the other character who sacrifices her life for Harry,[24] as well as other domestic women in the series whose depiction has been called sexist.

In her critique of sexism in *Harry Potter*, Jane Elliot decries several negative stereotypes: "the bossy, goody-goody girl," the "stern spinster teacher," and most relevant to my argument, "the mother whose only skill is self-sacrifice."[25] LaHaie, too, contends that "the series is built around the idea that a woman's primary purpose is to sacrifice for her children" (143). In their 2003 study of family dynamics in the series, Kornfeld and Prothro, after identifying stereotypical gender roles in the Dursley and Weasley families, observe, "Domineering fathers head the Crouch and Malfoy families ... while nurturing mothers in the Crouch and Potter families literally die to save their sons" ("Comedy, Conflict" 191). Self-sacrificing mothers have not, to say the least, been universally admired, especially in the series' early years. And if the domineering fathers were depicted approvingly or mothers did nothing but sacrifice, it would be legitimate to dismiss the mothers as "Angels in the House"; however, as with most other aspects of the series, its depiction of motherhood is more complex than that, amounting to a relational feminist reimagining of maternal power.

To be sure, neither Petunia Dursley nor Narcissa Malfoy makes the traditional housewife/ mother look good. Petunia embodies the worst housewife stereotypes: materialistic, gossipy, preoccupied with cleaning, and over-indulgent toward her son. That she becomes, if anything, even more obsessive about housework after her son and nephew enroll at boarding school reflects the Dursleys' traditionalism and, presumably, Vernon's pride that his income can support it. Similarly, Narcissa has no economic reason to work outside her home—nor has Lucius. The Malfoys presumably take pride in aristocratic idleness, and spoiled only child Draco resembles Dudley (SS 77).

On the other hand, at least three Order of the Phoenix members are mothers— Alice Longbottom, Molly Weasley, and Lily Potter—all formidable women and all active in the Order when their children were small.[26] We know least about Alice, but she and her husband were Aurors. The Ministry "only take the best" to become Aurors (OP 662). Like the Potters, they had "thrice defied" Voldemort—and lived, but later, outnumbered, they were tortured to insanity by young Barty Crouch and the Lestranges. In her only scene, Alice, who is confined at St. Mungo's, focuses exclusively on her son. Though timid, childlike, and nonverbal, Alice seems compelled to give what she can to Neville: empty gum wrappers. That readers are meant to be moved is underlined by the trio's responses: Harry "did not think he'd ever found anything less funny in his life"; Hermione is "tearful," and Ron speaks "hoarsely" (OP 515). Harry imagines that had Voldemort targeted Neville before Harry, Alice would have been the one to sacrifice: "Would Neville's mother have died to save him, as Lily had died for Harry? Surely she would" (HBP 139). But the text emphasizes that Alice is not only a woman willing to give everything for her child but also a "highly gifted" Auror (OP 514)—and that the two traits are fully consistent.

In the early books, Molly Weasley, the series' most fully developed mother, seems to justify Kornfeld and Prothro's critique of "stereotypical family roles" ("Comedy,

Conflict" 189). In pre-teen Harry's early perceptions, Molly is one-dimensional, the loving mother he never knew, who extends her care to Harry, feeding him delicious cooking, giving him Christmas sweaters, and trying to protect him from dangers. Her protectiveness often seems interfering to teenage Harry, somewhat confirming Elliott's view that "for female characters, even 'good' authority appears only in the shrill, limiting, rule-bound variety. Men make people feel free and safe in these books, while women merely tell them what to do" (n.p.). As the series progresses, though, Harry's and the reader's understanding of Molly deepens.

Lower on the economic scale than Petunia and Narcissa, Molly has economic incentives to work outside the home, especially once her seventh child enters school. Perhaps staying home had been more practical when several Weasley children were too young for Hogwarts: the series is silent regarding wizard daycare or elementary education, and distances between wizard households make sharing resources difficult; care theorists would argue that the Ministry has neglected to create social structures to reduce "care gaps" in magical culture—not unlike in our own. Possibly, by the time Ginny enters Hogwarts, the Ministry pressures holding back Arthur's career might also have hampered Molly's application for paid work. Knowing Molly, however, the reasons she stays home are more than practical. For example, it may have been largely Molly's decision that the family is so big: the fragment of Voldemort may have been on to something when it taunts Ron about "the mother who craved a daughter" (DH 375), for Ginny is, of course, the last-born Weasley. Molly seems to have freely chosen her role, as she relishes and is deeply skilled at domestic life. In a series that depicts many professional women—though perhaps not as many as it might—Molly exemplifies a woman who seems joyfully to have chosen to devote her life to caregiving. If modern feminism is about empowering women to choose whatever lives they find satisfying, Molly's choice should not be denigrated as inferior.

Molly's domestic skills turn out to be more intimidating than "cute and funny magical means" like Samantha's in the old sitcom *Bewitched* (Kornfeld and Prothro, "Comedy, Conflict" 190). Early in *Goblet of Fire*, when she prepares a meal while angry at the twins, she "point[s] her wand a little more vigorously than she had intended at a pile of potatoes in the sink, which shot out of their skins so fast that they ricocheted off the walls and ceiling" (58); shortly afterward, she "jabbed her wand at the cutlery drawer, which shot open. Harry and Ron both jumped out of the way as several knives soared out of it, flew across the kitchen, and began chopping the potatoes, which had just been tipped back into the sink by the dustpan" (GF 59). A wise person would not underestimate a woman who controls knives so efficiently.

I also take issue with Kornfeld and Prothro's comment about the "lack of respect that Mrs. Weasley receives from her children" ("Comedy, Conflict" 189). Consider the scene in which Harry arrives at the Burrow in the Ford Anglia. While the Weasley boys kid their mother at other moments, this is not one of them: "All three of Mrs. Weasley's sons were taller than she was, but they cowered as her rage broke over them" (CS 33). Molly is intimidating. Her anger is aroused by danger to her family. She shouts, "You could have *died*, you could have been *seen*, you could have lost your father his *job* —" (33). One might dismiss Molly as a spoilsport or a stereotypical strict mom, but, as Sarah Zettel observes, magical kids, if not kept in check, could endanger themselves and others; subsequent events confirm that her concerns are legitimate. Moreover, considering the results, Molly's strictness contrasts favorably with Petunia's indulgence.

Again, Molly's role in the Order at first seems primarily domestic—cleaning and cooking. Harry quickly perceives, however, that making number twelve Grimmauld Place a suitable headquarters rises above the condescending language used: "Snape might refer to their work as 'cleaning,' but in Harry's opinion they were really waging war on the house, which was putting up a very good fight, aided and abetted by Kreacher" (OP 117). Reclaiming a house inhabited for generations by a family whose crest says "Toujours Pur," for use by the Order of the Phoenix, represents the opening campaign in the war against Voldemort, metaphorically akin to clearing a room in urban combat. What greater illustration is there of the tensions between the two manifestations of cleanliness that we saw in Chapter Two—"purity" that oppresses, and cleaning to express love? Decontaminating rooms infested by venomous magical creatures and booby-trapped with dangerous hexes is hardly like wielding a bottle of Windex. Moreover, many relational feminists consider women's unique skills, including domestic skills, as the basis for their special capacities in the public sphere.

For cleaning is not Molly's only responsibility, as we learn when Sirius relays her advice against organizing Dumbledore's Army; Molly can't give the advice in person, Sirius explains, because "she's on duty tonight"—presumably guarding the hallway in the Ministry of Magic (OP 371). No mere "Ladies Auxiliary" member, Molly is a fellow resistance fighter. Like many Muggle women, she does what Arlie Russell Hochschild calls a "second shift," fulfilling the same responsibilities as other Order members, then, while the men relax, completing domestic tasks. The power of motherhood and of resistance are not mutually exclusive, any more than relational feminism and equality are mutually exclusive.

Molly most famously displays prodigious fighting skills in the Battle of Hogwarts.[27] As all fans know, Molly, freshly mourning Fred's death, intervenes as Bellatrix Lestrange battles Hermione, Luna, and Ginny, and "a Killing Curse shot so close to Ginny that she missed death by an inch" (DH 735). At once, Harry, invisible, moves in to help,

> but before he had gone a few steps he was knocked sideways.
> "NOT MY DAUGHTER, YOU BITCH!"
> Mrs. Weasley threw off her cloak as she ran, freeing her arms. Bellatrix spun on the spot, roaring with laughter at the sight of her new challenger.
> "OUT OF MY WAY!" shouted Mrs. Weasley to the three girls, and with a swipe of her wand she began to duel.
>
> (DH 736)

Motivated not only by the values shared by all those battling Death Eaters, but unambiguously, furiously, defending her youngest child, this angry mother confidently takes on Bellatrix, a witch of "prodigious skill and no conscience" (DH 461), who has previously killed her own cousin Sirius and niece Tonks. That Molly is an accomplished and determined duelist becomes clear as "Harry watched with terror and elation as Molly Weasley's wand slashed and twirled"; "Jets of light flew from both wands"; and "the floor around the witches' feet became hot and cracked" from being hit by spells. These descriptions indicate the magic's speed and intensity. Molly's own power is manifest as "Bellatrix Lestrange's smile faltered and became a snarl," showing how seriously she takes her opponent, for "both women were fighting to kill" (DH 736).

When Molly screams "Get back" to students trying to assist, the motive may be more than personal animus toward the witch who nearly killed Ginny. From the time Molly helps Harry access Platform 9 ¾ in Book One, we've known that she looks after all young people.[28] Maternal issues permeate the dialogue between Molly and Bellatrix, with Bellatrix cruelly mocking Molly about Fred's death and the possibility of leaving her children motherless:

> "What will happen to your children when I've killed you?" taunted Bellatrix, as mad as her master, capering as Molly's curses danced around her. "When Mummy's gone the same way as Freddie?"
>
> "You—will—never—touch—our—children—again!" screamed Mrs. Weasley.
>
> (DH 736)

In defeating Bellatrix, Voldemort's "last, best lieutenant" (DH 737), Molly demonstrates her magical prowess—enhanced, not diminished, by maternal defense of "our children," a phrase encompassing all children of the magical world. Rowling has said that Molly "would mother the whole world if she could" (*Women*). As Ruddick argues, preserving children's lives is the "constitutive maternal act" (19); moreover, feminist preservative motherhood is inherently resistant to any oppressive social order (225).[29] Bellatrix's sadistic mockery of Molly's maternal grief and protectiveness is consistent with Shira Wolosky's description of Bellatrix as a sort of anti-mother. Bellatrix is the opposite of self-abnegating; rather than willingly give her life for her child, she says at the beginning of *Half-Blood Prince* that she would give up her child to enhance her pride in serving Voldemort. It is thus appropriate that Molly Weasley, mother *par excellence*, conquers Bellatrix, individualist anti-mother, who mocks motherhood.

Maternal love can overcome fear and hate. Ruddick acknowledges that while maternal protectiveness can inspire prosocial behaviors and attitudes like peacekeeping and other forms of nonviolence, protective motherhood can also include "virulent forms of self-righteous hatred of the outsider" (177). Both Petunia's and Narcissa's maternal devotion manifests through hatred of the Other, ironically perceived in opposite ways. Yet one of the series' more stunning reversals is Narcissa's resisting Voldemort to protect Draco, first by enlisting Snape to circumvent Voldemort's dangerous plans for Draco, and later by lying to Voldemort in the Forbidden Forest that Harry is dead. Harry realizes that "Narcissa knew that the only way she would be permitted to enter Hogwarts, and find her son, was as part of the conquering army. She no longer cared whether Voldemort won" (DH 726). Indeed, as the final battle begins at the castle, Harry observes "Lucius and Narcissa Malfoy running through the crowd, not even attempting to fight, screaming for their son" (DH 735). Narcissa's lie, crucial to Harry's final triumph, is radical resistance, motivated by parental love that Voldemort cannot comprehend and that repeatedly stymies him. Although Narcissa's motives are entirely personal, when she prioritizes love over Voldemort's hate-based ideology, she inadvertently supports the resistance. Rowling has observed that Harry is saved by his own mother at the beginning of the series, and, at the end, "it's a mother who saves him again, because she's trying to get to her own son" (*Women*). Voldemort and Bellatrix are vulnerable to loving mothers because, as Dumbledore observes, "That which Voldemort does not value, he takes no trouble to comprehend," and, not understanding, he overlooks love's power (DH 709). Women can be as effective Aurors as men; women can, like Molly, master both wands and kitchen knives to protect their children.

Elliot dismisses Lily Potter's death as little more than "a stereotypical self-sacrifice that erases her from the books before they even begin," and early in the series, Lily seems simply a tragically dead mom, killed when Harry mysteriously survives. But the series gradually fleshes out Lily's character. Harry learns that she and James had been head boy and girl and both were "brave," Voldemort's word of praise at the climax of *Sorcerer's Stone* (294). From Slughorn, Harry learns that Lily Evans was not only "charming" and "vivacious" but also "one of the brightest [he] ever taught" (HBP 50), and "a dab hand at Potions" (191). Slughorn's describing Lily as giving "very cheeky answers" to his suggestion that she belonged in Slytherin House (HBP 70) and his observation that she had "nerve" and the "individual spirit" of a real potion-maker (378) indicate that she was nearly as inclined as James to resist authority. After having "thrice defied" Voldemort, Lily and James died at twenty-one, with only about two years in the Order before the prophecy drove them into hiding. Nevertheless, Lily was already extraordinarily skilled and powerful.

While it is true that Lily produced her greatest magic through her death, she is no passive victim. In Book One, Voldemort reveals that she "needn't have died," a statement neither Harry nor the reader yet understands. Not until nearly the end of the series do we learn that Snape had asked Voldemort to spare Lily; had she played along, she might have survived. However, when Voldemort tells her to "Stand aside, girl," Lily does the opposite:

> *At the sight of him, she dropped her son into the crib behind her and threw her arms wide, as if this would help, as if in shielding him from sight she hoped to be chosen instead....*
> "Not Harry, not Harry, please not Harry!"
> "Stand aside, you silly girl ... stand aside, now."
> "Not Harry, please no, take me, kill me instead—"
> "This is my last warning—"
> "Not Harry! Please ... have mercy ... have mercy.... Not Harry! Not Harry! Please—I'll do anything—"
> "Stand aside. Stand aside, girl!"
>
> (DH 344)

Voldemort says, "stand aside" three times, but she not only stands in front of Harry, arms outspread, as if "she hoped to be chosen instead," but she offers Voldemort incentive to spare Harry—"*I'll do anything*"—and proposes herself as an alternative: "*take me, kill me instead* —." In a 2005 interview, Rowling observed,

> James was immensely brave. But the caliber of Lily's bravery was, I think in this instance, higher because she could have saved herself.... [S]he was given time to choose. James wasn't. It's like an intruder entering your house, isn't it? You would instinctively rush them. But if in cold blood you were told, "Get out of the way," you know, what would you do? [...] She did very consciously lay down her life. She had a clear choice—
>
> ("Leaky Cauldron" Part 1)

Dumbledore accurately says that "Lily cast her own life between them as a shield" (DH 686) and in so doing, she gave Harry "a magical protection [Voldemort] could not penetrate" (HBP 510). Cook argues Lily's sacrifice "ends up saving the world," because had she not died for Harry, he could not have defeated Voldemort (86).

Criticism of Lily's sacrifice echoes arguments sometimes levied against the ethic of care: that it reproduces sexist ideologies, encouraging women to deny themselves in the service of men, that it treats women as means, not ends, in the same way house-elves are treated as means, not as ends in themselves. However, Gilligan distinguishes an ethic of care from "compulsive caregiving"—like Winky's—which contributes to bullying, especially when paired with compulsive masculine self-reliance—like that of Mr. Crouch (*Why* 70). Furthermore, willingness to sacrifice is not, obviously, an exclusively feminine—or house-elf—trait. In the Potterverse, the central example is Harry himself, but we see willing sacrifice in Ron's submission to the white queen in the *Sorcerer's Stone* chess match; and in Sirius's angry insistence that Wormtail "SHOULD HAVE DIED! ... DIED RATHER THAN BETRAY YOUR FRIENDS, AS WE WOULD HAVE DONE FOR YOU!" (PA 375). Fawkes puts himself in front of Dumbledore to absorb Voldemort's killing curse. Regulus dies so Kreacher can apparate the locket out of the Horcrux cave. Snape sacrifices his entire adult life and dies at Voldemort's hands to protect Lily's son. When Xenophilius Lovegood, fearing for Luna's safety, tries to prevent the trio from leaving his cottage, "He spread his arms in front of the staircase, and Harry had a sudden vision of his mother doing the same thing in front of his crib" (DH 419). Each intended or actual self-sacrifice is an act of defiance, a refusal to submit to another's will. And while Anne Collins Smith has a point that love, in *Harry Potter*, "is not wielded as a weapon; it simply overwhelms evil by its very existence" (88), love is far from passive. Each scene of sacrifice emphasizes the character's free, active choice. In each case, the impulse is protective. Voldemort kills others to express or enhance his own power and, in the most extreme cases, to protect himself from death by splitting his soul and creating Horcruxes. By contrast, Harry and his allies protect one another. Utterly solitary and so terrified of death that avoiding it is his primary motive, Voldemort cannot possibly grasp embracing death to protect others. In his D.A. lessons, Harry teaches his friends protective methods like *Expelliarmus*, the Shield Charm, and creating a Patronus: all means to protect not just oneself but others as well. Harry's invisibility cloak is the one Hallow that conceals from danger not just an individual but others. To defeat Voldemort, Harry walks willingly to what he anticipates will be certain death; in the end, while certainly armed and actively dueling, he employs only his "signature" defensive spell, *Expelliarmus*, which causes Voldemort's killing curse to rebound.

Love, the highest good in the *Harry Potter* series, is associated with self-sacrifice. Thus, it oversimplifies matters to dismiss house-elf behavior as merely manifesting false consciousness. If caring for others and sacrificing oneself for others were ignoble, weak, or foolish, how do we assess Harry's and Lily's behavior? By extension, the magical power of love suggests that house-elves' power may not only be something repressed through their enslavement but is also implicit in sacrifices that are slavery's ostensible penalty. That is, because they love their families and sacrifice themselves to serve them—much like mothers serving their families—the elves' magical power is, perhaps, enhanced. Indeed, this overlooked power suggests that the domestic realm in general contains more power than is generally acknowledged. As Hermione remarks, "Of course, Voldemort would have considered the ways of house-elves far beneath his notice, just like all the purebloods who treat them like animals. . . . It would never have occurred to him that they might have magic that he didn't" (DH 195). That is, the series redefines "power" in "feminine" rather than patriarchal terms.

The *Harry Potter* books question not only who holds power but the very nature of power. Those who appear insignificant and powerless—house-elves, mothers, teenagers—may wield more magic than the powerful realize. These groups may resist unjust rules and control in conventional ways, wielding wands or physically conquering their enemies with unacknowledged wandless magic—as Dobby conquers Lucius Malfoy. But the seemingly powerless may also resist patriarchal injustice and hate through the "force that is at once more wonderful and more terrible than death"—the love that house-elves, mothers, and Harry Potter share with those around them.

Notes

1 Among others who argue that the vision of the series is feminist are Katrin Berndt; Eliza T. Dresang, Ximena Gallardo-C. and C. Jason Smith; Mimi R. Gladstein; Anne Collins Smith; Shira Wolosky, "Gendered Heroism"; and Sarah Zettel.
2 See also Jack Zipes who asserted that the early novels are "formulaic and sexist" (171); Tison Pugh and David Wallace, also relatively early critics (2006), worried that "the ultimately regressive gender roles bear the potential to harm readers" (263). Christine Schoefer and Natasha Whitton likewise decry sexist stereotyping in the early books; Melanie J. Cordova argues that, owing to the third person limited point of view, the depiction of Hermione "relegates her to stereotype" throughout the series (21).
3 On the vexed issue of race in the series, see Chapter Two.
4 Rich distinguishes between "motherhood" as a male-defined patriarchal institution that oppresses women and "mothering," which can empower women. Patriarchal motherhood is relegated to the private sphere; mothering is social and political.
5 This analogy to domestic abuse is further elucidated by Lenore E. Walker's comparison between domestic violence and psychological violence, as defined by Amnesty International. This definition has eight elements, all but the first applicable to most house-elves: sexual abuse, emotional abuse, economic abuse, isolation, use of their children, threats, intimidation, and use of privilege.
6 See Berndt for a suggestive but all-too-brief comment on connections between the series and Mary Wollstonecraft's even earlier (1792) *A Vindication of the Rights of Woman*.
7 See Anne Bridger and Ellen Jordan's study of the S.P.E.W.
8 One of my students, Madelyn Saunders, suggested in class discussion that house-elves might have extraordinary powers not despite but because of their small size: magical power is compacted to a greater intensity in their tiny bodies.
9 I am grateful to Connor Brayton, Brad Dufek, and Connor Nielsen for their contributions to a class discussion that reminded me of the tradition of elfin mischief.
10 For discussions of this question, see Karen A. Brown, Kathryn N. McDaniel, and Steven W. Patterson.
11 Arthur's comment, "Now is not the time to discuss elf rights" (GF 139), sounds suspiciously like southern liberals' advice to Martin Luther King, Jr.
12 Mill does acknowledge that women suffering from domestic abuse—a "brutish master"—live in terror of their husbands—and at the time he was writing generally lacked the recourse of divorce.
13 "Beings," according to "Newt Scamander," in the book *Fantastic Beasts and Where to Find Them*, is the legal term established by the Ministry (xii), in 1811, which is, perhaps not coincidentally, just four years after the abolition of the slave trade in the U.K. There is no evidence that house-elves, though subject to some of the wizarding world's harshest regulations, have been consulted about them. Nevertheless, house-elves figure in the Ministry's Fountain of Magical Brethren, along with goblins and centaurs, both identified as "beings"—and have, despite the fountain's suggestion to the contrary, suffered from similar unjust treatment. In short, house-elves are not "beasts," and thus

not "service animals," but clearly slaves. Peter Dendle discusses house-elves in his study of wizard exploitation of magical beasts and seems to endorse the view that elves, however badly treated, are inferior to humans, a perspective I contest.

14 See discussion in Chapter Two.
15 For more on this issue, see the epilogue to this book.
16 A 2007 W.O.M.B.A.T. quiz on Rowling's former website revealed that house-elves "breed infrequently and only with their masters' permission" (Strand 178).
17 Theorists attempting to categorize the varieties of feminism in the present or historically or cross-culturally have identified anywhere from two approaches to well over a dozen feminisms, and while some of the names remain constant across various analyses (especially "liberal feminism," aka "equal rights feminism" and "Marxist/socialist feminism"), other names are more fluid in use or application. For example, "radical feminism" is applied to numerous, often quite divergent ideas. Anne Collins Smith makes a strong case for *Harry Potter*'s "radical feminism," but the term is readily misunderstood and has, unfortunately, been linked to the TERF ("Trans-Exclusionary Radical Feminist") controversy. However much Rowling deserves criticism for her positions about trans women, the series itself supports positions in keeping with a caring, "relational" label. For useful examinations of difference feminism, see Naomi Black, and the many studies identified in Offen's extensive notes.
18 Attempts to distinguish types of feminism depicted in the series are usefully considered alongside Jackie C. Horne's analysis of approaches to antiracism in the series.
19 See Eagly et al. and Paustian-Underdahl et al.
20 William MacNeil suggests that a relational feminist perspective (though he does not call it that) may help explain differences between (female) Winky's and (male) Dobby's attitudes toward freedom and that their situation suggests why Hermione's liberal approach fails: "rights discourse, and indeed the law itself, might be highly problematic strategies for change ... Specifically, how do you change a system's status inequities—its gender, race and class 'intersections' through the very instrument of those inequities, namely the law?" (557–58).
21 The similarities between Winky's dependence on butterbeer and Sybill Trelawney's on cooking sherry after Umbridge sacks her in *Order of the Phoenix* underline that both characters' firings are cruel and unwarranted.
22 Although Winky mentions her mother and grandmother, we learn nothing about house-elves' family lives, such as whether elf parents live together or how and by whom enslaved elf children are raised. This leaves open how much the children of the house-elves, like children of American mammies, are deprived of their mother's attention—if they are allowed to remain with her at all. Still, given that house-elf ownership is tied to a house and that house-elves stay with their family for generations, it is plausible that British wizard slave law conforms to British Muggle slave law, which abolished the slave trade in 1807—but unlike it in that British Muggles abolished slavery altogether in 1833. In other words, house-elves are inherited property but are not bought and sold. This may explain, too, the need for the Office for House-Elf Relocation, at which Newt Scamander worked (*Fantastic* 87)—but which seems to be defunct by Harry's era.
23 As Deborah Gray White has observed, obsequiousness was a survival mechanism among antebellum house servants in the American south. Dobby must unlearn the lessons of a lifetime serving the Malfoys.

24 A case might be made that several other characters (including James, Sirius, Dumbledore, Moody, and the combatants in the Battle of Hogwarts) die for Harry, though none so overtly and directly as Dobby and Lily.
25 Elliot's overall argument is astute and complex: that readers identify more with the series' rule-breaking boys than with its gendered authority figures: "Among the male characters, there's an opposition between bad authority (Snape) and good authority (Dumbledore). But for female characters, even "good" authority appears only in the shrill, limiting, rule-bound variety. Men make people feel free and safe in these books, while women merely tell them what to do."
26 Nymphadora Tonks Lupin is also both a mother and a highly skilled member of the Order of the Phoenix, though she dies too soon for readers to see her mothering behaviors. She joins the Battle of Hogwarts as a dedicated soldier would, leaving her baby in the safekeeping of her own mother.
27 See Louise Freeman's analysis of Molly's embodying of the Jungian archetypes of Mother and Amazon.
28 Louise Freeman speculates that Molly prompting Ginny to identify the platform number is no coincidence: she may already have noticed a solitary, confused-looking child with an owl.
29 For Ruddick, although motherhood can encourage injustice, "maternal thinking" encourages a "politics of peace." By contrast, of course, the mothers (and house-elves) in *Harry Potter* are engaged in warfare, but it is a "women's politics of resistance" that in Ruddick's words is aimed to "resist certain practices and or policies of their governors" (222).

4
"CREATIVE MALADJUSTMENT"
Creativity and Resistance in the *Harry Potter* Series

A chapter about creativity might seem irrelevant to a discussion of resistance in *Harry Potter*. Creative arts are almost completely absent from the series; and Harry, Ron, and Hermione don't seem particularly creative. But what if we expand our understanding of creativity? In 1967, months before he was assassinated, Martin Luther King, Jr., spoke to the American Psychological Association about what he called "creative maladjustment":

> There are some things concerning which we must always be maladjusted if we are to be people of good will. We must never adjust ourselves to racial discrimination and racial segregation.
> …
>
> Thus, it may well be that our world is in dire need of a new organization, The International Association for the Advancement of Creative Maladjustment. … And through such creative maladjustment, we may be able to emerge from the bleak and desolate midnight of man's inhumanity to man, into the bright and glittering daybreak of freedom and justice.
>
> ("Role" 10–11)

When we take "creative maladjustment" into account, a strong case can be made that Harry and his allies engage in creative resistance against unjust social structures and those who defend them. In this chapter, I will show that rule breakers in the magical resistance movement are indeed "creative." My primary interest is in creative problem solving and what Vlad Glăveanu calls "societal creativity," which reimagines society. Here, Harry's and his friends' rule breaking supports a remarkably creative and successful resistance effort.

DOI: 10.4324/9781003312260-5

As I have argued elsewhere,[1] "fine art" in the magical world is generally bad. Consider the sculptures at the Ministry of Magic, Umbridge's Technicolor kittens, Celestina Warbeck's ballads, or the songs composed by Draco Malfoy and Peeves the Poltergeist—the latter not, of course, human. The magical talking portraits are notable exceptions, but we never see anyone paint them. To be sure, "creativity" is not only about aesthetics. There are creative inventions or creative behaviors. Contemporary behavioral psychologists and academics in engineering, education, and business administration associate creativity with producing something with two traits: first, it is "novel," that is, original, unexpected, or surprising. What constitutes "novelty" depends on the field and is open to interpretation, but "novelty" engenders less debate than the second trait: being "useful" or "appropriate" or "adaptive concerning task constraints" (Sternberg and Lubart 3) or "effective" for solving problems, or having "value," variously defined. "Value" is favored in the arts, while "usefulness" is more favored for technology and the pure sciences.

Much of the creativity in the Potterverse is (magically) "useful," including conveniences like the Floo network, flying brooms, or Mrs. Scower's Magical Mess Remover. Nevertheless, we no more see these items created than most Muggles witness, say, the invention of iPads. So mundane are these inventions that they are studied in Hogwarts's most boring class, History of Magic, whose final exam entails "One hour of answering questions about batty old wizards who'd invented self-stirring cauldrons" (SS 263). Also useful but easily overlooked is creative problem solving. Creativity researchers give less attention to creativity in politics and social change than to creativity in other fields, but political creativity is crucial in *Harry Potter*.

Creativity as Rule Breaking

Psychologist J. P. Guilford, who is credited with initiating contemporary creativity studies, posited that problem solving involves two kinds of thinking: first, "divergent thinking," or idea generation, in which someone approaches a problem from several angles to generate approaches that "diverge" from what people generally think; and, second, "convergent thinking," or idea exploration, which prioritizes the findings generated by the divergent approaches, moves toward a "right answer," and devises steps to achieve solutions. "Divergent thinking" is primarily considered "creative," but creative problem solving requires both types of thought. Divergent thinking, by its nature, entails breaking rules of a particular field—whether it be musical theater or molecular science—to identify novel approaches. Creativity scholars also distinguish between two "cognitive styles" of problem solvers: either "adaptors," who conform to prevailing paradigms and make small changes, to "do things better" or "innovators," who break rules, proposing radical changes and "preferring to do things differently" (Kirton 622). In *Harry Potter*, "problems" are as mundane as finding a date to the Yule Ball or as serious as destroying a Horcrux or ending systemic oppression.

The series' most overtly creative characters are "innovators," who share a penchant for breaking rules. The Weasley twins experiment constantly to create clever joke items including Ton-Tongue Toffees to torment the gluttonous and their specialty: potions that help students cut class. Fred and George, who become legendary for pranks targeting Dolores Umbridge, end up, at first inadvertently, creating useful weapons to defend against the dark arts: extendable ears for spying, decoy detonators, shield cloaks, Instant Darkness Powder, and so on. The creators of the Marauder's Map are another set of creative pranksters. While the Marauders used the map for fairly ordinary rule breaking, it becomes one of Harry's most essential resistance tools. Another creative character with a frequent disregard for rules and a somewhat ambiguous past is Albus Dumbledore, discoverer of the twelve uses of dragon's blood (SS 103) and inventor of the Deluminator, essential to reuniting the central trio for their final insurgency against Voldemort (DH 125).

In Rowling's complex ethical universe, creating rules is not always good and breaking them not always bad—but also not automatically good or necessarily creative. Indeed, the series links creativity to much that is morally ambiguous or evil. Creativity researchers call creativity intended to cause harm "malevolent creativity."[2] This is the creativity of terrorists, hackers, and scam artists. In the wizarding world, it is often the realm of "dark magic"—and ethically challenged characters: Umbridge, Snape, Rita Skeeter, and Voldemort.

One of the most creative characters in the series is the ingeniously sadistic Dolores Umbridge, ironically, who excels at creating rules—and novel punishments for breaking them. Umbridge infiltrates Hogwarts to monitor Fudge's opponents, creating ever-more-powerful supervisory decrees and roles for herself, first "Hogwarts High Inquisitor" then headmistress. Infringing on teachers' academic freedom and censoring everyone's speech, Umbridge punishes Harry for "lying" about Voldemort's return, by having him write "I must not tell lies"—with an evilly inventive magic quill that etches the words in blood on the back of his hand. When Voldemort's Death Eaters gain control of the Ministry, Umbridge heads—possibly creates—the Muggle-born Registration Commission, which sends Muggle-born wizards to Azkaban, and she creates propaganda promoting her regulations. We shouldn't be too quick to dismiss the creation of rules as antithetical to creativity, for Rowling has observed that "The most important thing when you are creating a fantasy world is to set the rules ... Because without it—you have no conflict; you have no tension; you have no drama" ("Launch"). If there's one thing Umbridge creates with her rules, it's conflict.

Yet malevolent creativity is more often about breaking than making rules. Genuine rule-breaking creativity is, for example, the province of that ambiguous figure Severus Snape, in his youthful manifestation as the "Half-Blood Prince." He annotated his textbook with "imaginative little jinxes and hexes scribbled in the margins, which Harry was sure, judging by the crossings-out and revisions, that the Prince had invented himself" (HBP 238). Rather than doing what "the book says" (HBP 191), young Snape, an "innovative thinker," challenged official methods: "had taken issue with" various potion recipes and had written "alternative instruction[s]" (HBP 189). The potions *work*, better, in fact, than those brewed following the book's "official" directions. And while Snape turns out to be a "good" character, at the time he was annotating his textbook, he was in league with Voldemort's Death Eaters; many of his "self-invented spells" (HBP 238) are malicious—especially the incantation *Sectumsempra*, which slashes its target, as if "with an invisible sword" (HBP 522). Furthermore, since we learn the "Prince's" identity just when Snape seems least admirable, his creativity is linked with rule breaking at both its best and its worst.

Another creative rule breaker is "journalist" Rita Skeeter. An unregistered Animagus, she buzzes around Hogwarts although Dumbledore has forbidden it, uses Veritaserum on Bathilda Bagshot, no doubt illegally (its use is "controlled by very strict Ministry guidelines" (GF 517)), and steals Bathilda's photographs and other materials while composing *The Life and Lies of Albus Dumbledore*. Rita's false reporting borders on slander. Arguably, though, it's "inventive." Rita's Quick-Quotes Quill is certainly ingenious. She might be described less as a reporter than a fiction writer, who reconstructs reality to fit the story she prefers to tell.

Perhaps the most creative rule breaker is Lord Voldemort, also a sort of novelist, who concocts at least one ingenious *plot* against Harry in each episode. Indeed, the series' first use of the word "create" comes from Voldemort, toward the end of *Sorcerer's Stone*: "once I have the Elixir of Life," he tells Harry, "I will be able to *create* a body of my own" (SS 293–4; emphasis added). His ambition, to create a body to house a disembodied soul, is an act to rival God. At the end of *Goblet of Fire*, Voldemort uses the language of creation when he achieves what he calls a "true rebirth," through "a spell or two of my own invention" (656).

As we know, all Voldemort's evil—and his creative effort—is motivated by his goal to break a fundamental rule: that everyone dies. The boy born Tom Riddle "shed his name ... and *created* the mask of 'Lord Voldemort' behind which he has been hidden for so long" (HBP 277; emphasis added). Seeking immortality, Riddle/Voldemort learns about Horcruxes, whose formation is always described with the word "create": In fact, the words "experiment" and "create" are used most often in the series for Horcruxes' "creation."[3] Riddle learns that to evade death, a wizard would have to split his soul by committing murder and concealing a portion of his soul in a Horcrux.[4] But of course "the soul is supposed to remain intact and whole," as Slughorn explains: "Splitting it is an act of violation, it is against nature" (HBP 498). That is, it is a *creating* that *breaks* fundamental laws.

Voldemort has classic traits, both positive and negative, that psychologists have identified in creative people. Gregory J. Feist notes that researchers have found correlations between creativity and rebellion, nonconformity, and "asocial" traits like "introversion, independence, hostility, and arrogance," all applicable to Voldemort. Creative people frequently desire power ("Influence" 284). Howard Gardner, in a study of seven highly creative people, found all were unable to form deep emotional relationships. David Henry Feldman notes research showing that trauma is common in the childhoods of people who later made great creative achievements (175). J. Marvin Eisenstadt found that more than one-quarter of the geniuses he studied lost a parent by age ten and almost half by age twenty. These psychologists evince reluctance to speculate about cause and effect, but the series invites readers to employ the imaginative empathy Voldemort lacks, to understand young Riddle's childhood traumas. Voldemort is a fascinating character largely because our recognition of his evil is leavened somewhat by sympathy for his losses and admiration for his creative ingenuity. Harry and Voldemort share many traits and somewhat similar pasts, yet Voldemort is "asocial"; whereas Harry has a "saving people thing." But is Harry less creative?

In my earlier work on this topic, I argued that the series' most radical creativity comes from the greatest rule breakers: Voldemort and his supporters. In the intervening years of political and social change and with more re-readings, my perspective on rule breaking has evolved. I still contend that magical creativity—like creativity generally—entails rule breaking and that Voldemort is a creative rule breaker; however, I now recognize other forms of creative rule breaking by the series' protagonists. Harry and his allies defeat Voldemort and the ideology that supports him because, like other successful resistance figures, they engage in divergent thinking. They creatively identify problems, solve mysteries, and challenge the status quo.

Arguably, creativity is by its nature resistant, or, in psychologist Robert J. Sternberg's terms, defiant. Sternberg means "defy" in two ways: "to challenge the power of," and, significantly, to display "effective resistance" (51). Sternberg contends that creativity involves three types of defiance: defying the crowd, that is, the practices of a field such as physics or literary theory; defying oneself, meaning one's previous ideas or practices; and defying the Zeitgeist, meaning a field's—or a culture's—unconsciously accepted assumptions, paradigms, or ideologies. Sternberg's "defying the crowd" means recognizing that the usual way to do something is insufficient and then challenging it. "Defying oneself" is learning that some of one's previous views were wrong—and being open to learning new things. As I discuss elsewhere in this book, each of the characters is at a different point in learning to defy pure-blood privilege and wizarding privilege. Defying the magical world's Zeitgeist epitomizes the magical resistance movement—and real-world resistance.

"Can you imagine?"

As creators, Harry, Ron, and Hermione suffer a distinct disadvantage. The young friends are still mastering well-established spells and wizard lore or copying the Half-Blood Prince's spells and methods. Creativity scholars concur that to develop enough expertise to produce transformative innovations in any field ordinarily requires at least a decade of concentrated study—more time, of course, than Hogwarts's seven-year curriculum. That is, one must thoroughly understand a paradigm to be ready to defy it. With young witches and wizards, the situation is particularly fraught because, without training, their magical ability—their native creativity—can endanger themselves and others. Underage wizards who can't control magic create havoc, as when young Harry inadvertently releases a boa constrictor from its enclosure or blows up his infuriating Aunt Marge like a helium balloon. The word "creation" appears only once in the series in connection with one of the central trio: Hermione's "creation" of canaries in Transfiguration class—evidence not of inventiveness but of her usual academic superiority (HBP 284). What, then, enables our young heroes to creatively challenge equally or more creative foes? They possess strong imaginations, and they foster their creativity through daydreaming, cheating, and inventive lying. They also have traits typical of creative people: risk taking, low "conscientiousness," extraversion, rebelliousness, openness to new experiences, curiosity, resilience, maladjustment, and capacity to exploit luck.

As we have seen, following rules can be problematic. So is lacking imagination. Indeed, much of the evil depicted in the books derives from a lack of imagination among petty bureaucrats. The series mocks the conformity, blindness, and casual cruelty of those who insist on believing only the obvious or on rigidly adhering to regulations at the expense of common sense—or human decency. This pattern is established in the first chapter of the first book: Vernon Dursley, we are told, "didn't approve of imagination" (SS 5). Later, when attempting to expel Harry for protecting Dudley and himself with a Patronus, Cornelius Fudge accuses Harry of both an overactive imagination and defiance of rules: "'I would remind everybody that the behavior of these dementors, if indeed they are not figments of this boy's imagination, is not the subject of this hearing!' said Fudge. 'We are here to examine Harry Potter's offenses under the Decree for the Reasonable Restriction of Underage Sorcery!'" (OP 147).

As Fudge implicitly understands, imagination is "the human capacity to construct a mental representation of that which is not currently present to the senses" (Gotlieb 709). Harry emphatically does not imagine the dementors, but Fudge has a point: the word "imagine" is frequently linked to Harry. Sometimes he imagines in mundane ways, where "imagine" means something like "think": reviewing his fuzzy memories of his parents' deaths in a supposed car crash, Harry "couldn't imagine where all the green light came from" (SS 29). But this is not far from what we mean by "imagination," after all. Psychologists Rebecca Gotlieb et al., in "Imagination is the Seed of Creativity," suggest that "memory construction" entails imagination because it requires assembling materials into educated guesses (717). In turn, speculating how past events unfolded develops creativity: the ability to consider novel future outcomes (Gotlieb 718). Hence, when Dumbledore leads Harry through a series of memory exercises in Book Six, the memories and the speculation they inspire provide more than facts about Voldemort's past: they also prepare Harry for creative guesswork about where Voldemort hid his Horcruxes. And they help him anticipate Voldemort's next moves, as Harry cautions, "Can you imagine what [Voldemort]'s going to do once he realizes the ring and the locket are gone?" (DH 552).

Other speculations are more what we mean by "imaginative": when Harry meets Hagrid, for example, he tries to "imagine" him flying (SS 64); the following year, "Harry could just imagine the thirteen-year-old Hagrid trying to fit a leash and collar on" the as-yet-unidentified monster lurking in the Chamber of Secrets (CS 249). The first time Harry visits Honeydukes Sweet Shop, he "suppressed a laugh as he imagined the look that would spread over Dudley's piggy face if he could see where Harry was now" (PA 197). In examples of "prospective" imagination, Harry "pre-experiences" possible futures: "His stomach twisted as he imagined" being expelled for flying a broomstick without permission (SS 150). He "imagines" kissing Ginny in an empty corridor (HBP 289), smashing a cauldron over Snape's head (GF 301), and, possessing all three Hallows, becoming master of Death (DH 429). Such imaginative thinking aids in ethical decision-making, planning behaviors, and "self-regulation" (Gotlieb 710).

Harry's fantasy about Ginny is "fermenting in the depths of his brain, unacknowledged except during dreams or the twilight time between sleeping and waking" (HBP 472). As it happens, "mind-wandering is positively correlated with creativity" (Gotlieb 719). Harry must be creative indeed! Ironically, Hogwarts's least successful teacher, Professor Binns, may indirectly foster creativity, as his boring lectures put the class in a "deep stupor" (CS 148), with Dean Thomas "sitting with his mouth hanging open, gazing out of the window" (CS149). In short, Binns's students daydream. Those creative mischief-makers, the Weasley twins, also foster daydreaming with their "Patented Daydream Charms" (HBP 117). Daydreams are not intrinsically productive, so scholars associate them with creativity's "generating" stage. To create entails bringing ideas to fruition—through "convergent thinking." In the magical world, however, imagination and action sometimes ally more closely than for Muggles. For example, at the end of Book Two, when Harry needs to use Parseltongue, "He stared hard at [a] tiny engraving [of a snake], trying to *imagine* it was real"; by "willing himself to believe," he manages to speak Parseltongue and enter the Chamber of Secrets (300; emphasis added). Using imagination, one conquers Boggarts, those creatures that take the shape of one's deepest fears: the trick is "to … imagine how you might force it to look comical" (PA 136). Similarly, one conjures a Patronus by using imagination to think of something supremely happy. In each case, a spell follows, but imagination is intrinsic to the magic, or, as Travis Prinzi suggests, "it is not the charm itself, but the power to conjure the charm that defeats fear and depression" (66). Harry is master of the spells to defeat both Boggarts and dementors, and both spells are crucial to success against his foes.

The most important imagination in the series may be "social-emotional imagination" or "ability to conceive of multiple possible cognitive and affective perspectives and courses of actions" (Gotlieb 710). Social-emotional imagination enables empathy and is consistent with an ethic of care. To care, as philosopher Nel Noddings explains, requires "apprehending the other's reality, feeling what he feels as nearly as possible" (16). In this regard, Harry and Hermione are both extremely gifted. After viewing Dumbledore's memory of the trial of Death Eaters who tortured Neville's parents, Harry imagines the situation from several angles: First, he imagines his friend's suffering, but then he also grasps the fury of the trial's onlookers who demand extreme punishment for the perpetrators. Even more radically, he sympathizes with the pain and terror of young Barty Crouch, one of the torturers. Perhaps even more difficult, on viewing "Snape's worst memory," of being bullied by James and Sirius, Harry imaginatively identifies with his supposed antagonist: "he knew how it felt to be humiliated in the middle of a circle of onlookers" (OP 650). Understanding the "subjective reality" of others, including those with whom he disagrees, is, according to social justice researcher Leroy Pelton, an essential part of nonviolent activism (85). Harry's compassionate imagination helps him imagine how his father would feel about Sirius and Lupin killing Wormtail, which leads him to spare Wormtail, thus creating the magic bond that later saves Harry's own life. Harry's empathy for young Riddle, developed while viewing him in the Pensieve, enables Harry to surmise that Voldemort would hide Horcruxes at Hogwarts, "his first real home" (DH 289), and to realize that Tom, a fellow rule breaker, would know about the "the place where everything is hidden" in the Room of Requirement (DH 627); ironically, however, "Tom Riddle, who confided in no one and operated alone, might have been arrogant enough to assume that he, and only he, had penetrated the deepest mysteries of Hogwarts Castle" (DH 620), even when evidence from "generations of Hogwarts inhabitants" stares him in the face (HBP 526). He cannot empathize with others' guilty fears of detection. Even more crucially, Voldemort's plots fail because he can't understand Harry's capacity to sacrifice himself for those he loves, or, as Dumbledore says, Voldemort "was in such a hurry to mutilate his own soul, he never paused to understand [that is, to imagine] the incomparable power of a soul that is untarnished and whole" (HBP 511).

Even more than Harry, Hermione excels at social-emotional imagination. Hermione's emotional intelligence helps her explain Cho's conflicting emotions about Harry, recognize Harry's growing attraction first to Cho and later to Ginny, and help Ginny navigate her relationship with Harry in the early years. Such imaginative caring, when generalized beyond individuals, leads to social justice advocacy. Hermione's social-emotional imagination, at both its weakest and strongest, is manifest in her responses to house-elves. She recognizes the injustice of house-elf slavery and tries to redress it, but at first she does not empathize with their internalized acceptance of their condition; as a result, she tries to manipulate them into freedom. Naturally, she fails. Only in Book Seven does she demonstrate genuine empathy with Kreacher, enabling her to explain his loyalty to the Blacks.[5] At that point, Kreacher is won over, representing a small step toward justice for house-elves.

This is the kind of imagination Rowling described in her 2011 Harvard commencement address: "Imagination is not only the uniquely human capacity to envision that which is not, and therefore the fount of all invention and innovation.

In its arguably most transformative and revelatory capacity, it is the power that enables us to empathise with humans whose experiences we have never shared" ("Fringe"). Hermione, and with her help, Harry and Ron, strengthen this kind of imagination, as they empathize not only with other humans but with oppressed non-humans. From this empathy derives the other aspect of imagination Rowling described: "We do not need magic to change the world, we carry all the power we need inside ourselves already: we have the power to imagine better." This is the imagination of societal creativity.

"Harry invented": Lying, Rule Breaking, and Creativity

Related to memory construction and "prospection"—imagining possible futures—is counterfactual thinking: imagining alternative pasts and their hypothetical outcomes. For example, Harry speculates at the end of *Order of the Phoenix*, "If he had not gone to save Sirius, Sirius would not have died" (844), expressing his guilt feelings—the kind of thing we all do when we regret decisions. Harry feels similar regrets when he visits the Godric's Hollow cemetery and "imagined coming here with Dumbledore, of what a bond that would have been, of how much it would have meant to him" (DH 326). After learning about the prophecy, Harry speculates,

> Had Voldemort chosen Neville, it would be Neville sitting opposite Harry bearing the lightning-shaped scar and the weight of the prophecy. . . . Or would it? Would Neville's mother have died to save him, as Lily had died for Harry? Surely she would. . . . But what if she had been unable to stand between her son and Voldemort? Would there then have been no "Chosen One" at all? An empty seat where Neville now sat and a scarless Harry who would have been kissed good-bye by his own mother, not Ron's?
>
> (HBP 139–40)

Gotlieb et al. suggest that such "what-if thinking" supports creativity by providing practice at considering various possibilities. In this case, Harry is partly wishing his mother were still alive; partly speculating about Voldemort's reasons for selecting him, Harry, to attack first; and partly musing on the impacts of that decision. In many ways, he is continuing his conversation with Dumbledore when he had first heard the prophecy, when Dumbledore encouraged Harry to do more counterfactual thinking: "Imagine, please, just for a moment, that you had never heard that prophecy! How would you feel about Voldemort now? Think!" (HBP 511–12). Harry acknowledges that knowing the prophecy does not alter his determination to defeat Voldemort. Dumbledore encourages the creative effort to imagine a different past even though he knows it would not change the present or future; the counterfactual imaginative leap reinforces Harry's determination. Thinking counterfactually is a form of creative storytelling, by which Harry practices creatively thinking through alternative courses of action, useful when embarking on a resistance effort against the highly creative Voldemort.

Horace Slughorn creates another counterfactual tale: his altered "memory" of discussing Horcruxes with young Riddle. Or is it a lie? The distinction is a fine one, as skill at lying correlates with skill at counterfactual thinking. Liars tend to be creative: "both counterfactual thinking and lying require imagining possible alternatives. Nevertheless, lying can be an act of creativity in that individuals generate a new 'truth' to help achieve some goal they have involving the person to whom they are lying" (Gotlieb 719). As I discuss in Chapter Five, some critics believe Harry's penchant for lying undermines his status as a hero. But what if his lying enhances his success? Business professors Francesa Gino and Scott S. Wiltermuth, in a series of experiments, showed that dishonesty can increase creativity because both lying and creativity entail breaking rules. Harry's lies, while not always successful, frequently exercise his creativity. When Harry lies (a form of storytelling), his lies are often tagged "he invented." For example, interrogated by Snape about where he learned the *Sectumsempra* spell, "'It was—a library book,' Harry invented wildly. 'I can't remember what it was call—'" (HBP 524). Harry lies to protect his friends when Umbridge breaks up the D.A. meeting—and to preserve the forbidden insurgent group. He succeeds because Dumbledore encourages him to lie even more. Other times, lying directly assists Harry's fight against Voldemort, as when he lies about what he sees in the Mirror of Erised: "'I see myself shaking hands with Dumbledore,' he invented. 'I — I've won the House Cup for Gryffindor'" (SS 292). Under the spell of *Felix Felicis*, Harry tells truth or lies as needed to extract Slughorn's unaltered (true) memory. And in the Horcrux cave, regretfully obeying the headmaster's instructions, Harry plies Dumbledore with Voldemort's potion, lying that it will ease the headmaster's suffering. The climax of Harry's quest requires a series of deceptions, from multiple uses of Polyjuice potion, to denying his identity to Snatchers, to stretching the truth to Griphook about the sword of Gryffindor, to playing dead in the Forbidden Forest. Practice, as they say, makes perfect.

Hermione, of course, cements her friendship with Ron and Harry and begins her career as a rule breaker in *Sorcerer's Stone* by lying about their troll encounter, and she manages some of the series' most significant deceptions: she brews Polyjuice Potion (lying about identity), conceals her use of a Time-Turner, creates an elaborate lie about the "weapon" to lure Umbridge into the Forbidden Forest, and concocts a story about the sword of Gryffindor while being tortured in *Deathly Hallows*. Each lie helps forward the resistance. Even Ron, not the series' most creative character, embellishes his accounts of Sirius's attack in the dormitory and of the rescue during the Triwizard Tournament. He finesses a History of Magic exam with "invention": "Couldn't remember all the goblin rebels' names, so I invented a few" (GF 618). More productively, Ron devises the plan of enchanting the Weasley family ghoul to look like himself but with Spattergroit. Later, Ron lies to Snatchers about his identity, discovering a useful principle for liars: "It's a damn sight harder making stuff up when you're under stress than you'd think. I found that out when the Snatchers caught me. It was much easier pretending to be Stan, because I knew a bit about him, than inventing a whole new person" (DH 426). This learned expertise in lying helps Ron infer that Xenophilius Lovegood is *not* lying about the Hallows, an important step in the trio's victory over Voldemort. Along with Harry and Hermione, Ron employs Polyjuice Potion repeatedly, and impersonating Reg Cattermole enhances his compassion for Reg.[6] Trying out alternative identities—which in children we call "pretending"—helps foster imagination, that foundation for creativity.

Equally useful for fostering creativity is cheating. Creativity researchers Gino and Wiltermuth deduce that "after behaving dishonestly, people feel less constrained by rules, and are thus more likely to act creatively" (974). As a teacher, I've always winced when Harry and Ron copy homework or Hermione corrects their work—or does it for them. In these episodes, all three behave dishonestly, and Harry and Ron, as we say, cheat themselves of important knowledge. But perhaps it's not that simple. I agree with Robin Rosenberg that the Hogwarts curriculum "promotes memorization and punishes experimentation, creativity, and critical thinking skills" (5); if cheating counteracts that pattern, then perhaps it is educational after all. Certainly, Harry's and Ron's cheating on Divination homework entails inventing visions and dreams. Whether Harry cheats when he uses the Half-Blood Prince's annotations is debatable, as the annotations produce superior potions results—the course's purpose. And as Ron observes, "Could've been a catastrophe, couldn't it? But he took a risk and it paid off" (HBP192).

As it happens, a propensity for risk-taking accompanies creativity. Rowling observes of the twins' bet on the Quidditch World Cup: "It was a risk. They risked everything on it. That is Fred and George, isn't it? They are the risk-takers in the family. You've got Percy at one end of the family—conform, do everything correctly—and you've got Fred and George, who just take a totally different life path and were prepared to risk everything" ("Leaky," Part Three). The twins, two of Dumbledore's Army's most creative rule breakers, risk their bet, as we know, to fund their joke shop, which becomes a source of resistance resources. Risk-averse Percy, by contrast, collaborates with the increasingly totalitarian Ministry. Risk taking can also include risking ridicule for one's divergent ideas or behaviors, as Hermione does when she develops S.P.E.W., or Luna, most of the time.

Creativity researchers identify several other traits of creative people that might otherwise be seen as negative or antisocial, many of which characterize the magical resistance.[7] For example, business researchers Robert C Litchfield, Lucy L. Gilson, and Christina E. Shalley observed in teams that "*lower* aggregate conscientiousness resulted in *higher* creativity," with less conscientious teams performing better than more conscientious teams on tasks with flexible instructions—which certainly describes tasks the trio face. The researchers theorize that so long as more conscientious group members focus on the task, less conscientious members may be "procrastinating as ideas incubate in their minds, which could facilitate flexibility and divergent thinking" (365). Harry, Ron, and Hermione alternate among themselves as to which is most conscientiously focused on any task, each getting distracted in turn. Thus Harry, when he is failing to practice Occlumency, has the sudden insight that the hallway in his dreams really exists in the Ministry of Magic. When Hermione seems distracted by translating *The Tales of Beedle the Bard*, she observes the Deathly Hallows symbol and intuits its importance. Ron, after abandoning Harry and Hermione, buckles down and becomes their leader as Harry fixates on the Hallows; then Harry, in a classic "eureka moment," achieves clarity about his goals during the physical labor of digging Dobby's grave.

Other traits typical of creative people include extraversion, rebelliousness, "openness," resilience, and motivation. Feist notes that "extraversion" has two facets: "sociability-gregariousness" and "confidence-assertiveness." Creative people possess the independence, confidence, and assertiveness ("Function" 357). This distinction helps explain the apparent contradiction that some creativity researchers identify *malevolent* creativity with introversion rather than extroversion. Extraversion enhances creativity because "inclinations toward being enthusiastic, assertive, energetic, and action oriented [have] been associated with divergent thinking" (Litchfield 355) and with "rebelliousness." While rebellion is antisocial when too aggressive or combined with poor self-control, Paraskevas Petrou and his colleagues found that when employees pursue positive goals, disregarding authority enhances their creativity: that is, "the pathway from non-conformity to creativity requires that individuals are not rebellious for the mere sake of being rebellious but, rather, with a cause or because they seek improvements" (Petrou 817). Rebellious people often question accepted standards, freeing them to experiment with alternative approaches.

Rebellious people also tend to be open to new experiences, another contributor to creativity, because openness to "new and varied experiences, ideas, and values seems to make having novel and meaningful ideas more likely" (Feist, "Function" 354). People who are curious and seek fresh pursuits tend to put their novel ideas into practice, to "transform hypotheticals into ... observable and measurable creative output" (Gotlieb 722). An underlying premise of Harry's story is his openness to seeking adventures, forming hypotheses, and solving mysteries. Hermione shares a similar spirit. Ron, who grew up with magic, more often resists new ideas, but his family (except Percy) embraces the—to them—novel world of Muggle culture. Curiosity is essential to the trio's eagerness to learn what Fluffy is hiding, to identify Slytherin's heir, and to embark on an open-ended quest to identify, locate, and destroy Horcruxes. In contrast, openness to experience runs contrary to authoritarian tendencies (Stenner 81). Thus, Rowling says on the *Wizarding World* site that she used the name *Umbridge*, a homonym with *umbrage*, because "Dolores is offended by any challenge to her limited world-view; I felt her surname conveyed the pettiness and rigidity of her character."

Interrelated with "openness" is curiosity. From their first year, the three friends are, Hagrid says, constantly "meddlin' in things that don' concern yeh" (SS 193). By

Book Five, he observes, "Never known kids like you three fer knowin' more'n yeh oughta ... An' I'm not complimentin' yeh, neither. Nosy, some'd call it. Interferin'" (OP 423). In each novel, the friends solve one or more mysteries: What is attacking unicorns? What is in the Chamber of Secrets? Why is Sirius Black determined to kill Harry? What is hidden down the corridors of the Ministry of Magic? Who was the Half-Blood Prince? What is Draco's secret? What and where are the missing Horcruxes and the Deathly Hallows? As the series progresses, the mysteries become increasingly consequential, and curiosity rises from nosiness to serious investigation.

People who are curious and open to new experiences—creative people—have generally had "diversifying experiences": "unusual and unexpected events or situations that push people outside the realm of 'normality'" (Damian 102)—that loaded word in the Potterverse. Diversifying experiences may be positive, from travel abroad to being an immigrant, to hobbies, education, and reading (Damian 108); or they may include traumas like poverty, illness, or loss of loved ones. Such experiences enable people to perceive and approach things in unconventional ways, helping them develop the "cognitive flexibility necessary for coming up with creative ideas" (Damian and Simonton 376). Tom Riddle's childhood trauma, combined with his differences from the other orphans, may have contributed to his malevolent creativity, and Harry's childhood traumas may have influenced his openness and compassion. Those like Hermione and Harry, raised outside magical culture, have, from a wizarding perspective, diversifying experiences that give them fresh eyes on wizard "normality." Feeling disadvantaged in magical culture, Harry and Hermione readily perceive its power and status structures as well as its inequality and injustices. Outsider status contributes to Harry's willingness to say Voldemort's name and his and Hermione's resistance to "normal" opinions about house-elves, giants, and goblins.

By contrast, British magical culture is homogeneous and provincial, neither understanding nor caring to learn about Muggle innovations, and the Ministry tangles with other magical governments over trivia. Dean Keith Simonton's historical research indicates that political environments affect an era's creative output. The wizarding world's political situation—instability caused by wars and Ministry attempts to keep control—is not promising for creativity. The Ministry is too busy maintaining entrenched power to entertain alternative perspectives; indeed, it does its best to suppress novel ideas. The Triwizard Tournament departs from this insularity, and tournament tasks encourage creativity, designed as they are to test the champions' "magical prowess—their daring—their powers of deduction—and, of course, their ability to cope with danger" (GF 255). Significantly, though, after Voldemort returns, Dumbledore, not the Ministry, reaches out to the other Triwizard competitors; the Ministry retreats to insularity. The creativity of the Order of the Phoenix and Dumbledore's Army is a credit to their members' diversifying experiences with other cultures, including Muggles. In addition, Harry, Ron, and Hermione's unusual adventures in their first six years at Hogwarts provide successive "diversifying experiences" that enhance their creativity and resilience—another trait common to creative people.

Surviving ten years with the Dursleys and repeated traumatic battles with Voldemort amply demonstrate Harry's resilience, but in the context of creativity, resilience means persisting in the face of opposition, indifference, or ridicule—which Harry continues to face. Such resilience derives from being highly motivated, whether to explore things (curiosity), to put ideas into practice, or to achieve goals. Creativity theorists write a lot about "intrinsic motivation"—doing something for its own sake rather than extrinsic reward. One can be motivated without being creative, but to translate ideas into creative actions requires resilience and motivation. Of course, despite occasional discouragement, Harry is motivated to fight Voldemort and to resist the Ministry's injustices. His resilience and motivation are articulated most powerfully, perhaps, by Dumbledore in *Half-Blood Prince* when Harry asks if the prophecy means that he has to try to kill Voldemort: "Of course you've got to! But not because of the prophecy! Because you, yourself, will never rest until you've tried!" (511).

"Maladjustment" and Creativity

Openness to new experiences, resilience, and motivation: these sound like traits of well-adjusted people. So what does "maladjustment" have to do with creativity? King's phrase "creative maladjustment" plays, in part, on ancient assumptions about creativity: Plato, in the Phaedrus, described poetic inspiration as a "divine madness." Renaissance thinkers linked creativity with Melancholia; William Blake's poetry and art derived from visions; Samuel Taylor Coleridge attributed poems to opium dreams; and Robert Shumann credited his "Ghost Variations" to the ghost of Schubert or Mendelssohn. Mental illnesses have been linked with Sir Isaac Newton, Charles Darwin, Nikola Tesla, Albert Einstein, John Nash (*A Beautiful Mind*), and Steve Jobs. Depression is common among political luminaries, including Abraham Lincoln, Theodore Roosevelt, Winston Churchill, Mahatma Gandhi, and, yes, Martin Luther King, Jr.

But accusations of insanity have long been used to disparage those who resist social norms. China and both Soviet-era and present-day Russia have imprisoned political dissidents in psychiatric hospitals. Closer to home, many early Anglo-American feminists were diagnosed with "hysteria," and ambitious women like Charlotte Perkins Gilman were prescribed "rest cures"—to abstain from creative or intellectual work. When Martha Mitchell, the outspoken wife of Richard Nixon's Attorney General John Mitchell, alerted America to the administration's "dirty tricks," she was subjected to "rumors concerning her mental stability" (Cadden 14).[8] As Timothy Snyder has observed in connection with Nazi Germany, "It is those who were considered exceptional, eccentric, or even insane in their own time—those who did not change when the world around them did—whom we remember and admire today" (52).

Harry, like Martha Mitchell, is accused by his government of being delusional, precisely for telling the truth. Lucius Malfoy—who has the power to make things happen—tells Draco, "it's a matter of time before the Ministry has him carted off to St. Mungo's" (OP 361). When, at the end of *Goblet of Fire*, Fudge refuses to acknowledge Voldemort's return, his pretext is that young Crouch's confession is that of a "raving lunatic" (703) and Harry is having "hallucinations" (705). With Fudge "leaning on the *Prophet*" (OP 567) to continue such messaging, Harry is perceived as a "delusional" (OP 567) "nutter" (OP 221, 332, 525, 587) who has "lost his marbles" (567). Harry, we should remember, not only insists that Voldemort is back but also identifies powerful men as Death Eaters. By so doing, he challenges the authority of Fudge and the Ministry and contests their privilege.

Subsequently, he openly defies Umbridge, defender of both. Clinical psychologist Bruce E. Levine notes that since the 1980s the American Psychological Association has diagnosed "noncompliant children"—like Harry—with something called "oppositional defiant disorder" or ODD. To be diagnosed with ODD, "a youngster needs only *four* of the following eight symptoms for six months: often loses temper; often touchy or easily annoyed; often angry and resentful; often argues with authority figures; often actively defies or refuses to comply with requests from authority figures or with rules; often deliberately annoys others; often blames others for his or her mistakes or misbehavior; spitefulness or vindictiveness at least twice within the past six months"(Levine 100). Harry exhibits at least the first five of these eight during his fifth year (and other times); Snape and Umbridge would identify all eight. But Harry hardly defies for defiance's sake. Although the word "maladjusted" isn't used, Harry can, in Dr. King's words, "recognize that there are some things in our society, some things in our world, to which we should never be adjusted" ("Role" 10). And his maladjustment is used to discredit him.

Harry is not the only "maladjusted" one. To discredit Dumbledore's announcement of Voldemort's return and justify his demotion from Chief Warlock on the Wizengamot and removal from Chairmanship of the International Confederation of Wizards, the *Prophet* hints he is "getting old and losing his grip" (OP 95). Thereafter, the *Prophet* suggests Dumbledore "is no longer up to the task of managing the prestigious school of Hogwarts," rendering necessary the installation of Umbridge, to exert Ministry control (OP 308). Questioning someone's sanity, to suggest he is a failed leader, is a classic move to promote authoritarianism, as Karen Stenner has observed. No one questions Hermione's sanity, but her blood status and being a "know it all" make her an outsider. She is arguably more "maladjusted" than Harry, for her anti-racist stance regarding house-elves—which her peers treat as eccentric at best. Her activism inspires mockery, as when George remarks in the Gryffindor Common Room, "Going to try and lead the house-elves out on strike now, are you?" and in reaction, "Several people chortled" (GF 367).

From the perspective of dominant magical culture, Dobby is certainly "maladjusted." When he says, "Dobby likes being free!" other Hogwarts house-elves start "edging away from Dobby, as though he were carrying something contagious" (GF 378). When Hermione mentions elves' "rights" to "wages and holidays and proper clothes" and the freedom not to follow orders (GF 538), the house-elves look at Hermione "as though she were mad and dangerous." So intense is their response that Dobby looks "scared" and asks, "Miss will please keep Dobby out of this" (GF 539). Hagrid dismisses Dobby's desire for freedom with the assertion "yeh get weirdos in every breed" (GF 265). Combined, these responses illustrate that Dobby's attitudes are not merely unusual but somehow "sick." And this, in turn, echoes so-called "drapetomania, or the disease causing negroes to run away," an obviously illusory "species of mental alienation" first described in 1851 by Louisiana doctor Samuel A Cartwright (707). Dobby is indeed poorly "adjusted" to the injustices of house-elf enslavement.

Politically Resistant Curiosity

These characters may be "maladjusted" and rebellious, but are they creative? In his speech to the APA, Dr. King proposed an "Association for the Advancement of *Creative* Maladjustment." The "maladjustment" King had in mind entailed rejection of what he describes as "systemic" prejudices of white society ("Role" 9), in a culture that demanded that Black people *adjust* to Jim Crow, to go along to get along. To this day, "normal" society frequently describes protesters as pathological troublemakers. Levine has traced a pattern of linking anti-authoritarian behavior with psychiatric illness: disproportionately diagnosing rebellious young people with "oppositional defiant disorder" and Black men with schizophrenia. King turns such thinking on its head. As for "creative," since King's speech mentions civil disobedience and other direct action, "creative maladjustment" likely means "maladjustment" that resists social oppression, to *create* a more just society— or *perceived* maladjustment that inspires creative solutions to social problems.

One way to explain King's phrase "creative maladjustment" is to return to creative curiosity from this new angle. In the work of activists like Dr. King—and the magical resistance movement—we see "politically resistant curiosity." Early in his 1963 Letter from Birmingham Jail, King identifies four basic steps of nonviolent action: "(1) collection of the facts to determine whether injustices are alive, (2) negotiation, (3) self-purification, and (4) direct action" (290). Curiosity's role in the "collection of facts" is obvious. King's explanation of that step is brief—a list of injustices that had arisen in Birmingham. In his creative maladjustment speech, he argues that studying the root causes of problems faced by Black Americans is an important responsibility of social scientists: "White America needs to understand that it is poisoned to its soul by racism and the understanding needs to be carefully documented and consequently more difficult to reject" ("Role" 2). Pelton, in his study of nonviolence, argues that accumulating facts is an "essential preliminary step to all nonviolent action, that an activist must first convince himself, through both first-hand observation of a situation, consultation with others, and examination of his conscience. Only then does he attempt to persuade others" (83).

Political philosopher Perry Zurn identifies at least four ways resistance movements deploy curiosity, all applicable to *Harry Potter*. First is the way already mentioned: investigating a society's injustices, especially those experienced by marginalized groups. In magical culture, these groups include non-human magical beings like house-elves, goblins, centaurs, and merpeople, as well as giants, werewolves, and part-humans. As Voldemort's power rises, systemic discrimination against Muggle-borns increases, and of course the magical community routinely abuses Muggles and Squibs. Hermione's (unsuccessful) search for information about house-elf servitude in *Hogwarts: A History* exemplifies politically resistant curiosity.

Second, resistant curiosity shifts interest regarding "not only the topic of inquiry but the people being asked" (Zurn 239–40). Multilingual Dumbledore seeks input from merpeople, giants, house-elves, and centaurs. Hermione's biggest error with S.P.E.W. is neglecting to consult house-elves about their own preferences, a mistake she begins to rectify. Although we learn little about the Muggle Studies curriculum, it apparently fails to accomplish what a good ethnic studies course attempts: to decenter the thinking of witches and wizards by providing knowledge based in Muggle experiences; instead, as Hermione says, students "study them from the wizarding point of view" (PA 57), which is precisely the opposite.

The third aspect of politically resistant curiosity Zurn identifies is its attempt to change what is "recognized as a question or problem," to "destabilize the unquestioned character of race, prisons," and other institutions (240). Zurn focuses on King's work; on Michel Foucault's Prisons Information Group (activism that preceded *Discipline and Punish*); and on PISSAR, a "trans/crip coalition" that sought accessible bathrooms at U.C. Santa Barbara. Zurn's work readily applies to Azkaban, whose reform, especially removal of the dementors, Dumbledore advocates. More directly, Hermione questions house-elf enslavement, and Harry asks probing questions about Ministry law enforcement and Public Relations actions like imprisoning Stan Shunpike; all these situations generally go unquestioned by magical culture. A fourth angle of politically resistant curiosity, says Zurn, is asking "What do we need, what would a new future of care look like?" (240). The series' final pages only hint at a more progressive future that realizes Hermione's ambition to "do some good in the world!" (DH 124).

In his analysis of "Letter from Birmingham Jail," Zurn argues that "curiosity" operates in King's fourth step: the direct action itself. King says that direct action "seeks to create such a crisis and establish such creative tension that a community that has consistently refused to negotiate is forced to confront the issue. It seeks so to dramatize the issue that it can no longer be ignored" ("Letter" 291). King further clarifies that "tension" is "a tension in the mind so that individuals could rise from the bondage of myths and half-truths to the unfettered realm of creative analysis and objective appraisal ... that will help men to rise from the dark depths of prejudice and racism to the majestic heights of understanding and brotherhood" ("Letter" 291) King repeats the word *create*: "create a crisis," "creative analysis." Direct action is creative—creating an intellectual crisis that forces a community to engage in curiosity, to "confront the issue," and to engage in "analysis" and "objective appraisal" so that issues "can no longer be ignored," with the goal of defeating "myths and half-truths" and unthinking prejudice, to achieve "majestic heights of understanding." That is, direct action highlights issues the community has ignored, encouraging curiosity where before there had been indifference or lies. This is sometimes called epistemic curiosity: it inspires one to learn more; it is satisfied when one has acquired knowledge. We need not look to the 1960s to observe the accuracy of this analysis. Movements like #MeToo or the Black Lives Matter protests rely on "creative analysis": gathering and disseminating facts about sex crimes and systemic racism to awaken public awareness. Public protests create "tension"—awareness—and the consequent "curiosity" about the issues leads to people educating themselves, changing many people's attitudes and beginning to alter public policy.

Vladimir Nabokov has said, "Curiosity ... is insubordination in its purest form" (quoted in Zurn 228). In the early *Harry Potter* books, a "curious" response generally expresses innocent interest rather than insubordination. That changes midway through pivotal Book Four, when Harry sees the name of the Head of the Department of International Magical Cooperation on the Marauder's Map and "his curiosity got the better of him," so he reverses course, "to see what Crouch was up to" (GF 467). As we later learn, the "Bartemious Crouch" in Snape's office is the son, not the father, important information, had Harry acquired it; in any case, checking on a high-ranking Ministry official is hardly deferential. Harry's insubordinate "curiosity" arises again when Dumbledore catches Harry viewing his memory in the Pensieve without permission, and comments, "Curiosity is not a sin [...] But we should exercise caution with our curiosity ... yes, indeed" (GF 598). A year later, Harry will learn this advice for "caution" reflects Dumbledore's ill-conceived withholding of crucial facts about Harry's past and future, knowledge Harry receives too late. Apparently, he should have been more insubordinate the year before. Nevertheless, Harry does test the advice, as "curiosity held him in his chair" and he asks Dumbledore to explain what he witnessed: Igor Karkaroff's and Ludo Bagman's hearings, and the sentencing of the Longbottoms' torturers (GF 602). Harry's curiosity helps him with "collection of the facts to determine whether injustices exist." Curiosity proves essential to his (and readers') understanding of Ministry corruption on the one hand and, on the other, the backstory of Neville, whom Harry later learns was the other potential subject of Trelawney's prophecy. "Curiosity" is also at issue when Harry remains fascinated with what waits beyond the door in his dreams about Ministry of Magic corridors; when he peeks at Snape's worst memory in the Pensieve; and, significantly, in Slughorn's memory, whose comment is less cautious than Dumbledore's:

"It's natural to feel some curiosity about these things.... Wizards of a certain caliber have always been drawn to that aspect of magic...."

"Yes, sir," said Riddle. "What I don't understand, though—just out of curiosity—I mean, would one Horcrux be much use? Can you only split your soul once?"

(HBP 498)

This exchange illustrates that curiosity, like other traits including rule breaking and creativity, can be used for good or ill. So much depends on motive. As the series progresses, Harry's efforts to, in King's words, "collect the facts" increasingly aim at redressing injustice. After Dumbledore's death, as he contemplates his quest for Horcruxes, "He did not feel the way he had so often felt before, excited, curious, burning to get to the bottom of a mystery; he simply knew that the task of discovering the truth about the real Horcrux had to be completed before he could move a little farther along the dark and winding path stretching ahead of him" (HBP 635). Politically resistant curiosity has become serious business.

The other aspect of curiosity, the interest created in a direct action's "audience," is illustrated repeatedly as the resistance movement grows. Hermione's initial confrontation with Umbridge commences when she raises her hand until "more than half the class were staring at Hermione rather than at their books" (OP 241). As Hermione challenges Umbridge about using defensive spells, first Ron, then Harry, and "now several other people had their hands up too" (OP 242), all wanting practical lessons. The conflict climaxes, of course, when Harry drops Voldemort's name, then "Ron gasped; Lavender Brown uttered a little scream; Neville slipped sideways off his stool." Presently, "everyone was staring at either Umbridge or Harry" (244). When Harry mentions Cedric, the class "stared avidly from Harry to Professor Umbridge" (245). Although the immediate consequences are a scolding from Professor McGonagall, missed Quidditch tryouts, and nightmarish detentions with Umbridge, sharing the truth with "thirty eagerly listening classmates" (246) arouses curiosity in a big way:

> The news about his shouting match with Umbridge seemed to have traveled exceptionally fast even by Hogwarts standards. He heard whispers all around him as he sat eating between Ron and Hermione. The funny thing was that none of the whisperers seemed to mind him overhearing what they were saying about him—on the contrary, it was as though they were hoping he would get angry and start shouting again, so that they could hear his story firsthand.
>
> (250)

Harry's peers want to know more. Arousing curiosity makes recruiting Dumbledore's Army remarkably easy: more people than anticipated show up at the Hog's Head, "some looking rather excited, others curious" (339); many "had turned up in the hope of hearing Harry's story firsthand" (340). This frustrates Harry but looks different when we apply King's idea that direct action "seeks to create such a crisis and establish ... a tension in the mind so that individuals could rise from the bondage of myths and half-truths to the unfettered realm of creative analysis and objective appraisal" ("Letter" 291). The tension Harry creates changes minds and recruits resistance members. Subsequently, Harry's *Quibbler* interview piques Hogwarts's curiosity, and the issue goes into reprint—indicating wider curiosity—and Harry's mail reveals a shift of opinion among the wider British magical public.

Other instances in which direct action inspires creative tension include the twins' fireworks display—which rouses Hermione to remark, "Now you mention it [...] d'you know ... I think I'm feeling a bit ... *rebellious*" (OP 634). Their dramatic exit from Hogwarts stirs insurrection throughout the student body, as "a great number of students were now vying for the newly vacant positions of Troublemakers-in-Chief" (677). When Harry, Ron, and Hermione are operating undercover in *Deathly Hallows*, the magical resistance (curiously) listens to *Potterwatch* for news of them; *Potterwatch* and *The Quibbler* contribute to resistance fact gathering and communicating. The trio's creative and splashy adventure at Gringotts is immediately famous, and D.A. members create resistant curiosity when "We used to sneak out at night and put graffiti on the walls: *Dumbledore's Army, Still Recruiting,* stuff like that" (DH 575). One successful direct action inspires more.

Creative Maladjustment in Action in the *Harry Potter* Series

Creativity appears in *Harry Potter* in sometimes surprising ways. Dobby, for example, is definitely "maladjusted" and rebellious. But is he creative? Yes. As we have seen, something creative is inventive, unexpected, and useful or adaptive. Dobby's ploys, in *Chamber of Secrets*, to keep Harry from returning to Hogwarts are sufficiently unexpected that Harry doesn't suspect foul play when he gets no letters from his friends; the hover charm and destroyed pudding surprise first-time readers and effectively put Harry on track for expulsion. Equally inventive and impactful are blocking the entrance to Platform 9 ¾ and enchanting a Bludger—though the consequences are not what Dobby might have expected. Dobby's final act of resistance, unscrewing the Malfoys' chandelier while exclaiming, "Dobby is a free elf," surprises everyone and proves successful. It might also be said to illustrate another fictional mental illness invented by the antebellum apologist for slavery, Samuel Cartwright: "dysaesthesia aethiopica," also called "rascality," the tendency of freed slaves to "break, waste and destroy everything they handle ... as if for pure mischief" (709). Cartwright, of course, attributes "rascality" to "natural" laziness and stupidity, denying it could stem from "the debasing influence of slavery" (710). Dobby's responses demonstrate, however, that he is neither lazy nor stupid but determined and resourceful in his creative resistance.

Goblins, though associated mostly with banking—and historical goblin rebellions—are also creators of items with unique magical properties. Goblins crafted the Black family's goblets, Aunt Muriel's tiara, and the indestructible battle helmet Hagrid presents to the giants' Gurg. Since we are told that goblins produce all the finest magical metalwork, we may presume they made Ravenclaw's diadem, Hufflepuff's cup, and Slytherin's locket. The series' most important goblin creation is the sword of Gryffindor, which, Griphook explains, "was forged centuries ago by goblins and had certain properties only goblin-made armor possesses" (DH 298). Specifically, "Goblins' silver repels mundane dirt, imbibing only that which strengthens it" (DH 303)—an essential factor when Ron destroys the locket Horcrux with the sword, which had absorbed Basilisk blood five years before. Goblins so revere superior workmanship that, according to *Wizarding World*, the sword's maker, Ragnuk the First, was "finest of the goblin silversmiths, and therefore King (in goblin culture, the ruler does not work less than the others, but more skillfully)" ("Sword").

Goblins' value systems diverge from wizards' in another important way, their basis in creating: "To a goblin, the rightful and true master of any object is the maker, not the purchaser. All goblin-made objects are, in goblin eyes, rightfully theirs." Accordingly, goblins consider a wizard's purchase of a goblin-made item more like a lease and wizards' bequeathing such items to their heirs, "without further payment, little more than theft" (DH 517). That is why Griphook says, "That sword was Ragnuk the First's, taken from him by Godric Gryffindor! It is a lost treasure, a masterpiece of goblinwork! It belongs with the goblins!" (DH 505–6). Thus, even though, as bankers, goblins seem like the ultimate capitalists or collaborators, in fact, capitalism perverts the goblins' cultural model, as wizards insist on alienating goblins from their creative labor and treating their creations as mere commodities. Griphook's seizing the sword violates human property rules but reflects the value system of goblins, who live in a colonized culture, differing from house-elves in their history of rebellions. This glimpse into goblin epistemology illustrates that aspect of creative maladjustment that views a culture from the standpoint of disempowered groups. Goblins may share Griphook's indifference to other creatures' pain (DH 509), which would make them malevolent creators, whether or not theirs is a "malevolent creativity." The *Daily Prophet*'s oblique mention of "subversive goblin groups" (OP 308) may be propaganda to discredit a Dumbledore sympathizer or it may refer to an actual movement; but goblins are, by their very identity, "maladjusted" breakers of wizard norms and forces of creative resistance against wizard hegemony.

Hermione is easily dismissed as unimaginatively insisting on doing what "the book says" (HBP 191). In fact, she is among the resistance's most creative members. She smashes the "ten year rule": that to develop enough expertise to produce transformative innovations requires at least a decade of concentrated study (Weisberg 230–32). She conceives Dumbledore's Army, invents fake coins for communication, and designs the enchanted parchment that jinxes anyone who reveals the D.A.'s secret. And of course, Hermione defies the magical Zeitgeist by championing the rights of non-human magical beings. Part of "creative maladjustment" is recognizing that oppression, in King's words, is "not a consequence of superficial prejudice but [is] systemic" ("Role" 9) and refusing to "adjust" to it, a point Hermione makes to Ron.

No member of the D.A. defies norms more than Luna Lovegood, introduced as "Loony Lovegood." She epitomizes Snyder's advice that a major way to resist tyranny is to "stand out" (51). Luna is "slightly out of step in many ways" (Rowling, Albert Hall Interview) and often socially inappropriate: she sometimes laughs too loud, and she has a "knack of speaking uncomfortable truths" (HBP 311). As a result, she's frequently bullied—which she accepts with aplomb. Luna's "aura of distinct dottiness" derives partly from the fact that we first see her reading *The Quibbler*—upside down (OP 185)—and partly from her fashion choices. Appropriately, her odd radish-like earrings are Dirigible Plums, which supposedly "enhance the ability to accept the extraordinary" (DH 404). When Luna tells Harry she, too, sees thestrals and that "You're just as sane as I am," Harry is "Not altogether reassured" (OP 199).

In short, Luna's "maladjustment" is a given. Her divergent thinking, which invariably defies the Zeitgeist, derives from her creative parents and plenty of diversifying experiences, both positive and negative. For example, Luna sees thestrals because at age nine she witnessed her mother's death during a spell experiment that went wrong. Luna, through her father, facilitates the interview that helps reshape the resistance movement, and she is one of the few D.A. members, outside Harry's immediate circle, to accompany him to the Department of Mysteries; she is the one who, thinking outside the box, points out that there are ways besides brooms to fly there. In Book Seven, she helps Neville and Ginny lead the resistance at Hogwarts.

Most significant is the way Luna represents the creative power of love. Her capacity to "believe 10 impossible things before breakfast" makes her the "anti-Hermione," rejecting Hermione's skeptical rationalism ("Albert Hall Interview"). Luna goes with her heart and her faith. It is Luna who assures Harry he will see Sirius again (which he does), because she, too, had heard voices behind the veil at the Department of Mysteries; Hermione and Ron had not. The value Luna places on friendship is among her most salient traits. She says she enjoyed D.A. meetings because "It was like having friends" (HBP 138) and remarks happily that "Nobody's ever asked me to a party before, as a friend!" (HBP 311). Because they cherish friendship, Luna and Neville show up to help fight Death Eaters at the end of *Half-Blood Prince*: "Neville and Luna alone of the D.A. had responded to Hermione's summons the night that Dumbledore had died, and Harry knew why: They were the ones who had missed the D.A. most . . . probably the ones who had checked their coins regularly in the hope that there would be another meeting" (HBP 642).

The importance of friendship for Luna is best illustrated in her bedroom's décor, one of the series' few instances of aesthetically effective creativity:

> Luna had decorated her bedroom ceiling with five beautifully painted faces: Harry, Ron, Hermione, Ginny, and Neville. They were not moving as the portraits at Hogwarts moved, but there was a certain magic about them all the same: Harry thought they breathed. What appeared to be fine golden chains wove around the pictures, linking them together, but after examining them for a minute or so, Harry realized that the chains were actually one word repeated a thousand times in golden ink: *friends . . . friends . . . friends . . .*
> (DH 417)

Luna has not mastered whatever spells make magical portraits move; her art's "certain magic" comes from the more traditional portraiture magic of capturing its subjects' character—because Luna cares enough to understand them. The "certain magic" is love, the "power the Dark Lord knows not." The golden links among the pictured friends contrast with young Tom Riddle's Hogwarts connections, whom Dumbledore describes as "more in the order of servants" (HBP 444). Magical links of friendship do, as Dumbledore predicted, help defeat Voldemort.

Voldemort's domination of others, his mistaken belief in his own self-sufficiency, and his stark rejection of those he derides as Other and lesser are, as Carol Gilligan would note, intrinsic to the patriarchal Zeitgeist, which poisons not only Voldemort personally but wizard (and Muggle) culture more generally. Pointedly, in *Joining the Resistance*, Gilligan quotes Dr. King: "We are caught in an inescapable network of mutuality tied in a single garment of destiny. What affects one directly affects all indirectly" (18). Voldemort, of course, has no notion of mutuality.

After the Battle of Hogwarts, after Voldemort's death, and after the overthrow of the corrupt Ministry that supported him, the emphasis is on relationship, which replaces conflict and separation, even distinctions among Houses and species. As Harry wanders through the Great Hall, "Everywhere he looked he saw families reunited" (745), and that includes former enemies: "he spotted the three Malfoys, huddled together as though unsure whether or not they were supposed to be there, but nobody was paying them any attention" (744–45). Lucius and Narcissa Malfoy's love of Draco has contributed to Harry's victory. Connection based on power and fear is tenuous, but "communities of care," in Talia Schaffer's words, triumph.

"Accident, was it?": Luck and Creativity

One final issue: it is easy to minimize Harry's accomplishments according to his own self-deprecating assessment: "all that stuff was luck—I didn't know what I was

142 "Creative Maladjustment"

doing half the time, I didn't plan any of it, I just did whatever I could think of, and I nearly always had help—" (OP 327). The thing is: creative people embrace luck. Simonton emphasizes Louis Pasteur's statement, "Chance favors the prepared mind." To be "prepared," Simonton says, entails first, "an intense fascination with their field, an incessant curiosity about its phenomena and potentialities" ("Exceptional," 60). Harry is obviously no scientist, but he is incessantly curious about Voldemort's plots and eventually about his Horcruxes. During his adventures, he and his friends develop the second aspect Simonton considers necessary to prepare for luck: "considerable expertise" (61). Granted, they have only O.W.L. Level expertise in general magic, but they develop some skills far beyond expectations, especially during Harry's D.A. lessons. Perhaps their most important expertise is Harry's understanding of Voldemort's character, which, as Prinzi has argued, Harry comprehends better than Voldemort himself. In addition, Simonton argues that to take advantage of chance requires many "cognitive and dispositional traits" (61) discussed in this chapter, including divergent thinking, openness to experience, risk taking, nonconformity, and strong motivation (61–62).

Historian of science Ana Cecilia Rodríguez de Romo, comparing two neuroscientists, argues that the scientist responsible for creative breakthroughs benefited from luck in the sense that "'luck' is the capacity to take advantage of the opportunities that present themselves and to adapt to the unexpected" (284). This characterization matches Harry's description of his battles with Voldemort: "The whole time you know there's nothing between you and dying except your own— your own brain or guts or whatever" (OP 327). Faced with grave and unexpected dangers, from the possibility that Quirrell will see the Sorcerer's Stone in the Mirror of Erised to the prospect of being killed by Voldemort in Little Hangleton cemetery, Harry thinks fast and makes often-risky decisions—and risk is intrinsic to creativity. Among Harry's risky—and creative—acts are the insurgencies into the Ministry of Magic and Gringotts and riding a dragon to escape. And while Harry often has help, creativity applies to teams as much as to individuals.

Another piece of luck is that Voldemort, when he attempted to kill the infant Harry, created the seventh Horcrux, creating the mysterious link between them. But of course it was less bad luck than incomplete understanding—of the "power the Dark Lord knows not," the power of Lily Potter's sacrifice for her child; Simonton might call that "expertise." As a result, Voldemort, inadvertently "created" the means to his own undoing. As Dumbledore explains, "Voldemort himself created his worst enemy, just as tyrants everywhere do! Have you any idea how much tyrants fear the people they oppress? … He heard the prophecy and he leapt into action, with the result that he not only handpicked the man most likely to finish him, he handed him uniquely deadly weapons!" (HBP 510). That is, Voldemort has less control over his creative processes than he thinks he does. Despite his creativity, Voldemort's fundamental weakness is not just incapacity for love but failure of imagination, a creative capacity at which Harry excels. As Voldemort admits in the cemetery scene in *Goblet of Fire*, what he labels "the woman's foolish sacrifice" and the protection it provides represent "old magic, I should have remembered it, I was foolish to overlook it" (653). Even as he concedes this fact, though, he fails to call it by name, and he continues to believe, falsely, that his magic is stronger: "I can touch him now" (653).

Voldemort defies many laws, but unlike Harry, he fails to challenge the Zeitgeist: he is a tyrant who supports pure-blood privilege. Harry's victory derives from the "deadly weapon" he wields creatively: the magical power of love. Although Hermione's activism in defiance of systemic injustices is closer to what Dr. King meant by "creative maladjustment," I think King could also appreciate Harry's "signature move," the *Expelliarmus* charm, a form of nonviolent resistance Harry uses to protect innocents like Stan Shunpike; to avoid damaging his own soul through murder; and ultimately to defeat the "Deathstick," the supposedly unbeatable Elder Wand. Voldemort and the Death Eaters, representing the patriarchal wizarding Zeitgeist, mock use of the defensive spell as Harry's weakness, but it proves his greatest strength. However creative Voldemort is, he is bested by a more creative adversary. After all, what could be more creative than defeating your enemy by dying but not dying?

While it can be argued that Harry's "death" in the Forbidden Forest reflects Dumbledore's creative thinking, not Harry's, Harry writes the rest of the script. His forethought ensures that Neville knows to kill Nagini. Harry's instincts tell him to play dead and allow himself to be carried to the castle; to don the invisibility cloak at the first opportunity, and to use its cover to jinx Death Eaters and cast defensive spells to protect allies; and then to remove the cloak at the optimum moment. Creative resistance is performance, and Harry's miraculous "resurrection" is certainly a hit. Most of all, Harry, drawing on carefully researched wandlore, makes the creative mental leap that the wand he carries can defeat the Elder wand, but he employs its power not to kill but to deploy the defensive curse that will leave Voldemort "dead, killed by his own rebounding curse" (DH 744). Before this happens, Voldemort dismisses Harry as having "survived by accident" (737), but at that point, Harry challenges his view: "Accident, was it, when my mother died to save me? ... Accident, when I decided to fight in that graveyard? Accident, that I didn't defend myself tonight, and still survived, and returned to fight again?" All these victories in fact involve Harry's creative deployment of his unique magic, the magic of love. Still Voldemort misunderstands, screaming about "accident and chance and the fact that you crouched and sniveled behind the skirts of greater men and women" (DH 738), again insisting on autonomy rather than the magic of cooperation. It is no accident, but part of the magic, that each Horcrux is destroyed by a different ally.[9]

To conclude, then, the magical resistance beautifully illustrates Martin Luther King, Jr.'s concept of creative maladjustment. Though wizard culture, rife as it is with systemic oppression, mocks and abuses those who defy its norms, Dumbledore's Army refuses to "adjust" to an unjust society and defeats Voldemort's autocratic reign with love. And yes, it is creative. Their methods fit the definition: they are novel and surprising on the one hand, and effective on the other. And they break the rules.

Notes

1 See "The Ambivalent Portrayal of Creativity in *Harry Potter.*" *The Ravenclaw Chronicles: Reflections from Edinboro.* Edited by Corbin Fowler, Cambridge Scholars, 2014, pp. 122–40.
2 See Cropley et al.
3 Travis Prinzi cites Voldemort's assertion that he had "'gone further than anybody along the path to immortality' through certain 'experiments'"; Prinzi finds the "rather scientific" word "experiments" reinforces Voldemort's "position as a soul-discarding materialist" (152). My analysis of creativity complicates that perspective on "experimentation," by acknowledging that Voldemort is indeed a malevolent creator but noting that the word is also used for Fred and George Weasley, the only characters whose experiments are "shown" in the series.
4 Christina Phillips-Mattson notes, citing Craig Conley's *Magical Words: A Dictionary* (3rd edition, Weiser Books, 2008), that the killing curse, *Avada Kedavra*, with which Voldemort creates Horcruxes, derives from "'ebra kidibra,' an ancient Hebrew-Aramaic expression for, 'I will create with words,' 'I create like the word,' or 'I create as I speak'" (57–8).
5 Beatrice Groves makes a strong case that Hermione develops more emotional intelligence as the series progresses, starting out fairly obtuse in Book One.
6 See Chapter Three.
7 Many personality traits common to creative individuals are the converse of those with high disgust sensitivity (see Chapter Three). For example, people who are easily disgusted score high in conscientiousness but low in openness to new experiences (Page and Tan 195, 202).
8 When Mitchell was speaking with reporter Helen Thomas, her phone was pulled from the wall; she was, she said, "kidnapped," injected with tranquilizers, and beaten black and blue. The man she identified as her attacker, Stephen King, subsequently became Donald Trump's ambassador to the Czech Republic (Brockrell).
9 The notable exception being the diadem Horcrux, destroyed by Crabbe's Fiendfyre.

5

"DO YOU REALLY THINK THIS IS ABOUT TRUTH OR LIES?"

Honesty and Resistance in the *Harry Potter* Series

"Do you really think this is about truth or lies?" Professor McGonagall asks Harry rhetorically, the first time Dolores Umbridge gives him detention for "lying" about Voldemort's return (OP 249). The answer, of course, is that it is not—except that it is. The same is true of this chapter, which concerns the relationships among truth, lies, rule breaking, power, and resistance. Throughout the series, Harry is a seeker, not just for Golden Snitches and Horcruxes, but for answers to riddles, hidden secrets, and sometimes painful truths. He is also a surprisingly bad liar, frequently caught in his lies, despite how much he practices—as discussed in the previous chapter. Although the series generally endorses resisting the status quo and thus we might expect it would celebrate lying as a form of resistance, Harry (generally) takes the side of truth. This seems contradictory. I believe the contradiction is resolved by the fact that lying *is* the rule in the wizarding world's corrupt autocracy, where official lies and censorship undergird authoritarianism. Harry resists alternative facts and fake news. A saying that has been attributed to George Orwell applies nicely here: "In a time of universal deceit, telling the truth is a revolutionary act."[1] This chapter will argue that, paradoxically, in the wizarding world, truth *is* rule breaking, tends to challenge the status quo—and represents a powerful tool of resistance.

Harry Potter's relationship with the truth is complex. For starters, he tells a lot of lies; indeed, Mary Pharr identifies lying as Harry's "most obvious flaw" (16), and Laura Lee Smith observes that "the simple and unambiguous phrase 'Harry lied'" appears in all seven volumes (278). A good starting place, then, is to sort out the kinds of lies Harry tells, given that duplicity can take so many forms.[2] It is true that Harry frequently lies simply to evade trouble—lying in self-defense. As a rule breaker, Harry lies almost automatically to authority figures—about everything from excursions after curfew to divination homework to, later, his

DOI: 10.4324/9781003312260-6

success in Potions and even Horcruxes and Hallows. As Smith suggests, lying to disproportionately powerful antagonists places Harry in the mythic "trickster" tradition (278).

Many of Harry's lies are "social lies," to avoid hurting someone's feelings or to make them feel better. We traditionally distinguish social lies from lies told for our own advantage. Harry's social lies include telling Nearly Headless Nick that he's having a good time at Nick's death day party or the countless lies Harry, Ron, and Hermione tell Hagrid about his teaching. Harry lies to Ron about his Quidditch play, partly to make him feel better and partly to increase his confidence—and therefore his actual play, when he implicitly lies by pretending to spike Ron's pumpkin juice with Felix Felicis. The latter case might be likened to the "placebo effect."

Other lies are genuinely altruistic, told to protect others. Dumbledore lies about the DA to protect Harry. Harry lies in letters to Sirius, downplaying the pain in his scar, for fear that Sirius will return and be captured. Another seemingly altruistic lie is Hermione's lie about the mountain troll, ostensibly told to protect Harry and Ron but which, as Lana Whited has argued, wasn't strictly necessary, as Hermione could simply have said, truthfully, that the boys knew she was in the bathroom; by lying, though, Hermione makes much-needed friends (private communication). Sometimes Harry lies to avoid admitting his own flaws, but these lies make him uncomfortable. He feels guilty when he lies to Hermione and Hagrid that he's making progress on the Triwizard egg clue and each believes him. Likewise, when he tells everyone he's "fine" before the first Triwizard task, he starts "wondering why he kept telling people this, and wondering whether he had ever been less fine" (GF 351). Significantly, speaking with Sirius via Floo Network, he stops saying "fine" and, eases, relieved, into confidences.

Moral philosopher Sissela Bok has observed that to judge a lie, one should consider the perspective of the deception's target, and from a care ethic perspective, as Maurice Hamington contends, lies should be judged not by some absolute rule but by their impact on relationships (277). Clearly, few people like being lied to. For all the lies he tells, Voldemort nevertheless gets very touchy when people lie to him: it's a sure path to being tortured: "Tell the truth!" he commands Dumbledore when they first meet (HBP 269). Harry is enraged to discover the Dursleys have lied about his parents' deaths. Ron is hurt when he believes Harry has lied about entering the Triwizard tournament—though of course Harry is not lying, and Ron's distrust represents a failed test of his friendship. Much of Ron's suspicion can be dismissed as jealousy, but Harry's habit of lying doesn't help. False accusations of lying are among the most frustrating, especially where trust might be expected, as when the Dursleys refuse to believe that the "strange" things that happen around Harry are not his intention. After all, the Dursleys own lies have kept Harry ignorant of his magical powers. The most egregious false accusation of lying is, of course, Umbridge's accusing Harry of lying about Voldemort.

There are plenty of instances in which lying is overtly and obviously wrong. Gilderoy Lockhart enriches himself by claiming credit for other people's accomplishments. Umbridge conceals that she ordered the dementor attack on Harry and Dudley. She also lies about her family background and how she obtained Slytherin's locket. This might be interpreted as similar to Harry's lying to avoid getting in trouble—the necklace is stolen and then "taken as a bribe from a petty criminal"—but the lies conceal considerably more serious offenses than breaking curfew, especially in a high Ministry official. Furthermore, Umbridge bases her claim that "there are few pure-blood families to whom I am not related," on the probably fictitious Selwyn connection, to "bolster her own pure-blood credentials," precisely when she is persecuting others for their blood status (DH 261).[3] Draco's lie about Buckbeak and then about his arm, to avoid playing in the Quidditch match with Gryffindor, might seem merely self-serving, to avoid embarrassment, but it is actually the worst kind of malicious lie, hurting others with no meaningful benefit to anyone: an effort to get Hagrid sacked and Buckbeak executed. Tragically, when Kreacher lies about Sirius's whereabouts at the end of *Order of the Phoenix*, it does cost Harry's godfather's life. On the other hand, self-serving truth-telling can also kill, as Chantel M. Lavoie observes: to save his own life, Wormtail causes the Potters' deaths by telling Voldemort the truth about their location (85).

Detecting falsehood can create its own moral issues, especially two common magical lie-detecting methods, Veritaserum and Legilimency. Veritaserum resembles "truth serums," widely considered forms of torture; nevertheless, Dumbledore administers Veritaserum to Barty Crouch—who has been impersonating Mad-Eye Moody—to elicit the truth about Harry's abduction and Voldemort's return; as Laura Lee Smith argues, Dumbledore might have at least attempted to elicit the information using standard police interrogation techniques or asked permission to administer the potion (285). Veritaserum seems even more problematic when Rita Skeeter uses it to steal information from Bathilda Bagshot; when Snape threatens to use it on Harry in his fourth year, and Harry is horrified at what personal secrets might emerge; as well as when, the following year, Umbridge attempts to use it on Harry—and then, when Snape claims to have run out, nearly uses the Cruciatus curse instead, underlining the connection between Veritaserum and torture. As for Legilimency, the fact that, as Karin Westman notes, the characters who practice it "don't broadcast this talent" suggests that it functions as an underhanded invasion of privacy. Legilimency is of course Voldemort's stock in trade, not merely to detect lying but to control others. And yet Dumbledore, too, employs Legilimency—to learn from Kreacher how Harry and Sirius were enticed to the Department of Mysteries, and no doubt on other occasions.

It would be easy—too easy—to say the import of a lie or lie-detection method depends on who does it and why—though there's truth in that, too. Some lies in the series suggest an ends-justify-the-means ethic. In many cases, Harry lies to forward his efforts against Voldemort. He lies to Quirrell about what he sees in the Mirror of Erised, lies to Fudge about Dumbledore's Army, lies to Slughorn to obtain his memory (and also tells the truth when that works better), lies to the Snatchers about his identity, and even lies to Neville about his intentions as he heads to his expected death. His lie to Griphook about returning the sword of Gryffindor is an example of lying by means of a "mental reservation," saying one thing—"He can have it"—but, in his head, adding the "reservation"—"after we've used it on all of the Horcruxes" (DH 508). Pretending to be someone else using Polyjuice Potion is deception, and arguably so is concealing oneself and others under an invisibility cloak, but of course, Harry and company aren't the only ones who use Polyjuice Potion: Young Barty Crouch's impersonation of Mad-Eye is the most prominent and evil case in point. Both the Marauders and Rita Skeeter deceive others by being unregistered Animagi—with radically different motives.

In several instances, lying proves essential to the resistance. Apparently, Scrimgeour lies under torture to conceal Harry's whereabouts. Grindelwald delays Voldemort by lying that he never had the Elder Wand—and lies by omission in not revealing that it is a Hallow. Narcissa Malfoy lies that Harry is dead, and though her motive concerns protecting her son rather than forwarding the resistance, the effect is the same.[4] Crucially, Snape succeeds as a double agent by lying to Voldemort through Occlumency. Occlumency allows Snape to retain Voldemort's trust, to foil the plot to have Draco kill Dumbledore, and to deceive Voldemort about plans to move Harry before Harry's seventeenth birthday. But a life of lying to everyone except Dumbledore leaves Snape a broken human, living a lie and suppressing his emotions and his better side. These are examples of lying, as the young Dumbledore and Grindelwald might say, "For the Greater Good," but given that slogan's context, violating norms "for the greater good" is ethically questionable. Dumbledore describes the phrase as "empty words" and admits he was lying to himself about Grindelwald (DH 716). Perhaps, too, Harry's difficulty mastering Occlumency reflects his fundamental honesty (McDaniel, "Mischief").

Voldemort obviously engages in all manner of dishonesty (stealing, framing others for murders he commits, deceiving Harry about the Department of Mysteries). Indeed, David and Catherine Deavel argue that the essence of Voldemort's evil is deceit, convincing his followers that there is no good or evil, only power. Among Voldemort's final acts is lying about Harry's death: "He was killed while trying to sneak out of the castle grounds," said Voldemort, and there was relish in his voice for the lie, "killed while trying to save himself—" (DH 731). This lie, intended to debase Harry in his followers' eyes, builds on all that preceded it. No doubt he considers the lie essential to persuading his opponents to stand down in support of "the new world we shall build together," composed of people of "noble stock" (DH 729, 731), because, centrally, Voldemort is devoted to the "Big Lie" of wizard superiority.

What Is Truth?

To sort all this out, let's consider a larger question: "What is truth?" People who study lying consider this a separate issue because, as. J. A. Barnes says, truthfulness and lying have to do with the liar's beliefs and intentions, so lying is a moral issue; in contrast, truth and falsity are matters of ontology and epistemology. That is, Barnes explains, "Truth remains a contested concept" (13). I contend, however, that this contest is relevant to understanding truthfulness and lies in *Harry Potter*. There are four approaches to truth that operate most overtly in the series: the "correspondence theory," "pragmatic theory," "coherence theory," and "constructivist theory" of the truth.

Explained simply, correspondence theory, the oldest and most straightforward theory of truth, holds that something we say or believe is true if it corresponds to actual facts. This theory assumes, of course, that facts exist and can be verified.

A second way of thinking about truth, known as "pragmatic" theory, is what it sounds like: it involves evaluating a truth based on how useful it is. Muggles assess scientific theories by testing hypotheses. Robin S. Rosenberg has argued that wizards are very weak at this kind of thinking, that their lack of science training contributes to wizard "learned helplessness" (13–14)—and, I would add, to wizard credulity, their weakness at testing truth claims with evidence. The Weasley twins' penchant for experimentation may be related to their well-developed bullshit detectors. We see a "pragmatic" approach when Muggle-raised Harry and Hermione, along with Ron, solve a different set of mysteries in each book, by developing and testing theories. Of course, knowing the truth is useful when making everyday decisions about everything from dressing for the weather to vaccinations to what defensive spells to teach at Hogwarts.

Another theory of truth, the "coherence theory," posits that people assess the truth of something based on how consistent it is with other things they hold to be true. Any proposed fact must fit with other accepted facts in a unified and coherent system. When, in *Harry Potter*, our heroes attempt to solve a mystery— what is Fluffy guarding and from whom? What is in the Chamber of Secrets, and who opened it?—they organize clues into a coherent theory, upon which to base appropriate actions. Sometimes this approach works; an important example is the Deathly Hallows. As Hermione observes after Xenophilius Lovegood explains them, "Harry, you're trying to fit everything into the Hallows story"; he responds, "*Fit everything in?* ... Hermione, it fits of its own accord!" (DH 429). In this case, it does. Unfortunately, a coherence approach to truth may invite confirmation bias, the phenomenon in which people only accept information that confirms their coherent worldview. Harry's certainty that Snape is trying to steal the Sorcerer's Stone and his obliviousness to Quirrell's suspicious behavior derives from the consistency of these beliefs with other "truths" he "knows" about his professors. It takes Harry seeing Quirrell with Voldemort under his turban and Fudge seeing

Voldemort at the Ministry to re-jigger their belief systems—and even then, Harry continues to distrust Snape.

Thus, a core weakness in a coherence approach to truth is that if the original system is flawed, it supplies a flawed basis for assessing reality, and, indeed, it invites multiple competing realities or, as we might now say, "alternative facts." Politicians' fondness for "alternative facts" is hardly new. In 1945, Orwell remarked of "political thinking," "People can foresee the future only when it coincides with their own wishes, and the most grossly obvious facts can be ignored when they are unwelcome" (297). Hannah Arendt argues that extreme ideological consistency is a hallmark of totalitarianism: "What convinces the masses are not facts, and not even invented facts, but only the consistency of the system of which they are presumably part" (460). In recent years, Americans have observed the corrosive effects when a political faction embraces only the alternative facts that correspond to their worldview. Similarly, Fudge refuses to believe Sirius is innocent because that fact is inconsistent with the system of beliefs he and his government have operated in for more than a decade, in which Sirius is a confessed murderer and ally of Voldemort, Peter Pettigrew is dead, and Voldemort is too. Likewise, Snape persists in seeing Harry as "mediocre [and] arrogant as his father … delighted to find himself famous, attention-seeking and impertinent." Dumbledore correctly observes, "You see what you expect to see" (DH 679). In Harry's fifth year, the *Prophet* "won't print a story that shows Harry in a good light. Nobody wants to read it. It's against the public mood. … People just don't want to believe You-Know-Who's back." (OP 567). The Ministry, the *Prophet*, and the *Prophet*'s readers who only want to read one kind of story and avoid any other, construct an almost impermeable information silo, endangering the entire wizarding world.

The final approach to truth that is crucial to the *Harry Potter* series is sometimes called constructivism and is a manifestation of postmodernist ideas that knowledge and reality are not objective but subjective. Truth, therefore, is socially constructed, based on convention, and reflects whoever in a culture has the power to shape ideas. In British magical culture, the Ministry, working in uneasy collaboration with the *Prophet*, is the power center of truth control. As Michel Foucault has observed, power is "disciplinary," a punning term that elides concepts of punishment and education. This is why it is appropriate that the Senior Undersecretary to the Minister of Magic acquires a supervisory role at Hogwarts. After McGonagall asks Harry, "Do you really think this is about truth or lies?" she confirms that "the Ministry of Magic is trying to interfere at Hogwarts"—that is, to control the education of young minds (OP 249). It is more a matter of power than of truth. Umbridge's "post-truth" constructivist position—that truth is what the Ministry says is true—is precisely what Harry opposes. Although there are instances where the series touches on pragmatic and coherence approaches to truth, explorations of truth in the series boil down to a conflict between constructivist and correspondence theories. On balance, correspondence wins.

Although I believe the series critiques postmodern ideas of truth, I grant it has postmodern elements. Quite a few critical articles on the series cite postmodernism, though some do so merely to place the series in the present era.[5] That's easy to concede. I also concede that the series may be considered postmodern in its form. Signe Cohen describes the series' "postmodern bricolage of shards of cultural knowledge" and says that "it is precisely this blurring of religious, cultural, and historical elements that appeals to contemporary readers' postmodern sensibilities" (55). Laura Yiyin Lee sees in Harry an "alternative heroism for the postmodern age." This may be so but says nothing about postmodern *thinking*. Closer to home, Robert Scholes advances an interesting argument that scientific thinking and magical approaches represent two different constructions of reality: Scholes writes, "It is as if, in this universe when science and magic parted company, they did not turn into true and false natural philosophy but into two true and different visions of the world" (208). That is, the entire wizard worldview is a construct—and so is our own scientific worldview. Similarly, Drew Chappell argues that the child characters in the series "deconstruct the adult world from an 'outsider' perspective" (281). They can "often see through hegemonic structures" and "They react to imposed dualities and easy answers with skepticism and questioning" (291). Pharr finds the series postmodern in that its theology and the nature of magic remain fuzzy, reflecting "the general distrust of code" in contemporary culture (9).

I believe these observations are accurate, and to that extent, I agree that the series embodies a postmodern perspective. According to (postmodern) constructivism, people's beliefs about what is true derive from their culture and its conventions. Thus, what we consider "facts," especially such matters as race, gender, and class, derive from constructed social assumptions that shape how we interpret our world. Travis Prinzi's discussion of postmodernism in the series emphasizes the ways it challenges cultural metanarratives (belief structures that shape a culture), with particular emphasis on the idea that "history is written by the winners." Unquestionably, the series suggests that widely held wizard assumptions about blood status, giants, or Muggles are socially constructed. John Granger identifies ten traits of postmodernism that Rowling shares, including many I have mentioned, and sums up his argument, that Rowling is "a writer of her times writing for a postmodern audience of readers." The books, he explains, "reveal her disregard for conventional and historical genre lines and taboos, her 'incredulity toward metanarrative,' that is, a loathing of dogma and ideology in an almost dogmatic fashion in choice of themes, narratological perspective, and story line, and her profound suspicion of and skepticism about the motives of institutional carriers of these metanarratives (school, home government, media)" (*Unlocking* 199). My argument somewhat resembles Granger's point that despite Rowling's postmodernism in other regards, she rejects "postmodern relativism" (209), but Granger focuses on the series' religious underpinnings—whose importance I certainly acknowledge—rather than on epistemological issues.

Thus, the series *embodies* a postmodern perspective in many ways, but, somewhat paradoxically, it rejects a postmodern perspective of truth. The characters whose worldviews are most consistent with a postmodern view that truth is a construct are characters like Voldemort/Quirrell, Umbridge, Rita Skeeter, and Ministers of Magic Fudge and Scrimgeour. Harry, at his core, takes a correspondence approach to truth: that facts do exist and can be verified.

The most overt constructivist statements come from Umbridge in her role as a professor. In a near parody of a postmodern academic, she teaches not defensive spells but a "theory-centered" course (OP 239). To be sure, theory is important and valuable. A good grasp of underlying principles can help with tackling difficult skills or concepts. Remus Lupin, one of Harry's best teachers, often introduces underlying principles before teaching a spell. That's the case with his first lesson, on defeating Boggarts, and the most important lesson he teaches Harry, on the Patronus charm. Horace Slughorn introduces Golpalott's Third Law (albeit not very effectively) to establish principles for creating an antidote to a potion, and when Harry struggles to learn a summoning charm, Hermione has him study the theory to help. But in none of these cases does theory substitute for practice. When Hermione objects to a purely theoretical approach, arguing, "Surely the whole point of Defense Against the Dark Arts is to practice defensive spells?" Umbridge dismisses her condescendingly. On the contrary, says Umbridge, only a "Ministry-trained educational expert" is "qualified to decide what the 'whole point' of any class is," and she claims (falsely, of course), that "Wizards much older and cleverer than you have devised our new program of study" (OP 242). In short, the Ministry has defined knowledge, and, what's more, will evaluate it on the principle that "a theoretical knowledge will be more than sufficient to get you through your examination, which, after all, is what school is all about" (OP 243). Never mind, of course, that it would not suffice.

Having embraced "teaching to the test," Umbridge disdains relevance to the "real world," in an exchange questioning not only practical knowledge but also what is "real":

> "And what good's theory going to be in the real world?" said Harry loudly, his fist in the air again.
> Professor Umbridge looked up.
> "This is school, Mr. Potter, not the real world," she said softly.
> "So we're not supposed to be prepared for what's waiting out there?"
> "There is nothing waiting out there, Mr. Potter."
>
> (OP 244)

Voldemort, Umbridge thus asserts, is "nothing." In criticizing the standard curriculum, Umbridge challenges its premises. After all, the title "Defense Against the Dark Arts" presumes people need to resist wizards wielding dark magic. More to the point, Umbridge rejects the reality known to Harry (and the reader): "you have been informed that a certain Dark wizard is at large once again. *This is a* lie. ... I repeat, *this is a lie*. The Ministry of Magic guarantees that you are not in danger from any Dark wizard. If you are still worried, by all means come and see me outside class hours. If someone is alarming you with fibs about reborn Dark wizards, I would like to hear about it" (OP 245; emphasis in the original). Umbridge repeatedly claims that accounts of Cedric's murder and Voldemort's return are lies, fibs. Simply not real. Rather, they are "stories" (fictions) designed merely to alarm and to get attention (265). Umbridge poses as a reliable arbiter of truth, as an educator, and as "Hogwarts High Inquisitor." The title *Inquisitor* implies someone inquiring after truth—but, of course, readers will think of the brutal Spanish Inquisition, designed to root out heresy. And heresy, as the *Oxford English Dictionary* helpfully tells us, is a "religious opinion or doctrine ... held to be contrary, to ... orthodox doctrine of the Christian Church," or, to speak more generally, an opinion "at variance with those *generally accepted* as authoritative" (emphasis added). In short, Umbridge comes to Hogwarts to instill and enforce the *orthodox* view of Truth endorsed by the Ministry. For Umbridge, if the Ministry says it's truth, it is Truth, and because she is an educator, this becomes an issue not only of power but of epistemology enforced by power. Implicitly, her position is "It's true because I have the power to say what is true."

The Ministry's constructivist approach is institutional. Nothing changes after Scrimgeour replaces Fudge—indeed, Scrimgeour may be worse, since Fudge may have been lying to himself about Voldemort;[6] Scrimgeour apparently has a steely eyed grasp on reality. The policy of both is that truth is merely a construct. In *Half-Blood Prince*, Scrimgeour remarks to Harry, "Does it really matter whether you are 'the Chosen One' or not? [...] Well, of course, to *you* it will matter enormously [...] But to the Wizarding community at large ... it's all perception, isn't it? It's what people believe that's important" (344). For this reason, he asks Harry "to be seen popping in and out of the ministry from time to time," because "that would give the right impression" (345). And when he asks if Harry actually is the Chosen One and Harry retorts, "I thought you said it didn't matter either way," Scrimgeour says, "I shouldn't have said that. It was tactless." Harry's response gets to the root of the issue:

> "No, it was honest," said Harry. "One of the only honest things you've said to me. You don't care whether I live or die, but you do care that I help you convince everyone you're winning the war against Voldemort. I haven't forgotten, Minister. ..."
>
> He raised his right fist. There, shining white on the back of his cold hand, were the scars which Umbridge had forced him to carve into his own flesh: *I must not tell lies.*
>
> (HBP 347)

Rejecting the Ministry's constructivist approach, Harry angrily refuses to collaborate, partly because he disapproves of Ministry public relations ploys like falsely imprisoning Stan Shunpike: "You're making Stan a scapegoat, just like you want to make me a mascot"—both (misleading) symbols that mask actual reality. Harry insists that it's the Ministry's "duty to check that people really are Death Eaters before you chuck them in prison" (HBP 346). That is, their actions should reflect reality. Harry does not understand a phenomenon Arendt explains, that elites in a totalitarian system are not supposed to believe their own propaganda but cynically to "dissolve every statement of fact into a declaration of purpose"—which is to "organize the masses" (503, 504). As Timothy Snyder observes, "Post-truth is pre-fascism" (*On Tyranny* 71). This is not to say that the British wizarding world has become totalitarian under Fudge or Scrimgeour, but it is moving in that direction, a trend that facilitates Voldemort's coup. Constructivist perspectives are more than an intellectual issue. As Bok observes, "to the extent that one has radical doubts about the reliability of all knowledge, to that extent the moral aspects of how human beings treat one another, how they act, and what they say to each other, may lose importance" (10). Radical intellectual relativism fosters ethical relativism.

In refusing to cooperate with Fudge and Scrimgeour, Harry objects to another kind of lie, the lie by omission, the Ministry's history of ignoring the truth about Voldemort and insisting that Harry do the same. Lies of omission seem almost as innocent as social lies when, in *Prisoner of Azkaban*, Molly Weasley attempts to withhold the supposed fact that Sirius Black wants to kill Harry and when she later tries to exclude the young people from the Order of the Phoenix's plans. Ironically, one of Dumbledore's strongest comments about Truth covers a lie of omission. When Harry, in typical Harry fashion, says at the end of *Sorcerer's Stone*, "Sir, there are some other things I'd like to know, if you can tell me . . . things I want to know the truth about . . ." Dumbledore's response is evasive—more evasive than is apparent to a first-time reader: "'The truth.' Dumbledore sighed. 'It is a beautiful and terrible thing, and should therefore be treated with great caution. However, I shall answer your questions unless I have a very good reason not to, in which case I beg you'll forgive me. I shall not, of course, lie'" (SS 298). We later learn that this is the first of several occasions when Dumbledore, while not lying directly, does lie by omission, neglecting to inform Harry why Voldemort attacked him—the prophecy, the nature of whose truth is debatable. Dumbledore's "very good reason not to" provide complete information, much like Molly's, is his desire to protect Harry. Ironically, of course, concealing the truth has precisely the opposite effect. Dumbledore finally admits that "I cared more for your happiness than your knowing the truth, more for your peace of mind than my plan, more for your life than the lives that might be lost if the plan failed" (OP 838), and of course the result of Harry's incomplete information is Sirius's death, among several other unhappy consequences. Withholding important, though painful, truths from young people, these examples suggest, does more harm than good, no matter how good the intentions.

"There will be no need to talk."

So says Dolores Umbridge to fifth-year students at the beginning of her first Defense Against the Dark Arts class and again in the second class (OP 240, 316). Thereafter, Umbridge punishes Harry for insisting that Voldemort murdered Cedric; and, in the second class, she refuses to acknowledge students' questions, taking five points from Gryffindor for Hermione's "disrupting my class with pointless interruptions" (her opinions about the textbook) (317). Fundamental to Umbridge's assault on truth are both lies by omission and silencing of others, evidence—if we needed it—of her authoritarianism. As Carol Gilligan and David A .J. Richards point out, "Constitutional Democracy has at its core a normative conception of respect for ... voices speaking from personal conviction." Unfortunately, they say, openness to hearing others' voices is fundamentally "in tension with a patriarchal conception of authority" (240). Censorship is endemic to authoritarianism: autocrats need to regulate all information, which means both shaping the state's message and stifling competing ideas. In turn, resistance to patriarchal authority is based on hearing these different voices, especially voices of care.

Within hours of the publication of Harry's interview in *The Quibbler*, Umbridge issues Educational Decree Number Twenty-Seven: "Any student found in possession of the magazine *The Quibbler* will be expelled" (OP 581). Furthermore, "The teachers were, of course, forbidden from mentioning the interview by Educational Decree Number Twenty-six" (582), instituted following the Death Eaters' escape from Azkaban: "Teachers are hereby banned from giving students any information that is not strictly related to the subjects they are paid to teach" (551). So students are forbidden from getting accurate information about real-world subjects from either professors or independent reading. However, as Hermione exultingly observes, censorship tends to backfire: "If [Umbridge] could have done one thing to make absolutely sure that every single person in this school will read your interview, it was banning it!" (OP 582). Students whisper among themselves about the story and teachers covertly express approval. The issue sells out and goes into extra editions. The sheer act of accessing and sharing censored information constitutes resistance and fosters further resistance, a phenomenon reminiscent of samizdat in Soviet bloc countries.[7]

Because attending to all voices is so important, it is deeply troubling that when Harry inherits Kreacher, his first command is "Kreacher, shut up!" which renders Kreacher completely, angrily mute (HBP 52). But it is equally significant that although Kreacher recounts the story of the deposit and retrieval of Slytherin's locket from the Horcrux cave because Harry orders him to do so, Harry wins Kreacher's loyalty by listening politely and with growing compassion. Harry's listening and treating Kreacher as "a being with feelings as acute as a human's" (OP 832) change Kreacher's attitude toward Harry from contempt to devotion. Harry need no longer tell him to "shut up" or forbid him from calling Hermione a "Mudblood." Listening to others' voices is not only the right thing to do; it is the expedient thing and contributes to the resistance.

Probably Fudge believes silencing the truth about Voldemort's return benefits the Ministry—or at least Fudge's career—and will serve the magical community as well. Lies—whether overt lies or lies of omission—told with the justification that they benefit the public good have come to be called "blue lies," a term originating in lies told by police to protect other police or to support a case against an alleged criminal, but now applied to any lie justified as benefiting the collective. The Ministry's "Office of Misinformation" (HBP13) ostensibly safeguards the wizarding world by maintaining the Statute of Secrecy—a classic blue lie that "protects" one community while excluding another. It's a short step from modifying Muggle memories to manipulating information for the magical community. At the core of the Ministry's mission is "protection" from discovery by Muggles, who, ironically, are considered inferior to witches and wizards. One could reasonably ask what, then, makes Muggles so dangerous. Bok has described lies told by authorities for "the public good" as "the most dangerous body of deceit of all" (166). The lies authorities tell represent one of the greater evils in *Harry Potter* beginning with the Dursleys' lie to Harry about his parents' death and escalating with Rita's lies and Ministry propaganda in the *Daily Prophet*; they become literally painful when Harry starts carving "I must not tell lies" into his hand as punishment, ironically, for telling the truth.

Constructivism and the Potterverse's Big Lie

A constructivist approach to truth underlies government propaganda: truth becomes what those in power determine it to be. Most critics agree that the magical world's idea of pure-blood superiority echoes Nazi Germany's myth of Aryan superiority and the Jewish threat, the big lie that inspired Hitler's famous contention that people will more easily fall victim to a big lie than to a small one. Hitler's Minister of Propaganda, Joseph Goebbels, is widely—though probably falsely—credited with saying:

> If you tell a lie big enough and keep repeating it, people will eventually come to believe it. The lie can be maintained only for such time as the State can shield the people from the political, economic and/or military consequences of the lie. It thus becomes vitally important for the State to use all of its powers to repress dissent, for the truth is the mortal enemy of the lie, and thus by extension, the truth is the greatest enemy of the State.[8]

Whether Goebbels said it or not, it is an apt description of how propaganda works. While the lies about Voldemort's return and Harry's and Dumbledore's unreliability are smaller than the broad social lies about pure-blood superiority, the same principle applies to both: repeat the lie often enough and people believe it, hence the constantly repeated jibes about Harry's instability. In her study of strongman leaders, Ruth Ben-Ghiat describes propaganda as "a set of communication strategies designed to sow confusion and uncertainty, discourage critical thinking, and persuade people that reality is what the leader says it is" (93). This description perfectly matches what Tracy Bealer describes as the Ministry's "carefully manufactured reality" ("(Dis)Order" 177). The supposed reality that Fudge, the Ministry, and Umbridge wish to reinforce throughout Harry's fifth year is that Voldemort has not, in fact, returned and that Cedric's death was a "tragic accident" (OP 245). Their success is illustrated by skepticism toward Harry even by his friend Seamus Finnegan—who thinks he's a "nutter"—not to mention most of the other Hogwarts students, Seamus's mother, and much of the public. Fudge and Umbridge put great effort into repeating the lie and repressing dissent.

By contrast, when Rita interviews Harry, Hermione insists Rita tell "The true story. All the facts" (OP 567). Hermione's demand assumes a correspondence position: that truth exists, can be objectively assessed—and should be shared. When Umbridge forces Harry to carve "I must not tell lies" into his hand, she is, ironically, attempting to force him to lie. If he shuts up about Voldemort's return, he will be lying by omission. And he rejects Scrimgeour's selecting for "Truth" what is most convenient to the Ministry and omitting the rest. Pharr observes that Umbridge "magically carves the boy's most obvious flaw—the ease with which he lies—onto the back of his right hand" (16). But Harry is the hero of the series because he is committed to truth that is not based on the wizarding world's social constructs, as reinforced by wizarding leadership. Harry's truth in this instance is what *corresponds* to fact. Indeed, Kathryn N. McDaniel speculates that Harry's carving "I must not tell lies" into his hand "actually helps to 'entrench' him into his truth-telling position. It's literally become his *brand*" ("Mischief").

Mostly, Harry doesn't just talk about truth; he seeks it. For direct statements about truth, we must—as is often the case—turn to Dumbledore. Dumbledore says the Mirror of Erised "will give us neither knowledge or truth. Men have wasted away before it, entranced by what they have seen, or been driven mad, not knowing if what it shows is real or even possible" (SS 213). In short, the truth is not what we want it to be but what is "real." At the end of *Prisoner of Azkaban*, Dumbledore assures Harry that his actions "made all the difference in the world, Harry. You helped uncover the truth. You saved an innocent man from a terrible fate" (PA 425). The truth in this case is Sirius's innocence, though the Ministry continues to broadcast his "guilt" because it fits their preferred narrative. At the end of *Goblet of Fire*, upon learning of Voldemort's return, Dumbledore's first action is to disseminate the truth and to insist that Snape and Sirius cooperate with one another because "unless the few of us who know the truth stand united, there is no hope for any of us" (GF 712). Then, at the end-of-year feast, he honors Cedric and announces Voldemort's return to the school, this time explicitly rejecting lies of omission and acknowledging,

> The Ministry of Magic ... does not wish me to tell you this. It is possible that some of your parents will be horrified that I have done so—either because they will not believe that Lord Voldemort has returned, or because they think I should not tell you so, young as you are. It is my belief, however, that the truth is generally preferable to lies, and that any attempt to pretend that Cedric died as the result of an accident, or some sort of blunder of his own, is an insult to his memory.
>
> (GF 722)

For truth to be preferable to lies, for it to be something on which to base actions, there must *be* truth, and even—or perhaps especially—the young should hear it. Ironically, even as Dumbledore argues for trusting young people with the truth, he is still concealing the prophecy from Harry. Nevertheless, his speech is the perfect foil to Umbridge's beginning-of-term address in the next novel and the constructivist approach she will embrace.

Truth-Telling as Resistance to Propaganda: *Prophets* and *Quibblers*

Assaults on truth are among the most serious forms of oppression carried out by the Ministry, abetted by the *Daily Prophet*. Inadvertently at first and later directly, the *Prophet*'s assault on truth facilitates Voldemort's worst schemes, such as the oppression of Muggle-borns. Harry's resistance to "fake news" (not, of course, Rowling's term) constitutes one of his most important rebellions, despite being lower key than the resistance that culminates in his duel-to-the-death with Voldemort.

In *Harry Potter*, journalism, mainly the *Daily Prophet*, functions in several ways. Both Harry and Hermione subscribe to the *Prophet*, whose reports are frequently offered "straight," for plot exposition. From *Prophet* stories we learn about an attempted theft from vault seven hundred thirteen; the *Prophet* reports that Muggles spotted a flying Ford Anglia; that Scrimgeour has become the new Minister of Magic; and that Snape is the new Hogwarts Headmaster. The accurate headlines and reports demonstrate that responsible, factual journalism is crucial for an informed citizenry.

In a free society, we expect journalists to maintain a skeptical, even adversarial relationship with the government, not simply to relay press releases but to challenge government statements and investigate government actions. Early on, the *Prophet* seems to meet that expectation, for we first encounter it as Hagrid reads it en route to Diagon Alley and remarks, "Ministry o' Magic messin' things up as usual" (SS 64). When Sirius and Buckbeak escape, Fudge sighs, "The *Daily Prophet's* going to have a field day!" (PA 420), and the report on the riot at the World Cup with its references to "Ministry blunders" inspires Percy's complaint that Rita Skeeter has "got it in for the Ministry of Magic" (GF 147). Adversarial Rita certainly is, but not necessarily accurate, as illustrated by her report of Mr. Weasley's statements at the World Cup. One reporter's practice does not necessarily reflect editorial policy, as other examples indicate that the *Prophet* prints what the Ministry wants people to read. Early in *Prisoner of Azkaban*, Mr. Weasley remarks, "I don't care what Fudge keeps telling the *Daily Prophet*, we're no nearer catching Black than inventing self-spelling wands" (65), one of the first indications of Ministry press manipulation. Subsequently, the *Prophet*'s original account of Sirius's crime and capture is revealed to be inaccurate, undermining the reader's trust in the paper. That skepticism is only strengthened by Fudge's comment, "This whole Black affair has been highly embarrassing. I can't tell you how much I'm looking forward to informing the *Daily Prophet* that we've got him at last" (PA 416–17). Fudge judges the *Prophet*'s reporting exclusively by how it reflects upon him; he has no interest in hearing about Sirius's innocence.

The *Daily Prophet*'s credibility is completely undermined after Harry meets Rita and her Quick-Quotes Quill. Rita's story that is ostensibly about the Triwizard champions instead is "all about Harry, the names of the Beauxbatons and Durmstrang champions (misspelled) had been squashed into the last line of the article, and Cedric hadn't been mentioned at all" (GF 314). If a journalist's first responsibility is accuracy, Rita obviously fails, as illustrated by her rumor-mongering about the World Cup and then her patently fabricated reporting on Harry and intentionally hostile portraits of Hagrid and Hermione. In *Goblet of Fire*, the political flaws of mainstream journalism are satirized less than are the dangers of tabloid-style gossip, for Rita is depicted as more interested in self-promotion (*"writes Rita Skeeter, Special Correspondent"*) and focuses more on Harry's (fabricated) tears about his parents than the competition. She supplies "human interest" stories for *Witch Weekly*, a parody of Muggle "women's magazines," illustrating how readily journalism can be perverted for profit and entertainment. Rita selects stories based on whether there's a "market for a story like that" (OP 567), not newsworthiness. Eagerly matching "the public mood," she routinely identifies Hermione as "Muggle-born" and traffics in negative stereotypes of giants and werewolves. Although no one avoids personal biases, and true objectivity may be elusive if not impossible, Rita's reporting supports her personal vendettas. There's a good reason people are repeatedly warned "not to annoy Rita Skeeter" (GF 542).

Harry also learns the hazards of annoying the Ministry, as the *Prophet*, never inclined to fact-check Ministry statements, increasingly becomes its mouthpiece. When Hermione proposes that Rita interview Harry about Voldemort's return, Rita refuses: the *Prophet* won't run the story because "Fudge is leaning on the *Prophet*," or as Hermione says more baldly, "the *Prophet* won't print it because Fudge won't let them" (OP 567). Instead, the *Prophet*, controlled by the Ministry, engages in what political sociologists Davita Silfen Glasberg and Deric Shannon describe as "soft repression," meaning social controls such as state surveillance or "public ridicule and stigmatization" of insurgents (160). At first, after Harry and Dumbledore announce Voldemort's return, "hard repression" of organized resistance, such as physical reprisals, would backfire. Two years later, of course, Umbridge identifies Harry as "to be punished" (DH 252), but in the early days, the *Prophet*, the Ministry's surrogate, launches snide innuendoes about Harry as an unbalanced attention seeker and Dumbledore as senile. A responsible newspaper would distinguish opinion from facts, pursue evidence, seek multiple perspectives, verify information from multiple sources—and identify sources as much as possible. It would also acknowledge reporting errors when they occur. The *Prophet* does none of these things. Rather, it becomes essentially an arm of state media.

As Snyder has observed, lack of a variety of news sources is an invitation to tyranny ("Deathly"). The *Prophet* seems at first to be British magical culture's only news source, supplemented by apparently trashy publications like *Witch Weekly* and *The Quibbler*. As John S. Nelson observes, Harry starts depending on Muggle news when the *Prophet* proves inadequate (19). Initially, *The Quibbler* is a joke, with its "revelation" that Sirius is the lead singer for a wizard rock band and its obsession with Crumple-Horned Snorkacks. In contrast to a "prophecy," a "quibble" is a minor disagreement over something trivial. Nevertheless, the magazine's default position of "quibbling" at least identifies it as disagreeing, and although its "scoops" are absurd, at least *The Quibbler* recognizes Fudge as a threat—albeit for the wrong reasons. As Luna explains, "my father is *very* supportive of any anti-Ministry action! ... He's always saying he'd believe anything of Fudge, I mean, the number of goblins Fudge has had assassinated! And of course he uses the Department of Mysteries to develop terrible poisons, which he feeds secretly to anybody who disagrees with him" (OP 395). Xenophilius Lovegood could benefit as much as Rita from rigorous fact-checking, but he's skeptical of Ministry pronouncements, and his motives at any rate are not financial: "He publishes important stories that he thinks the public needs to know. He doesn't care about making money" (CP 568), unlike the *Prophet* (or *Profit?*), which "exists to sell itself" (567).

In the quotation attributed to Goebbels, the truth is described as "the mortal enemy of the lie, and thus by extension, the truth is the greatest enemy of the State." Thus, it is appropriate that Harry's interview describing Voldemort's return, which Hermione insists Rita reproduce verbatim, not with the usual "Quick-Quote" flourishes, offers what the *Prophet*, under Ministry control, has blocked: an unvarnished account that corresponds to reality. Ironically, that issue of *The Quibbler* sells more copies than any previous issue, and Xenophilius eventually sells the story to the *Prophet* for reprinting—after its veracity is undeniable. In the meantime, Harry's fan mail illustrates how fully truth is the "mortal enemy of the lie." Though some readers remain skeptical, Harry receives letters like this: "Having read your side of the story ... I am forced to accept that you are telling the truth" (OP 579–80), and Umbridge's censorship renders the interview the most popular item at school. Harry's story, because it is in fact true, conquers the falsehoods and lies of omission spread by the Ministry. Suppression of truth loses again.

After Voldemort's silent coup topples Ministry leadership, the propaganda machine operates in multiple media: the Ministry's new sculpture depicting wizard domination; Alecto Carrow teaching Muggle Studies at Hogwarts; Umbridge's pamphlets about "MUDBLOODS and the Dangers They Pose to a Peaceful Pure-Blood Society"; posters of Harry as "Undesirable Number One"; and front-page stories in the *Prophet* claiming that Muggle-borns have stolen magic and announcing that Harry is wanted for questioning in Dumbledore's death. Each is designed to foster confusion and shape people's sense of what is true, to forward Voldemort's ideology. But the Ministry no longer provides the only messages: they are challenged by *Potterwatch* and *The Quibbler*. Ron describes *Potterwatch* as "the only [radio program] that tells the truth about what's going on! Nearly all the programs are following You-Know-Who's line, all except *Potterwatch*" (DH 437). Part of *Potterwatch*'s mission is to provide actual news, such as a summary of what has happened to allies like Hagrid and Xenophilius Lovegood; a "report [on] those deaths that the *Wizarding Wireless Network News* and *Daily Prophet* don't think important enough to mention"—including Muggle deaths (DH 439)—and information on how "the new Wizarding order" affects Muggles and how magic folk can protect their Muggle neighbors. *Potterwatch* also features editorial commentaries to counter anti-Muggle propaganda. These include Kingsley's advice that "it's one short step from 'Wizards first' to 'Purebloods first,' and then to 'Death Eaters' ... We're all human, aren't we? Every human life is worth the same, and worth saving" (DH 440). And Lupin's bracing words of encouragement, in response to being asked whether he thinks Harry is still alive: "'I do,' said Lupin firmly. 'There is no doubt at all in my mind that his death would be proclaimed as widely as possible by the Death Eaters if it had happened, because it would strike a deadly blow at the morale of those resisting the new regime. "The Boy Who Lived" remains a symbol of everything for which we are fighting: the triumph of good, the power of innocence, the need to keep resisting'" (DH 441). Lupin both challenges Ministry propaganda and explicitly advocates continued resistance.

The Quibbler, too, advocates resistance: "Xeno says, front page of every issue, that any wizard who's against You-Know-Who ought to make helping Harry Potter their number-one priority" (300). *The Quibbler*, like *Potterwatch*, now provides reliable reporting that undermines the state media's propaganda. When Dirk Cresswell doubts Harry, based on *Prophet*'s "pretty good case against him," Ted Tonks retorts, "The *Prophet*? ... You deserve to be lied to if you're still reading that muck, Dirk. You want the facts, try the *Quibbler*. ... Xeno is printing all the stuff the *Prophet's* ignoring" (299). Unfortunately, in classic authoritarian style, Voldemort's Ministry silences Xenophilius by taking Luna hostage. Nevertheless, *Potterwatch* and *The Quibbler* exemplify the power of an independent, adversarial press.

Magical Culture's Big Lie

In the weeks and months following the 2020 U.S. election, the phrase "The Big Lie" came to refer to repeated claims that Donald Trump won the election, that his victory was stolen from him by voter fraud in Democratic cities—not incidentally heavily populated by people of color. Trump's Big Lie motivated and inspired the January 6, 2021, insurrection at the U.S. Capitol Building, aimed at overturning the election. The phrase "The Big Lie" was consciously adopted from Hitler's and (supposedly) Goebbel's remarks that if you tell a lie big enough and often enough, people will readily believe it. Hitler's original big lie was that Jews' lies caused Germany's loss of the Great War; it became Hitler's own assertion that "international Jewry" were the source of all of Germany's and Europe's problems, thus justifying their extermination. Similarly, wizarding culture's big lie claims the intrinsic superiority of magical humans over other magical beings such as house-elves, centaurs, goblins, and merpeople; as well as the superiority of "pure-blood" wizards over those of mixed blood, and the superiority of both over Muggle-born wizards, Squibs, and Muggles.

As Dumbledore says at the end of *Order of the Phoenix*, "The fountain we destroyed tonight told a lie. We wizards have mistreated and abused our fellows for too long, and we are now reaping our reward" (834). Dumbledore is referring to the golden "Fountain of Magical Brethren," depicting a house-elf, centaur, and goblin, "all looking adoringly up at the witch and wizard" (OP 127). The statue implies not only wizard superiority but that other magical beings prefer subordination. Almost from the first, Harry recognizes and resists the fountain's lie: "from what Harry knew of goblins and centaurs, they were most unlikely to be caught staring this soppily at humans of any description. Only the house-elf's attitude of creeping servility looked convincing" (OP 156). As art, that is, the fountain fails the mimesis test: it does not correspond accurately to the truth Harry has observed. However, it effectively conveys its intended message. The fountain's location, in the Ministry lobby, conveys what philosopher F. G. Bailey calls a "basic hegemonic lie," a lie reflecting a culture's dominant ideology (122). The fountain communicates wizard superiority, albeit euphemistically. After the Fountain's destruction, the Ministry, under Voldemort's control, replaces it with the statue "Magic is Might." Nothing subtle about that title, or the statue itself:

> Now a gigantic statue of black stone dominated the scene. It was rather frightening, this vast sculpture of a witch and a wizard sitting on ornately carved thrones
>
> ...
>
> Harry looked more closely and realized that what he had thought were decoratively carved thrones were actually mounds of carved humans: hundreds and hundreds of naked bodies, men, women, and children, all with rather stupid, ugly faces, twisted and pressed together to support the weight of the handsomely robed wizards.
> "Muggles," whispered Hermione. "In their rightful place."
>
> (DH 241–2)

These statues, no less than the *Prophet*'s reporting, are propaganda, communicating Muggles' supposed inferiority and turning them into objects of disgust. The lies conveyed by the Ministry—as by any government—frequently surpass simple untruths about the sanity or worth of opponents, and they may be conveyed without words. The Voldemort-controlled Ministry uses the big lie of pure-blood superiority to justify murdering Muggles and imprisoning Muggle-borns. This big lie no more began with Voldemort than the lie about Jews began with Hitler. It is, as Bailey says, a "basic hegemonic lie" that has permeated magical culture for centuries. The statues are less art than propaganda. Rowling's commentary on more uplifting art is, as we shall see, more subtle.

"Is this real?"

The issue of truth reaches its greatest complexity and ambiguity in the series' final pages. Throughout the seven books, things that have seemed true very often are not, and the truth is often belied by false appearances: Quirrell, not Snape, plots against Harry; Sirius is innocent, and Scabbers is an Animagus; Mad-Eye Moody is really Barty Crouch, and so on. And yet, just when we think we finally have the truth sorted out, we're confronted with the dialogue between Harry and Dumbledore at King's Cross Station. Toward the end of his near-death experience, Harry asks Dumbledore, "Is this real? Or has this been happening inside my head?" Dumbledore replies, "Of course it is happening inside your head, Harry, but why on earth should that mean that it is not real?" (DH 723). In a 2008 interview, Rowling said, "That dialogue is the key; I've waited seventeen years to use those lines" ("To Be Invisible").

"That dialogue is the key"—to what? A reasonable theory, since the scene depicts a near-death experience, is that it suggests there are spiritual truths beyond our day-to-day comprehension. The scene shares traits with reports of actual near-death experiences, but it offers no physiological or psychological explanation, only Dumbledore's theory about the power of Lily's blood, which might be considered a theological idea. John Granger's interpretation, in *Harry Potter's Bookshelf*, is that "Is this real?" refers to the "agonizing postmodern dilemma," namely, "Is it just the deluded product or projection of my prejudices and assorted mental filters?" (136). Granger reads the scene in the context of Harry's other choices to believe, in *Deathly Hallows*: the scene confirms Rowling's comment that the series' final book reflects her "struggling with religious belief" in the face of postmodern relativism (qtd. in Granger, 133). There seems some truth to that theory. In any case, Harry's experience, we are assured, is real, but it remains mysterious. Of course, the scene can remain real and not "deluded" even if it is a "projection" of Harry's psyche. After all, as Tolonda Henderson shows in "Harry Potter and the Management of Trauma," everything Harry "learns" in the scene is something he either knows already or could have deduced from the information he possesses. It "really" helps him cope with his situation and work through his questions about it.

Perhaps we should read the dialogue as "meta," commenting on the fact that in the mysterious process that is "reading," the scene takes place entirely within the head of the person whose eyes scan the pages and convert black marks into words and images. Within the fictional world of *Harry Potter and the Deathly Hallows*, the "real world" is an invented school named Hogwarts that trains witches and wizards, whose gifts are only "real" within the book's pages—and its readers' minds. King's Cross Station, unlike Hogwarts, is real, but Platform 9 ¾, where, presumably, the scene unfolds, is entirely fictional. Most witches and wizards believe the "Tale of the Three Brothers" is pure fiction. However, like the legend of the Chamber of Secrets, it turns out to "have a basis in fact" (CS 149)—to the extent anything in the Potterverse is "fact"—and the "historical" Peverell brothers were the story's three brothers. But, as Dumbledore speculates, "Whether they met Death on a lonely road . . . I think it more likely that the Peverell brothers were simply gifted, dangerous wizards who succeeded in creating those powerful objects. The story of them being Death's own Hallows seems to me the sort of legend that might have sprung up around such creations" (DH 714). Like much of what we know of ancient history that was originally transmitted orally, the "facts" are mixed up with cultural commentary, and in that regard, Ron is correct that "that story's just one of those things you tell kids to teach them lessons, isn't it? 'Don't go looking for trouble, don't pick fights, don't go messing around with stuff that's best left alone! Just keep your head down, mind your own business, and you'll be okay'" (DH 414).

Thus Dumbledore's observation, "Of course it is happening inside your head, but why on earth should that mean that it is not real?" invokes the "realness" of literature in the sense that Aristotle asserted that poetry (literature generally) is more "philosophical" than history, because rather than merely recording what has happened, poetry represents what *could* happen; history deals with particulars, while poetry deals with universals (*Poetics* 9.1451b5–8). Yet fiction, like lying, is something the teller knows is not true. And so does the reader. We open *Harry Potter and the Sorcerer's Stone* sharing the author's understanding that the story did not, in fact, happen and none of these people exist. As Samuel Taylor Coleridge explains in *Biographia Literaria*, readers encountering fictional characters "transfer from our inward nature a human interest and a semblance of truth sufficient to procure for these shadows of the imagination that willing suspension of disbelief for the moment which constitutes poetic faith." Having suspended our disbelief, we cry when Sirius dies, when Dumbledore dies, when Dobby dies. These "lies" feel painfully real.

However readily Voldemort lies, he cannot grasp the powers of fiction: "That which Voldemort does not value, he takes no trouble to comprehend. Of houseelves and children's tales, of love, loyalty, and innocence, Voldemort knows and understands nothing. *Nothing.* That they all have a power beyond his own, a power beyond the reach of any magic, is a truth he has never grasped" (DH 709–10). What is that "power beyond the reach of any magic" that fiction possesses? A widely cited study by Loris Vezzali and his collaborators strongly suggests that "the greatest magic of Harry Potter" is that its readers exhibit less prejudice against stigmatized out-groups than do non-Potter fans. *Harry Potter* readers reject Voldemort's big lie, his bigoted ideology, in favor of Harry's compassion and tolerance. Reading makes us more compassionate and accepting. It undermines the big lie that some people are superior to others.

The series' lessons about lying and truth are more ambiguous. Surely it endorses Harry's position that truth does exist, and that what is true is not merely what the powerful decide it is. Nevertheless, sorting truth from lies is rarely simple. The truth, as Dumbledore observes, "is a beautiful and terrible thing, and should therefore be treated with great caution" (SS 298). Despite the difficulties of sorting out truth and lies, one must insist upon the truth but, in a pinch, equivocate or even lie to protect one's cause or people in need of care.

Notes

1 Ironically, no one can locate where Orwell says this, suggesting that the attribution itself is untrue (O'Toole).
2 My discussion has been shaped by Sissela Bok's analysis in *Lying: Moral Choice in Public and Private Life* and J. A. Barnes's in *A Pack of Lies: A Sociology of Lying*.
3 Umbridge's profile in *Wizarding World* states that her father worked in the Magical Maintenance department, and her mother was a Muggle ("Dolores Umbridge"). To bolster her power and prestige by concealing an "inferior" connection, she paid her father to retire early from the Ministry, and she never saw her mother and Squib brother after the family split when she was in her teens.
4 Why doesn't Voldemort detect this lie with Legilimency? Presumably because he arrogantly assumes his curse, employing the "Deathstick," is infallible.
5 See, for example, Griesinger and Wood. For Griesinger, Harry Potter, as fantasy, answers the cynicism and skepticism of postmodernism with hope for a better, more meaningful future.
6 Diana Mertz Hsieh discusses the damage done by self-deception, focusing primarily on the Dursleys but touching on Fudge's self-deception and also exploring the ways the series depicts honesty as advantageous.
7 I am grateful to Kathryn N. McDaniel for reminding me of this parallel ("Mischief").
8 Regarding the false attribution to Goebbels, see Schultze and Bytwerk.

EPILOGUE

"Mischief Managed"?

In the Epilogue to *Harry Potter*, as Harry's son Albus boards the Hogwarts Express for the first time, now-wife Ginny reassures Harry that "He'll be all right." Harry, "absentmindedly" touching his scar, responds, "I know he will." The series concludes, "The scar had not pained Harry for nineteen years. All was well" (DH 759).

"All was well."

Yes.

And no.

Voldemort, this narrative reassures us, is gone for good—or at least the Horcrux is. Draco Malfoy and Harry can interact civilly, if coolly. According to Rowling, in interviews, Ministry corruption has been eliminated by Minister of Magic Kingsley Shacklebolt, while Harry and Hermione lead important Ministry departments. If the scenario imagined in *Harry Potter and the Cursed Child* can be trusted, Harry's son, Dumbledore's namesake, will be sorted into Slytherin[1] and become best friends with Scorpius Malfoy, and Hermione is the Minister of Magic.

Is so much improvement possible?

The years between 2016 and 2020, when the bulk of this book was written, were marked by the rise of "the resistance" in the United States. With 2021's inauguration of a new President, many felt relief, that "All was well." But of course, problems remain, in our world as much as in Harry's. As Rowling said in her 2007 Carnegie Hall interview, "I wanted Harry to leave our world and find exactly the same problems in the wizarding world." In fact, he does. He finds bigotry, privilege, and discrimination. He finds a corrupt government, censorship, and a press that sometimes collaborates with the corrupt government. He finds patriarchal values, both in the narrow sense of sexism and in the broader sense of valorization of autocracy and suppression of democratic values, including care for others. Harry defeats Voldemort, but of course patriarchy remains, along with other problems shared by the wizarding and Muggle worlds. The defeat, however satisfying, of one charismatic leader, goes only so far, if underlying ideologies remain intact. Indeed, blaming a single individual for the evils of his regime may even strengthen the fundamental social problems that brought him to power in the first place. Better individual leaders only go so far if the system is weak.

The Epilogue to Harry Potter leaves a lot of loose ends, for not even 4100 pages can cover everything; and six pages—or nineteen years—can hardly solve every lingering issue. This epilogue, too, will leave some loose ends, but it offers a few final thoughts.

The Unresolved-House-Elf Dilemma

One of the biggest criticisms levied against the series' ending is that the problem of house-elf enslavement remains unresolved.[2] Indeed, although the last line of the epigraph is "All was well," the final line of the final true chapter has Harry "thinking now only of the four-poster bed lying waiting for him in Gryffindor Tower, and wondering whether Kreacher might bring him a sandwich there" (DH 749). Has Harry learned nothing? Perhaps the fact that he "wonders" if Kreacher "might" bring the sandwich suggests some uncertainty. Perhaps not. The series' epilogue, not unlike *Hogwarts: A History*, is completely silent about house-elf rights.

This lack of resolution is consistent with the series' depiction of systemic cultural flaws of all sorts. To quote Sirius Black one final time: "The world isn't split into good people and Death Eaters" (OP 302). Like the best fantasy worlds, the Potterverse functions as a commentary on the real ("Muggle") world, and thus, like our own, it is a flawed culture with deeply embedded social evils, many of which are discussed in this book. House-elf enslavement—as well as discrimination against other sentient beings like goblins, centaurs, and merpeople—is symptomatic of flaws so deeply embedded in the culture that even the most likable characters, like Hagrid, the Weasley family, and Harry himself at the end of the series, fail to question them. Dumbledore wisely observes that Kreacher's betrayal of Sirius illustrates that "We wizards have mistreated and abused our fellows for too long, and we are now reaping our reward" (OP 834). Yet while Dumbledore does not mistreat the Hogwarts house-elves, his melioristic kindness does nothing to eliminate the fundamental moral evil of their enslavement. So long as it continues, wizards will continue to reap what they sow.

Brycchan Carey, Meredith Cherland, Rachel McCarthy James, and Farah Mendlesohn, among others, criticize Hermione's efforts to assist the house-elves as condescending, manipulative, and "irrational" (Cherland 275, Mendlesohn 306) and observe that she denies the house-elves agency.[3] Yes, Hermione's methods in S.P.E.W. are insensitive and ineffective, but at least she's trying, and she learns from her mistakes. As Rowling said after the publication of *Goblet of Fire*, Hermione's activism was a depiction of a "growing process, of realizing you don't have quite as much power as you think you might have and having to accept that. Then you learn that it's hard work to change things and that it doesn't happen overnight. Hermione thinks she's going to lead them to glorious rebellion in one afternoon and then finds out the reality is very different" (Interview with Evan Solomon).

If, as Rowling has asserted, Hermione later works in the Department for the Regulation and Control of Magical Creatures (followed by becoming Minister of Magic), it seems plausible that, having grown more realistic, she will indeed be "instrumental in greatly improving life for house-elves and their ilk" ("J.K. Rowling Web Chat"). Considering how Hermione interacts with Kreacher, we can be reasonably confident that house-elves' opinions will be respected in that process. They will no longer be "shockingly underrepresented" (GF 225). Privilege, moreover, partly entails assuming that one's own value systems are "normal" and the only ones that count. Perhaps, magical humans will learn from house-elves' capacity for love. Carey (2009) rightly points out that "improving" house-elves lives is not "emancipation" (171); nevertheless, that Ron and (to a much lesser extent) Harry can have their consciousness raised regarding house-elves is a small step in the right direction, and Hermione's plans could make even more difference. Perhaps, too, Travis Prinzi is right in speculating that Dobby's sacrifice to save Harry Potter will become legendary among house-elves—"a rallying point and an inspiration for future house-elf liberation movements" (256). However, to suggest that house-elf liberation should come primarily from house-elves themselves is to overlook the fact that house-elf oppression is a systemic problem in which wizards hold the power. Wizard privilege is a wizard problem. And power structures that rest on unpaid and largely unnoticed care work will continue to reinforce other unjust power relations based on gender, race (however defined), class, and magical ability.

By the same token, magical culture, like our own, suffers when it fails to appreciate the unique powers of house-elves, not to mention those of centaurs, goblins, and other magical beings. It is weakened by pure-blood snobbery: consider the impact of inbreeding on the Gaunts. Wizarding ignorance of Muggle technology deprives them of useful inventions; more fundamentally, being stuck in a pre-Enlightenment intellectual and legal system, thanks to the Statute of Secrecy of 1689, fosters the social and political backwardness discussed in Chapter One, not only regarding slavery but also the scientific method and concepts of individual liberty, genuinely representative government, due process, feminism, or equality before the law. The disadvantages deriving from wizard ethnocentrism offer object lessons for privileged Muggles indifferent to cultures different from their own.

While defeating a single evil wizard—albeit an extremely powerful one—may be the work of seven school years, it is unreasonable to expect to cure in the same period, or even in several generations, an entrenched social ill that has endured for at least a millennium. That is part of the effectiveness of depicting a wizarding world no less flawed in its institutions than the Muggle world. Regarding sexism, racism, and other problems I have discussed in this book, the series encourages readers to "imagine better" and to resist injustice with the mysterious power of love. Apparently, it has somewhat succeeded. When Anthony Gierzynski and his team surveyed Millennials, they found that *Harry Potter* fans were less authoritarian than non-fans, more politically active and open to diversity, and less likely to support torture or violence. That Rowling has herself fallen short in imagination about transgender rights does not negate the power of her books' invitation to embrace others' differences and to question the status quo.

When Good Wizards Do Bad Things

In a provocative review of *Goblet of Fire*, Joan Acocella wondered how the later books would resolve "the question about power—is it reconcilable with goodness?" (78). Magic is obviously a form of power, and if there's one thing the series makes clear it's that magic can be used for both good and evil. In the end, Harry wields the "power that the Dark Lord knows not," explicitly choosing not to pursue the Elder Wand, the physical symbol of power as it is conventionally understood. Instead, he deploys what Gene Sharp would identify as the jiu-jitsu of nonviolent resistance, deflecting Voldemort's lethal power. But not every decision Harry makes is virtuous, nor are all the decisions made by his allies.

One could of course write a chapter or an entire book about ethics and Harry Potter—and several people have.[4] There is no need for me to duplicate their excellent work. Nevertheless, this seems a good place to reiterate that not all rule breaking in *Harry Potter* is virtuous and that sorting out the good from the bad is not necessarily easy. It is not enough to say, "Well, that rule was broken for the greater good." After all, the series effectively undermines that argument by putting it in Dumbledore's letter to Grindelwald:

> Your point about Wizard dominance being FOR THE MUGGLES' OWN GOOD—this, I think, is the crucial point. Yes, we have been given power and yes, that power gives us the right to rule, but it also gives us responsibilities over the ruled. We must stress this point, it will be the foundation stone upon which we build. Where we are opposed, as we surely will be, this must be the basis of all our counterarguments. We seize control FOR THE GREATER GOOD. And from this it follows that where we meet resistance, we must use only the force that is necessary and no more.
>
> (DH 357)

Significantly, the idea of domination "for the Muggles' own good" originated with Grindelwald, the series' other Hitler stand-in—and Dumbledore predicts there will be "resistance" to their plan. Even as a seventeen-year-old, Dumbledore mentions "responsibilities"—a word from the ethic of care. But his primary impulse at seventeen is fundamentally patriarchal, in the sense of anti-democratic. Despite his mild demurrals, young Albus uses "the greater good" as a pretext to "seize control." Dumbledore's dalliance with Grindelwald and his ideas about power led indirectly to Ariana Dumbledore's death and Albus's subsequent rejection of arguments for Muggle domination. As Hermione argues, he was relatively young, and he did change; the series emphasizes, through many of its major characters, that people are capable of learning and growing; and such changes matter.

However, those facts do not alter the reality that "For the Greater Good" became, says Hermione, "Grindelwald's slogan, his justification for all the atrocities he committed later. ... They say 'For the Greater Good' was even carved over the entrance to Nurmengard," the "prison Grindelwald had built to hold his opponents" (DH 360). It is a dangerous slogan, amounting to justifying any means so long as they lead to a supposedly virtuous goal. Dumbledore—or Harry's subconscious—in the King's Cross scene has no patience for his youthful rationalizing: "Oh, I had a few scruples. I assuaged my conscience with empty words. It would all be for the greater good, and any harm done would be repaid a hundredfold in benefits for wizards" (DH 716). Talk about acting "for the greater good," Dumbledore is saying, amounts to Orwellian doublethink, "empty words" designed not only to say the opposite of what one means but to convince oneself as well. And of course "benefits for wizards" means for a privileged minority, hardly the "greater good" in any real sense. As Timothy Snyder points out, "magical thinking," that is, accepting blatant contradictions, is a key step toward tyranny (*On Tyranny* 67).

For a time, Harry himself falls into acting as though the ends justify the means. At first, reading Dumbledore's letter disappoints and infuriates him, leading to a crisis of doubt that only dissipates as he is burying Dobby. Significantly, though, as he contemplates lying to Griphook about the sword of Gryffindor, he remembers the phrase "for the greater good," specifically in its place over the gates of Nurmengard—and then "He pushed the idea away. What choice did they have?" (DH 508). Denying the possibility of choice is always dangerous. Then, having manipulated Griphook with a lie by mental reservation, the group enters Gringotts, aided by Harry's successful deployment of the Unforgivable Imperius Curse on the goblin bank teller Bogrod and the Death Eater Travers. The episode is partly a study of the psychology of breaking ethical taboos for "the greater good." Before Harry casts the spell, the plot to retrieve the Horcrux is nearly foiled by Bogrod's suspicions; at Griphook's prodding, "Harry raised the hawthorn wand beneath the cloak, pointed it at the old goblin, and whispered, for the first time in his life, '*Imperio!*'" When, immediately afterward, Travers asks about "Bellatrix's" supposed "new wand," Harry finds using an Unforgivable Curse easier: "Harry acted without thinking: Pointing his wand at Travers, he muttered, '*Imperio!*' once more" (DH 531). Although Travers and Bogrod are "standing there looking blank," Harry doubts the curse's efficacy:

"I don't think I did it strongly enough, I don't know...."

And another memory darted through his mind, of the real Bellatrix Lestrange shrieking at him when he had first tried to use an Unforgivable Curse: "You need to *mean* them, Potter!"

(DH 533)

At this stage, readers may excuse Harry's behavior because it is necessary and because he himself seems torn—but he obviously does "mean" it. And Harry soon uses the curse yet a third time, after the trio's spells, including the Imperius Curse, are washed away by the waters of the Thief's Downfall. This time we see neither hesitation nor narrative comment about lack of hesitation: "'*Imperio!*' Harry said again; his voice echoed through the stone passage" (DH 535). Now, unquestionably, Harry does "really mean it." His cursing has evolved from tentativeness to near reflex and from a whispered command to an echoing shout—granted, partly because secrecy is no longer required. This decreasing discomfort with his actions illustrates the ease with which someone can adjust to carrying out illicit behavior.

The sequence also depicts the temptations of power. The first time, "A curious sensation shot down Harry's arm, a feeling of tingling warmth that seemed to flow from his mind, down the sinews and veins connecting him to the wand and the curse it had just cast" (DH 531). The "tingling warmth" suggests a distinctly pleasurable sensation deriving from the power, an impression reinforced the second time Harry Imperiuses Bogrod: "he felt again the sense of heady control that flowed from brain to wand" (DH 535). "Heady" tells us that the sensation is intoxicating, even exhilarating. Depriving another of free will is clearly evil, but the control it represents is seductively attractive—part of what makes it so dangerous.

Aaron Schwabach has observed that although Harry performs the Imperius Curse with "several unfriendly witnesses"—Bogrod, Travers, and Griphook—he eludes the supposedly mandatory Azkaban sentence. Possibly Harry benefits from privilege derived from his popularity—hardly unprecedented in the wizard world's distinctly flawed justice system—or possibly from a "necessity defense": he had to perform the curse to defeat Voldemort (Schwabach 73)—not that that argument had worked well when Harry defended Dudley with a Patronus. Harry's uses of the Imperius Curse are obvious examples of acting "for the greater good," of the ends justifying the means. Harry's making an evil person like Travers act in the interest of good is, to be sure, far better than Voldemort's and the Death Eaters' habit of forcing good people to do evil deeds. But while readers may get a kick out of Harry's use of the Cruciatus Curse against Amycus Carrow, when Amycus spits on McGonagall, was it necessary, for the greater good or otherwise? He could as easily have stunned Amycus. We should not overlook the flaws in Harry's decisions or the privilege that allows him to get away with them.

If we take the King's Cross scene as an extended interior dialogue, what Harry learns from "Dumbledore" about the harm done by "empty words" about the "greater good" is Harry's reckoning with his own values prior to his final showdown with Voldemort. To be sure, Harry has already shown himself capable of resisting the temptations of power by disposing of the Resurrection Stone, but it is after this scene—and the entire episode of symbolic death and rebirth—that Harry renounces the phallic Elder Wand. Most important, he avoids the most serious Unforgivable Curse, *Avada Kedavra*, by defeating Voldemort with *Expelliarmus*.

Harry's justification to Aberforth Dumbledore of some of Albus's more manipulative decisions speaks more to his own character than Dumbledore's: "sometimes you've *got* to think about more than your own safety! Sometimes you've *got* to think about the greater good! This is war!" (DH 568). Yes, this is war, which always complicates ethical questions, and in this conversation, Harry speaks to risking his own life, while Aberforth's point was that his brother frequently endangered the lives of others, notably Harry. Dumbledore, significantly, never dismisses his manipulation of Harry "for the greater good" as "empty words"—perhaps because those plans work. Is that justification enough? Justifying everything that "my side" does on the grounds of "the greater good" is dangerous, and indeed advocates of nonviolent resistance studies find it counterproductive.[5]

By the end of the series, few characters or actions are shown to be unequivocally or simply good or evil. Humans are depicted as complex, flawed creatures, and in some circumstances, no choice is purely good or purely bad. It remains true, however, that free choice—as opposed to blind obedience—is central to the *Harry Potter* series, as seen in Dumbledore's observation, "It is our choices, Harry, that show what we truly are, far more than our abilities" (CS 333). The various ways in which wizards control one another are all violations of this crucial emphasis on choice, and people often must choose between two bad options. Much of what maintains a serious reader's interest in the *Harry Potter* series is its nuance and complexity, its resistance of easy answers.

Part of Harry's maturation involves facing the reality that those he had admired—first his father and Sirius, and later Dumbledore and Lupin—were far from perfect. James and Sirius had been privileged and arrogant. They had bullied the impoverished and less popular Severus Snape and patronized Peter Pettigrew and to a lesser degree Remus Lupin. Lupin could have done more to rein them in; later, he nearly abandons his wife and child, though Harry helps him think better of that. Dumbledore dallied with the idea of Muggle domination and was at least partially responsible for his sister's death.

And Harry himself is far from perfect, which of course helps make him an interesting character. As Shira Wolosky has observed, the presence of a piece of Voldemort within Harry "is itself a figure of good and evil in human nature, a mixture not simply bounded by stark opposition" (*Riddles* 119). Even with the Horcrux excised, Harry remains human and flawed, as his continued willingness to exploit Kreacher exemplifies. While Harry's rule breaking, as I believe this book has shown, is generally one of his virtues, there are times when our experience of identifying with the "hero" perhaps lulls us into accepting too readily that he doesn't always make the best choices. The mature reader, like the maturing Harry, needs to grapple with ethical complexity in the magical resistance movement, as in life itself.

Historian Timothy Snyder, in his influential little book, *On Tyranny: Twenty Lessons from the Twentieth Century*, urges readers to surround themselves with books, among them, *Harry Potter and the Deathly Hallows*. Snyder, like me, believes the novel "offers an account of tyranny and resistance" and urges, "If you or your friends or your children did not read it that way the first time, then it bears reading again" (62–63). Of course, I fully agree. My own book has argued, at perhaps unconscionable length, precisely Snyder's point, exploring, in addition, the tyranny of unquestioned, oppressive social norms, which also must be resisted. If its thesis has surprised you, I hope it will inspire you to reread the series with resistance to tyranny in mind.

At the end of *Half-Blood Prince*, at Dumbledore's funeral, Harry remembers his mentor's advice: "he and Dumbledore had discussed fighting a losing battle … It was important, Dumbledore said, to fight, and fight again, and keep fighting, for only then could evil be kept at bay, though never quite eradicated" (644–45). Evil is never eradicated, but it can be resisted. So we must continue to resist, to fight threats of autocracy in our own culture. Or, to quote another of Harry's mentors—and a sign at the 2017 Women's March on Washington—we need constant vigilance.

Notes

1 John S. Nelson has noted with disappointment that Hogwarts has apparently failed to make much-needed reforms, including abolition of Slytherin House (278–79).
2 Among those faulting the lack of resolution of the house-elf problem are Lisa Anatol, Brycchan Carey, Peter Dendle, Megan Farnel, Alyssa Magee Lowery, Mary Pharr, and Aaron Schwabach.
3 Lauren Camacci has suggested that criticism of Hermione's house-elf activism requires assuming that she is white (comment during the Southwest Popular and American Culture Association conference, Albuquerque, NM, 22 February 2019).
4 See for example Edmund Kern's *The Wisdom of Harry Potter*, Moshe Rosenberg's *Morality for Muggles*, and the section on "Morality in Rowling's Universe" in Baggett and Klein's *Harry Potter and Philosophy*. Nearly every extensive study of the series almost necessarily touches on ethical questions. See my discussion in the Introduction.
5 See Gene Sharp, for example.

WORKS CITED

Abanes, Richard. *Harry Potter and the Bible*. Horizon Books, 2001.
Abrams, Ruth. "Of Marranos and Mudbloods: Harry Potter and the Spanish Inquisition." *Harry Potter and History*, edited by Nancy R. Reagin, John Wiley and Sons, 2011, pp. 219–41.
Acocella, Joan. "Under the Spell." Review of *Harry Potter and the Goblet of Fire*, by J. K. Rowling. *The New Yorker*, 31 July 2000, pp. 74–78.
Amnesty International. *Torture in the Eighties*. Amnesty International Publications, 1984.
Anatol, Giselle Liza. "The Fallen Empire: Exploring Ethnic Otherness in the World of Harry Potter." *Reading Harry Potter: Critical Essays*, edited by Giselle Liza Anatol, Praeger, 2003, pp. 163–78.
―――. Editor. *Reading Harry Potter: Critical Essays*. Praeger, 2003.
―――. "The Replication of Victorian Racial Ideology in Harry Potter." *Reading Harry Potter Again: New Critical Essays,* edited by Giselle Liza Anatol, Praeger, 2009, pp. 109–26.
Arendt, Hannah. *The Origins of Totalitarianism*. Penguin, 2017.
Baggett, David, and Shawn E. Klein, editors. *Harry Potter and Philosophy: If Aristotle Ran Hogwarts*. Open Court Publishing Company, 2004.
Bailey, F. G. *The Prevalence of Deceit*. Cornell UP, 1991.
Barnes, J. A. *A Pack of Lies: Towards a Sociology of Lying*. Cambridge UP, 1994.
Barratt, Bethany. *The Politics of Harry Potter*. Palgrave Macmillan, 2012.
Bealer, Tracy. "Consider the Dementor: Discipline, Punishment, and Magical Citizenship in Harry Potter." *Dialogue: The Interdisciplinary Journal of Popular Culture and Pedagogy*, vol. 6, no. 3, 2019, pp. 36–47. http://journaldialogue.org/issues/v6-issue-3/consider-the-dementor/.
―――. "(Dis)Order and the Phoenix: Love and Political Resistance in Harry Potter." *Reading Harry Potter Again: New Critical Essays,* edited by Giselle Liza Anatol, Praeger, 2009, pp. 175–90.
Becker, Ernest. *The Denial of Death*. Free Press, 1997.
Bell, Christopher E. "Does Harry Ever Cheat at Quidditch?" *Facebook* Exchange, 16 Apr. 2019.

———, Editor. *Hermione Granger Saves the World: Essays on the Feminist Heroine of Hogwarts*, McFarland & Company Publishing, 2012.

———. "Heroes and Horcruxes: Dumbledore's Army as Metonym." *Wizards vs. Muggles: Essays on Identity and the Harry Potter Universe*, edited by Christopher E. Bell, McFarland & Company Publishing, 2016, pp. 72–88.

———. "Riddle Me This: The Moral Disengagement of Lord Voldemort." *Legilimens! Perspectives in Harry Potter Studies*, edited by Christopher E. Bell. Cambridge Scholars Publishing, 2013, pp. 43–65.

———. "'You Have Your Mother's Eyes': Biracial Identity Development in Harry Potter." Chestnut Hill Harry Potter Academic Conference, 2020, Chestnut Hill, PA, 17 Oct. 2020, www.youtube.com/watch?v=6u7iL0N7u6c.

Ben-Ghiat, Ruth. *Strongmen: Mussolini to the Present*. W.W. Norton, 2020.

Beowulf: A New Verse Translation. Translated by Seamus Heaney, W.W. Norton, 2001.

Berndt, Katrin. "Hermione Granger, or, a Vindications of the Rights of Girl." *Heroism in the Harry Potter Series*, edited by Katrin Berndt and Lena Steveker, Ashgate Publishing Co., 2011, pp. 159–76.

Biggers, Jeff. *Resistance: Reclaiming an American Tradition*. Counterpoint Press, 2018.

Black, Naomi. *Social Feminism*. Cornell UP, 1989.

Blake, Andrew. *The Irresistible Rise of Harry Potter*. Verso, 2002.

Bok, Sissela. *Lying: Moral Choice in Public and Private Life*. Vintage Books, 1999.

Boulukos, George. *The Grateful Slave: The Emergence of Race in Eighteenth-Century British and American Culture*. Cambridge UP, 2008.

Bowlby, John. "On Knowing What You Are Not Supposed to Know and Feeling What You Are Not Supposed to Feel." *Canadian Journal of Psychiatry*, vol. 24, no. 9, 1979, pp. 403–8.

Brennan, David. "Eric Trump Calls Black Live Matter Protesters 'Animals.'" *Newsweek*, 21 June 2020, www.newsweek.com/eric-trump-calls-black-lives-matter-protesters-animals-rally-tulsa-1512374.

Bridger, Anne, and Ellen Jordan. *Timely Assistance: The Work of the Society for Promoting and the Training of Women, 1859-2009*. MRM Associates, 2009.

Brockrell, Gillian. "'I'm a Political Prisoner': Mouthy Martha Mitchell Was the George Conway of the Nixon Era." *Washington Post*, 21 Mar. 2019, www.washingtonpost.com/history/2019/03/21/im-political-prisoner-how-martha-mitchell-became-george-conway-nixon-era/.

Brown, Karen A. *Prejudice in Harry Potter' World: A Social Critique of the Series, Using Allport's The Nature of Prejudice*. Virtualbookworm.com Publishing, 2008.

Cadden, Vivian. "Martha Mitchell: The Day the Laughing Stopped." *McCall's*, vol. 100, July 1973, pp. 12+.

Calvert, Peter. *A Study of Revolution*. Clarendon Press, 1970.

Camacci, Lauren R. "The Face of Evil: Physiognomy in Potter." *Open at the Close: Literary Essays on the Harry Potter Novels*, edited by Cecilia Konchar Farr, UP of Mississippi, 2022, pp. 188–200.

———. "The Multi-Gaze Perspective in *Harry Potter*." *The Rhetorical Power of Children's Literature*, edited by John Saunders, Lexington Books, 2017, pp. 149–71.

———. "The Prisoner of Gender: Masculinity in the *Potter* Books." *Wizards vs. Muggles: Essays on Identity and the Harry Potter Universe*, edited by Christopher E. Bell, McFarland & Company Publishing, 2016, pp. 27–48.

Campbell, Lori M. "J. R. R. Tolkien and the Child Reader: Images of Inheritance and Resistance in *The Lord of the Rings* and J. K. Rowling's *Harry Potter*." *How We Became*

Middle-Earth: A Collection of Essays on The Lord of the Rings, edited by Adam Lam et al., Walking Tree, 2007, pp. 291–310.

Carey, Brycchan. "Hermione and the House-Elves: The Literary and Historical Contexts of J. K. Rowling's Antislavery Campaign." *Reading Harry Potter: Critical Essays*, edited by Giselle Liza Anatol, Praeger, 2003, pp. 103–15.

———. "Hermione and the House-Elves Revisited: J. K. Rowling, Antislavery Campaigning, and the Politics of Potter." *Reading Harry Potter Again: New Critical Essays*, edited by Giselle Liza Anatol, Praeger, pp. 73.

Cartwright, Samuel A. "Report on the Diseases and Physical Peculiarities of the Negro Race." *New Orleans Medical and Surgical Journal*, vol. 7, May 1851, pp. 691–715.

Castro, Adam-Troy. "From Azkaban to Abu Ghraib: Fear and Fascism in *Harry Potter and the Order of the Phoenix*." *Mapping the World of the Sorcerer's Apprentice: An Unauthorized Exploration of the Harry Potter Series Complete Through Book Six*, edited by Mercedes Lackey and Leah Wilson, Benbella Books, 2005, pp. 119–32.

Cawston, Amanda, and Alfred Archer. "Rehabilitating Self-sacrifice: Care Ethics and the Politics of Resistance." *International Journal of Philosophical Studies*, vol. 26, no. 3, 2018, pp. 456–77.

Chappell, Drew. "Sneaking Out after Dark: Resistance, Agency, and the Postmodern Child in JK Rowling's Harry Potter Series." *Children's Literature in Education: An International Quarterly*, vol. 39, no. 4, Dec. 2008, pp. 281–94.

Chattaway, Peter T. "Review: *Harry Potter and the Prisoner of Azkaban* (dir. Alfonso Cuarón, 2004)." Filmchat, *Patheos*, 4 June 2004, www.patheos.com/blogs/filmchat/2004/06/review-harry-potter-and-the-prisoner-of-azkaban-dir-alfonso-cuaron-2004.html. Accessed 4 May 2019.

Chaudhry, Lakshmi. "Harry Potter and the Half-Baked Epic." *The Nation*, 13 Aug. 2007, pp. 5–6.

Chenoweth, Erica, and Orion A. Lewis. "Unpacking Nonviolent Campaigns: Introducing the NAVCO 2.0 Dataset." *Journal of Peace Research*, vol. 50, no. 3, 2013, pp. 415–23.

Chenoweth, Erica, and Maria J. Stephan. *Why Civil Resistance Works: The Strategic Logic of Nonviolent Conflict*. Columbia UP, 2011.

Cherland, Meredith. "Harry's Girls: Harry Potter and the Discourse of Gender." *Journal of Adolescent & Adult Literacy*, vol. 52, no. 4, 2008, pp. 273–82.

Chevalier, Noel. "The Liberty Tree and the Whomping Willow: Political Justice, Magical Science and Harry Potter." *Lion and the Unicorn: A Critical Journal of Children's Literature*, vol. 29, no. 3, Sept. 2005, pp. 397–415.

Christian, Barbara. *Black Feminist Criticism: Perspectives on Black Women Writers*. Pergamon Press, 1985.

Clarke, Kenneth. *The Nude: A Study in Ideal Form*. Princeton UP, 1990.

Cohen, Signe. "A Postmodern Wizard: The Religious Bricolage of the Harry Potter Series." *Journal of Religion and Popular Culture*, vol. 28, no. 1, 2016, pp. 54–66.

Cohen, William A. "Introduction: Locating Filth." *Filth: Dirt, Disgust, and Modern Life*, edited by William A. Cohen and Ryan Johnson, U of Minnesota P, 2005, pp. vii–xxxvii.

Cole, Kristen L. "Transcending Hogwarts: Pedagogical Practices Engendering Discourses of Aggression and Bullying." *Wizards vs. Muggles: Essays on Identity and the Harry Potter Universe*, edited by Christopher E. Bell, McFarland & Company Publishing, 2016, pp. 149–67.

Collins, Patricia Hill. *Black Feminist Thought: Knowledge, Consciousness, and the Politics of Empowerment*. Routledge Classics, 2009.

Cook, Tanya. "The Politics of Motherhood in the Wizarding World." *The Sociology of Harry Potter: 22 Enchanting Essays on the Wizarding World*, edited by Jenn Sims, Zossima Press, 2012, pp. 79–90.

Cooley, Ron W. "Harry Potter and the Temporal Prime Directive: Time Travel, Rule-Breaking, and Misapprehension in *Harry Potter and The Prisoner of Azkaban*." *Scholarly Studies in Harry Potter: Applying Academic Methods to a Popular Text*, edited by Cynthia Whitney Hallett and Debbie Mynott, Edwin Mellen Press, 2005, pp. 29–42.

Cordova, Melanie J. "'Because I'm a Girl, I Suppose!': Gender Lines and Narrative Perspective in *Harry Potter*." *Mythlore: A Journal of J. R. R. Tolkien, C. S. Lewis, Charles Williams, and Mythopoeic Literature*, vol. 33, no. 2 [126], 2015, pp. 21–35.

Cropley, David H., et al. "Malevolent Creativity: A Functional Model of Creativity in Terrorism and Crime." *Creativity Research Journal*, vol. 20, no. 2, Apr. 2008, pp. 105–15.

Cross, Jennifer. "The Banality of Evil: Collaborators and Appeasement in Harry Potter." Harry Potter and the Pop Culture Conference, DePaul University, 29 Apr. 2017.

Curtis, Valerie. "Why Disgust Matters." *Philosophical Transactions of the Royal Society B: Biological Sciences,* vol. 366, no. 1583, 2011, pp. 3478–90.

Dahlen, Sarah Park, and Ebony Elizabeth Thomas, Editors. *Harry Potter and the Other: Race, Justice, and Difference in the Wizarding World*. UP of Mississippi, 2022.

Damian, Rodica Loana. "Where Do Diversifying Experiences Fit in the Study of Personality, Creativity, and Career Success?" *The Cambridge Handbook of Creativity and Personality Research*, edited by Gregory J. Feist et al., Cambridge UP, 2017, pp. 102–23.

Damian, Rodica Loana, and Dean Keith Simonton. "Diversifying Experiences in the Development of Genius and their Impact on Creative Cognition." *The Wiley Handbook of Genius*, edited by Dean Keith Simonton, Wiley, 2014, pp. 375–93.

Das, Soma. "Of the Patil Twins." *Inside the World of Harry Potter: Critical Essays on the Books and Films*, edited by Christopher E. Bell, McFarland & Company Publishing, 2018, pp. 44–58.

Deavel, David, and Catherine Deavel. "A Skewed Reflection: The Nature of Evil." *Harry Potter and Philosophy: If Aristotle Ran Hogwarts*, edited by David Baggett and Shawn E. Klein, Open Court Publishing Company, 2004, pp. 132–47.

DeMitchell, Todd A., and John J. Carney. "Harry Potter and the Public School Library." *Phi Delta Kappan*, vol. 87, no. 2, Oct. 2005, pp. 159–65.

Dendle, Peter. "Monsters, Creatures, and Pets at Hogwarts: Animal Stewardship in the World of Harry Potter." *Critical Perspectives on Harry Potter*, edited by Elizabeth E. Heilman, Routledge, 2009, pp. 163–76.

de Romo, Ana Cecilia Rodríguez. "Chance, Creativity, and the Discovery of the Nerve Growth Factor." *Journal of the History of the Neurosciences*, vol. 16, no. 3, July 2007, pp. 268–87.

Douglas, Mary. *Purity and Danger: An Analysis of the Concepts of Pollution and Taboo*. Routledge, 1966.

Dresang, Eliza T. "Hermione Granger and the Heritage of Gender." *The Ivory Tower and Harry Potter: Perspectives on a Literary Phenomenon*, edited by Lana A. Whited, U of Missouri P, 2002, pp. 211–42.

Durkheim, Émile. *The Rules of Sociological Method*. Translated by Sarah A. Solovay and John H. Mueller, edited by George E. G. Catlin, 8th edition, the Free Press of Glencoe, 1962.

Dyer, Richard. *White*. Routledge, 1997.

Works Cited

Eagly, Alice H., et al. "Transformational, Transactional, and Laissez-Faire Leadership Styles: A Meta-Analysis Comparing Women and Men." *Psychological Bulletin*, vol. 129, no. 4, July 2003, pp. 569–91.

Eisenstadt, J. Marvin. "Parental Loss and Genius." *American Psychologist*, vol. 33, no. 3, Mar. 1978, pp. 211–23.

Elliott, Jane. "Stepping on the Harry Potter Buzz." *Bitch Magazine: Feminist Perspectives to Pop Culture*, 2001, www.bitchmagazine.com. Internet Archive Wayback Machine, web.archive.org/web/20080205035511; www.bitchmagazine.org/archives/3_01potter/potter.shtml. Accessed 10 May 2017.

Engster, Daniel. *The Heart of Justice: Care Ethics and Political Theory*. Oxford UP, 2007.

Engster, Daniel, and Maurice Hamington. Introduction. *Care Ethics and Political Theory*, edited by Daniel Engster and Maurice Hamington, Oxford UP, 2015, pp. 1–16.

Farnel, Megan. "Magical Econ 101: Wealth, Labor and Inequality in *Harry Potter* and Its Fandom." *From Here to Hogwarts: Essays on Harry Potter Fandom and Fiction*, edited by Christopher E. Bell, McFarland & Company Publishing, pp. 28–53.

Farr, Cecila Konchar. Introduction. *Open at the Close: Literary Essays on Harry Potter*, edited by Cecilia Konchar Farr, UP of Mississippi, 2022, pp. xi–xxix.

Feist, Gregory J. "The Function of Personality in Creativity: The Nature and Nurture of the Creative Personality." *The Cambridge Handbook of Creativity*, edited by James C. Kaufman and Robert. J. Sternberg, Cambridge UP, 2010, pp. 113–30.

———. "The Influence of Personality on Artistic and Scientific Creativity." *Handbook of Creativity*, edited by Robert J. Sternberg, Cambridge UP, 1999, pp. 273–96.

Feldman, David Henry. "The Development of Creativity." *Handbook of Creativity*, edited by Robert J. Sternberg, Cambridge UP, 1999, pp. 169–86.

Freeman, Louise M. "The Weasley Witches: From Snitches to Stitches to 'Not-My-Daughter-You-Bitches.'" *Potterversity: Essays and Conversations*, edited by Kathryn N. McDaniel. Forthcoming, 2023.

Furness, Hannah. "JK Rowling Invented Quidditch after a Row with Her Boyfriend." *The Telegraph*, 18 May 2013, www.telegraph.co.uk/culture/books/10065868/JK-Rowling-invented-Quidditch-after-a-row-with-her-boyfriend.html. Accessed 21 July 2019.

Gabriel, Trip. "Ohio Lawmaker Asks Racist Question About Black People and Hand-Washing." *New York Times*, 11 June 2020.

Gaines, Cork. "Gregg Popovich Says the U.S. Has Become 'an Embarrassment to the World' in Speech Slamming Trump and White Privilege." *Business Insider*, 25 Sept. 2017, www.businessinsider.com/gregg-popovich-trump-anthem-protests-2017-9.

Gallardo, Ximena C., and C. Jason Smith. "Cinderfella: J. K. Rowling's Wily Web of Gender." *Reading Harry Potter: Critical Essays*, edited by Giselle Liza Anatol, Praeger, 2003, pp. 191–205.

Gardner, Howard. *Creating Minds: An Anatomy of Creativity Seen Through the Lives of Freud, Einstein, Picasso, Stravinsky, Eliot, Graham, and Gandhi*. Basic Books, 1993.

Garfinkle, Richard. "Why Killing Harry Is the Worst Outcome for Voldemort." *Mapping the World of Harry Potter*, edited by Mercedes Lackey and Leah Wilson, Benbella Books, 2005, pp. 179–94.

Genovese, Eugene D. *Roll, Jordan, Roll: The World the Slaves Made*. Pantheon, 1974.

Gierzynski, Anthony. *Harry Potter and the Millennials: Research Methods and the Politics of the Muggle Generation*. Johns Hopkins UP, 2013.

Gilligan, Carol. *The Birth of Pleasure: A New Map of Love*. Vintage, 2003.

———. *In a Different Voice: Psychological Theory and Women's Development*. Harvard UP, 1982.

———. *Joining the Resistance*. Polity Press, 2011.
Gilligan, Carol, and David A. J. Richards. *The Deepening Darkness: Patriarchy, Resistance, and Democracy's Future*. Cambridge UP, 2009.
Gilligan, Carol, and Naomi Snider. *Why Does Patriarchy Persist?* Polity Press, 2018.
Gino, Francesa, and Scott S. Wiltermuth. "Evil Genius? How Dishonesty Can Lead to Greater Creativity." *Psychological Science*, vol. 25, no. 4, 2014, pp. 973–81.
Gladstein, Mimi R. "Feminism and Equal Opportunity: Hermione and the Women of Hogwarts." *Harry Potter and Philosophy: If Aristotle Ran Hogwarts*, edited by David Baggett and Shawn E. Klein, Open Court Publishing Company, 2004, pp. 49–59.
Glanzer, Perry L. "Harry Potter's Provocative Moral World: Is There a Place for Good and Evil in Moral Education?" *Phi Delta Kappan*, Mar. 2008, pp. 525–28.
Glasberg, Davita Silfen, and Deric Shannon. *Political Sociology: Oppression, Resistance, and the State*. Pine Forge Press, 2011.
Glăveanu, Vlad. "Developing Society: Reflections on the Notion of Societal Creativity." *Creativity, Culture, and Development*, edited by A. G. Tan and C. Perleth, Springer, 2015, pp. 183–200.
Gotlieb, Rebecca J. M., et al. "Imagination Is the Seed of Creativity." *The Cambridge Handbook of Creativity*, edited by James C. Kaufman and Robert J. Sternberg, 2nd ed., Cambridge UP, 2019, pp. 709–31.
Granger, John. *Harry Potter's Bookshelf: The Great Books Behind the Hogwarts Adventures*. Berkley Books, 2009.
———. *Unlocking Harry Potter: Five Keys for the Serious Reader*. Zossima Press, 2007.
Griesinger, Emily. "The Search for 'Deeper Magic': J. K. Rowling and C. S. Lewis." *The Gift of Story: Narrating Hope in a Postmodern World*, edited by Emily Griesinger and Mark Eaton, Baylor UP, 2006, pp. 317–31.
Groves, Beatrice. *Literary Allusion in Harry Potter*. Routledge, 2017.
Guilford, J. P. "Creative Abilities in the Arts." *Psychological Review*, vol. 64, no. 2, 1957, pp. 110–18.
Hall, Susan. "Harry Potter and the Rule of Law: The Central Weakness of Legal Concepts in the Wizard World." *Reading Harry Potter: Critical Essays*, edited by Giselle Liza Anatol, Praeger, 2003, pp. 147–62.
———. "Justice in the Wizarding World." *Selected Papers from Nimbus-2003 Compendium: We Solemnly Swear These Papers Were Worth the Wait*, edited by Penny Linsemayer, et al., HP Education Fanon, Inc., 2005, pp. 61–74.
———. "Marx, Magic, and Muggles: Class Conflict in Harry Potter's World." *Harry Potter and History*, edited by Nancy R. Reagin, John Wiley and Sons, 2011, pp. 269–92.
Hamington, Maurice. "Politics Is Not a Game: The Radical Potential of Care." *Care Ethics and Political Theory*, edited by Daniel Engster and Maurice Hamington, Oxford UP, 2015, pp. 272–92.
Harris, Trudier. *From Mammies to Militants: Domestics in Black American Literature*. Temple UP, 1982.
Harry Potter and the Half-Blood Prince. Directed by David Yates. Warner Bros, 2009. DVD.
Heilman, Elizabeth E., editor. *Harry Potter's World: Multidisciplinary Critical Perspectives*. Routledge, 2003.
Heilman, Elizabeth E., and Trevor Donaldson. "From Sexist to (Sort-Of) Feminist: Representations of Gender in the Harry Potter Series." *Critical Perspectives on Harry Potter*, edited by Elizabeth E. Heilman, Routledge, 2009, pp. 139–61.
Henderson, Tolonda. "Chosen Names, Changed Appearances, and Unchallenged Binaries: Trans-Exclusionary Themes in *Harry Potter*." *Harry Potter and the Other: Race, Justice, and Difference in the Wizarding World*, edited by Sarah Park Dahlen and Ebony Elizabeth Thomas, UP of Mississippi, 2022, pp. 164–77.

———. "*Harry Potter* and the Management of Trauma." *Open at the Close: Literary Essays on Harry Potter*, edited by Cecilia Konchar Farr, UP of Mississippi, 2022, pp. 212–22.

Hochschild, Arlie Russell, and Anne Machung. *The Second Shift: Working Families and the Revolution at Home*. Penguin, 2012.

Horne, Jackie C. "Harry and the Other: Answering the Race Question in J. K. Rowling's Harry Potter." *Lion and the Unicorn*, vol. 34, no. 1, Jan. 2010, pp. 76–104.

Howard, Susan. "'Slaves No More': The Harry Potter Series as Postcolonial Slave Narrative." *Harry Potter's World Wide Influence*, edited by Diana Patterson, Cambridge Scholars Publishing, 2009, pp. 35–47.

Hsieh, Diana Mertz. "Dursley Duplicity: The Morality and Psychology of Self Deception." *Harry Potter and Philosophy: If Aristotle Ran Hogwarts*, edited by David Baggett and Shawn E. Klein, Open Court Publishing Company, 2004, pp. 22–37.

Hubley, Doug. "Civil Rights Hero John Lewis to Class of '16: 'Get in Trouble—Good Trouble,'" *Bates College News*, 2016, www.bates.edu/news/2016/05/29/civil-rights-hero-john-lewis-to-class-of-16-get-in-trouble-good-trouble/. Accessed 12 Mar. 2021.

Hurst, Alexander. "Donald Trump and the Politics of Disgust: The Republican presidential front-runner is disgusted by a lot of things. And it's resonating with voters." *New Republic*, 31 Dec. 2015, newrepublic.com/article/126837/donald-trump-politics-disgust.

Inbar, Yoel, et al. "Disgust Sensitivity, Political Conservatism, and Voting." *Social Psychological and Personality Science*, vol. 3, no. 5, Sept. 2012, pp. 537–44.

James, Rachel McCarthy. "Hermione Granger and the Failures of Feminism." *Deeply Problematic*, 1 Mar. 2011, www.deeplyproblematic.com/2011/03/hermione-granger-and-failures-of.html.

James, Stanlie M. "Mothering: A Possible Black Feminist Link to Social Transformation?" *Theorizing Black Feminisms: The Visionary Pragmatism of Black Women*, edited by Stanlie M. James and Abena P.A. Busia, Routledge, 1993, pp. 44–54.

Johnston, Hank. "Analyzing Social Movements, Nonviolent Resistance, and the State." *Social Movements, Nonviolent Resistance, and the State*, edited by Hank Johnston. Routledge, 2019, pp. 1–24.

———. *What Is a Social Movement?* Polity Press, 2014.

Kasibhatla, Bharati. "S.P.E.W./spew, or; Hermione Spews a Badge." *Selected Papers from Nimbus-2003 Compendium: We Solemnly Swear These Papers Were Worth the Wait*, edited by Penny Linsemayer, et al., HP Education Fanon, Inc., 2005, pp.121–31.

Kellner, Rivka Temina. "J. K. Rowling's Ambivalence Towards Feminism: House Elves—Women in Disguise—in the 'Harry Potter' Books." *Midwest Quarterly: A Journal of Contemporary Thought*, vol. 51, no. 4, 2010, pp. 367–85.

Kelman, Herbert and V. Lee Hamilton. *Crimes of Obedience: Toward a Social Psychology of Authority and Responsibility*. Yale UP, 1989.

Kendi, Ibram X. *How to Be an Anti-Racist*. One World, 2019.

Kern, Edmund M. *The Wisdom of Harry Potter: What Our Favorite Hero Teaches Us about Moral Choices*. Prometheus Books, 2003.

King, Martin Luther, Jr. "Letter from Birmingham Jail." *A Testament of Hope: The Essential Writings and Speeches of Martin Luther King, Jr.*, edited by James M. Washington, HarperCollins, 1991, pp. 289–302.

———. "The Role of the Behavioral Scientist in the Civil Rights Movement." *Journal of Social Issues*, vol. 24, no. 1, 1968, pp. 1–12.

Kirton, Michael. "Adaptors and Innovators: A Description and Measure." *Journal of Applied Psychology*, vol. 61, no. 5, 1976, pp. 622–29.

Köhler, Ulrike Kristina. "Harry Potter—National Hero and National Heroic Epic." *International Research in Children's Literature*, vol. 4, no. 1, 2011, pp. 15–28.

Kornfeld, John and Laurie Prothro. "Comedy, Conflict, and Community: Home and Family in *Harry Potter*." *Harry Potter's World: Multidisciplinary Critical Perspectives*, edited by Elizabeth E. Heilman, Routledge, 2003, pp. 187–202.

———. "Comedy, Quest, and Community: Home and Family in *Harry Potter*." *Critical Perspectives on Harry Potter*, edited by Elizabeth E. Heilman, Routledge, 2009, pp. 121–37.

Kringelbach, Morten L., et al. "On Cuteness: Unlocking the Parental Brain and Beyond." *Trends in Cognitive Sciences*, vol. 20, no. 7, July 2016, pp. 545–58.

Lacassagne, Aurélie. "Othermothering and Othermothers in the *Harry Potter* Series." *Journal of the Motherhood Initiative for Research & Community Involvement*, vol. 7, no. 1, spring/summer 2016, pp. 111–25.

LaHaie, Jeanne Hoeker. "Mums Are Good: Harry Potter and Traditional Depictions of Women." *Critical Insights: The Harry Potter Series*, edited by Lana A. Whited and M. Katherine Grimes, Grey House Publishing, 2015, pp. 123–45.

Lavoie, Chantel M. "The Good, the Bad, and the Ugly: Lies in Harry Potter." *Reading Harry Potter Again: New Critical Essays*, edited by Giselle Liza Anatol, Praeger, 2009, pp. 77–87.

Law, Wendy N., and Anna K. Teller. "Harry Potter and the Development of Moral Judgment in Children." *The Law and Harry Potter*, edited by Jeffrey E. Thomas and Franklin G. Snyder, Carolina Academic Press, 2010, pp. 149–66.

LeBlanc, Douglas. "The Trouble with Harry: Authors Weigh in on the Potter Debate and Alternative Stories." News Watch, *Christian Research Journal*, vol. 31, no. 1, 2008, pp. 4–6.

Lee, Laura Yiyin. "Alternative Heroism for the Postmodern Age: J. K. Rowling's Harry Potter Series." *Wenshan Review of Literature and Culture*, vol. 7, no. 1, Dec. 2013, pp. 65–92, www.wreview.org/index.php/archive/40-vol-7-no-1/122-alternative-heroism-for-the-postmodern-age-jk-rowling-39-s-harry-potter-series.html.

Levine, Bruce E. *Resisting Illegitimate Authority: A Thinking Person's Guide to Being an Anti-Authoritarian—Strategies, Tools, and Models*. A. K. Press, 2018.

Lewis, Mark-Anthony. "Uncle Remus's Shack: Tokenism in the Wizarding World." *Potterversity: Essays and Conversations*, edited by Kathryn N. McDaniel. McFarland & Company Publishing, Forthcoming, 2023.

Lipińska, Joanna. "The Xenophobic World of Wizards: Why Are They Afraid of the 'Other'?" *Harry Potter's World Wide Influence*, edited by Diana Patterson, Cambridge Scholars Publishing, 2009, pp. 117–23.

Litchfield, Robert C., et al. "Can Teams Have a Creative Personality?" *The Cambridge Handbook of Creativity and Personality Research*, edited by Gregory J. Feist et al., Cambridge UP, 2017, pp. 354–71.

Lopes, Juliana Valdes. "All Was Well? The Sociopolitical Struggles of House-Elves, Goblins, and Centaurs." *Open at the Close: Literary Essays on the Harry Potter Novels*, edited by Cecilia Konchar Farr, UP of Mississippi, 2022, pp. 178–87.

Lowery, Alyssa Magee. "Harry Potter and the Ill-Begotten Celebratory Sandwich: Misguided Activism in S.P.E.W." Southwest Popular/American Culture Association Annual Conference, 22 Feb. 2019, Albuquerque, NM.

Lurie, Alison. *Don't Tell the Grown-Ups: Subversive Children's Literature*. Little, Brown, 1990.

MacNeil, William P. "'Kidlit' as 'Law-And-Lit': Harry Potter and the Scales of Justice." *Law and Literature*, vol. 14, no. 3, 2002, pp. 545–64.

Mayes-Elma, Ruthann. *Females and Harry Potter: Not All That Empowering*. Rowman & Littlefield, 2007.

McCarthy, A.J. "J. K. Rowling Defends Free Speech—and Donald Trump." *Slate*, 17 May 2016, slate.com/human-interest/2016/05/j-k-rowling-defends-donald-trumps-right-to-be-bigoted-and-free-speech-video.html. Accessed 28 Feb. 2022.

McCauley, Patrick. *Into the Pensieve: The Philosophy and Mythology of Harry Potter*. Schiffer Publishing, Ltd., 2015.

McDaniel, Kathryn N. "Dumbledore's Army and the White Rose Society: Youth Justice Movements in the Wizarding World and Nazi Germany." *Harry Potter for Nerds II: Essays for Fans, Academics, and Lit Geeks*, edited by Kathryn N. McDaniel and Travis Prinzi, Unlocking Press, 2015, pp. 251–69.

———. "The Elfin Mystique: Fantasy and Feminism in J. K. Rowling's *Harry Potter* Series." *Past Watchful Dragons: Fantasy and Faith in the World of C. S. Lewis*, edited by Amy H. Sturgis, Mythopoeic Press, 2007, pp. 183–207.

———. "Re: Mischief Managed!" received by Beth Sutton-Ramspeck, 12 July 2022.

———. "The 'Real House-Elves' of J. K. Rowling: the Elfin Mystique Revisited." *Harry Potter for Nerds II: Essays for Fans, Academics, and Lit Geeks*, edited by Kathryn N. McDaniel and Travis Prinzi, Unlocking Press, 2015, pp. 63–92.

McElya, Micki. *Clinging to Mammy: The Faithful Slave in Twentieth-Century America*. Harvard UP, 2007.

McIntosh, Peggy. "White Privilege and Male Privilege: A Personal Account of Coming to See Correspondences through Work in Women's Studies." *On Privilege, Fraudulence, and Teaching as Learning: Selected Essays 1981-2019*, Routledge, 2019, pp. 17–27.

Mendlesohn, Farah. "Crowning the King: Harry Potter and the Construction of Authority." *Journal of the Fantastic in the Arts*, vol. 12, no. 3 [47], 2001, pp. 287–308.

Milgram, Stanley. *Obedience to Authority: An Experimental View*. Harper & Row, 1974.

Mill, John Stuart. *The Subjection of Women. Sexual Equality: Writings by John Stuart Mill, Harriet Taylor Mill, and Helen Taylor*, edited by Ann P. Robson and John M. Robson. University of Toronto Press, 1994, pp. 303–400.

Neal, Connie. *What's a Christian to Do with Harry Potter?* WaterBrook Press, 2001.

Nelson, John S. *Defenses Against the Dark Arts: The Political Education of Harry Potter and His Friends*. Lexington Books, 2021.

Noddings, Nel. *Caring: A Feminine Approach to Ethics and Moral Education*. U of California P, 1984.

Nowak, Tenille. "The Nuances of Rule-Breaking." *Teaching with Harry Potter: Essays on Classroom Wizardry from Elementary School to College*, edited by Valerie Estelle Frankel, McFarland & Company Publishing, 2013, pp. 21–31.

Nussbaum, Martha. *Hiding from Humanity: Disgust, Shame, and the Law*. Princeton UP, 2004.

Offen, Karen. "Defining Feminism: A Comparative Historical Approach." *Signs: The Journal of Women in Culture and Society*, vol. 14, no. 1, pp. 119–57.

Olatunji, Bunmi O., et al. "Multimodal Assessment of Disgust in Contamination-Related Obsessive-Compulsive Disorder." *Behaviour Research and Therapy*, vol. 45, no. 2, Feb. 207, pp. 263–76.

Omolade, Barbara. *The Rising Song of African American Women*. Routledge, 1994.

Orwell, George. "London Letter to *Partisan Review* (Winter 1945)." *George Orwell: As I Please, 1943-1946*, edited by Sonia and Ian Angus, 2000, volume 3, pp. 295–99.

Ostry, Elaine. "Accepting Mudbloods: The Ambivalent Social Vision of J. K. Rowling's Fairy Tales." *Reading Harry Potter: Critical Essays*, edited by Giselle Liza Anatol, Praeger, 2003, pp. 89–101.

O'Toole, Garson. "In a Time of Universal Deceit—Telling the Truth Is a Revolutionary Act. George Orwell? V. G. Venturini? David Hoffman? Charlotte Despard? Antonio Gramsci? Anonymous? Apocryphal?" *Quote Investigator*. 24 Feb. 2013, quoteinvestigator.com/2013/02/24/truth-revolutionary/.

Page, Andrew C., and Benjamin J. Tan. "The Intersection of Disgust and Contamination Fear." *Disgust and its Disorders: Theory, Assessment, and Treatment Implications*, edited by Bunmi O. Olatunji and Dean McKay. American Psychological Association Press, 2009, pp. 191–209.

Park, Julia. "Class and Socioeconomic Identity in Harry Potter's England." *Reading Harry Potter: Critical Essays*, edited by Giselle Liza Anatol, Praeger, 2003, pp. 103–15.

Patterson, Steven W. "Kreacher's Lament: S.P.E.W. as a Parable on Discrimination, Indifference, and Social Justice." *Harry Potter and Philosophy: If Aristotle Ran Hogwarts*, edited by David Baggett and Shawn E. Klein, Open Court Publishing Company, 2004, pp. 105–17.

Paustian-Underdahl, Samantha C., et al. "Gender and Perceptions of Leadership Effectiveness: A Meta-Analysis of Contextual Moderators." *Journal of Applied Psychology*, vol. 99, no. 6, Nov. 2014, pp. 1129–45.

Pelton, Leroy. *The Psychology of Nonviolence*. Pergamon Press, 1974.

Petrou, Paraskevas, et al. "Rebel with a Cause: When Does Employee Rebelliousness Relate to Creativity?" *Journal of Occupational and Organizational Psychology*, vol. 93, no. 4, Dec. 2020, pp. 811–33.

Pharr, Mary. "A Paradox: The Harry Potter Series as Both Epic and Postmodern." *Heroism in the Harry Potter Series*, edited by Katrin Berndt and Lena Steveker, Ashgate Publishing Co., 2011, pp. 9–23.

Phillips-Mattson, Christina. "Spellwork and the Legacy of Nonsense." *Open at the Close: Literary Essays on the Harry Potter Novels*, edited by Cecilia Konchar Farr, UP of Mississippi, 2022, pp. 48–64.

Plott, Elaina "What Does Tucker Carlson Believe?" *The Atlantic*, 15 Dec. 2019, www.theatlantic.com/politics/archive/2019/12/tucker-carlson-fox-news/603595/.

Post, Jerrold M. "Narcissism and the Charismatic Leader-Follower Relationship." *Political Psychology*, vol. 7, no. 4, 1986, pp. 675–88.

Prinzi, Travis. *Harry Potter & Imagination: The Way between Two Worlds*. Zossima Press, 2009.

Pugh, Tison, and David Wallace. "Heteronormative Heroism and Queering the School Story in J. K. Rowling's Harry Potter Series." *Children's Literature Association Quarterly*, vol. 31, no. 3, 2006, pp. 260–81.

Puppet String News. "2,267 Caravan Invaders Have Tuberculosis, HIV, Chickenpox and Other Health Issues." *Puppet String News*, 29 Nov. 2018, www.puppetstringnews.com/blog/2267-caravan-invaders-have-tuberculosis-hiv-chickenpox-and-other-health-issues.

Rangwala, Shama. "A Marxist Inquiry into J. K. Rowling's Harry Potter Series." *Reading Harry Potter Again: New Critical Essays*, edited by Giselle Liza Anatol, Praeger, 2009, pp. 127–42.

Reagin, Nancy R. "Was Voldemort a Nazi? Death Eater Ideology and National Socialism." *Harry Potter and History*, edited by Nancy R. Reagin, John Wiley & Sons, 2011, pp. 127–52.

Reilly, Rick. *Commander in Cheat: How Golf Explains Trump*. Hachette Books, 2019.

Rich, Adrienne. *Of Woman Born: Motherhood as Experience and Institution.* W.W. Norton, 1976.

Robinson, Fiona. "Care Ethics, Political Theory, and the Future of Feminism." *Care Ethics and Political Theory*, edited by Daniel Engster and Maurice Hamington, Oxford UP, 2015, pp. 293–312.

Rose, Jonathan A. "'Loony, Loopy, Lupin': (Sexual) Nonnormativity, Transgression, and the Werewolf." *Open at the Close: Literary Essays on the* Harry Potter *Novels*, edited by Cecilia Konchar Farr, UP of Mississippi, 2022, pp. 154–66.

Rosenberg, Moshe. *Morality for Muggles: Ethics in the Bible and the World of Harry Potter.* KTAV Publishing House, 2011.

Rosenberg, Robin S. "What Do Students Learn from Hogwarts Classes?" *The Psychology of Harry Potter*, edited by Neil Mulholland, BenBella Books, 2006, pp. 5–17.

Rowling, J. K. "Azkaban." *Wizarding World*, 10 Aug. 2015, www.wizardingworld.com/writing-by-jk-rowling/azkaban. Accessed 25 May 2019.

———. "Dolores Umbridge." www.wizardingworld.com/writing-by-jk-rowling/dolores-umbridge 2015. Accessed 26 Jan. 2021.

———. *Fantastic Beasts and Where to Find Them, by Newt Scamander*, revised edition. Scholastic, 2017.

———. "The Fringe Benefits of Failure, and the Importance of Imagination." Harvard Commencement Address. *Harvard Magazine*. 5 June 2008, www.harvardmagazine.com/2008/06/the-fringe-benefits-failure-the-importance-imagination. Accessed 29 May 2011.

———. *Harry Potter and the Chamber of Secrets.* Scholastic, 1999.

———. *Harry Potter and the Deathly Hallows.* Scholastic, 2007.

———. *Harry Potter and the Goblet of Fire.* New York: Scholastic, 2000.

———. *Harry Potter and the Half-Blood Prince.* New York: Scholastic, 2005.

———. *Harry Potter and the Order of the Phoenix.* New York: Scholastic, 2003.

———. *Harry Potter and the Prisoner of Azkaban.* New York: Scholastic, 1999.

———. *Harry Potter and the Sorcerer's Stone.* New York: Scholastic, 1998.

———. "Harry Potter: The Final Chapter." Interview with Meredith Viera. *NBC News*, 29 July 2007. www.nbcnews.com/id/wbna20001720#.XNdXYdh7mM8. Accessed 11 May 2019.

———. "J. K. Rowling at Carnegie Hall Reveals Dumbledore is Gay, Neville Marries Hannah Abbott, and Much More." Interview, 20 Oct. 2007. *The Leaky Cauldron*, www.the-leaky-cauldron.org/2007/10/20/j-k-rowling-at-carnegie-hall-reveals-dumbledore-is-gay-neville-marries-hannah-abbott-and-scores-more/. Accessed 24 Jan. 2022.

———. "J. K. Rowling at the Royal Albert Hall," Interview by Stephen Fry, 26 June 2003. *Accio Quote*, www.accio-quote.org/articles/2003/0626-alberthall-fry.htm.

———. "J. K. Rowling Interview." Interview with Evan Solomon. *CBC News World: Hot Type*, 13 July 2000, www.accio-quote.org/articles/2000/0700-hottype-solomon.htm.

———. "J. K. Rowling Web Chat Transcript," *The Leaky Cauldron*, 30 July 2007, www.the-leaky-cauldron.org/2007/07/30/j-k-rowling-web-chat-transcript/.

———. "Launch Day interview aboard the Hogwarts Express." Interview with Stephen Fry. *Bloomsbury Press*, 8 July 2000, www.accio-quote.org/articles/2000/0700-bloomsbury-fry.html. Accessed 29 May 2011.

———. "The Leaky Cauldron and MuggleNet interview, Joanne Kathleen Rowling: Part One." Interview by Melissa Anelli and Emerson Spartz. *The Leaky Cauldron*, 16 July 2005, www.accio-quote.org/articles/2005/0705-tlc_mugglenet-anelli-1.htm. Accessed 28 Nov. 2021.

———. "The Leaky Cauldron and MuggleNet interview, Joanne Kathleen Rowling: Part Two." Interview by Melissa Anelli and Emerson Spartz. *The Leaky Cauldron*, 16 July

2005, www.accio-quote.org/articles/2005/0705-tlc_mugglenet-anelli-2.htm. Accessed 28 Nov. 2021.

———. "The Leaky Cauldron and MuggleNet interview, Joanne Kathleen Rowling: Part Three." Interview by Melissa Anelli and Emerson Spartz. *The Leaky Cauldron*, 16 July 2005, www.accio-quote.org/articles/2005/0705-tlc_mugglenet-anelli-3.htm. Accessed 31 Dec. 2021.

———. "Malfalda." "Extra Stuff." *J. K. Rowling Official Site*. Internet Archive Wayback Machine. web.archive.org/web/20110722014536; www.jkrowling.com/textonly/en/extrastuff_view.cfm?id=3.

———. "Ministers for Magic." *Wizarding World*, 10 Aug. 2015, www.wizardingworld.com/writing-by-jk-rowling/ministers-for-magic. Accessed 22 May 2019.

———. "New Interview with J. K. Rowling for Release of Dutch Edition of 'Deathly Hallows.'" *The Leaky Cauldron*, 2007, www.the-leaky-cauldron.org/2007/11/19/new-interview-with-j-k-rowling-for-release-of-dutch-edition-of-deathly-hallows/.

———. "Order of Merlin." *Wizarding World*. 10 Aug. 2015, www.wizardingworld.com/writing-by-jk-rowling/order-of-merlin.

———. "PotterCast Interviews J. K. Rowling, part one." Interview by Melissa Anelli, John Noe, and Sue Upton. *PotterCast #130*, 17 Dec. 2007, www.accio-quote.org/articles/2007/1217-pottercast-anelli.html.

———. "Pure-Bloods." *Wizarding World*, 2015, www.wizardingworld.com/writing-by-jk-rowling/pure-blood.

———. *Quidditch Through the Ages, by Kennilworthy Whisp*. Arthur A. Levine Books, 2001.

———. "Remus Lupin." *Wizarding World*, 10 Aug. 2015, www.wizardingworld.com/writing-by-jk-rowling/remus-lupin.

———. "The Sword of Gryffindor." *Wizarding World*, 11 Aug. 2015, www.wizardingworld.com/writing-by-jk-rowling/the-sword-of-gryffindor.

———. *The Tales of Beedle the Bard*. Scholastic, 2007.

———. "To Be Invisible . . . That Would Be the Best." Interview with Juan Cruz. *El País*, 7 Feb. 2008. Translated by Felicia Grady, 8 Feb. 2008. *Mugglenet*, www.mugglenet.com/2008/02/translation-j-k-rowling-interview-el-pais/.

Rozin, Paul, Jonathan Haidt and Clark McCauley. "Disgust: The Body and Soul Emotion in the 21st Century." *Disgust and its Disorders: Theory, Assessment, and Treatment Implications*, edited by Bunmi O. Olatunji and Dean McKay, American Psychological Association Press, 2009, pp. 9–29.

Ruddick, Sara. *Maternal Thinking: Toward a Politics of Peace*. Ballantine Books, 1989.

Sawchuk, Craig N "The Acquisition and Maintenance of Disgust: Developmental and Learning Perspectives." *Disgust and its Disorders: Theory, Assessment, and Treatment Implications*, edited by Bunmi O. Olatunji and Dean McKay, American Psychological Association Press, 2009, pp. 77–97.

Saxena, Vandana. *The Subversive Harry Potter: Adolescent Rebellion and Containment in the J. K. Rowling Novels*. McFarland & Company Publishing, 2012.

Schaffer, Talia. *Communities of Care: The Social Ethics of Victorian Fiction*. Princeton UP, 2021.

Schock, Kurt. "The Practice and Study of Civil Resistance." *Journal of Peace Research*, vol. 50, no. 3, 2013, pp. 277–90.

Schoefer, Christine. "Harry's Girl Trouble: The World of Everyone's Favorite Kid Wizard is a Place where Boys Come First." *Salon*, 30 Oct. 2000, www.salon.com/2000/01/13/potter/.

Scholes, Robert. *The Crafty Reader*. Yale UP, 2001.

Schott, Christine. "The House Elf Problem: Why Harry Potter is More Relevant Now Than Ever." *The Midwest Quarterly*, vol. 16, no. 2, winter 2020, pp. 259–73.

Schuck, Raymond I. "'The Anti-Racist-White-Hero Premise': Whiteness and the *Harry Potter* Series." *Wizards vs. Muggles: Essays on Identity and the Harry Potter Universe*, edited by Christopher E. Bell, McFarland & Company Publishing, 2016, pp. 9–26.

Schultze Quentin J., and Randall L. Bytwerk. "Plausible Quotations and Reverse Credibility in Online Vernacular Communities." *ETC: A Review of General Semantics*, vol. 69, no. 2, Apr. 2012, pp. 216–34.

Schwabach, Aaron. "Harry Potter and the Unforgivable Curses." *The Law and Harry Potter*, edited by Jeffrey E. Thomas and Franklin G. Snyder, Carolina Academic Press, 2010, pp. 67–90.

Sharp, Gene. *From Dictatorship to Democracy: A Conceptual Framework for Liberation*. 4th U.S. Edition, The Albert Einstein Institution, 2010.

Simonton, Dean Keith. "Exceptional Creativity and Chance: Creative Thought as a Stochastic Combinatorial Process." *Beyond Knowledge: Extracognitive Aspects of Developing High Ability*, edited by Larisa V. Shavinina and Michel Ferrari, Lawrence Erlbaum Associates, Publishers, 2004, pp. 35–68.

———. "Sociocultural Context of Individual Creativity: A Transhistorical Time-Series Analysis." *Journal of Personality and Social Psychology*, vol. 32, no. 6, Dec. 1975, pp. 1119–33.

Simpson, Jacqueline. "On the Ambiguity of Elves [1]." *Folklore* (London, UK), vol. 122, no. 1, Apr. 2011, pp. 76–83.

Skulnick, Rebecca and Jesse Goodman. "The Civic Leadership of *Harry Potter*: Agency, Ritual, and Schooling." *Harry Potter's World*, edited by Elizabeth E. Heilman, Routledge, 2003, pp. 261–77.

Smith, Anne Collins. "Harry Potter, Radical Feminism, and the Power of Love." *The Ultimate Harry Potter and Philosophy: Hogwarts for Muggles*, edited by Gregory Bassham and Tom Morris, John Wiley and Sons, 2010, pp. 80–93.

Smith, David Livingstone. *Less than Human: Why We Demean, Enslave, and Exterminate Others*. St. Martin's Press, 2011.

Smith, Laura Lee. "Who Deserves the Truth? A Look at Veracity and Mendacity in *Harry Potter*." *Harry Potter for Nerds II: Essays for Fans, Academics, and Lit Geeks*, edited by Kathryn N. McDaniel and Travis Prinzi, Unlocking Press, 2015, pp. 271–92.

Snyder, Timothy. *On Tyranny: Twenty Lessons from the Twentieth Century*. Tim Duggan Books, 2017.

———. "The Deathly Hallows: How Literature Helps Us to See Evil in Politics." Chestnut Hill Harry Potter Conference, 2020, Chestnut Hill, PA, 16 Oct. 2020, www.youtube.com/watch?v=JYwb8gsNNsQ.

Stenner, Karen. *The Authoritarian Dynamic*. Cambridge UP, 2005.

Sternberg, Robert J. "A Triangular Theory of Creativity." *Psychology of Aesthetics, Creativity, and the Arts*, vol. 12, no. 1, 2018, pp. 50–67.

Sternberg, Robert J., and Todd I. Lubart. "The Concept of Creativity: Prospects and Paradigms." *Handbook of Creativity*, edited by Robert J. Sternberg, Cambridge UP, 1999, pp. 3–15.

Stevenson, Keri. "The First Gift: Owls as Paragons of the Non-Human." *Inside the World of Harry Potter: Critical Essays on the Books and Films*, edited by Christopher E. Bell, McFarland & Company Publishing, 2018, pp. 116–29.

Stowe, Harriet Beecher. *Uncle Tom's Cabin or, Life Among the Lowly*, edited by Ann Douglas. Penguin Books, 1986.

Strand, Emily. "Dobby the Robot: The Science Fiction in *Harry Potter*." *Mythlore*, vol. 38, no. 1, fall/winter 2019, pp. 175–98.
Thomas, Jeffrey E., and Franklin G. Snyder, editors. *The Law and Harry Potter*. Carolina Academic Press, 2010.
Tilly, Charles. *From Mobilization to Revolution*. Addison-Wesley, 1978.
Tompkins, Jane P. "Sentimental Power: *Uncle Tom's Cabin* and the Politics of Literary History." *Sensational Designs: The Cultural Work of American Fiction, 1790-1860*. Oxford UP, 1985, pp. 122–46.
Troester, Rosalie Riegle. "Turbulence and Tenderness: Mothers, Daughters, and 'Othermothers' in Paule Marshall's *Brown Girl, Brownstones*." *Sage: A Scholarly Journal on Black Women*, vol. 1, no. 2, 1984, pp. 13–16.
Tucker, Nicholas. "The Rise and Rise of Harry Potter." *Children's Literature in Education*, vol. 30, no. 4, Dec. 1999, pp. 221–34.
Turner-Vorbeck, Tammy. "Pottermania: Good, Clean Fun or Cultural Hegemony?" *Critical Perspectives on Harry Potter*, edited by Elizabeth E. Heilman, 2nd ed., Routledge, 2009, pp. 329–41.
Valverde, Miriam. "Misleading Headline Claims Thousands of Caravan Migrants Have HIV, Tuberculosis, Other Diseases." *PolitiFact*, 4 Dec. 2018, www.politifact.com/factchecks/2018/dec/04/puppetstringnewscom/misleading-headline-claims-thousands-caravan-migra/. Accessed 21 Apr. 2022.
Vezzali, Loris, et al. "The Greatest Magic of Harry Potter: Reducing Prejudice." *Journal of Applied Social Psychology*, vol. 45, no. 2, February 2015, pp. 105–21.
Walczak, Laurie Barth. "Sexuality, Protest, Elves, and White Womanhood: Hermione and S.P.E.W." *Selected Papers from Nimbus-2003 Compendium: We Solemnly Swear These Papers Were Worth the Wait*, edited by Penny Linsemayer, et al. HP Education Fanon, Inc., 2005, pp. 146–52.
Walker, Lenore E. A. *Abused Women and Survivor Therapy: A Practical Guide for the Psychotherapist*. American Psychological Association Press, 1994.
Walling, Carrie Booth. "The History and Politics of Ethnic Cleansing." *The International Journal of Human Rights*, vol. 4, no. 3–4, 2000, pp. 47–66.
Way, Niobe. *Deep Secrets: Boys' Friendships and the Crisis of Connection*. Harvard UP, 2011.
Weber, Max. *The Theory of Social and Economic Organization*. Translated by A. M. Henderson and Talcott Parsons. Oxford UP, 1947.
Weisberg, Robert W. "Creativity and Knowledge: A Challenge to Theories." *Handbook of Creativity*, edited by Robert J. Sternberg, Cambridge UP, 1999, pp. 226–50.
Wente, Sarah. "The Making of a New World: Nazi Ideology and Its Influence on Harry Potter." *A Wizard of Their Age: Critical Essays from the Harry Potter Generation*, edited by Cecilia Konchar Farr et al., State University of New York Press, 2015, pp. 89–112.
Westman, Karin E. "Perspective, Memory, and Moral Authority: The Legacy of Jane Austen in J. K. Rowling's *Harry Potter*." *Children's Literature*, vol. 35, 2007, pp. 145–65.
"What are the Differences between Muggle and Wizarding World Law?" *Wizarding World*, 13 Feb. 2018, www.wizardingworld.com/features/differences-between-muggle-and-wizarding-world-law. Accessed 27 May 2019.
White, Deborah Gray. *Ar'n't I a Woman? Female Slaves in the Plantation South*. W.W. Norton, 1985.
Whited, Lana A., and M. Katherine Grimes. "What Would Harry Do? J. K. Rowling and Lawrence Kohlberg's Theories of Moral Development." *The Ivory Tower and Harry*

Potter: Perspectives on a Literary Phenomenon, edited by Lana A. Whited, U of Missouri P, 2002, pp. 182–208.

Whitton, Alexis E., et al. "Moral Rigidity in Obsessive-Compulsive Disorder: Do Abnormalities in Inhibitory Control, Cognitive Flexibility and Disgust Play a Role?" *Journal of Behavior Therapy and Experimental Psychiatry*, vol. 45, no. 1, Mar. 2014, pp. 152–59.

Whitton, Natasha. "'Me! Books! And Cleverness!' Stereotypical Portrayals in the Harry Potter Series." *Women Writers*, 15 May 2004, www.womenwriters.net/summer04/reviews/harrypotter/htm. Accessed 1 May 2017.

Windarti, Estiningsyas Retno. Abstract, *A Postcolonialist Analysis on the Portrayal of House-Elves As Slaves in J.K Rowling's Harry Potter and Goblet of Fire*. Program Studi Pendidikan Bahasa Inggris FBS-UKSW, 2014. repository.uksw.edu/handle/123456789/5471.

Wolosky, Shira. "Gendered Heroism: Family Romance and Transformations of the Hero-Type." *Wizards vs. Muggles: Essays on Identity and the Harry Potter Universe*, edited by Christopher E. Bell. McFarland & Company Publishing, 2016, pp. 110–30.

———. *The Riddles of Harry Potter: Secret Passages and Interpretive Quests*. Palgrave Macmillan, 2010.

The Women of Harry Potter, Part 1. Warner Bros. Entertainment, Inc., 2011, www.youtube.com/watch?v=kNk5q2Qy9No, posted 4 Jan. 2013. Accessed 30 Jan. 2022.

Woolf, Virginia. "Professions for Women." *The Death of the Moth and Other Essays*. Harcourt Brace Jovanovich, 1970, pp. 235–42.

Yang, Jeff. "A New Virus Stirs up Ancient Hatred." *CNN Opinion*, 30 Jan. 2020, www.cnn.com/2020/01/30/opinions/wuhan-coronavirus-is-fueling-racism-xenophobia-yang/index.html.

Zettel, Sarah. "Hermione Granger and the Charge of Sexism." *Mapping the World of the Sorcerer's Apprentice*, edited by Mercedes Lackey and Leah Wilson, Benbella Books, 2005, pp. 83–99.

Zipes, Jack. *Sticks and Stones: The Troublesome Success of Children's Literature from Slovenly Peter to Harry Potter*. Routledge, 2001.

Zurn, Perry. "Curiosity and Political Resistance." *Curiosity Studies: A New Ecology of Knowledge*, edited by Perry Zurn and Arjun Shankar, U of Minnesota P, 2020, pp. 227–45.

INDEX

Abanes, Richard 2, 36
Accio (summoning charm) 36, 152
Acocella, Joan 169
"alternative facts" *see* propaganda
American Psychological Association 119, 134
Amnesty International 48, 116n5
Anatol, Giselle Liza 28n5, 56, 173n2
Animagi 43, 47, 48, 68, 122, 148, 163; See also Black, Sirius; Pettigrew, Peter; Skeeter, Rita
Amortentia (love potion) 6, 13, 29n15, 100–101
antisemitism 9, 48, 63–64, 70, 156, 162, 163, 169
antiracism 55–56, 58, 76, 81–82, 117n18
apparition 30, 80; by house-elves 91, 115
Archer, Alfred 11
Arendt, Hannah 150, 154
Aristotle 164
Aurors 10, 44, 109, 113
authority 2, 3, 4, 12, 20, 45, 77, 85, 89, 104, 107, 110, 118n25, 145, 153, 156; legitimate 5, 7; systems of 7; types of (Weber) 7
authoritarianism vii, 3, 10, 21, 26–27, 28, 38, 41, 46, 47, 49, 79, 133, 145, 150, 154, 160, 169, 170–71; creativity, contrary to 130; and disgust 60–61, 71; and Ministry of Magic 21, 25, 27, 41, 145, 161; patriarchy, relationship to 12–13, 155, 160, 166; and resistance 3, 10, 21–22, 24, 27–28, 49–50, 113, 129, 130, 133, 134, 140, 142, 145, 155, 173; and Voldemort 8, 13, 53, 143–44, 161
authoritarian dynamic (Stenner) 25, 130, 133; embraced by women 113, 153; and social norms 26, 49
Avada Kedavra 4, 5, 19, 53, 111, 114–115, 143, 144n4, 172; *see also* death; Unforgivable Curses
Azkaban Prison 25, 42, 46, 47, 171; as death sentence, potential 48, 54n6; escape from 104, 155; and Muggle borns 47–48, 54n6, 65, 80, 121; punishment without trial 40, 45, 46, 66; reform of 10, 135; and Sirius Black 45, 75, 103, 159; as torture 47–48

Bagman, Ludo 35–36, 43, 46, 47, 136
Bagshot, Bathilda 70, 122, 147
Bailey, F. G. 162–63
Barnes, J. A. 149, 165n2
Barratt, Bethany 102
Barthes, Roland viii
basilisk 96, 106, 139;
Battle of Hogwarts 10, 82, 102, 111–13, 118n26, 118n27, 141
Battle of the Ministry 10, 17, 114–15, 126, 140, 149–50
Bealer, Tracy 8–9, 17, 48, 157
beasts, magical, and creatures 83n4, 101, 116–17n3; Blast-Ended Skrewts 88;

Index

Boggarts 125, 152; Crumple-Horned Snorkacks 160; doxies 73; gnomes 74; permitted at Hogwarts 36–37; unicorns 131; vela 74; *see also* basilisk; dragons; Fawkes; Fluffy; ghouls; trolls
Becker, Ernest 60
Beauxbatons 159
beings (magical category) 5, 12, 13, 56, 57, 67, 162, 168; distinguished from beasts 66, 116–17n13; legal rights and disabilities of 40, 65, 67, 78, 92, 96, 135, 140, 167; *see also* Code of Wand Use; Department for the Regulation and Control of Magical Creatures
Bell, Christopher E. 8, 13, 35, 39, 64–65, 85
Ben-Ghiat, Ruth 157
Beowulf 91
Berndt, Katrin 23, 116n1, 116n6
Bewitched 110
Big Lie, the 165; United States 161–62; wizard 148, 157, 162–63, 165; World War II 156–57, 162, 163
Biden, President Joseph R. 166
binary thinking 15, 54n9, 55, 76, 83, 151, 172
Binns, Professor 67, 125, 164
Black family 13, 66, 73, 88, 92, 95, 111, 126, 139; family tree tapestry 72, 103; and house-elf heads 95, 101
Black Lives Matter movement 64, 136
Black, Naomi 117n17
Black, Regulus 8, 88, 101, 103, 115
Black, Sirius 1, 8, 17, 24, 31, 35, 39, 69, 75, 79, 101, 103, 111, 126, 146, 147, 157, 159, 163, 167, 172; Animagus 47–48; bully 126, 172; and cleaning 72–73, 75; considered dangerous criminal 42, 43, 103, 128, 131, 150, 154, 159; death of 17, 18, 91, 92, 112, 127, 140, 154, 164; Kreacher, treatment of 75, 88, 92, 95, 101, 102, 167; in *The Quibbler* 160; rescued by Harry and Hermione 1–2, 31, 45, 48, 158; and sacrifice 114, 118n24; source of information about First Wizarding War 43, 44, 45, 47; and wizard justice system 45, 47, 74, 150, 154, 159; *see also* Marauders
Black, Walburga (Sirius's mother) 63, 66, 73, 95, 101, 102–103
Blake, Andrew 4
Blake, William 98, 132

blood 38, 58, 60, 62, 63, 64, 65, 68, 121, 139, 163
blood status 39, 48, 55, 63–65, 79, 81, 133, 147, 151; blood traitor 25, 76, 103; half blood 9, 56, 69, 162; as metaphor for race 55–56, 156; Muggle-born ("mudblood" as status) 48, 55, 56, 57, 63, 65–66, 81, 84n10, 161, 162; pure blood 24, 25, 26, 55, 56, 62, 63, 65, 73, 79, 81, 83n5, 106, 111, 115, 123, 143, 147, 156, 161, 162, 163, 168; Squib 47, 56, 57, 71, 84n13, 135, 162, 165n3; *see also* mudbloods; privilege
Bogrod 170, 171
Bok, Sissela 146, 154, 156, 165n2
Boot, Terry 39, 52
Boulukos, George 102
Bowlby, John 14
Brayton, Connor 116n9
Bridger, Anne 116n7
broomsticks, magical 34–35, 36, 37, 120, 125, 140; Nimbus Two Thousand 35; Nimbus Two Thousand and One 35
Brown, Karen A. 83n2, 116n10
Brown, Lavender 67, 137
Buckbeak 31, 45, 48, 147, 158
bullying 3, 14, 15, 23, 29n18, 35, 57, 114, 126, 129, 140, 172
Burbage, Charity 63
Burrow, the 58, 60, 73, 74, 110
butterbeer 1, 52, 62, 75, 94, 95, 103–104, 117n21
Bytwerk, Randall L. 165n8

Calvert, Peter 10
Camacci, Lauren R. 29n17, 83n8, 173n3
Campbell, Lori M. 8
care ethics vii, viii, 11–19, 25, 29n16, 29n19, 32, 39, 70, 75–76, 80, 93, 100, 103, 110, 112–13, 114, 115, 117n17, 118n29, 125–26, 135, 141, 146, 154, 155, 165, 166, 168; as distinguished from patriarchal ethic of rights, 11, 99–100, 117n17, 117n20, 134, 166, 169–70
Carey, Brycchan 23, 98, 102, 106, 107, 167, 168, 173n2
Carlson, Tucker 64
Carrow, Alecto 19, 20, 25, 39, 63, 67, 161
Carrow, Amycus 19, 25, 39, 62, 171
Cartwright, Samuel A. drapetomania 131; dysaesthesia aethiopica 138
Castro, Adam-Troy 28n10

Cattermole, Mary 19, 78–81
Cattermole, Reg 78–81, 129
Cawston, Amanda 11
Cedarville, Arkansas 2
censorship 2, 27, 38, 73, 75, 121, 145, 155, 159, 160, 161, 166; backfires 155, 160; *see also* voice and silence
centaurs 19, 56, 65, 66, 67, 68, 116n13, 135, 162, 167, 168
Chamber of Secrets, the 22, 28n1, 63, 66, 96, 125, 131, 149, 164
Chang, Cho 17, 126
Chappell, Drew 151
charismatic leader 7, 28, 28n9, 52, 167
Chattaway, Peter T. 2
Chaudhry, Lakshmi 8
cheating 2, 4, 33, 35–36, 62, 124, 129
Chenoweth, Erica 9–10, 29n13
Cherland, Meredith 29n19, 167
Chevalier, Noel 4, 31, 39
Choice 5–7, 12, 22, 26, 34, 36, 52, 68, 91, 92–93, 94–98, 100, 102, 106–107, 108, 110, 114, 115, 137, 163, 170, 172–73
Christianity, Christian themes 2, 24, 36, 58, 70, 108, 153; *see also* self-sacrifice
Christmas 64, 72, 96, 110
Churchill, Winston 132
Civil Rights movement, US vii, 9, 11, 20, 26, 27, 132–38, 140, 141, 143
Clarke, Kenneth 93
class, social 4, 15, 26, 35, 56, 60, 66, 76, 79, 81, 86–87, 97, 99, 102, 117n20, 131, 151, 168
cleaning 72, 78, 82; care, expression of 27, 70, 80; as control 71, 72; literal 70–71; love and 27, 58, 72, 73–75, 101; without magic 72; number twelve Grimmauld Place 72–73, 111; as resistance 27, 111, 58, 72, 75–76; Scourgify 71; Sirius and 72; Snape denigrates 72, 111; and social class 79–80, 87; Molly Weasley and 72, 73, 104, 111; Tergeo 71; to wipe 75
cleanliness 26, 55, 82; and authoritarianism 60, 71, 72; grooming 71–72, 74–75; negative associations 58, 75–76; obsessive compulsive disorder 27, 60, 71; Petunia Dursley 71, 73, 109; positive associations 59, 70, 74–76; Tonks's response to 71, 73; and xenophobia/racism 27, 65, 70, 72, 73, 83n10, 111; Wool's Orphanage 14, 73
Cohen, Signe 151
Cohen, William A. 58

Cole, Kristen, L. 56
Cole, Mrs. 14; *see also* Wool's Orphanage
Coleridge, Samuel Taylor 132, 164
collaboration, as vice 24–25, 48, 76, 129, 139, 150, 153, 154, 166; as virtue 9, 11, 100, 129, 141–42, 143, 157
Collins, Patricia Hill 105
Committee for the Disposal of Dangerous Creatures 45
Compassion *See* empathy
conformity/nonconformity 3, 4, 49, 120, 122, 124, 129, 130, 142
Confundus charm 22
consent 6, 7, 8, 13, 29n15, 89, 95
consumerism 4, 107, 139
contamination 26, 61, 62–63, 68, 69, 71, 73, 111; *see also* disgust
Cook, Tanya 104, 119
cooking *see* food and cooking
Cooley, Ron W. 3
Cordova, Melanie J. 116n2
Corruption, political *see* Ministry of Magic, corruption of
courage 23, 49, 51, 52, 107, 113–14
COVID-19 64
Crabbe, Vincent 144n9
creative maladjustment 119, 132–36, 138–45; Dobby 134, 138; Dumbledore 133, 143; goblins 102, 139; Harry 133, 143; Hermione 133–34, 139–43; Luna 140–41
creativity 119; adaptors 120; in the arts 119–20, 122, 132, 141; in business 120, 128, 129; and cheating 124, 129; and conscientiousness, low 124, 129–30, 144n7; convergent thinking 120, 125; counterfactual thinking 127–28; creating rules 121; cultural influences on 131–32; and curiosity 130–31, 132, 134–38; and daydreaming 124, 125; divergent thinking 27, 120, 123, 124, 129–30, 139, 140, 142; and diversifying experiences 131–32, 140; and experimentation 120–21, 122, 129, 144n3; and expertise 123, 129, 137, 139, 142–43; and extraversion 124, 130; innovators 11, 120, 121; invention 120–22, 125, 126, 128–29; and luck 124, 141–42; and lying 124, 128–29; malevolent 121–23, 130, 131, 139, 144n3; and memory 124, 126–28; and mental illness 132–34, 138; and motivation 130, 132, 142; and mysteries,

192　Index

solving 123, 130–31, 136–37; novelty 120, 130, 131, 138, 144; openness 130, 132, 142, 144n7; problem solving, creative 120, 123, 130; rebelliousness 122, 124, 130, 133, 134, 136; resilience 124, 130, 132; risk taking 124, 129, 142; rule breaking and 119, 120–23, 126, 128, 129, 133, 136–37, 139, 144; in science 120, 123, 142, 144n3; societal 119, 121, 123, 126–27; ten year rule 123, 139; traits of creative people 122–23, 124–32; usefulness/value 120, 121–22, 129, 130, 131, 138, 144; and trauma 122, 123, 131; Zeitgeist, defying the, as resistance 123, 131, 132–36, 139–41, 143; *see also* creative maladjustment; imagination; politically resistance curiosity; Voldemort, creativity of

creativity studies 119–23, 124, 125, 127–32, 142

creatures *see* beings, Department for the Regulation and Control of Magical Creatures

Cresswell, Dirk 43, 161

criminality 1, 5, 10–11, 14, 25, 43, 46, 48, 65, 71, 136, 147, 156, 159

criticisms (negative) of series 28n5, 39; as conservative 4, 8, 34; gender roles, depiction of 4, 56, 85–87, 108–11, 113, 114, 116n2, 118n25; house-elf slavery, depiction of 4, 85, 86–87, 90, 95, 98, 106, 107, 115, 167–68, 173n2; occult, depiction of 2–3; race, depiction of 4, 55–56, 83n2, 85–87, 90, 107, 155–56; rule breaking, justification of 2–3, 36; social class, depiction of 86–87; S.P.E.W 22–23, 29n19, 167, 173n3; transgender issues 118n17

Cropley, David H. 144n2

Cross, Jennifer 76

Crouch, Bartemius, Sr. 25, 75, 100, 103–5, 109, 114, 136; and Department of Magical Law Enforcement 40, 44, 46–47, 72; Harry thinks he sees on Marauder's Map 136; under Imperius Curse 6; neatness 71–72; and Winky 72, 88, 90, 94, 95, 100, 103–5

Crouch, Barty, Jr. 27, 72, 90, 95, 100, 133; confession 91, 104–5, 147; under Imperius Curse 6, 91, 104; produces Dark Mark 91; receives Dementor's Kiss 19–20, 45; tortures Longbottoms 47, 109, 126

Crouch, Barty, Jr., disguised as Mad-Eye Moody 6–7, 17, 35–36, 44, 104, 136, 147, 148, 163; and cheating during the Tri-Wizard Tournament 35–36; teaches Unforgivable Curses 6–7

Crouch family 98, 103

Crouch, Mrs. 25, 104, 109

Cruciatus Curse 5, 7, 38–39, 41, 45, 109, 126, 136, 146, 147, 171

Dahlen, Sarah Park 83n2

Daily Prophet, the 8, 63; attacks on Harry and Dumbledore 20, 133, 139, 159–60; inaccuracies vii, 54, 158, 159, 161; Ministry manipulation of 28, 48, 54n1, 133, 150, 156–57, 158–62; profit motive 48, 150, 160; as source of reliable information 158, 160; *see also* journalism; propaganda; Skeeter, Rita

Dark Mark 61, 91, 100

Darwin, Charles 61, 132

Das, Soma 5

Davis, Bryan 2

death 5, 18, 19, 22, 25, 31, 32, 37, 45, 47–48, 53, 54n6, 67, 70, 78, 95, 102, 104, 107–8, 111, 112, 132, 147, 148, 153; fear of 32–33, 60, 69–70, 83, 115, 122; Harry's near-death experience at King's Cross 18, 59, 163–64; of individual characters 8, 10, 17–18, 19, 22, 23, 44, 58, 66, 69, 70, 74, 91, 92, 106–8, 109, 111, 112–15, 118n24, 118n26, 124, 127, 140, 143, 146, 147, 148, 154, 156, 157, 158, 161, 164, 170, 172; love is a force more terrible than 26, 32–33, 100, 116; Master of 33, 70, 125; murder 1, 5, 7–8, 9, 18, 22, 25, 31, 33, 40, 41, 44, 53, 57, 62, 63, 66, 70, 84n10, 103, 111, 112, 113, 114–15, 122, 126, 131, 142, 143, 148, 150, 153, 154, 155, 163; "Tale of the Three Brothers, The" 13, 164; *see also Avada Kedavra*, Hallows; Horcruxes; self-sacrifice

Death Eaters 3, 7, 9, 22, 24, 25, 29n18, 38–39, 44, 45, 46, 52, 58, 62, 64, 83n10, 102, 104, 112, 115, 121, 122, 126, 133, 137, 140, 141, 143, 154, 161, 170, 171; escape from Azkaban 155; at Quidditch World Cup 90–91, 100, 104; "the world isn't split into good people and" 8, 39, 44, 167

Deathstick *see* Elder Wand

Deavel, Catherine 148

Deavel, David 148
Decree for the Reasonable Restriction of Underage Sorcery 7, 41–43, 46, 123–24; *see also* surveillance; Trace
Defense Against the Dark Arts 52, 67; class 6, 16, 20, 152–53, 155; exams 152; Harry teaching 24, 52, 115, 142; textbook 155; *see also* Dumbledore's Army; Lupin, Remus; Umbridge, Dolores
dehumanization 5, 13, 62–65, 83n8, 90, 96–97
Delacour, Fleur 74, 76
Delacour, Gabrielle 36
Delacour, Madame 74
Deluminator 121
dementors 10, 16, 20, 45, 47–48, 125, 135; attack on Harry and Dudley 38, 42–43, 78, 124, 147, 171; Dementor's Kiss 19–20, 45, 48; *see also* Azkaban, Patronus
democracy 8, 9, 12, 19, 21, 23, 25, 40–41, 44, 66, 155, 161–62, 168–70
Dendle, Peter 83n4, 101, 116–17n13, 73n2
de Romo, Ana Cecilia Rodríguez 142
Department for the Regulation and Control of Magical Creatures 23, 24, 43, 65, 99, 160, 168
Department of Magical Games and Sports 35–36, 43 *see also* Bagman, Ludo
Department of Magical Law Enforcement 10, 24, 79, 166; at World Cup 43; misconduct 43–45, 72; *see also* police misconduct
Department of Mysteries 10, 31, 54n1, 140, 147, 148, 160; Unspeakables 31
Diagon Alley 158
Diggory, Cedric 18, 36, 137, 153, 155, 157–58, 159
dirt 26–27, 55, 56, 64, 67, 68, 70, 82, 90, 139; Black, Walburga and 73; culturally defined 57–58, 60, 63; decay 69, 73; definitions 57; feces 57, 60, 61, 62, 64, 73; "matter out of place" 57, 58, 70; as misdirection 58, 59, 68; negative associations 58, 59, 67–68; at number twelve Grimmauld Place 59, 63, 72–73; poor grooming 58, 59, 67–68, 74–75; positive associations 58–59, 73, 75–76; synonyms 57
disgust 27, 82, 144n7; "anal retentive" personality 60–61; animal reminder disgust 60, 62–65, 67–70, 72, 82, 83n8; and anti-immigrant attitudes 60, 64; and antisemitism 62, 63–64; as biologically determined 60, 61, 83n5; contamination disgust 61, 62–64, 70; as culturally influenced 26, 54n7, 57, 60, 62–66, 70, 83n5; and disease 60, 61, 64, 65, 68; and fear 62, 69–70; and miscegenation 63–64, 71; moral 62; and obsessive compulsive disorder 27, 60–61; oppression, to justify 62–65, 75, 76, 78–79; political conservatism and disgust sensitivity 60, 62, 71–72, 76; and propaganda 62, 63; and racism 26, 63–65, 69–70; and rule breaking 60, 61, 75–76; sexual 60, 3–64, 68–69; and social class 60, 63
disgust studies 58, 60–62, 69, 83n5, 83n6
disinformation 54n138, 1
dissent, suppression of 8, 48, 156, 157, 159–60
Divination (class) 66, 129, 145–46
Dobby 23, 27, 35, 52, 59, 75, 77, 78, 86, 87, 88, 92, 93, 103, 105–6, 117n23; creativity of 138; disobedience by 42, 85, 95, 96, 106; as free elf 86, 90, 94, 95, 105–7, 117n20, 134, 138; grave, dug by Harry 105–7; Harry, love for 105–7; Harry, protects 91, 93, 104–107; hover charm, produces 40, 42, 91, 104, 138; maladjusted 44, 95, 134; political consciousness of 96–97, 102, 106; proto-resistance by 89, 91, 92, 94, 95–97, 12, 106, 138, 168; self-sacrifice 106–8, 118n24, 164, 168; *see also* house-elves
domesticity 27, 60, 76, 90, 111; as empowering 85, 87, 99, 100, 104, 108; perceived as inferior 71, 72, 87, 88, 93, 98, 108, 110, 111, 115
domestic abuse/violence 87–88, 116n5, 116n12
Donaldson, Trevor 85
Douglas, Mary 26, 57, 58, 60, 70
dragons 15, 21, 35, 36, 74, 77, 83n4, 88, 121, 142
Dresang, Eliza T. 116n1
Dufek, Brad 116n9
Dumbledore, Aberforth 59, 172
Dumbledore, Albus 14, 15, 39, 45, 47, 59, 91, 114–15, 118n25, 122, 127, 166; changes 7, 33, 97, 121, 170; as charismatic leader 7; creativity of 121, 127, 143; *Daily Prophet* criticizes him 20, 133, 139, 156, 159–60; death of 22, 137, 140, 161, 164, 173;

on death 18, 70, 82, 100; and the Elder Wand 13; Fudge, distrusted by 20, 21, 159–60; gay 69, 84n11; and gender norms 12–13, 15; and giants 44, 135; and the greater good 169–72; at Harry's hearing 7, 41, 46; Harry, love for 18, 126, 150, 154; hiring decisions 66; in Horcrux cave 5, 91, 128; and house-elf slavery 92, 94, 101, 135, 162, 167; and house points 38, 49; and the invisibility cloak 37–38; on laws of magic 26, 31, 32–33, 126; Legilimency, use of 147; lies of omission 154; on Lily's death 114, 163; on love 12, 17, 18, 32, 70, 100, 105–6, 107, 114, 126, 141; memories in Pensieve 47, 124, 126, 136; Minister of Magic, declined position of 7, 40; on Ministry corruption 41, 47, 48, 135; plans, with Grindelwald, for wizard domination over Muggles 3, 28, 33, 148, 169–72; plot to kill him 25, 148; on prophecy 127, 132, 142; as resistance leader 5, 22, 25, 31, 51, 131, 135, 157–58, 173; and the Resurrection Stone 33, 70; rules, disregard for 5, 26, 31, 32–33, 37–38, 49, 121; rules, respect for 5, 36–37; Snape and 44, 148, 150; "Tale of the Three Brothers, The," commentary on 13, 164; on truth and lies 128, 146, 148, 154, 157–58, 163, 164, 165; Veritaserum, use of 147; Voldemort, assessments of 7, 17, 18, 21, 70, 113, 126, 141, 142; Voldemort, mission to defeat 5, 33, 124, 137, 141, 143, 154; on Voldemort's name 50–51; wisdom of 6, 17, 18, 70, 82, 100, 101, 132, 136, 142, 154, 157, 162, 163, 165, 170–72; "Warlock's Hairy Heart, The," commentary on 32;
Dumbledore, Ariana 56, 170, 172
Dumbledore's Army viii, 21, 52–53, 111, 115, 128, 129, 131, 140, 148; democratic structures 21; "Dumbledore's Army, still recruiting" 39, 138; Hermione instigates its founding 22, 139–40; recruitment 21, 137–38; as resistance operation 9–10, 21, 22, 24, 39, 138, 143–44; and the White Rose Society 28n11
Dumezweni, Noma 83n1
Durkheim, Émile 10–11
Durmstrang 159
Dursley, Dudley 54n4, 125; Harry saves from dementors 38, 42–44, 78, 124, 127, 147, 171; overindulged 15, 109, 111; and Ton-Tongue Toffee 3
Dursley family 16, 40, 77, 78, 87, 110, 132; authoritarian 49; lies 146, 156, 165n6; normalcy of 48–49, 58, 77, 109
Dursley, Marge 42, 64–65, 71, 124; named for Margaret Thatcher 64
Dursley, Petunia 15, 64, 104, 110; cleaning 27, 58, 71, 73, 109; disgust sensitivity 58, 71; as mother 15, 86, 104, 109, 111, 112–13
Dursley, Vernon 11, 49, 64, 71, 77, 109, 124
Dyer, Richard 70

Eagly, Alice H. 117n19
Edgecombe, Marietta 52, 139–40
Eichmann, Adolf 5, 7
Einstein, Albert 132
Eisenstadt, J. Marvin 122–23
Elder Wand 13, 77, 82, 143, 148, 169, 172; phallic 13, 18, 82, 143, 172; *see also* Hallows
elf rights *see* house elves, S.P.E.W.
Eliot, George (*The Mill on the Floss*) 88
elitism 52, 53, 63, 79, 87, 165n3
Elliott, Jane 109, 110, 113, 118n25
"The Elves and the Shoemaker" (Grimms) 93
Empathy 4, 5, 17, 18–19, 29n18, 80, 108, 123, 125–27, 129, 131, 155, 165
Engster, Daniel 11
Enlightenment, the 43, 168
epistemology 136, 139, 149, 151, 153
espionage 17, 19, 78, 121
ethics 2–8, 28n7, 31–32, 34–39, 44, 49, 56, 58, 62, 97, 100, 121, 137, 146–49, 154, 167, 169–73, 173n4; choices 22, 26, 36, 125, 170–73; "ends justify the means" 147, 170–72; principles 11–12, 33, 39, 57, 96; *see also* care ethics; choice; "greater good"; lies and lying
ethnic cleansing 27, 65, 70, 84n10
ethnocentrism 55, 67, 135, 168
Eurocentrism 56, 67
examinations 117n16, 120, 128, 152; O.W.L.s 24, 142
Expelliarmus (disarming spell) 115, 143, 149; makes killing curse rebound 10, 19, 53, 115, 143, 169, 172

"fake news" *see* propaganda
Fantastic Beasts and Where to Find Them 66, 89, 116n13

Farnel, Megan 87, 101, 173n2
Farr, Cecila Konchar ix
Faulkner, William (*The Sound and the Fury*) 105
Fawkes 114–15
Federalist Papers, The 41
Feist, Gregory J. 122, 130
Feldman, David Henry 122
Felix Felicis potion 34, 128, 146
feminism xii, 87, 89, 110, 116n6, 116n7, 117n17, 117n18, 132, 168; difference feminism 99, 117n17; liberal (rights) feminism 99, 100, 117n17; Marxist/socialist feminism 99, 117n17; multicultural feminism 99; radical feminism 117n7; relational feminism 11–12, 27, 87, 99–101, 104, 108, 111, 112, 116n4, 117n20; social feminism 99; trans-exclusionary radical feminism vii, 117n17
feminist interpretations 15, 85–89, 99–101, 104–5, 116n1, 117n17; series as sexist 4, 56, 85–87, 99, 108–11, 113, 114, 116n2, 118n25
fiction 83n1, 108, 122, 127–28, 131, 153; fantasy as commentary 2, 88, 110, 165n5, 167–69; truth of 163–65
Figg, Arabella 15, 56
Filch, Argus 15, 37, 39; cleaning 57, 71; sadism 20, 52; Squib 56
Finnigan, Seamus 157
Firenze 19, 66, 67
First Amendment (free speech, freedom of assembly) ix, xii, 2, 38
First Wizarding War 6, 40, 44, 72
Flamel, Nicolas 36, 37, 122
Fletcher, Mundungus 75, 147
Flitwick, Professor Filius 25
Floo Network 74, 120
Fluffy 36, 37, 130, 149
food/cooking 3, 15, 19, 31, 61, 72, 77, 88, 101; feasts 24, 157; Molly Weasley 73, 104, 110, 111, 113; Aunt Petunia's pudding 40, 42, 50, 91, 104, 138; treacle tart 36
Forbidden Forest 18, 25, 37, 38, 113, 128, 143
Ford Anglia 5, 110, 158
Foucault, Michel 150
Fountain of Magical Brethren, the 116n13, 162–63
Freeman, Louise M. 118n27, 118n28
free will 5, 6, 95, 171; and moral responsibility 6; *see also* house-elves

Freud, Sigmund 60–61
Friedan, Betty 88, 99
Frye, Northrop 3
Fudge, Cornelius 19, 148, 154; appearances, focus on 20, 45, 72, 156, 159; authoritarianism 9, 21, 41, 44, 121, 133, 154; coherence approach to truth 149–50; constructivist approach to truth 152–53; Dementor's Kiss, authorizes 19–20, 45, 48; and the *Daily Prophet* 133, 157, 158–59; Dumbledore, fear of 21; and *The Quibbler* 160; rule of law, subversion of the 7, 41, 42–43, 45, 46, 124; self-deception 153; Umbridge as deputy to 19, 20, 21, 121, 133, 157; Voldemort, suppression of truth about 19–20, 44, 46, 124, 133, 156, 159–60; *see also* Ministry of Magic

Gallardo-C., Ximena 29n17, 116n1
Gandhi, Mahatma 132
Gardner, Abby viii
Gardner, Howard 122
Garfinkle, Richard 8
Gaunt family 13, 59, 168
Gaunt, Merope (Riddle) 13, 69
gender 29n17, 54n9, 56, 87, 116n1, 117n20, 118n25, 168, 169; redefined 15, 19, 24n17; stereotyping 56, 85, 86, 109, 116n2, 151
genocide 25, 27, 44, 65, 70, 84n10
Genovese, Eugene D. 105
ghouls 68, 73, 128
giants 5, 44, 66, 68, 77–78, 84n10, 91, 131, 135, 139, 151, 159
Gierzynski, Anthony 169
Gilligan, Carol 11–15, 17; and patriarchy 12–15, 18–19, 32, 100, 114, 141, 155
Gilman, Charlotte Perkins 132
Gino, Francesa 128, 129
Gladstein, Mimi R. 116n1
Glanzer, Perry L. 28n3
Glasberg, Davita Silfen 159–60
Glăveanu, Vlad 11, 119, 127
Goblet of Fire 35, 36
goblins 19, 43, 54n1, 128, 148, 160, 170, 171; creative workmanship 139; discrimination against 5, 56, 65, 76, 81, 92, 96, 102, 116n13, 131, 135, 162, 167, 168; ownership, understanding of 67, 139; wars 57, 67
Godric's Hollow 127
Goodman, Jesse 4, 8, 34, 39

196 Index

Goebbels, Joseph 156–57, 160, 161–62, 163, 165, 165n8
Gotlieb, Rebecca J. M. 124–30
Granger, Hermione 16, 31, 36, 73, 76, 83n1, 111, 116n2, 140, 141, 146, 149, 158, 159, 162, 170; academic excellence 30–31, 38, 39, 45, 123, 152; and care ethics 12, 29n19, 117n20; creativity 119, 123–24, 129–31, 138, 139–40; criticisms of 22, 29n19, 98, 167; dynamic character 126, 135, 144n5, 167–68; empathy 73, 101, 109, 125–27; and ethics 22; and feminism 85, 89; future career 10, 24, 48, 135, 166, 168; and Harry's *Quibbler* interview 155, 157, 159, 160; Hopkirk, Mafalda, impersonation of 78–80; and house-elves 22–24, 48, 50, 57, 82, 88–91, 94, 97–98, 99, 101, 102, 115, 126, 127, 131, 134, 135, 140, 167–68, 173; lies 12, 128, 146; Luna, contrast with 140; magical skill 36, 80, 152; McLaggen, jinxes 33; as Muggle-born 50, 57, 63, 81, 155–56, 159; outsider's perspective 50, 57, 77, 82, 131, 133, 135, 149; and Polyjuice Potion 22, 36, 129; and race 83n1, 171n3; and research 18, 57, 73, 89–90, 135; as resistance leader 19, 22–24, 52–53, 83, 121, 131, 137; ridiculed 38, 77, 81, 133; Ron, love for 33, 74, 80–82, 107; rule breaking 12, 21, 22, 28n2, 31, 33, 36, 37–38, 45, 48, 52–53, 73, 75, 78, 129, 138, 146, 155, 171; rules, respect for 16, 22; S.P.E.W. (Society for the Promotion of Elvish Welfare) 20, 22–24, 81, 88–89, 99, 129, 135, 167–68; systemic injustice, recognition of 22–24, 49–50, 52–53, 57, 81, 143; and Umbridge, Dolores 24, 137, 152, 155; uses Voldemort's name 52–53; *see also* Dumbledore's Army; S.P.E.W
Granger, John 151, 163
Grawp 19, 68
"greater good, the" 28, 148, 169–72
Greyback, Fenrir 19, 67–68
Griesinger, Emily 28n3, 107, 165n5
Grimes, M. Katherine 28n4
Grindelwald, Gellert 9, 148, 169–70
Gringotts Bank 8, 19, 21, 39, 102, 138, 142, 170
Griphook 19, 82, 92, 102, 128, 139, 148, 170, 171
Groves, Beatrice 29n17, 144n5
Gryffindor, Godric 139

Gryffindor House 16, 33, 34, 38, 98, 128, 133, 147, 155, 167; traits 23, 107
Guilford, J. P. 120

Hagrid, Rubeus 25, 35, 38, 44, 50, 54n4, 58, 67, 68, 73–5, 77–78, 125, 130–31, 139, 146, 158, 161; Azkaban, sent to 40, 45, 66; and Buckbeak 45, 147; and gender roles 15, 104; and house-elves 86, 88, 89, 97, 98, 103, 134, 167; on Voldemort 13, 51
Haidt, Jonathan 62
Half-Blood Prince *see* Snape, Severus
Hall, Susan 13, 39, 43, 54n1, 54n3
Hallows 125, 129, 130, 131, 146, 148, 149, 164; "Master of Death" 33, 70, 92, 125; *see also* Elder Wand; invisibility cloak, Resurrection Stone; "Tale of the Three Brothers"
Hamilton, V. Lee 5
Hamington, Maurice 11, 39, 146
Hanrahan, Brie vii, xii
Harry Potter and the Chamber of Secrets 5, 22, 40, 41–42, 45, 52, 54n8, 71, 90, 91, 94, 96–97, 105, 106, 123, 125, 138
Harry Potter and the Cursed Child 83n1, 166
Harry Potter and the Deathly Hallows 5, 6, 10, 12, 16, 17, 18–19, 21, 22, 25, 28n8, 39, 48, 50, 53, 59, 65–66, 67, 74, 77–81, 106–107, 111–14, 126, 128, 138–39, 141, 162–65, 166, 169–73
Harry Potter and the Goblet of Fire 6–7, 16, 19, 23, 35, 37, 69, 71–72, 73, 77–78, 90–91, 104–105, 110, 122, 133, 136, 142–3, 157, 159, 162–65, 167–68, 169
Harry Potter and the Half-Blood Prince 5, 13, 15, 25, 33, 36, 37, 46–47, 96, 112, 121–22, 123, 127, 129, 132, 133, 137, 140, 153, 173
Harry Potter and the Half-Blood Prince (film) 61
Harry Potter and the Order of the Phoenix 7, 8, 17, 19, 20–21, 22, 24, 41, 52–53, 66, 68–69, 71, 106, 117n21, 127, 137, 147, 152–55, 157, 159–60, 162
Harry Potter and the Prisoner of Azkaban 1–2, 31, 38, 42, 45, 147, 154, 157, 159
Harry Potter and the Prisoner of Azkaban (film) 2
Harry Potter and the Sorcerer's Stone 2, 16, 22, 34–35, 37, 38, 49, 50–52, 75, 77, 86, 107, 113, 114, 122, 128, 154, 164
Harry Potter films 2, 4, 76

Hedwig 58
Heilman, Elizabeth E. 38n5, 85
Henderson, Tolonda xin1, 54n9, 163
heroism 4, 7, 34, 54n8, 56, 85, 87, 107–8, 124, 128, 149, 151, 157, 172–73
history 9, 28n11, 56, 57, 58, 60, 87, 90, 97, 99, 100, 117n17, 131, 135, 139, 142, 151, 164, 173
History of Magic class 56, 67, 120, 128
Hitler, Adolf 9, 19, 48, 63–64, 156, 162, 163, 169
Hochschild, Arlie Russell 111
Hogshead pub 59
Hogwarts: A History 135, 167
Hogwarts Express 51, 60, 166
Hogwarts School of Witchcraft and Wizardry 1, 5, 7, 8, 16, 20–21, 23, 24, 34, 41, 42, 55, 56, 63, 71, 75, 77, 82, 90, 91, 110, 113, 120, 122, 123, 125, 126, 129, 131, 133, 137, 138, 140, 141, 149, 157, 158, 161, 164, 173n1; history of 5, 7, 90, 91; Ministry interference at 3, 19, 20, 24, 38, 121, 150, 153; privilege, reinforcement of 23, 34, 56, 57, 63, 65–67, 86; rules 1, 2, 22, 26, 34, 36–39, 61; *see also* Battle of Hogwarts; house-elves
Hogsmeade 1, 37, 42
Hokey 23, 40, 66, 87, 92, 94
Hooch, Madame Rolanda 15, 34
Hopkirk, Mafalda 78–80 *see also* Granger, Hermione
Horcruxes 19, 128, 137, 145–46; cave 5, 91, 115, 128, 155; creation of 14, 18, 27, 32, 115, 122, 144n4; Harry as 17, 142, 166, 172; Hufflepuff's cup 139, 170; quest for 17, 19, 74, 81, 120, 124, 126, 130, 131, 137, 142, 143, 145, 170; Ravenclaw's diadem 139, 144n9; Riddle's diary 63; remorse and 18–19, 53; ring 124; Slytherin's locket 73, 81, 88, 101, 110, 115, 124, 137, 139, 147, 155
Horne, Jackie C. 23, 86, 117n18
House Cup 16, 38, 49, 128
house-elves 5, 6, 19, 26, 29n19, 40, 42, 56, 66, 71, 72, 117n10, 118n16, 126, 131, 133, 135, 13n3; American 89; analogies to enslaved humans 85, 87, 88–90, 92, 95, 101, 102, 104–5, 107, 108, 116n11, 117n22, 117n23; in Battle of Hogwarts 101–2; "beings" 96, 117n13; and clothing 59, 74–5, 87, 93; depiction of as racist 85, 86–87, 90, 107; disagreement with masters 94, 95; disobedience by 85, 87, 88, 95–96, 101–3, 106–7; enslavement of, characters' attitudes towards 76, 77, 81, 82, 86–87, 88–9, 92, 98; enslavement of as culturally determined 89, 92–93, 94, 95, 97–98, 100, 117n23; enslavement of as "natural" 27, 88–90, 93, 94, 97, 106; enslaving enchantments 27, 92–95, 105; families of 88, 92–93, 100–7, 115, 117n16, 117n22; feared by wizards 91–92; free will 94–99, 101–7; history of 57, 89–90, 92–93, 96–97, 98, 103, 135, 139; Hogwarts house-elves 23, 62, 90, 91, 94, 98, 134; humor and 86–87; inferiority, supposed 90–91, 115–16; internalized racism 88, 97, 98; legal status 22, 23, 24, 65, 66, 92, 96, 99, 102; loopholes in orders, exploiting 95; love and 27, 76, 85, 89, 94, 98, 100–7, 115–16; Medieval precursors 91, 117n9; obedience by 89, 94–96, 103, 106–7; Office for House-Elf Relocation 117n22; powers of 27, 85, 87, 90–92, 107–8, 115–16, 117n8, 117n9, 168; prospects for future change 95, 96–97; punishment of 94–95, 106, 117n12; resistance and 85, 87, 91–92, 95–97, 101, 102, 105–7, 134, 168; rules governing behavior of 85, 94–95; and social class 86, 87, 99; unresolved issue 4, 23, 28, 98, 167–9, 173n2; and wands 23, 65, 91–92, 115; "willing slaves" 86, 94, 97, 98, 102–7, 134, 162; women, resemblances to 27, 85, 87–88, 96, 97–101, 104, 106–7, 117n5, 117n12, 117n20; *see also* Dobby; Hokey; Kreacher; S.P.E.W.; Winky
House points 16, 28n2, 38, 49, 155
housewives 27, 73, 86–88, 104, 109
Howard, Susan 106, 107, 122
Hsieh, Diana Mertz 156n6
Hufflepuff, Helga 90
Huffman, Stephen 64
humor 61, 68, 73, 76, 83n7, 86–87, 109, 110, 125

imagination 108, 121, 124–29, 139, 142, 164, 169; and empathy 108, 123, 126–27
imperialism *see* eurocentrism
Imperius Curse 5–8, 16–17, 21, 25–26, 28n8, 95, 170–71; resisting 6–8, 16–17, 21, 25–26, 28n8, 95, 170–71

Inferi 70
in-groups and out-groups 26, 49, 55, 62, 63, 64, 164–65
Inquisitorial Squad 38
International Statute of Wizarding Secrecy 41–42, 43, 54n4, 63, 156, 168
interpretive frames 50
intersectionality 56, 87, 117n20
invisibility cloak 1, 2, 37–38, 75, 91, 104, 115, 143, 148, 170; *see also* Hallows
iPads 120

James, Rachel McCarthy 29n19, 167
James, Stanlie M. 105
January 6, 2021 insurrection 162
Jim Crow 90, 134
Jobs, Steve 132; *see also* iPads
Johnston, Hank 20, 24
Jordan, Ellen 116n7
Jordan, Lee 22, 62
Jorkins, Bertha 43, 83n3
Journalism 158–59; *see also* news media

Kant, Immanuel 96
Karkaroff, Igor 35–36, 46–47, 136
Kasibhatla, Bharati 23, 29n19
Kellner, Rivka Temina 87, 99
Kelman, Herbert 5
Kendi, Ibram X. 81
Kern, Edmund M. 3–4, 28n3, 28n4, 173n4
King, Martin Luther, Jr. 11, 20, 116n11; creative maladjustment 27, 119, 132–35, 140, 143; "Letter from Birmingham Jail" 134–38, 141
King's Cross Station 15, 18, 59, 70, 163–64, 170, 171–2; Platform 9 ¾ 30, 112, 118n28, 138, 164; *see also* Potter, Harry, near-death experience
Knockturn Alley 59
Kohlberg, Lawrence (stages of moral development) 4, 11
Köhler, Ulrike Kristina 34
Kornfeld, John 86, 109–10
Kreacher 27, 29, 75, 82, 87, 88, 106, 115, 167; at Battle of Hogwarts 101–2; Black family, love for 95, 96, 101–3, 126; and Black family possessions 73, 88, 103; disobedience by 95, 101–2; gratitude 101–2, 104, 126; Harry, attitudes towards 96, 101–2, 104, 155; Harry as master 94, 96, 155, 172; and Harry's sandwich 82, 167; and locket 73, 78; rebelliousness 73, 88, 93, 95–96, 101, 111; Sirius,

responsibility for death of 88, 92, 147, 167

Lacassagne, Aurélie 104
LaHaie, Jeanne Hoeker 29n19, 86, 109
Lavoie, Chantel M. 147
laws and legal systems, Muggle and Wizarding 7, 9, 34, 36, 48, 54n7, 63, 66, 67, 77, 96, 122; due process 19, 40, 66, 159; equality before the law 43, 46, 168; flaws and injustices 10–11, 13, 21, 23, 26, 30, 34, 39, 40–48, 53, 54n3, 54n6, 65, 66, 79, 99, 117n20, 117n22, 135, 143, 171; legislative process 38, 40–41, 47, 66, 96, 116n13; pro-pureblood laws 24; rule of law 13, 23, 26, 39, 44, 47, 72; separation of powers 43; time travel 31; trials and hearings 7, 19, 40, 41, 43, 45–47, 78, 124, 126, 136; *see also* Azkaban, magical law enforcement; resistance; trials and legal hearings
laws of magic 26, 30–33, 54n5, 122; Adalbert Waffling's Fundamental Laws of Magic 32; Gamp's Law of Elemental Transfiguration 31; Golpalott's Third Law 30–31, 152; saving a fellow wizard's life 31; scientific laws, similarity to 26, 30–31; wands 31; *see also* love
Law, Wendy N. 28n4
Leaky Cauldron, the 58
Lee, Laura Yiyin 151
Legilimency 165n4; for control 147; and emotions 17; and empathy 17; as invasive 147; *see also* Voldemort, connection to Harry
Lestrange, Bellatrix 7, 47, 65, 95, 106, 109, 136, 170–71; as "anti-mother" 112; Weasley, Molly, battle with 111–12
Lestrange, Rabastan 47, 109, 136
Lestrange, Rodolphus 47, 109
Levine, Bruce E. 133, 134
Lewis, John (Congressman) vii, 26
Lewis, Mark-Anthony 66
Lewis, Orion A. 29n13
library restricted section 36, 37
lies and lying vii; "alternative facts" ("fake news," "post-truth") 150, 154, 158; altruistic 128, 146, 154; Animagi and 148, 163; "basic hegemonic lie" (Bailey) 105, 135–36, 162–63; "Big Lie" 148, 156–57, 161–63, 165; "blue lies" 156; counterfactual thinking 127–28; as creative 124, 128; by Crouch, Barty 6,

147, 148, 163; detecting 44–45, 147; by Dumbledore 128, 146, 154; by the Dursleys 146, 156; ethical considerations 2, 129, 146–49, 154; false accusations of lying 28, 121, 133, 145, 146, 152–53, 154, 156; fiction as 122, 127–28, 153, 164; by Fudge, Cornelius 154, 156, 157, 159; Goebbels, Joseph 156–57, 160, 162; by Grindelwald, Gellert 148; by Harry 2, 5, 27, 128, 145–46, 147–48, 160; Harry as resisting lies 145, 150, 153–54, 157–58, 160, 162; by Hermione 12, 128, 146; Hitler, Adolf 162; "I must not tell lies" 38, 62, 121, 153, 156, 157; by Kreacher 91, 92, 96, 147, 167; by Ministry of Magic 27–28, 45, 54n1, 160–63, 152–59; resistance, lies that contribute to the 75, 128–29, 147–48; lies of omission 136, 154–58; by Lockhart, Gilderoy 147; by Malfoy, Draco 45, 146; by Malfoy, Narcissa 25, 113, 148; malicious 146; mental reservation 128, 148, 170; occlumency as 148; Orwell, George on 145, 150, 165n1; Polyjuice Potion as 128, 129, 148; by Ron 128–29; as rule breaking 128; self-deception 69, 141, 143, 148, 153, 165n6, 170; by Scrimgeour, Rufus 148, 153, 157; as self defense 128–29, 145–46; by Skeeter, Rita 146, 154; by Slughorn, Horace (altered memory) 128; by Snape, Severus 148; social lies 146, 154; target, effect on 146; and totalitarianism 145, 150, 154, 155–57, 160; and trickster tradition 145; by Umbridge, Delores 147, 150, 152, 155, 156, 165n3; Umbridge, Delores, false accusations of lying by 28, 121, 145, 146, 152–53, 155, 157; Voldemort and 122, 146, 148, 164; *see also* Big Lie; censorship; creativity; *Daily Prophet*; Goebbels, Joseph; Polyjuice Potion; propaganda; truth

Lincoln, Abraham 132

Lipińska, Joanna 67

Litchfield, Robert C. 129

Little Hangleton cemetery 7, 142–43

Lockhart, Gilderoy 83n3, 147

Longbottom, Alice 47, 109, 126, 136; as Auror 44, 109; as mother 109, 127

Longbottom, Frank 44, 47, 126, 136

Longbottom, Neville 28n2, 44, 52, 109, 137, 141, 148; house points, wins 49; Remembrall incident 15, 35;

as resistance leader 19, 20, 39, 140; Voldemort's other intended victim 109, 127, 136

Lopes, Juliana Valdes 66

love 13, 15, 25n15, 32, 70, 81, 89, 103, 131, 142, 168; dangers of 100–101, 105, 112; vs. hierarchy 13, 82; as motivation 7, 25, 58, 72, 73–74, 80, 100–101, 104–8, 111, 113, 115, 126, 14; vs. patriarchy 12, 13, 14, 27, 143–44; as power 12, 17, 18, 26, 32–33, 53, 59, 62, 70, 100–101, 107–8, 113, 115–16, 126, 140, 141, 143–44, 164, 169; and resistance 8–9, 12, 17, 25, 27, 72, 101, 105, 112, 113, 141, 143–44; *see also* Amortentia; cleaning; house-elves; self-sacrifice

Lovegood, Luna 74, 115, 160, 161; creativity of 140–41; and friendship 140–41; ostracized 49, 129, 140; resistance fighter 19, 111, 140; thestrals, ability to see 140

Lovegood, Xenophilius 115, 129, 140, 149, 160, 161

Lowery, Alyssa Magee 173n2

Lurie, Alison 3

Lupin, Nymphadora *see* Tonks, Nymphadora

Lupin, Remus 68, 73, 126; discrimination against 40, 60, 66, 67, 77; flaws 172; infiltrates werewolves 19; poverty 59–60; on resistance 21, 22, 161; Snape's hostility towards 67; as teacher 60, 67, 68, 152; Tonks, marriage to 56, 172; on Voldemort's methods 21

lycanthropy 60, 66, 68; metaphor for HIV 69, 84n11; *see also* werewolves; Lupin, Remus

MacNeil, William P. 35, 47, 54n3, 86, 117n20

"Magic Is Might" sculpture 93, 160–61, 62

Malfoy, Draco 5, 25, 28n2, 35, 65, 68, 75, 96, 109, 113, 120, 131, 133, 141, 148, 166; Aryan appearance 9; bigotry 55, 57, 59–60, 63, 65, 76, 81; and Buckbeak 45, 147; bullying 15, 29n18, 35; claim he has "no choice" 7; privilege 56

Malfoy family 52, 77, 109, 141; authoritarian 49, 109; and Dobby 23, 59, 75, 93–96, 103, 105, 106, 107, 117n23, 138

Malfoy, Lucius 35, 45, 85, 91, 93, 106, 109, 113, 115, 141; power 91, 133

Malfoy, Narcissa 65, 92, 109, 110, 112–13; and disgust 60; lies 25, 113, 148; resisting Voldemort by protecting Draco 8, 25, 113, 141
Malfoy, Scorpius 166
mammy figure 92, 105; *see also* othermothers; Winky
Marauders 68, 121, 148
Marauder's Map, the 1–2, 75, 121, 136
March for Our Lives 29n12
masculinity 12, 14–15, 18–19, 72, 87, 114; redefinitions 12, 15, 29n17
Maternal thinking 100, 112, 118n29
Maxime, Madame Olympe 35, 44
Mayes-Elma, Ruthann 86
McCauley, Clark 42
McCauley, Patrick 15
McDaniel, Kathryn N. 10, 28n11, 29n19, 87–88, 95, 116n10, 157, 165n7
McElya, Micki 105
McGonagall, Minerva 21, 38, 137, 145, 171; overrides Hogwarts rules to recruit Harry 34–35; as resistance participant 25, 62, 150; and Time-Turner 31; and Voldemort's name 50–51
McIntosh, Peggy 56–57, 66, 81
McLaggen, Cormac 33
Meihls, Ashley 84n12
memory 16, 17, 59, 68, 124, 126, 127, 128, 129, 136–37, 148, 158, 171; *see also* Pensieve
memory modification 6, 43, 45, 83n3, 156
Mendelssohn, Felix 132
Mendlesohn, Farah 22–23, 35, 86, 95, 163, 167
mental illness xiii, 32, 47, 101, 109, 132–34, 138; Harry and Dumbledore, allegations of 133–34, 157; Oppositional Defiance Disorder 133–34; *see also* creative maladjustment; creativity; dementors
merpeople 66–67, 68, 135, 162, 167
Meteolojinx Recanto 80
#MeToo 136
Milgram, Stanley 5, 7, 20
Mill, John Stuart (*The Subjection of Women*) 88–89, 92, 94, 96, 97, 101, 116n12; critique of argument that women's subjection is "natural" 88–89, 92, 98; liberal feminism 99; "no enslaved class ever asked for complete liberty at once" 95, 101; women's subjection as cultural 89, 97, 98; "willing slaves" 89, 97, 99; women's subjection resembles slavery 27, 88–89, 92, 94, 95, 97, 99
Mill on the Floss, The (Eliot) 88
Ministers of Magic 40–41, 47; selection process 7, 25, 40–41; *see also* Granger; Hermione; Fudge, Cornelius; Scrimgeour, Rufus; Shacklebolt, Kingsley; Thicknesse, Pius
Ministry of Magic 1–2, 6, 12, 17, 19, 20, 23, 34, 25, 30, 31–32, 37, 40, 42–43, 56, 61, 66, 78, 83n3, 92, 110, 111, 116n13, 119, 122, 130, 131, 136, 149–50, 158, 165n3; Accidental Magic Reversal Squad 43; corruption of 2, 7, 8, 9, 10, 19, 20, 21, 24–26, 27–28, 38, 39, 40–48, 49–50, 54n1, 110, 129, 132, 133, 136, 141, 145, 150, 153–54, 156, 160, 166; Department of International Magical Cooperation 43, 136; Goblin-Liaison Office 43; Improper Use of Magic Office 43, 78; incursions into 17, 19, 21, 78–80, 142; Magical Maintenance 78–80, 165n3; Misuse of Muggle Artifacts Office 43; Office for the Detection and Confiscation of Counterfeit Defensive Spells and Protective Objects 43; under Voldemort's control 7, 8, 10, 21, 25, 39, 47, 62, 63, 65, 93, 121, 141, 160–63; *see also* Battle of the Ministry; dementors; Department of Magical Law Enforcement; Department for the Regulation and Control of Magical Creatures; Ministers of Magic; laws and legal theories; privilege; propaganda; Umbridge, Dolores; truth, constructivist theory of
Mirror of Erised, the 38, 128, 142, 148, 157
miscegenation *see* disgust/blood purity
misdirection (things not what they seem) 58, 59, 68, 90–91, 163
Mitchell, Martha 132–33, 144 n.8
Moaning Myrtle 40, 44
Moody, Alastor "Mad-Eye": as Auror 44; "Constant vigilance" 173; death of 74, 118n24; *see also* Barty Crouch, Jr., disguised as Mad-Eye Moody
Morales, Andrea 83n7
mothers 13, 15, 74, 78, 80, 86, 104, 109, 113, 115, 118n27, 118n29, 140, 157, 165n3; *see also* Black, Walburga; Dursley, Petunia; Longbottom, Alice; Malfoy, Narcissa; mammy figure; othermothers;

Potter, Lily; Tonks, Nymphadora; Weasley, Molly
motherhood 112; as disempowering 86, 87, 116n14; as empowering 87, 104, 105, 109, 111, 113, 115–16, 116n4
Mrs. Skower's All-Purpose Magical Mess Remover 71; *see also* cleaning"
"mudbloods" (Muggle-borns) 22–24, 26, 27, 43, 45, 48, 55, 57, 58, 62, 63, 65, 66, 72, 76, 79, 81, 101, 103, 133, 135, 156, 158, 159, 161; *see also* Granger, Hermione; Muggle-born Registration Commission; racism
Muggle-Born Registration Commission 9, 19, 43, 47, 48, 54n6, 79, 80, 121, 163
Muggle-Worthy Excuse Committee 43
Muggles 3, 7, 17, 26, 30, 33–34, 40–47, 49, 54n1, 54n7, 71, 72, 76, 77, 83n10, 84n13, 88, 111, 125, 130, 131, 141, 158, 159, 167–69; attributes and accomplishments of 20, 23, 24, 54n1, 67, 131, 149, 160, 168; inferiority of, perceived 5, 40, 45, 53, 56, 57, 63, 65, 66, 67, 70, 77, 83, 93, 151, 156, 161, 162, 165n3; manipulation of 43, 44, 45, 59, 83, 156; Muggle-baiting 40, 57, 81; murder of 9, 57, 62, 66, 69, 161, 163; oppression of 3, 5, 26, 49, 56, 63, 65, 66, 135, 169–70, 172; refusal to see magic 59; *see also* laws and legal systems
Muggle Studies 63, 67, 135, 160–61; *see also* Burbage, Charity; Carrow, Alecto
murder *see* death; Horcruxes
Muriel, Aunt 139
My Lai massacre 5

Nabokov, Vladimir 136
Nagini 8, 70, 143
narcissism 7, 8, 28n9
Nash, John 132
Nazi ideology 9, 48, 63–64, 132, 156, 162–63, 169; Aryans 9, 63–64, 70, 156; *see also* antisemitism; Hitler, Adolf; World War II
Neal, Connie 28n3
Nearly Headless Nick 146
news media vii, 8, 54n1; adversarial 158–159, 161; fact checking 83n5, 83n9, 149, 152, 158–160; importance of 28, 168; manipulation of by government 27–28, 48, 54n1, 133, 139, 150, 156–57, 159, 160; reliability of 158–60; *see also* censorship; *Daily Prophet*;

journalism; propaganda; *Potterwatch*; *Quibbler*; Skeeter, Rita
Newton, Isaac 31, 32
Nielsen, Connor 116n9
Nixon, Richard M. 132
Noddings, Nel 11, 29n19, 125
nonconformity *see* conformity/ nonconformity
norms, "normal" 10–11, 19, 26, 48–49, 53, 54n7, 55, 56, 58, 60, 71, 76, 77, 78, 84n11, 89, 99, 101, 131, 132, 134, 148, 155, 168, 173; Muggle norms 3, 49, 55; wizard norms 1, 2, 3, 8, 11, 26, 27, 30, 49–51, 53, 67, 71, 78, 82, 99, 131, 139, 140, 143
Nowak, Tenille 3
number twelve Grimmauld Place 59, 63, 72–73, 111
Nuremberg Trials 5
Nurmengard Prison 170
Nussbaum, Martha 62, 69

obedience 5, 94, 97, 128, 172; arguments for 2, 4, 5, 17; arguments against 4–8, 10–11, 49; crimes of 5; and the Imperius Curse 5–7, 8, 16, 21, 95; *see also* house-elves; rule breaking
obedience research 5, 7, 20, 53
Obliviate charm *see* memory modification
Occlumency 29n18, 130; as resistance 17, 148; Harry's inability 17, 148; Harry's success at 17; *see also* Legilimency
Offen, Karen 99–100, 117n17
Office of Misinformation 43, 156
Olatunji, Bunmi O. 83n6
Ollivander, Garrick 19, 31, 51–52, 59
Omolade, Barbara 105
Order of the Phoenix, the vii, 8, 9, 11, 19, 22, 24, 25, 50, 61, 73, 109, 111, 113, 118n26, 131, 154
Orwell, George 94, 145, 150, 165n1, 170
Ostry, Elaine 83n2
othering 13, 49, 56, 57, 58, 62, 64, 66–67, 76, 83n2, 86, 97, 112–13, 141
"othermothers" 104–5

Park, Julia 86–87
Parseltongue 15, 125
Pasteur, Louis 142
Patil, Padma 52, 56
Patil, Parvati 56
patriarchy 4, 11, 82–3, 143, 166–67; autonomy 12, 14, 18, 100, 141, 143;

emotional detachment / stoicism 14, 17–18; vs. democracy 12, 19, 155, 166, 169–70; hierarchy 12–13, 19, 56, 87, 100, 141, 155, 166; vs. relationships 12, 13, 15, 25, 32, 85, 100, 115–16; and self-sacrifice 15, 27, 115–16; vs. vulnerability 18, 32–33, 62, 100; *see also* care ethics
Patronus 16, 124, 152, 171; and care 16, 115; and imagination 125; *see also* dementors
Patterson, Steven W. 96, 116n10
Paustian-Underdahl, Samantha C. 117n19
Peeves 120
Pelton, Leroy 20, 107, 126, 134–35
Pensieve 14, 46, 59, 126, 136
Petrou, Paraskevas 130
Pettigrew, Peter ("Wormtail") 150, 172; betrayal of Potters 1, 7, 68, 114, 147; hand 7, 70; Harry saves his life 31, 126; and obedience 7–8, 72; possible homosexuality 68–69; ratlike traits 68; as Scabbers 37, 68, 163
Peverell brothers 73, 164; *see also* "Tale of the Three Brothers, The"
Pharr, Mary 145, 151, 157, 173n2
Phillips-Mattson, Christina 144n4
Philosopher's Stone *see* Sorcerer's Stone
Piaget, Jean 11
Pince, Madam 59
PISSAR 135
Plato 10–11, 132
police misconduct 43–44, 65, 66, 72, 79, 135, 156
politics viii, 2, 4, 5, 8–10, 11–13, 19, 23–24, 29n16, 30, 39, 43, 48, 49, 55–56, 60, 66, 95, 99, 100, 101, 103, 107, 116n4, 118n29, 120, 131, 132, 134–35, 137–38, 150, 156, 159–63, 168, 169
politically resistant curiosity 134–38; and audience 137–38; epistemic curiosity 136; *see also* creativity; creative maladjustment
Polyjuice Potion 10, 22, 36, 58–59; as deception 128–29, 148; as means to empathy 78–81, 129
Popovich, Gregg 82
Portkeys 35, 39
portraits, magical 63, 73, 102–103, 120, 141
Post, Jerrold M. 28n9
postmodernism 150–52, 163, 165n5; *see also* truth, constructivist theory of

potions text book 5, 59, 121–22, 123, 129, 131, 146–47
Potter, Albus 166
Potter, Harry *passim*; as adult 10, 44, 166; boa constrictor, releases 15, 124; and cheating 34–36, 129; and coherence approach to truth 149–50, 165; conscientiousness, deficiency of 130–31; and correspondence approach to truth 152, 157; and curiosity 130–32, 135, 136–38, 145, 154; delusional, accusation of being; diversifying experiences 131–32; dynamic character 19, 28 n.7, 51, 107, 127, 155, 167, 168, 172–73; empathy 15–19, 23, 93, 102, 125–26, 131; and *Expelliarmus* 115, 143, 169, 172; flaws 82, 167, 169, 170–73; and gender 15, 18–19; as Horcrux 17, 18, 142, 172; imagination of 124–27, 142; infancy 15; as Kreacher's master 95–96, 101, 103–4, 167; love/care, capacity for 15–18, 114–16, 143; and luck 141–43; lying 2, 5, 27, 128–29, 145–48, 160; lying, false accusations of 121, 133, 145, 146, 152–53; as "maladjusted" 133; and Marauder's Map 1–2; messiness of 58, 71, 73–4; near-death experience 18, 59, 163–64, 170, 171–72; nonviolence of 2, 10, 28n11, 115–16, 126, 143, 169; obedience by 4–5, 6; and Occlumency 17, 130, 148; openness to new experiences 130, 131;and oppositional defiant disorder 133; as outsider 49–51, 55, 77–78, 82, 131, 151; as point of view character 4, 28n7, 29 n.19, 41, 49–51, 55, 57, 58, 76–78, 90–91, 109–11, 113, 116n2, 118n25, 136, 138, 151, 152, 154, 171, 172–73; privilege 35, 46, 54n2, 82, 171; propaganda, rejection of 48, 145, 153–54, 158, 162; and the prophecy 127 132, 142, 154; and Quidditch 4, 34–35; resilience 132; Riddle Tom /Voldemort, similarities with 15, 122–23, 126, 131; rules, breaking of 1–4, 15–16, 31, 34–36 41–43, 45–46, 48, 145–6, 170–73; as role model (or not) for readers 2–3, 164–65, 169, 172–73; scar 166; and trauma 15, 18, 122–23, 131, 132, 163;and Voldemort, death of 10, 18–19, 115, 141, 143, 158, 166–67, 171–72; Voldemort, mercy towards 18–19; and Voldemort's name 50–53, 137;

Voldemort, understanding of 126, 142; Wizengamot hearing 7, 20, 41–43, 46, 124; Zeitgeist (wizarding), resists 11, 49–50, 143

Potter, James 38, 68–69, 113, 126, 159; as Black 64–65; bravery of 114; bully 72, 126, 150, 172; death of 15, 58, 113, 124, 146, 147, 156; Harry's shifting view of 16, 172; privileged 74, 172; sacrifice 118n24; *see also* Marauders

Potter, Lily 64, 72, 86, 109, 115, 118n29; bravery 114, 159; characterized 113; critique of 108–109, 113, 114; death of 1, 15, 18, 53, 58, 62, 69, 124, 127, 146, 147, 156; love (power) 87, 100, 107, 113, 114, 142, 163; self-sacrifice 53, 100, 107, 108, 109, 113, 114, 115, 118n24, 127, 142, 143; skills 113; Voldemort, defiance of 109, 113

Potterwatch 19, 21, 22, 28, 138, 161

power 14, 28, 40, 44, 48, 49, 53, 58, 61, 66, 86, 89, 105, 121, 122, 123, 141, 145, 146, 148, 150, 153, 161, 164, 167; magical 6, 7, 8, 9, 17, 22, 26, 27, 32, 33, 37, 47–48, 50, 52, 60, 61, 65, 66, 67. 80, 85, 90–96, 101, 102, 107, 112, 113–16, 116n8, 125, 126, 135, 142, 143, 146, 163, 164, 168–70, 171–72; political 4, 7, 8, 9, 20, 23, 28, 38, 39, 40–41, 53, 78, 81, 89, 95, 97, 99–100, 131, 133, 156, 165, 165n3, 167–73; "power the Dark Lord knows not," the 27, 85, 107, 141, 142; and resistance 4, 9, 12, 87, 111, 139, 145, 173; redefined 17, 24, 27, 53, 80, 85, 87, 99–101, 104, 107–108, 110, 111, 113–16, 116n4, 126, 127, 140, 141, 142, 143, 161, 164–65, 169; *see also* house-elves; love

powers, separation of *see* laws and legal systems

Prefects, prefect system 12, 38, 61

press *see* news media

Prime Minister, Muggle 31, 40

Prinzi, Travis 28n9, 28n10, 68, 108, 125, 142, 144n3, 151, 168

privilege 26–27, 49, 56, 82, 133, 166, 168, 172; and intersectionality 56, 76, 81–82; invisibility of 56, 57, 66–67, 75, 81, 89, 168; as systemic 57, 65–67, 81

privilege, male 56, 89, 99, 116n5

privilege, pure-blood 26, 55, 56, 65, 81, 123, 143, 172

privilege, white 26, 56, 57, 76, 81, 89

privilege, wizard 23, 26, 27, 55, 56–57, 58, 65–67, 76, 78, 82, 83n3, 89, 99, 116n5, 123, 168, 170

propaganda 22, 48, 54n1, 105, 121, 156, 161–63; "alternative facts" 145, 150, 154, 158; public relations 48, 135, 153–54; ridicule and stigmatization of opponents 139, 156–57, 159; and totalitarianism 154, 156, 157; visual 160–61, 162–63; World War II 62, 63, 156

prophecy 113, 127, 132, 136, 142, 154, 158, 160

Prophecy, Hall of 17

protective spells 43, 44, 53, 115; *Protego* (Shield Charm) 53, 115; *see also Expelliarmus*; Patronus

Prothro, Laurie 86, 109–10

Pugh, Tison 116n2

Punishments 2, 5, 11, 37, 42, 47, 49, 98, 100, 105, 106, 129, 150; arbitrary 26, 38, 40, 42, 47; cleaning 38, 72; cruel and unusual 47, 48; detention 5, 28n2, 38, 39, 137, 145; expulsion 7, 16, 20, 34, 37, 40, 41–43, 124, 125, 138, 155; lines 38, 62; physical abuse 20, 25, 28, 37–38, 39, 42, 70, 94–95, 100, 106, 121, 155, 156, 159–60; points, loss of 16, 28n2, 38, 155; without trial or hearing 45–46, 126; wand loss 42–43, 65, 82; *see also* Azkaban; Cruciatus Curse; dementors; house elves; Umbridge, Dolores

public relations *see* propaganda

Puppet String News 64

queer theory/queerness viii–ix, xin1, xii–xiii, 3, 84n11, 60, 68–69, 169

Quibbler, The 140; Harry's interview 21, 38, 138, 155, 160; as resistance publication 19, 28, 138, 160, 161

Quidditch 33–36, 46, 57, 71, 77, 137, 146, 147; bludger 33, 91, 138; cheating in 4, 33–34, 36, 62; rules of 26, 34, 36; Seeker 34–36, 145; Snitch 34, 54n2, 68–69, 145

Quidditch Through the Ages 33–34, 36

Quidditch World Cup 35, 43, 59–61, 83n3, 90–91, 100, 104, 129, 158–59

Quick-Quotes Quill 122, 159, 160

Quirrell, Professor Quirinus 7–8, 142, 148, 149–50, 152, 158, 163

race (Muggle) 49, 55–56, 63–65, 69–70, 76, 81, 82, 83n1, 83n2, 83n10, 86–87, 107, 117n20, 119–135, 138, 151, 168
"race traitors" 9, 25, 56, 76, 103
racism vii, 169; internalized 68, 88, 96, 98, 126; Muggle 49, 55–57, 60, 63–65, 70, 81, 131, 134–36, 138, 140; "post-racial" 86; racial discrimination 56–57, 60, 65–66, 68, 119, 134–36, 168; systemic vii, 2, 9, 19, 22, 23–24, 26, 27, 28, 13, 43, 47, 48, 54n6, 55–57, 62–63, 65–67, 75–76, 78–82, 83n3, 83n10, 90, 93, 102, 117n20, 120, 121, 134–36, 139, 140, 143, 160–61, 163, 167, 168; wizard 4, 13, 24, 25, 26–27, 53, 55, 57, 62–63, 65–67, 69–70, 72, 73, 76–79, 81, 86, 101, 103, 155–56; *see also* antiracism; antisemitism; criticisms of the series; privilege; whiteness; xenophobia
Rangwala, Shama 90
readers and reading viii–ix, 4, 13, 17, 26, 29n19, 30, 31–32, 34, 35, 36–37, 40, 41, 44, 45, 48, 49, 54n1, 55, 58, 59, 61, 69, 77, 78, 82, 86–87, 88, 90–91, 93, 100, 103, 108, 109, 110, 113, 116 n.2, 123, 131, 136, 138, 140, 150, 151, 152, 153, 154, 155, 159, 160, 161, 163–65, 169, 170, 171, 172–73
Reagin, Nancy R. 28n10
Reilly, Rick 33
resistance 9, vii, 2, 4, 6, 7, 8–9, 14, 15–17, 21–24, 26–28, 30, 39, 45, 48, 49, 50–51, 53, 55, 56, 75, 76, 83, 85, 86, 90, 91, 92, 97, 104, 106–107, 111, 119, 121, 123, 128, 129, 131, 132, 134, 138–140, 145, 148, 152, 158, 161, 162, 166, 169, 173; civil disobedience 3, 134; cooperation, importance of 9, 17, 20, 100, 129, 140–41, 143, 157; and coups ix, 10, 154, 160; definitions 9–10, 19, 27, 29n13; direct action 134–38; and empathy 15–16, 126; history of 9–11, 11n28, 19; love as 27, 58, 72–76, 85, 105, 113–116, 140–41, 148; movements 9–10, 19, 21, 24, 25, 27, 39, 50, 53, 83, 119, 134, 135, 136, 137, 139, 140, 173, 168; and nonviolence 2, 9, 28n11, 29n13, 112, 126, 134–35, 143, 169, 172, 173n5; to patriarchy 12–13, 15, 18–19, 85, 87, 112, 113–116, 118n29, 155–56; performance and 20–21, 135–36, 137–82, 143; refusal decisions 20, 24–25, 48, 115, 133, 140, 143, 153–54; repression of 8, 9, 39, 156, 157, 159–60; and revolution 10, 11, 28, 29n13, 145; samizdat 155; sedition 25; terrorism 25, 83n10, 121; *see also* creative maladjustment; creativity; Dumbledore's Army; Order of the Phoenix
Resurrection Stone 33, 70, 172; *see also* Hallows
Rich, Adrienne 87, 116n4
Richards, David A. J. 155
Riddle, Tom, Jr. 18, 52, 53, 73; diary 52, 63; conception 13, 29n15; early adulthood 66; has followers not friends 7, 126, 141; frames others for his crimes 40, 44, 66; and Gaunts 13, 168; Harry, similarities to 15, 122–23, 126, 131; at Hogwarts 7, 126; infancy, childhood, and adolescence 13–14, 36, 37, 73, 123, 131; and Horcruxes 63, 71, 122, 128, 136–37; Slytherin, Heir of 13, 63, 71, 130; *see also* Voldemort; "Voldemort" (name); Wool's Orphanage
Riddle, Tom, Sr. 13, 53, 63
Roberts, Mr. 83n3
Robinson, Fiona 11, 100
Room of Requirement, the 28n1, 39, 126
Roosevelt, Theodore 132
Rose, Jonathan A. 84n11
Rosenberg, Moshe 28n3, 173n4
Rosenberg, Robin S. 129, 149
Rowling, J. K. 29n16, 69, 70, 88, 92, 93, 94, 107, 158; on children's brain development 13–15; criticism of viii–ix, xii–xiii, 56, 86–87, 106; and feminism viii–ix, xii–xiii, 86–87, 99, 117n17; and free speech ix, xii; on future events in the Potterverse 10, 12, 24, 48, 166, 168; Harvard commencement address 108, 126–27; on historical parallels 9; interpretive comments 9, 13–15, 23, 29n15, 29n18, 33, 40, 48, 69, 83–84n11, 84n13, 89–90, 102, 112, 113, 114, 117n16, 129, 130, 140, 163, 166, 167–68; and postmodernism 151, 163; on Quidditch 33; and resistance 4, 23; and rules 121; on taboos 50; "TERF" controversy viii–ix, xii–xiii, 117n17, 169
Rozin, Paul 62
Ruddick, Sara 11, 112, 118n29
Rules 11, 27, 30, 61, 85, 87, 93, 110; legitimate 2, 3–5, 13, 169; Ministry 1, 7, 26, 30, 39–43, 54n4, 65–66, 71, 78;

norms 1, 2, 13, 26, 48–53, 55, 76; and patriarchy 11–15, 25, 86, 89; school 1, 2, 3, 15–16, 22, 26, 30, 33, 34, 35, 36–39; sports 4, 26, 30, 33–36, 54n2; *see also* laws and legal systems
rule breaking viii, 1–4, 8, 9, 11, 21, 22, 24, 26–28, 28n2, 34, 36–39, 48, 49–50, 60, 75–76, 82, 85, 106, 115, 118n25, 124, 126, 133, 139, 144, 145–46, 169–72; and creativity viii, 27, 119, 120–23, 128, 129; inappropriate 3–5, 13, 26, 35, 121–23, 137, 169–70; of magical laws 30–33; of Ministry regulations 41, 42–44, 45, 46, 47; of school rules 34–35, 36–39; of sports rules 33–36, 43; *see also* creative maladjustment
Runcorn, Albert 43, 80

Saunders, Madelyn 116n8
Saxena, Vandana 3, 87
Scabbers *see* Pettigrew, Peter
Scamander, Newt 66, 116n13, 117n22
Schaffer, Talia 15, 16, 141
Schock, Kurt 9–10
Schoefer, Christine 116n2
Scholes, Robert 131
Schott, Christine 29n19, 90
Schubert, Franz 132
Schuck, Raymond I. 55–56
Schultze Quentin J. 165n8
Schumann, Robert 132
Schwabach, Aaron 171, 173n2
science 31, 54 n.1, 120, 142, 144n3, 151; scientific laws 26, 30–31; scientific method 31, 149, 168
Scrimgeour, Rufus 9, 10, 24, 25, 31–32, 46, 48, 148, 158; constructivist approach to truth 152, 153–54, 157
Sectumsempra 4–5, 122, 128
self-sacrifice 16, 98, 108–16; as Christlike 107–8; and gender 15, 19, 98, 108–9, 113–16; as magical 53, 107–8, 113–16, 126, 142–43; as resistance 114–15, 126, 168
separation of wizarding and Muggle worlds 41–42, 43, 54n1, 56–57, 131, 156, 168
Shacklebolt, Kingsley 19, 24, 44, 161, 166
Shakespeare, William 3
Shannon, Deric 159
Sharp, Gene 10, 24, 169, 173n5
Shunpike, Stan 46, 48, 128–29, 135, 143, 153–54
Simonton, Dean Keith 131, 142

Simpson, Jacqueline 93
Skeeter, Rita 44, 147, 148, 152, 156, 157, 158–60; creativity of 27, 121, 122; *The Life and Lies of Albus Dumbledore* 122, 169–70; Quick-Quotes Quill 122, 159, 160
Skulnick, Rebecca 4, 8, 34, 39
slavery 62, 86–87, 94, 98, 101, 105, 106, 107, 134, 138, 168; British legal history 116n13, 117n22; grateful slave trope 101–3, 105–6; mammies 92, 104–5, 117; as "natural" 27, 88–90, 106–7; Neo-Confederate myths 105; women, comparison to subjection of 27, 88–90, 92, 94, 97, 99; *see also* house-elves; Mill, John Stuart
Slughorn, Horace 32, 57, 59, 100–101, 105, 113, 122, 128, 136–37, 148, 152
Slytherin, Heir of *see* Riddle, Tom
Slytherin House 35, 38, 62, 113, 166, 173n1
Slytherin, Salazar 13, 63, 130, 139, 147, 155
Smith, Anne Collins 29n17, 115, 116n1, 117n17
Smith, David Livingstone 62–64
Smith, Hepzibah 23, 66, 92, 94
Smith C. Jason 29 n.17, 116n1
Smith, Laura Lee 145, 146, 147
snakes 15, 61, 62–63, 69–70, 124, 125; *see also* Nagini
Snape, Severus 4–5, 16, 44, 68, 69, 75, 118n25, 125, 128, 136, 147, 149–50, 163; bullied 72, 126, 172; and cleaning 72, 111; creativity of 121–22; as Death Eater 7, 44, 122; and dirt 59, 72, 74; emotions, suppression of 17, 18, 148; as "Half-Blood Prince" 4, 59, 121–22, 123, 128, 129, 131; Harry, dislike of 17, 38, 133, 150; as Headmaster 158; Lily, love for 113, 115; Lupin, effort to out him 67; memories 17, 68–69, 74, 126, 136; Occlumency 17, 148; punishes students 38; self-sacrifice 115; Sirius, conflict with 72, 157; unbreakable vow, makes with Narcissa 25, 113; and Veritaserum 147; Voldemort, resistance to 8, 25, 148
Snatchers 50, 128–29, 148
Snider, Naomi 14
Snyder, Franklin G. 54n3
Snyder, Timothy 41, 132, 140, 154, 160, 170, 173
social injustice vii, 4, 8, 10, 24, 26, 27, 28, 47–53, 55, 56–57, 60, 62–67, 78–79, 81,

89–90, 93–98, 105, 116n13, 126–27, 119, 131, 133–36, 138, 139–40, 143–44, 158, 161–63, 167, 169; tokenism 56, 66; *see also* systemic oppression
Socrates 10–11
Sorcerer's Stone, the 16, 37, 142, 149, 158
Sorting Hat 23, 58
soul 32, 50, 70, 126, 144; damaged by committing murder 18, 32, 69–70, 122, 126, 143; *see also* dementors, Horcruxes, Voldemort
Sound and the Fury, The (Faulkner) 105
Soviet Union 132, 155
spell damage 31, 59; Dumbledore's hand 31; George's ear 31
spells, household 74, 110
S.P.E.W. (Society for the Promotion of Elfish Welfare) 20, 22–24, 81, 88–89, 98, 99, 126, 129, 134, 135, 167–68
S.P.E.W. (Society for Promoting the Employment of Women) 89, 99, 116n7
sports (Muggle) 30, 33–34, 35–36, 82
Squibs 47, 56, 57, 71, 84n13, 135, 162, 165n3
Statute of Secrecy *see* International Statute of Wizarding Secrecy
St. Brutus's Secure Center for Incurably Criminal Boys 11
Stenner, Karen 25, 49, 133
Stephan, Maria J. 9
Sternberg, Robert J. 123
Stevenson, Keri 58
St. Mungo's Hospital for Magical Maladies and Injuries 59, 71, 78, 80, 109, 133
Stowe, Harriet Beecher (*Uncle Tom's Cabin*) 107–8
Subjection of Women, The see Mill, John Stuart
surveillance 42, 44, 48, 50–51, 121, 159
sword of Gryffindor 128, 139, 148, 170
systemic oppression vii, 2, 4, 8, 9, 12, 22, 23–24, 26, 27, 28, 36, 40, 43, 49–50, 55, 65–67, 72, 76, 81–82, 89–90, 93, 94, 96, 102, 117n20, 119, 120, 132, 134–36, 140, 143–44, 154, 166–69, 171

"Tale of the Three Brothers, The" 13, 77, 164
Tales of Beedle the Bard, The 32, 130
Teller, Anna K. 28n4
Tesla, Nikola 132
Thatcher, Margaret 64
thestrals 67, 140

Thicknesse, Pius 6, 10, 21, 25–26
Thomas, Dean 19, 67, 125
Thomas, Ebony Elizabeth 83n2
Thomas, Helen 144n8
Thomas, Jeffrey E. 54
Tilly, Charles 10
Time-Turners 31, 45, 128
Tompkins, Jane P. 107–8
Tonks, Andromeda 65, 118
Tonks, Nymphadora (Lupin) 19, 44, 65, 71, 73, 112, 118, 172
Tonks, Ted 161
Torture 5, 37, 41, 44, 47, 48, 109, 126, 128, 136, 146, 147, 148, 169; *see also* Cruciatus Curse; Veritaserum
Totalitarianism *see* autocracy
Trace charm 44
transgender issues viii-ix, xin1, xii-xiii, 54n9, 117n17, 135, 169
trauma 14, 15, 18, 25, 122–23, 131, 132, 163, 170
Travers 170–71
Trelawney, Sibyll 62, 66, 117n21, 136
trials and legal hearings 19–20, 40, 45, 46–47; of Buckbeak 45; of Ludo Bagman 46, 136; of Barty Crouch, Jr. and the Lestranges 47, 126, 136; of Harry Potter 7, 20, 41, 43, 46, 124, of Igor Karkaroff 46, 136; *see also* Muggle-born Registration Commission
trickster figure 146
Triwizard Tournament 33–34, 35–36, 72, 106, 128, 131, 146, 159
Troester, Rosalie Riegle 105
trolls 12, 68, 78, 83n4, 128, 146
Trump, Donald ix, 8, 9, 33, 64, 144n8, 161–62, 166–67
Trump, Eric 64
truth and truth telling 1, 27, 60, 140; in art and fiction 2, 88, 162–65; coherence theory of 149–50; constructivist theory of 28, 86, 149, 150–54, 156–57, 160–63, 165; correspondence theory of 28, 149, 150, 152, 154, 157–58, 160–61, 162, 165; Dumbledore on 154, 157–58, 163, 164–65; epistemology 136, 149, 151, 153; Orwell, George on 145; pragmatic theory of 149, 150, 151; as resistance 12, 27–28, 39, 137–38, 145, 148, 155–58, 159–62, 165; self-serving 147; spiritual 163; and young people 154, 157–58; *see also* Legilimency; lies; propaganda; *Quibbler, The*; Veritaserum

Tucker, Nicholas 4
Turner-Vorbeck, Tammy 4, 28n5
tyranny *see* authoritarianism

Umbridge, Dolores 119, 128; anti-werewolf legislation 40, 62; authoritarianism of 3, 12–13, 38, 72, 133, 147, 153, 155; bigotry of 40, 43, 47, 62, 66, 72, 121, 147, 165n3; censorship by 38, 75, 121, 155, 160; constructivist approach to truth 28, 150, 152–53, 155, 157, 158; creativity of 27, 121; dementor attack, authorization of 20, 38, 147; Educational Decrees 38, 72, 121, 155; family 146, 165n3; Fudge, Cornelius, support for 20, 21, 121, 133, 152–53, 157; Harry, punishes for "lying" 27–28, 121, 137, 145, 146, 152–53, 157; Hogwarts Headmistress 3, 19, 24–25, 38, 121; Defense Against the Dark Arts, teaching of 20, 21, 24, 38, 62, 137, 152–53, 155; inspires disgust 62; magical quill 38, 62, 121, 137, 153, 157; Muggle-Born Registration Commission 43, 47, 54n6, 121; name 130; neatness 72; propaganda pamphlets 24, 62, 121, 160–61; resistance to 3, 19, 20–21, 24–25, 39, 61, 75, 121, 128, 133, 137, 155, 160; sadism 20–21, 38, 62, 117n21, 121, 147, 160; and Veritaserum 147
unbreakable vow 25, 113
Uncle Tom's Cabin (Stowe) 86, 107–8
Unforgivable Curses 3, 4, 5–6, 28, 35–36, 41, 44, 170–71, 172; *see also* Avada Kedavra; Cruciatus Curse; Imperius Curse
United Nations 83n10
US Defense Department 9, 20

Veritaserum 6, 44–45, 122, 147; as torture 147
Vezzali, Loris 164–65
voice and silence ix, 12, 21, 39, 50–52, 53, 94–95, 105–6, 108, 140, 155–56, 161; *see also* censorship
Voldemort 1–2, 33, 35, 36, 38, 39, 46, 72, 109, 111, 109, 129, 149–50, 152, 161, 171; ambivalence about his body 61, 69–70; and anal retentiveness 61; and animal reminder disgust 61, 62, 65, 68, 69–70; authoritarianism 7, 8, 10, 13, 21–22, 53, 143–44; autonomy, lack of friends 7, 10, 14, 18–19, 115, 122, 126, 141, 143; blood status and parentage of 9, 53, 69; on blood status 62, 65, 69; as charismatic leader 7–8, 26; control of others 6–7, 54n8, 109, 141, 147; creativity of 27, 121, 122–23, 127–28, 142, 143, 144n3; death of 10, 18–19, 115, 141, 143, 158, 166–67, 171–72; death, fear of 32–33, 69–70, 115, 122; Dumbledore's comments about 7, 17, 18, 21, 70, 113, 126, 164; Dumbledore, plot to kill 25, 113, 148; and Elder Wand 143, 148; and fiction 122, 164–65; first rise to power 6, 40; and genocide 27, 65, 83n10; Harry, attack on in infancy 96, 109, 113–14, 127, 147, 154; Harry, attacks on 7, 17–19, 21, 122, 132, 142, 147; Harry, connection to 17, 172; Hitler and Stalin as models for 9, 70, 156, 161–163; Hogwarts, affection for 126; Horcruxes 17, 110, 115, 122–23, 124; and house-elves 91, 97, 101, 115; imagination, failure of 142; Legilimency 17, 147, 148; and Lily Potter 62, 113–14, 142–43, 163; and love 8–9, 13–14, 25, 17, 26, 27, 32–33, 53, 62, 85, 107, 113, 115, 126, 141, 142–43, 164–65; and lying 146, 147–48, 160–63, 165, 165n4; magic, incomplete understanding of 17, 26, 27, 32–33, 53, 91, 113, 114, 126, 142–43, 164–65, 169; Ministry, takeover and control by 6, 8, 10, 13, 21, 25–26, 45, 47, 50, 53, 54n1, 63, 65, 66, 93, 121, 154, 160–61; Muggles and Muggle-borns, hatred of 9, 13, 26–27, 47, 49, 53, 58, 62, 63, 65–66, 69–70, 93, 135, 143, 148–49, 158, 160–61, 165; narcissism 7, 8, 28n9; and patriarchy 13, 14–15, 17, 18–19, 27, 32, 141; power of 6, 7, 8, 9, 14, 26, 32, 33, 37, 50, 52, 85, 96, 102, 107, 113, 115, 122, 135, 141, 148, 164–65, 167, 168, 169; "rebirthing" ceremony 7–8, 69, 122, 142; as resistance leader 25–26; return of 16, 20, 21, 27–28, 44, 53, 131, 133, 145, 146, 147, 150, 152, 154, 155, 156–58, 159–60; rule breaking 3, 13, 14–15, 26, 32, 120–21, 122, 123; snakelike 69–70; soul 17, 18, 32, 70, 110, 126, 144n3, 171; wizarding culture, conformity with 13, 49, 141, 143, 156–57, 158, 160–63, 167; *see also* Big Lie; dehumanization; Horcruxes; racism; Riddle, Tom, Jr.; "Voldemort" (name)

"Voldemort" (name) 33, 137; alternative ways of naming 50, 51–52, 54n8; Harry's use of "Riddle" 53, 54n9; jinx on name 44, 50; "Lord" 7; protective spells, neutralizes 44, 50; reluctance to say "Voldemort" 50–53; Riddle's reasons for adopting the name 52, 122; and "U-No-Poo" 61; willingness to say "Voldemort" 24, 50–53, 131

Walczak, Laurie Barth 83n2
Walker, Lenore E. A. 116n5
Wallace, David 116n2
Walling, Carrie Booth 83n10
wands 13, 18, 29n13, 29n14, 42–43, 61, 65, 74, 81, 91, 102, 104, 110, 111, 112, 113, 115, 159, 170, 171; Code of Wand Use 65, 92; wandlore 31, 51–52, 53, 92, 143; *see also* Department for the Regulation and Control of Magical Creatures; Elder Wand; house-elves
Warbeck, Celestina 120
"Warlock's Hairy Heart, The" 32
Way, Niobe 18
weapons 19, 29n13, 115, 121, 128, 142, 143, 17; *see also* nonviolence; wands
Weasley, Arthur 17, 43, 79–80, 159; career at Ministry of Magic 43, 110, 111; and house elves 23, 94, 116n11; legislation with loopholes, writes 44; and Muggles 62, 67, 84n13; Nagini, nearly killed by 17
Weasley, Bill 74
Weasley family 5, 54n8, 68, 73, 74, 77, 128, 167; blood status 65, 76, 82; and gender roles 109–11; poverty 35, 60, 76
Weasley, Fred 35, 73, 110; creativity 120–21, 125, 129, 144n3; death of 111, 112; and disgust 61; and house elves 3, 90, 97; and Marauder's Map 1, 75; resistance 3, 19, 20, 21, 24–25, 39, 61, 121, 138; risk taking 129; rule breaking 3, 37, 61, 129, 138; scepticism 149; as scientist 31, 144n3, 149
Weasley, George 35, 73, 110; creativity 120–21, 125, 129, 144n3; and disgust 61; ear 31; and house elves 3, 97, 133; and Marauder's Map 1, 75; resistance 3, 19, 20, 21, 24–25, 39, 61, 121, 138; risk taking 129; rule breaking 3, 37, 61, 129, 138; scepticism 149; as scientist 31, 144n3, 149

Weasley, Ginny 19, 110, 111, 112, 118n28, 125, 126, 140, 141, 166; possessed by Voldemort 54n8
Weasley, Molly 76, 77, 84n13; domesticity 60, 75, 87, 104, 110–11, 113; and Harry 15, 73, 104, 109–12, 127; as mother 15, 86, 104, 109–12, 118n27, 118n28; power 110–13, 118n27; protectiveness 86, 110–12, 113, 154
Weasley, Percy 37, 130, 158; fondness for rules 12, 39, 71–2, 129
Weasley, Ron 5, 15, 21, 37, 47, 50, 51, 91, 108, 110, 130, 137, 140, 149; Cattermole, Reg, impersonating 78–81, 129; and cheating 129; and cleaning 38, 58, 72, 73–74; and creativity 119, 123, 128–29, 131–32; criticism of 76; and disgust 61, 62, 63, 68; dynamic character 27, 29n19, 58, 76–83, 92, 101–2, 107, 108, 127, 168; "everyone knows" 77–78, 81–82; friendship 12, 16, 20, 23, 50, 76, 77, 114, 128, 130–31, 141, 146; Hermione, influence on him 23, 29n19, 50, 107; Hermione, romance with 29n19, 33, 73–74, 76–77, 80–82, 107; and house-elves 29n19, 76, 81–82, 94, 97, 100, 101–2, 107, 108, 168; information about magical culture, source of 63, 76–78, 81–82, 164; insecurities 34, 76, 110, 146; ironic distance from 77; and lying 128–29, 146; movies, depiction in the 76; and poverty 15, 76; and Quidditch 33, 34, 77, 146; and resistance 19, 39, 78–82, 137, 138, 139, 161; wizard ideology, internalized 23, 58, 76–78, 81–82, 130; and wizard privilege 27, 58, 76–83
Weasley's Wizard Wheezes, joke products 20–21, 24, 61, 78, 80, 117, 120–21, 125, 129; as defenses against dark arts 3, 121, 129
Weber, Max 7
Weil, Simone 92
Wente, Sarah 28n10
werewolves 19, 40, 45, 60, 63, 66, 67–68, 69, 71, 76, 77–8, 84n11, 135, 159; *see also* Greyback, Fenrir; Lupin, Remus
Westman, Karin E. 28n7, 83n3, 147
Whisp, Kennilworthy 34
White, Deborah Gray 117n23
Whited, Lana A. 28n4, 146
whiteness 69–70; *see also* privilege

white savior trope 56, 106
Whitton, Alexis E. 83n6
Whitton, Natasha 116n2
Wiltermuth, Scott S. 128, 129
Windarti, Estiningsyas Retno 90
Wingardium Leviosa 30
Winky 6, 13, 88, 95, 96, 117n22; alcohol abuse 62, 75, 94, 95, 103–4, 117n21; and Battle of Hogwarts 102; Crouch family, abuse by 87–88, 94, 100–101, 103–5, 106, 114; Crouch family, love for 97–98, 100–101, 103–5, 106; freedom, hatred of 75, 86, 94, 95, 98–100, 103–4, 117n20; as "mammy" figure 104–5; misdirection in her depiction 90–91; power of 91
Witch Weekly 159, 160
Wizarding Wireless Network News 161
Wizarding World (website) 40, 42, 54n6, 83n2, 83n5, 83n11, 130, 139, 165n3
Wizengamot 133; legislation 40; tribunal 20, 41, 46
Wollstonecraft, Mary 116n6
Wolosky, Shira 29n17, 112, 116n1, 172
Women's March on Washington 29n12, 173
women's suffrage 82, 89, 96

Women, Victorian 15, 88, 89, 97–99, 101, 104; Women's National Anti-Suffrage League 89; *see also* Mill, John Stuart
Wool's Orphanage 14, 15, 73
Woolf, Virginia 98–99, 109
"world isn't split into good people and Death Eaters, the" 8, 39, 44, 167
World War I 162
World War II; antisemitism 63, 156, 162, 163; resistance 9, 11, 19, 28n11; propaganda 62; wizarding history parallels i, 9, 19, 28n11; *see also* antisemitism; Big Lie, the; Eichmann, Adolf; Goebbels, Joseph; Hitler, Adolf; propaganda
Wormtail *see* Pettigrew, Peter

xenophobia 26, 62, 72; *see also* antisemitism; racism

Yang, Jeff 64
Yaxley, Corban 79

Zeitgeist, defying the 2, 11, 27, 50, 123, 140, 141, 143, 145, 169
Zettel, Sarah 111, 116n1
Zipes, Jack 4, 116n2
Zurn, Perry 135–36

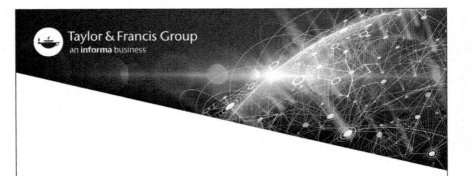